A LONG SHADOW

An Antonia Conti Thriller

DAVID BECKLER

THOMAS & MERCER

Text copyright © 2022 by David Beckler
All rights reserved.

Published by Thomas & Mercer, Seattle

www.apub.com

Amazon, the Amazon logo, and Thomas & Mercer are trademarks of Amazon.com, Inc., or its affiliates.

ISBN-13: 9781542034685
ISBN-10: 154203468X

Cover design by Dominic Forbes

Printed in the United States of America

I dedicate this book to Tricia, who has not only supported me on every step of my journey but encouraged me whenever I received setbacks. She's always believed in my writing and whenever I wavered, assured me Antonia would find a home.

CHAPTER 1

Antonia winced as the shorter woman ploughed through her blonde opponent's jab and landed three blows to unprotected ribs before catching her with an uppercut. The blonde fell to one knee, blood streaming from her mouth. The amateur recording of Antonia's next opponent wobbled, but even through the TV screen Antonia could sense the shorter woman's fury. She imagined the same fists ripping into her ribcage as Milo paused the footage.

Milo waved the remote at the screen. 'See her lining up the uppercut? She dropped her left.'

'A right hook and she's history,' Darius said. 'And she so telegraphed it.'

'You'll take her easy, Antonia,' Milo assured her. 'She's only one-seventy, so you've got height and reach on her.' Light glinted off his shaved skull, a huge brown cannonball. 'We got three weeks to sharpen you up.' He grinned and winked at her.

Her mouth dry, Antonia didn't reply. It was easy for them; most of the Dekker brothers' opponents gave up when they saw either of the monsters across the ring and spent the fight keeping out of their way.

Milo killed the screen and Darius said, 'Want a lift home?'

'I'll walk.' She rose out of the shabby armchair in the small TV room at the side of the gym, picked up her backpack and headed for the door. 'Thanks, guys.'

The empty gym smelt of sweat and liniment. Darius had lowered the lights and the heavy bags cast long shadows across the wooden floor. Her trainers made no sound as she reflected on what she'd watched. Despite the brothers' reassurances, Antonia wasn't sure she'd prevail against her unbeaten opponent. Although she'd sparred hundreds of rounds, she'd never fought someone fuelled by so much anger. The memory of a coachload from the gym going to support one of the other fighters in his first bout still mortified her. Despite showing promise in training, he'd frozen at the first bell and had never since visited the gym. The fear she'd do the same haunted her.

Outside, she hesitated. Normally high on the endorphins after a workout, tonight a sense of dread weighed on her. Only the brothers' battered silver Land Cruiser remained in the gloomy car park and she paused beside it. She could say she'd changed her mind.

Don't be a wuss, Antonia. She shouldered her backpack and set off for home.

The familiar route seemed different tonight, the darkened industrial buildings lining it appearing sinister. She shivered and hurried between the pools of light surrounding the scattered lamp posts. Icy air infiltrated layers of clothing and she promised herself a mug of hot chocolate when she got home. Cheered by the prospect, she walked faster.

Instead of fading, the sense of unease grew stronger. *The fight isn't for three weeks. Forget it and pull yourself together.*

Angry voices called out ahead and she faltered. The sounds came from an opening on her left. She glanced up at the nearest camera, for the first time welcoming its intrusive surveillance. As she approached, she saw that the opening led down a narrow pot-holed lane. In the shadows, thirty metres away, two jeering men bent over a bundle on the ground. One of them kicked it. An old man cried out in pain.

Antonia stepped towards them, shouting, 'Leave him alone!'

The men spun round, seeming unsurprised to see her, and she hesitated. Ignoring the old man, they advanced towards her. Chests thrust out and arms bent, they looked huge, and hostility flooded out of them. *Oh hell, you've done it now.*

Ten metres from her, the men halted. In their mid-twenties, both stood over one-eighty and although not athletes, looked like they could take care of themselves.

The one at the front leered. 'Leave him alone, or else . . . ?'

A gust of wind carried the odour of beer and curry from them. If she ran now, she'd get away, but she couldn't abandon an old man. Although the same height as the one who spoke, she was half his bulk. A sudden movement from the other one made her heart jump until she realised he was pointing behind her.

'Cameras, Arkady,' he said, frowning.

The man called Arkady glared at the camera and then at her as he raised his palms in a gesture of appeasement. 'Come on,' he said and edged past her towards the main road. His small, mean eyes appraised her, making her skin tingle. His principal emotion as he passed Antonia confused her. She expected anger, but she sensed satisfaction, as if he'd achieved something. His companion followed, a scar from his mouth to his ear giving him a macabre grin.

When they reached the corner, Arkady stopped and turned back to her. Her stomach tensed. 'See you around,' he said, blowing her a kiss, and Scar-face laughed.

They left, and she exhaled. Their victim, an unkempt old man, crouched in the gutter retrieving his belongings and she went to help him.

3

'You okay?' she said, rescuing a grimy, fluorescent-pink sleeping bag from a puddle of filthy water.

A claw-like hand snatched it from her grasp. 'Get your thieving Black hands off!' She recoiled as the old man straightened, his toothless mouth twisted into a sneer. 'Unless you want to give me a gobble,' he said, cackling and spraying spittle.

Cheeks burning, Antonia turned away from him, then stopped. Arkady had reappeared, and now stood between her and the main road along with half a dozen others, the hostility emanating from them like a physical barrier. Her insides fluttered and she checked behind her, along the lane. She didn't even know where it led. The old man, seeming unhurt by the kicking, scurried away and vanished into the darkness.

She remembered what Scar-face had said about the camera. If she stayed within range of surveillance cameras, she should be safe. She set off down the lane away from them. *Don't run, and don't look back. They're just trying to scare you.* The men's heavy steps echoed off the buildings.

Determined to stay calm, she checked the nearest camera. It hung broken, the letters ASL sprayed on the wall under it. Anti-Surveillance League. Although sympathetic to their cause, she cursed them. *Keep calm, there's another one ahead.* She got closer and saw the black paint across the lens. Time slowed. Her pulse raced and the men's steps grew louder. She ran.

She'd pushed herself in the gym and her legs felt leaden. Angry shouts followed her. Heavy footwear thudded on to the road. Images of what they'd do to her filled her with terror. *Save your energy, concentrate on running.* The freezing air scoured her throat. She groped for the mental exercises Milo made her rehearse to block out her fear. The straps of her backpack slapped her shoulders with each stride on the uneven roadway. The sounds of her pursuers grew fainter and she risked a glance behind her. Two men trailed in her wake but she didn't see the others. In a few minutes these last two would give up.

She saw the pothole too late and her foot caught the edge. Her ankle gave way and she stumbled, flailing her arms. Her other foot smashed into the kerb and pain ripped through her knee. She staggered two steps, almost going down. Her pursuers let out yells of triumph. Antonia gritted her teeth and ran.

The knee stiffened with every step but she forced her legs to move, hoping it would ease. The men sounded closer. She must think. If she stayed in the lane, they'd catch her, but if she left it, they'd wait for the others. On her right lay an alleyway. She swerved into it, ignoring the pain as she changed direction, concentrating on keeping her footing.

A shout told her they'd seen her. A distant reply followed a few seconds later, then silence. The path split and she took the left branch. The alley opened out and in front of her lay a stretch of inky water, slick in the faint light. City Road Basin; she'd doubled back on herself. She hesitated, unsure which way to go.

A shout in the distance sounded forlorn. They'd lost her. She relaxed and listened. A yell in reply, much nearer, jolted her into action. She ran left, along a lane bounded by a wall and the water. Each step on the uneven ground jarred her knee. Voices echoed over the water, closer than she expected. They were gaining on her.

A few yards in front, a darker shadow in the wall led to an opening. She plunged through it before skidding to a halt. She found herself in an enclosed courtyard lined with large steel bins. Paralysed for a moment, she turned back, but the men were almost on her. She hobbled to the furthest container and threw herself into it. The stench of rotting garbage made her heave, but she eased the lid shut. Had they seen her? Her pulse pounded in her ears as she listened. When she didn't hear anything for several minutes, she began to hope they'd passed her.

Then a roar of anger and a voice said, 'Where the fuck's she gone?'

She gulped, gagging again at the stink of putrefaction.

'You sure she came down here?' another voice panted.

'Where else would she go?'

'She's probably carried on along the path,' the uncertain one said. 'Come on, Pavlo, we'll soon catch her.'

'What if she *did* come down here?'

'What if she *didn't?*'

She held her breath, willing them to go. A bin lid clanged, sending shockwaves through the soles of her trainers. Plastic rustled and bottles clinked. *Blast!*

'You going to fucking help, or what?' Pavlo said.

'Waste of time,' the other man mumbled, but another lid clanged.

Antonia swallowed. Should she wait until they discovered her or jump out now, surprise them? Would her knee let her?

'Come on, Pavlo, I'm going back.'

'Don't you want the money?'

What does he mean?

'The others might have caught her.'

'Those fat fuckers. No way.' Pavlo's voice came closer.

She could almost taste his anger and she prepared herself, tensing her muscles and inhaling. Bad knee or not, she would do serious damage to whoever found her. Another bin opened, the lid striking the side of hers. She bit back a cry.

'Come on, search under those bags,' Pavlo ordered.

'Shit, it's all over my hands. What the fuck's this stinking crap—'

'Don't be a pussy.'

'Fuck off!' A lid banged shut.

'Where the fuck you going?' Pavlo demanded.

'We don't even know she came down here.'

'Hang on . . .' Something smashed into her bin, making it reverberate. The sound faded and Pavlo muttered a frustrated, 'Shit!'

Their voices grew faint but not daring to hope they'd left, Antonia waited. Her thighs trembled with the effort of keeping her out of the vile-smelling sludge at the bottom of the bin and a chill leached into her weary body. After what seemed an age, she lifted a corner of the lid and drank down the freezing air.

Silence greeted her, so she straightened, easing the cover back against the wall. She flexed her legs, massaging them and grimacing as her circulation returned. Once sure they worked, she grabbed the side of the bin and clambered out. Something made her hesitate; a sensation of danger still close. A dog barked in the distance and a lorry laboured up an incline, its engine complaining. The everyday sounds calmed her and she set about retracing her steps.

Pavlo's words raced round her mind as she tried to make sense of them. *Don't you want the money?* They must have thought she was an illegal. She remembered the outcry when the new company running homeland security suggested offering a bounty for each illegal immigrant handed in. She hadn't realised they'd gone ahead. The stretch of water lay in front of her and she stepped into the open.

A noise like a large animal scratching at the floor made her turn. A bulky figure was almost atop her, charging her with a cry of, 'Got you, bitch!'

Pavlo.

He drove his lowered shoulder into her, hitting her mid-thigh and jarring her teeth. Caught off balance, she flew backward, screaming until icy water engulfed her.

The shock of entering the freezing water paralysed Antonia. Pavlo seized her legs, dragging her under. Foul liquid entered her mouth and nose and she fought not to retch. The numbness faded and she kicked out, twisting her hips. The grip on her thighs loosened, so she kicked again and he released her legs. She struck for the surface but a fist thudded into her shoulder, spinning her. Hands closed around her neck, squeezing. She tore at the fingers digging into her flesh, but couldn't dislodge them. She lashed out, aiming for his head. But the water dragged at her arms, slowing her punches and robbing them of power.

Energy drained from her with each blow she attempted. Her lungs caught fire but she clamped her mouth shut, resisting a desperate need to breathe. A roaring filled her ears and bright lights flashed in front of her. Then anger seized her. How dare this man end her life? After everything she'd survived. She pushed her exhausted body into a final effort. Thrashing feet struck a solid surface and she pushed against it. Her trainers slipped before gripping on a rough patch and she propelled herself through the water. As she emerged from the icy liquid, she gulped for air.

Still blinking to clear her vision, she lashed out. When her hand hit solid flesh and caused him to grunt, she struck again. Encouraged by a cry of pain, she pulled her fist back. Before she could throw the punch, he seized her in a powerful bear hug, pinning her arms to her sides. She fought to free them as he crushed her against his body. The grip intensified, squeezing air out of her lungs. Panic made her mind go blank. Then a small voice told her to stop struggling and let her body go limp.

Pavlo pushed her under the water. As it closed over her, she made herself stay calm. Her feet found the bottom and scrabbled for purchase on its slimy surface, but she kept her upper body limp. After long seconds his hold relaxed. She drove with her thighs, shooting out of the water and smashing her forehead into his face. Bone crunched, and he cried out.

Before he could react, she hit him in the throat. With a strangled cough, he fell back. She made for the bank, scrambled out and lay on the side, panting, muscles screaming for rest. *Come on, don't stop now.* With an effort she pushed herself to get up and crawled away from what had almost been her grave.

A hand seized her ankle and Antonia's heart somersaulted. With the last of her strength, she jerked her leg, attempting to free it, but the grip tightened. Then he pulled her towards the water and an involuntary whimper escaped her lips.

CHAPTER 2

Chapman eased his car along the rutted lane, dodging the potholes picked out in his headlights. A flickering blue light reflected off the concrete fence as the lane opened out. A row of cars and vans stood alongside the wall. He parked on the end and got out. Icy air enveloped him and shuddering, he thrust his hands into his pockets, wishing he'd stayed in bed with Brigitte.

Ahead of him figures moved in front of a body of water. Spotlights illuminated the surface and as he got closer, the outlines of the underwater rescue team rippled. A slick black body-bag lay by the side of the water. With a resigned sigh he stepped forward and, unzipping the top half, shone his torch on the victim.

He inspected the smashed features, studying the injuries, unsettled such sights no longer touched him. 'Someone didn't like you, did they?' he said to the body, and resisted the urge to make a promise he might not be able to keep.

'Morning, guv,' a familiar voice said, adding, 'Sorry: Sergeant.'

Are you taking the piss? He studied the young constable but couldn't tell if she'd made a genuine slip. 'Who's in charge of the scene?'

'Dobrowski, from CrimTech, Sarge.'

The first good news of the day. A slender figure detached from a group at the water's edge then came towards him, her white coveralls flapping.

'Good morning, Russell, introducing yourself to our key witness?'

'Jo, I didn't know you covered murders.'

As usual, she appeared to have fixed her hair and make-up at her leisure. Chapman suppressed a yawn. Did she ever sleep? He wouldn't mind finding out.

'My promotion came through last week, Senior Crime Scene Technician Jolanta Dobrowski at your service.' She gave a mock salute. 'So, you'll see a lot more of me.'

'Congratulations.' At least he'd now have something to look forward to on these calls. 'Anything you can tell me about the casualty?'

'The divers recovered the body,' she said, 'and I'm pretty sure drowning *isn't* the cause of death.'

Chapman addressed the constable, hovering a few feet away. 'I suppose there's no sign of our anonymous caller.'

'Sorry, Sarge.'

'Any witnesses?'

'There might be CCTV from over there.' She pointed at a building across the canal where three blinking red lights showed.

The backlit logo on the wall behind the cameras displayed the silhouette of a swooping raptor framed in a stylised shield. 'They're owned by GRM as well, aren't they, Jo? Like your lot?'

Dobrowski smiled and her pale-blue eyes glittered. 'Strictly speaking CrimTech have nothing to do with them. But yes, we're part of the same group. One big happy family.'

He spoke to the constable. 'Has someone gone over there?'

'Inspector Harding, Sarge.'

'Why the hell did *he* go? He's supposed to be here. In charge.' The constable shrugged and he dismissed her. 'Has he spoken to you, Jo?'

'We've spoken.' Dobrowski coloured. 'On the way here.'

Lucky bastard, so the rumours were true. In the circumstances, her immaculate appearance impressed him even more. He shivered and pushed his hands further into his pockets before going to look for the inspector to find out how he wanted to proceed.

As he walked towards the alley, a tall figure came out of the gloom. 'Russell, glad you could make it.'

Chapman blew out his cheeks. 'Some of us can't afford to live in the city, Ian.' *Not any more.*

Harding moved close and murmured, '"Inspector" or "boss" in front of the troops please, Russell.' He stepped past and continued, 'Let's examine our victim, Sergeant.'

'Yes, boss,' he said, clenching his fists and following in the inspector's wake.

◆ ◆ ◆

The sense of panic that had seized Antonia since her mother hid her grew and she fought the desire to escape. The dried hides her mother had piled over her smelt musty and dust tickled her nose, but she knew she mustn't sneeze. Sounds from outside penetrated the hides – men shouting, followed by a woman's screams – and she cringed, making herself as small as possible. 'Whatever happens, don't come out,' her mother had said, and Antonia knew from her expression that she meant it.

The sounds came closer and she pressed her hands over her ears. Then it grew quiet and she listened. A shrill cry came from nearby, making her jump, her heart thumping so fast she couldn't count the beats. Again, the woman screamed, her voice familiar but alien. Mamma!

Antonia threw the hides off her and scrambled to her feet. From the next room, muffled by the blanket that covered the doorway, came sobbing and a woman begging. There was no mistake, it was her mother. She shoved the blanket aside and ran into the room. Two men knelt with their backs to her, holding her mother down while a third lay on top of her. Antonia picked up the water jug that stood on a chair and smashed it into the back of the nearest man's head.

Water splashed from the jug, but it didn't break and he slumped forward to the floor. The one lying on Mamma stopped and looked back, surprise etched on his features. She swung the heavy pot again, aiming at the other man who'd been holding her mother down, but he blocked her arm and it smashed on the earthen floor.

'Run, Antonia!' her mother screamed, but she hesitated.

The man who'd blocked the jug scrambled to his feet and, seeing his expression, she ran. A huge hand seized her arm and pulled her back. With a yell of rage her mamma broke free of the man atop her and attacked the man holding Antonia's arm. He let go and Antonia ran, ignoring the cries behind her. She burst out of the house, into what should have been bright sunlight, and stopped. Smoke filled the air, making her eyes water, and around her, bodies lay scattered in bloody pools.

Men wearing long robes and carrying weapons moved among the smoke. The men watched her with little interest, then shouts came from behind her. With angry cries, the men came for her. She ran for the river, her fleet feet picking their way over the familiar paths. At the edge of the village, she headed into the bush. The men's voices receded, then a new sound. Hooves. She glanced over her shoulder and saw the horses, their riders' robes flowing behind them.

She had to reach the river. The hooves grew louder until she could hear the men, yelling in triumph and breathing hard. A stitch cut through her side, but gritting her teeth, she ran on. A man yelled something, then fire slashed across her back. The pain worse than the time

13

the jackal bit her. She staggered but kept her balance. Another blow landed and this time the pain was even worse. She turned her head, desperate to avoid the next one.

Her foot caught on the edge of an animal burrow and she went flying, landing in a heap. Hooves thundered and she looked up in time to see a huge body bearing down on her. She closed her eyes and curled into a ball as the hooves slashed through the air . . .

Antonia opened her eyes. Sweat slicked her body and her pulse raced. Dawn light crept round the edge of her curtains and after a few seconds she recognised her bedroom. She lay on her back and filled her lungs but couldn't get rid of the hollowness in her chest. As she untangled herself from the bedding, she tried to dismiss the nightmare but the odour of smoke persisted.

A faint shout came from downstairs. 'Antonia, breakfast!'

This smell *wasn't* a hangover from her dreams and her stomach rumbled, reminding her she'd not eaten since yesterday afternoon. She swung her legs out of bed, rose and stretched. Her shoulder ached from where the thug in the canal had punched her and her throat hurt, but to her relief, neither knee nor ankle complained too much when she flexed them.

'Antonia!'

'Coming, Eleanor,' she shouted, hurrying into the bathroom.

Filthy water had seeped out of the clothes she'd worn last night, forming a pool on the tiled floor. The stench of mud and slime replaced the odour of burnt breakfast. After switching on the lights, she examined herself in the mirror. The thick pink scars tracking round her torso appeared to glow in the harsh light and goosebumps peppered her long, muscular limbs. The bruises where fingers had dug into her neck were almost invisible against her dark skin, and she moved nearer the glass, checking for cuts. She didn't want to get Weil's disease, or worse. Apart from a small swelling above her right eye she couldn't see any marks on her face. The memory of her attacker's cry when she kicked him made her smile. He'd think twice before attacking a woman again.

She showered and dressed in the cheap garments she now wore, looking forward to the day she could return to wearing her own clothes. Weariness drained her. The prospect of working undercover on a story had seemed so exciting, but she couldn't wait for it to end. After dumping the wet clothes in her washing machine, she set off downstairs.

In Eleanor's kitchen, the aroma of bacon and burnt toast lingered. One of the downlights above the red Aga flickered and Antonia remembered, with a stab of guilt, that she'd promised to change it. Eleanor Curtis sat in her wheelchair stroking Max, whose purring almost drowned out the *Today* programme in the background. A large mug steamed on the scrubbed pine table in front of her. The cat leapt off the old woman's lap, wrapping himself round Antonia's legs as she greeted Eleanor and poured herself a coffee.

Eleanor studied Antonia's forehead. 'Did you do that at the gym?'

'Yes,' Antonia said, 'I got caught with a kick.'

'You'll ruin your looks. Men don't like girls with broken noses and black eyes.'

Antonia placed her mug on a coaster and winked. 'Some do.' Max leapt on to the table and rubbed his forehead against her hand. He let out an indignant mewing when she picked him up. 'Come on, Max, you know you're not allowed.'

'Alan told me his mole's expecting Reed-Mayhew to receive important papers today.'

'Some financial documents. GRM are paying senior people in government to favour their contracts. We're hoping to find out exactly who.'

'You've got evidence on some, haven't you?' Eleanor studied her over her mug.

'Only low-level officials. Not the big fish.'

'That's no surprise. Reed-Mayhew's very good at covering his tracks. And he's not above using threats and violence to do so.'

'I knew about the blackmail and threats, but violence?'

Eleanor had spent years trying to bring Reed-Mayhew and his growing empire down. Sometimes, Antonia suspected she'd set up The Electronic Investigator just to do that. Had he attacked her? Eleanor never discussed how she had ended up in the chair.

Eleanor put her mug on the table. 'We couldn't prove anything, but he had a former employee's house firebombed because he threatened to expose him. The poor guy finished up in intensive care. He recovered, but never said another word. His wife and kids escaped the fire, but I suppose were still targets.'

'I didn't know that.' The offhand and arrogant way senior staff treated junior staff hadn't impressed her, but she never suspected they'd resort to something like this. Antonia experienced a sudden urge to never again set foot in the offices of GRM.

Eleanor looked like she wanted to take her words back and gave a reassuring smile. 'That was a while ago, when he was young and rash. He doesn't need to do that now. He relies on bribes, blackmail and legal threats. He's got dirt on anyone who's anyone.'

Despite Eleanor's reassurance, the strength of the urge remained. 'I was thinking of getting out once I've recovered the papers.'

Eleanor raised her eyebrows. 'Have we got enough evidence? Once you're out, there's no going back in.'

She couldn't let Eleanor think she was scared. 'I'm worried about the ID for my cover. Since the bomb at King's Cross they're increasing security checks on the Tube. If I'm caught using fake documents . . .'

'I told you, the people we get the papers from supply government agencies.' Eleanor sighed. 'If Alan's happy with what you've managed to—'

16

'I'm the one who's in there risking my neck, not Alan.'

'Yes, Antonia, but you volunteered for this.'

Antonia held the old woman's gaze, reading the sympathy but behind it a resolve. Sometimes, Antonia felt that the fact she was her adoptive mother as well as her employer made Eleanor treat her more harshly.

Eleanor looked away first. 'I'll speak to Alan during our editorial conference and if we've got enough material . . .'

'Thank you.' If it was Alan Turner's decision, getting him to do what she wanted shouldn't give Antonia a problem.

Eleanor drained her mug and let Max jump on to her lap. 'What about your investigation into Monika's disappearance? I'm surprised you're giving up on her. She's one of your few close friends.'

'I haven't given up on her.' Antonia's cheeks grew hot.

'Oh, you've found out what happened to her. Fantastic, I can't wait to read—'

Antonia banged the table, making Max jerk. 'You're the one who said I'm wasting my time. "She's done a bunk and is doubtless shacked up with some guy with a platinum card on an exotic island." Quote.'

Eleanor laughed. 'And you're the one who persuaded us GRM had something to do with her disappearance.'

'I was wrong.'

Eleanor studied her. 'Really? What about the other young women who've gone missing from there?'

'It's probably a coincidence. GRM is a huge company and so many women disappear every year . . .'

'You can't possibly believe that.'

Antonia concentrated on buttering a slice of toast, irritated at Eleanor for making her feel so guilty. Despite her conviction that someone at GRM was behind the disappearance of at least three young women, including Monika, she'd not found the evidence, but until a few minutes ago she'd have sworn she wouldn't give up until she did.

'As you said, Antonia, you're the one risking discovery. Let Alan know you'd like to finish working undercover, or would you rather I told him?' Eleanor's tone conveyed a mixture of sympathy and disappointment.

I'm not giving up! she wanted to shout, but she was. 'I'll tell him myself.'

'This morning, or will you go in today?'

'Of course I'll go in today. And I'll keep going until I get . . .' Tears stung her eyes and she rose. 'I don't want to be late.'

The old lady's triumph followed her out of the house as she hurried towards the Tube weighed down by a sense of dread.

◆ ◆ ◆

Still smarting from her run-in with Eleanor, Antonia rushed to Angel Tube station. Monika had been the first close friend Antonia had made since leaving the care system and, despite Eleanor's disapproval, they'd stayed close. It was Monika who had introduced her to the gym, the only place she felt really safe. Monika's disappearance while working at GRM had been the catalyst that had led Antonia to volunteer for the undercover assignment. Despite Eleanor and Turner considering more experienced freelancers, Antonia knew her enthusiasm had swung the decision. She couldn't back out now, and anyway, she'd made better progress than Eleanor suspected, though she knew not to share her plans.

The usual queue of commuters passing through the screening devices at the entrance to the station moved at a steady pace past the bored security staff. Antonia suspected a determined terrorist would have no trouble getting weapons and explosive devices into the underground system and these security checks represented a PR exercise to reassure passengers.

She passed through the security checkpoint as a train drew into the platform. A short woman, her black hair streaked with grey, waited to one side, scanning the new arrivals until she saw Antonia. A relieved smile lit up her face.

The sight of Sabirah reminded Antonia of the insignificance of her problems. They got seats together and Sabirah took out her phone to text her kids, reminding them to eat breakfast, like she did every morning. Didn't she realise the government and media companies tracked you through those things?

A middle-aged man in paint-spattered dungarees stared at Antonia. She'd hoped the shapeless work clothes would decrease interest from his type but it didn't always work. He switched his attention to Sabirah and sneered – so, not a lecher but a racist. Antonia glowered at him until he looked away. She wanted to punch him, but instead watched the screen fixed to the side of the carriage. Between adverts for easy loans and betting shops, the news comprised the usual talking heads discussing the latest terrorist bombing. As if they knew anything. She scrutinised the other passengers hunched up against the cold and, like her, wearing baggy tracksuits under quilted coats.

Her attention drifted back to the screen, but she wasn't concentrating until a familiar scene appeared. She straightened and focused on the image, which showed the site of her fight with Pavlo. A tall, well-dressed man spoke to a reporter. In the background a diver surfaced holding her backpack. She'd given up seeing it ever again. She watched, fascinated. Why were the divers searching there?

A gentle elbow in her side made her start. 'Patience, we have to go.'

'Sorry.' Antonia leapt out of her seat, reaching the doors before they closed.

Sabirah's solid figure moved ahead of her towards the exit. Many of their fellow passengers were regulars and Sabirah exchanged greetings with them. Antonia replayed the images from the screen, trying to remember if anything in the backpack could identify her. She didn't think so, but her anxiety persisted. As they neared the exit, the atmosphere changed. The easy resignation of the other passengers gave way to fear and, underneath it, a suppressed anger.

She peered over the figures in front of her to see why. A team of Border Force Operatives waited beyond the travel-card readers, wearing grim expressions, their arms folded. With their peaked caps and dark uniforms they just needed guns to pass for representatives of any police state.

The crowd shuffled forward. Antonia reached out and squeezed Sabirah's shoulder. Her friend's body trembled. 'Walk tall and look them in the face,' Antonia whispered.

The guards scrutinised them and one, a tall blond, smiled at her. She glared at him until the smile died. His companion intercepted Sabirah.

'Citizen's ID card,' he demanded.

'I don't have one, sir,' Sabirah said, her voice almost inaudible. 'I have a Permit to Reside.'

The man clicked his fingers as she fished for it in her voluminous handbag. He snatched it and examined the document. Antonia needed all her self-control not to intervene.

'On your way to work?' he asked.

Sabirah whispered, 'Yes, sir.'

'This expires in six weeks.' He held up the card.

'Yes, sir, I know,' she said, on the verge of tears.

Antonia couldn't contain herself any longer. 'Is there a problem?'

'No, miss.' He returned Sabirah's ID and held out his other hand. 'Not with hers, but I've not seen yours yet.'

Antonia hesitated. Despite her dark complexion, she normally passed for British. She reached into her top and produced a creased plastic rectangle with her picture printed on one side and shoved it into his hand. In the three months she'd been using it, nobody from Border Force had properly scrutinised it. She chewed her lower lip as he examined it. *Serves you right, giving Eleanor the excuse you're worried about the exposure of your ID.*

'Patience Okoye?'

Her breath caught in her throat. 'Yes.'

'You should take better care of this.'

He returned the card and dismissed her. Antonia walked beside Sabirah in silence, humiliation and anger enveloping her.

Chapman strode into the headquarters of GRM Partners, his mind half on his ex-wife's text telling him his daughter couldn't make it at the weekend. He was sure Rhona had invented the school outing to punish him for bringing Abby home late.

Alongside him, Detective Constable Alice Sanchez kept pace, her shiny brown hair swinging with each stride. A muscular, hard-eyed man in a too-tight suit moved to intercept them but returned to his post by the front door when Sanchez flashed her ID.

Behind the imposing dark wooden reception desk sat a young blonde woman, well groomed and wearing a smart suit. She smiled at him, and Chapman self-consciously pulled in his stomach and stood straighter before showing her his ID.

'Detective Sergeant Chapman, Crime Squad.' He produced the sealed clear bag containing the coded identity badge they'd found in the backpack recovered from the City Road Basin. 'We need to know who you issued this to.'

'I'll have to get someone from HR. Do you want to take a seat?' She gestured to a pair of brown leather chesterfields in front of the opposite wall.

Chapman declined and paced in front of the desk contemplating his response to Rhona's text, having deleted his initial angry retort.

Next to him, Alice Sanchez studied her surroundings. 'Imposing, isn't it?'

He halted and studied the spacious chamber. Polished marble floors and pale wood panelling on the walls. His gaze drifted towards the huge chandeliers hanging down in cascades of glittering crystal. 'Makes you wonder how they can afford this if they're making all their money from government contracts.'

'If they're efficient enough to do it, why not?'

The way newer officers like Sanchez accepted private companies making money out of running public services still surprised him. Didn't she see the way it eroded their jobs? 'A waste of money if you ask me, designed to impress credulous fools.'

She blushed and looked away, making him feel like he'd kicked a puppy.

Heels clacked on the tiled floor, breaking the uncomfortable silence. A small woman with shoulder-length blonde hair and wearing the same Tom Ford suit his ex-wife owned walked towards him, and for a horrible instant he thought it *was* Rhona.

'Officers, I'm Sylvia Wise.' She held out a hand. 'How can I help you?' Her smile reminded him of a TV evangelist's.

'DS Chapman, and this is DC Sanchez. We need to identify the person issued with this.' He handed her the badge – the only information on it the company logo and a computer chip.

She examined it through the clear bag. 'Can you tell me why?'

'We just need the name,' Chapman said.

'We take the privacy of our staff seriously and without a court order, I can't give you any—'

'Can't, or won't?'

Wise stepped back.

'Sylvia,' Sanchez said, smiling, 'we're investigating a serious crime and would really appreciate your help.'

Wise's lips compressed. 'I'm sorry, it's company policy.' She didn't seem sorry.

'We'll be back.' Without waiting for Sanchez, Chapman made for the exit.

A semi-circular flight of steps led down to the crowded pavement and he swore as he waited at the bottom of it. What a waste of time.

'What happened there?' Sanchez said.

Chapman strode towards the car, annoyed he'd let the woman get to him. 'People like her piss me off. Hiding behind "company policy" when all they're doing is exercising what little power they have.'

'You didn't handle her very well. You could have finessed—'

'When you're sergeant, you can decide how to handle it.'

Sanchez opened her mouth to speak but walked away, blinking.

Chapman swore, half at himself. The truth of her words made them sting all the more. Now he'd have to see if Harding would sort out the court order and save them having to return to the station. He retrieved his phone and activated the secure connection.

Harding picked up straight away. 'Russell?'

'Ian, they're refusing to play ball. We'll need a court order.'

Harding chuckled. 'Not a surprise. With their bid for the squad in the offing, they aren't going to go out of their way to help us.'

'What do you mean?'

'They're preferred bidder. I thought everyone knew.'

'But they aren't privatising The Met.'

'That *was* the plan, but the Home Secretary's commissioned an efficiency review.'

Acid filled Chapman's throat. Every force subjected to an *efficiency review* ended up in private hands and that always meant cuts. He didn't have tenure since his demotion, so he'd end up out on his ear when the new company took over, unless they gave him a zero-hours contract on minimum wage. *Fucking great.*

'You still there?' Harding said.

'Yeah, sure.'

'You'd better sort out the paperwork, Sergeant. I'm afraid I've got to see the DCI.'

'Right, boss, I'll come back and do it.' Chapman ended the call before he said something he'd regret later.

'Everything all right, Sarge?' Sanchez said.

'Bloody marvellous.'

They walked to their car, deep in thought. Had Harding made a mistake? Maybe GRM weren't preferred bidder. He'd not heard any rumours, and despite his current lowly status, he still had contacts in the senior ranks. Mind you, Harding had even better sources. A committed networker, he probably had a DCI's job lined up with the new firm. With an effort, Chapman ignored his concerns; no point worrying about what hadn't happened yet. If he fucked this up, he wouldn't need to wait for a change in regime.

◆ ◆ ◆

Two hours later, Chapman and Sanchez were back in front of the GRM reception desk. He checked the clock on the wall behind it; they'd been here eleven minutes and he began to think Wise was making him wait on purpose.

Seeming to be still smarting from his earlier putdown, Sanchez looked everywhere but up at the atrium. Chapman scanned the space, determined not to let Wise irritate him. A huge painting hung above the entrance, placed so everyone leaving could see it. Painted in the style of the pictures of eighteenth-century landowners he'd seen in the National Portrait Gallery, it showed a man in front of a stately pile. He peered at the title: 'Gustav Reed-Mayhew'. It had to be an ancestor of the owner, then he saw the date, 1975–. *Bloody hell. Mr Big himself. Pompous ass.* With hazel eyes and short brown hair parted at the side, Reed-Mayhew resembled a mid-level accountant rather than the chief executive of one of the biggest outsourcing companies in the country.

Thinking Sanchez was behind him, Chapman opened his mouth to comment when Wise said, 'Admiring our leader, Sergeant Chapman?'

'I thought he'd look a bit more aristocratic, what with his double-barrelled surname.' He'd read somewhere that Reed-Mayhew had adopted the name to hide his modest background. How did that work if everyone knew that was what you'd done?

Her eyes glazed and lips parted as she studied the portrait. 'He's a self-made man. That's what's so admirable about him, don't you think?'

He mumbled, 'Yeah, very admirable.' He waved the court order. 'I've got the—'

'Here you are, Sergeant.' She smirked and held up a pink folder.

He opened the file and studied the photo before scanning the details with a sinking feeling. Not only did the badge they'd found in the backpack in the canal not belong to the victim, but its owner couldn't be a suspect, although she might have seen something.

Wise walked away.

'Hang on.'

She halted, her smile gone. 'Yes?'

25

'Can I speak to this' – he read the name on the file – 'Patience Okoy?'

'It's Okoye,' she said, frowning at him. 'I'll get a message to her.'

'Right – Okoye,' he said, his face growing warm. *How was he supposed to know?* 'And we could do with somewhere private to interview her.'

Her frown deepened, and she sighed. 'You'll have to sign in and get a badge.'

Antonia's pulse raced as she checked the corridor outside Reed-Mayhew's office. With a breathless thanks when she saw it was empty, she wheeled the trolley out and locked the door behind her. With so few people working on this floor, she didn't think she'd see anyone else, but anybody used to seeing the squat figure of Sabirah cleaning these offices would wonder what she was doing here. If they investigated and discovered what she'd done, she'd have wasted all those weeks of undercover work. And more worryingly, she'd also heard rumours of what Reed-Mayhew's private security guys did to those who crossed him, something Eleanor's horror story over breakfast had reinforced. Dismissing her fears, she set off for Sabirah's work station. She needed to return the trolley before she was spotted.

Voices came from the corridor and she ducked into the cleaner's cupboard, pulling the door shut, her heart thudding.

'—the Serb's doing it tonight,' a man's voice said.

She couldn't hear the reply but the speaker sounded like a man. A door opened and closed, cutting them off. *That was close – concentrate, Antonia.* She opened the door a crack and checked the corridor again before wheeling her trolley out. The sooner she got out of here . . .

She'd gone a few steps when the sound of footsteps made her jump. Where did he come from? She hadn't heard a door. The skin on her neck prickled, but she kept walking and told herself not to hurry. A tall thin man walked by and studied her. She recognised Mishkin, GRM's chief of security, from her briefing notes. He wore a three-piece pin-striped suit and gleaming white shirt with a flash of scarlet tie at his throat. She ignored him, stopping her trolley to concentrate on putting on a pair of disposable gloves.

He halted and demanded, 'What are you doing here?'

Seized by panic, Antonia couldn't think of an answer. She bent forward, pretending to search the locker near the bottom of the trolley.

'I asked you a question.'

'Sorry, sir?' She made herself look at him. His intense glare made her insides flutter. There was something familiar about it, but she couldn't place him.

'You're not our normal woman. What are you doing on this floor?'

The cover story she'd rehearsed flew out of her mind. Straightening, she took a deep breath. 'I ran out of floor cleaner, sir.' She gestured towards the cleaner's storeroom where Sabirah kept her supplies. Even to her it sounded lame.

He studied her with expressionless eyes, making her skin crawl. A strong scent of sandalwood wafted towards her and a distant memory stirred, adding to her unease.

'I suggest you return to your own floor.'

She didn't think she could speak, so just nodded. Then she watched as he made his way along the corridor and didn't exhale until he turned the corner.

A buzzer sounded, jolting her into the present. She took out her comms unit and read the message. 'Report to hygiene post F23.'

Blast! Someone must have noticed her missing. Still thinking about her encounter with Mishkin, she reached the twenty-third floor where Wise, the woman from personnel, waited with two strangers. Wise had already berated her for losing her security pass, so what did she want now?

Antonia studied the visitors. The man, around forty and stocky, needed a shave and his brown hair a comb. His younger companion had dark hair cut in a bob and a complexion suggesting she spent a lot of time outdoors. The man's blue eyes appraised Antonia, his thoughts clear. The pair gave off the air of police. She must forget her encounter with Mishkin and concentrate. The Border Force guards must have said something about her ID.

'This is Patience Okoye,' Wise said.

'Is anything wrong?' Antonia said, trying to keep her voice level. If she explained why she'd needed the fake ID, they might let her off, but she'd have well and truly blown her cover.

Wise indicated the visitors. 'These officers want to speak—'

'Sergeant Chapman.' The man produced an ID card, showing a well-groomed but grim-faced likeness. 'And Constable Sanchez. We're investigating a murder. We found a body in the City Road Basin.'

Panic gripped Antonia and her knees threatened to buckle. Pavlo must have drowned, and she'd left her DNA all over him.

CHAPTER 3

Eleanor waited in her hallway for the lift to take her down to the basement offices of The Electric Investigator, wondering how best to deal with Antonia. The doors opened with a swish and she wheeled her chair through the gap, catching her knuckle against the edge. The doors slid shut and she examined her hand, relieved the skin hadn't broken. It would just give Alan another excuse to lecture her about getting a power-chair. She might as well be in a coffin.

'Hello, Mrs Curtis,' Miles's cheerful baritone called as she rolled into the main office.

'Good morning, Miles. Love the waistcoat,' she said, pointing at the gaudy fabric covering his substantial midriff. His bushy beard seemed even more luxuriant, reminding her of her grandfather's.

Miles beamed and moved the box of files blocking her way. 'We need more space,' he muttered, an unwelcome reminder of rows she'd had with Alan on that subject.

She couldn't handle another one today. Her priority was making sure they wrapped up the GRM story; she'd pursued Gustav Reed-Mayhew for a long time and wasn't going to let him off the hook. She'd almost got him once, when he was still a smallish fish, but the firebombing had ended that opportunity. Telling Antonia about it had been a mistake, but at least she hadn't mentioned that the young accountant had been speaking to The Investigator. Now, Reed-Mayhew, with his huge government contracts, was anything but a small fish, but she wouldn't give up.

She tapped on Alan Turner's door before pushing it open. He unwound his legs before scrambling to his feet and edging round the untidy desk to push the visitor's chair aside. She manoeuvred herself into position while he returned to his seat and she exhaled in relief when he made it back to his chair without his long arms knocking anything off his desk. With receding hair and a perpetually furrowed brow, her nephew looked older than his thirty-three years. Had she done the right thing appointing him as editor? She didn't doubt his ability, but worried the responsibility weighed too heavily on his narrow shoulders. He pushed the black-rimmed glasses up his nose and cleared his throat.

'The monthly figures are good,' he said, handing his tablet across to her. 'We've added a few thousand subscribers but the uplift in temporary passes is most pleasing.'

Eleanor took it and read with a sense of satisfaction; she'd worked hard building up The Investigator. 'I presume the story about baby trafficking attracted most of the new readers?'

'Amongst others. The celebrity angle made sure we got plenty of interest and we've added about ninety thousand.'

She detected more than a hint of self-congratulation in his manner. *Okay, so you were right, Alan. Even our socially enlightened readers enjoy stories about celebrities.* 'How many do you think we'll keep?'

'Based on past figures, about thirty per cent will take out a subscription.'

Eleanor whistled. 'Those are serious numbers. It should take us into the top ten.'

'Seven,' he said, then cleared his throat again and studied his screen. 'We should consider monetising it.'

'Not again, Alan! You know my views.'

'But we don't have to compromise our values.' He opened his email browser. 'Since those figures came out, I've been contacted by several companies prepared to sponsor us, no strings attached. We wouldn't even need to place their ads or logos. They believe in what we do.'

'But they always want their pound of flesh, and will want to influence editorial policy, especially if the story involves them or their competitors.' The pulse in her temple pounded and she hoped she wouldn't develop a migraine.

'We need more space,' he said, sweeping an arm round the overcrowded room. 'The money will enable us to get somewhere bigger, so we can grow. Investigate more cases . . .'

'Please, Alan, I don't want to discuss it.' They could do with more money, but getting sponsorship always led to compromises.

The room felt as if someone had sucked the air out of it. Alan leant back in the chair and studied the ceiling. Eleanor tried to read his expression. *Don't let's fall out.*

He grinned. 'I'll tell them, thanks, but Mrs Curtis says no.'

'They'll call me a dippy old hippy,' she said, returning his smile. 'What about the GRM story?'

'The evidence is stacking up. GRM have been paying bribes to get contracts and keep them. They're also involved in manipulating the news cycle to benefit themselves—'

'In what way?' Was Reed-Mayhew that powerful now?

'I'm not entirely sure, but I've heard he's got dirt on most of the top people running the press. I'm expecting our mole to contact me, so should have a better idea afterwards. If I can persuade him to make a statement, we'll have a very strong centrepiece.'

'How likely is that?'

Turner looked less happy. 'Not very, if I'm honest.'

'I don't think it's wise to expose the poor man.'

'Oh, really?' Alan repositioned his glasses. 'He's planning to leave.'

Eleanor pondered how much to tell him. 'I'd imagine GRM have tied him up in contracts and he'd get hammered in the courts.' *Or worse.*

'What about Whistleblower Protection?'

Eleanor couldn't suppress a snort of laughter.

'Yeah, you're right.' Alan gave a rueful smile. 'At least once Antonia gets those documents he told us about we shouldn't need him, and even our solicitors will be satisfied.'

'Good.' At least Antonia's threat to pull out wouldn't jeopardise the main story. 'It's a pity she couldn't hide the voice-activated recorder in Reed-Mayhew's office.'

'Too much chance of it being discovered. His security team sweep it every day. Even tampering with his shredder isn't without risk.'

'Yes, I realise.' She hesitated before making her next suggestion. 'How would you feel if we dropped the investigation into Monika Hogan's disappearance?'

'Have you mentioned it to Antonia?' Turner leant forward.

Despite her exasperation with the girl, Eleanor didn't want Alan to think Antonia had lost her nerve. 'Keeping her in GRM is a risk, especially as she's not making much progress—'

'But she is. Didn't she mention it?'

Eleanor tried to hide her irritation. 'What's happened?'

'Antonia spoke to two men Monika hung out with when she worked at GRM, and she's sure at least one of them knows something.' Turner clicked a button and read off the screen. 'Zack Wichrowski and Gareth Beynon.'

'What do we know about them?'

'I've ordered background checks from ICS. And . . .'

She waited for her nephew to continue. 'And w*hat*?'

Turner examined his hands. 'Antonia met them for a drink.'

'You're not serious?' So much for Antonia's concern of discovery, silly girl. 'How could you let her?'

'I didn't! I told her it wasn't a good idea, but you know Antonia . . .'

'It's more than *not a good idea*. If these men were behind Monika's disappearance, we don't want Antonia anywhere near them.'

Turner blew air through his lips. 'As you said, we close down the investigation?'

'As soon as possible.' A weight lifted off her. Sometimes Antonia needed protection from herself. *Remind you of anyone, Eleanor?* But at least she'd had the sense to back away from fights when it became obvious she couldn't win. Antonia didn't have that switch.

Antonia fought to keep her feelings of panic from showing as Chapman studied her. Convinced he was about to accuse her of killing Pavlo, she tensed, ready to run. His gaze returned to the lump on her forehead as if he knew how she'd got it.

After an eternity, he said to Wise, 'Can we have the private room now?'

The words reached Antonia through a thick fog and she tried to control her heartbeat. Wise set off along the corridor, her clacking heels beating a tattoo on the floor.

'Come on, we'd better keep up.' Chapman winked at Antonia and followed.

She hesitated for a moment, thrown by his attitude, before falling into step behind him. Conscious of Sanchez bringing up the rear, she needed to concentrate on what she should tell them about last night. What the hell happened after she escaped from

Pavlo? She'd left him floundering in the canal, wet and furious, but very much alive.

Wise paused outside a door, consulted a screen set into the wall and, shielding her hand, keyed in an access code. The door swung open with a hiss, and she strode into the darkened room. A soft glow coming from the walls and ceiling increased until it bathed the chamber in bright light. She gestured at a pale wooden table surrounded by a dozen steel-framed chairs.

'Call when you're ready to leave,' she said, pointing at a telephone handset in the middle of the table. '9147.'

When Wise had swept out, Antonia studied the two officers. Chapman came across as amenable but Sanchez didn't conceal her dislike.

Chapman waited until the door closed behind Wise. 'Why don't we make ourselves comfortable?' he said, directing Okoye to a chair on the opposite side of the table.

Okoye walked round and took the seat. Taller than he, even wearing flat shoes, she had golden brown skin and strong features. He wondered which part of Africa she came from. The unflattering clothes hid a good body, slim but not skinny.

A furrowed-browed Sanchez scrutinised him as he studied Okoye.

'Set up the recorder please, Alice.'

While she arranged the portable camera, he inspected the lump above Okoye's right eye. Did her man hit her? *Bastard.* Why did women put up with that shit?

'Can you say your name?' Sanchez said.

Okoye leant forward, but Chapman held up his hand. 'No need, it will pick your voice up from there.'

'Patience Okoye,' she said in a firm voice.

Chapman questioned the air of panic appearing to grip her when he'd introduced himself. Perhaps she was an illegal. If so, he didn't want to know. 'Ms Okoye, we're making enquiries about a body we found in the City Road Basin this morning,' he said. She opened her mouth and blinked but recovered so fast he wasn't sure if he'd imagined it. Never mind. If Sanchez hadn't noticed, they'd analyse the images later. 'Do you know the area?'

'Yes.' Her voice caught. 'I live near there.'

'When were you there last?'

She bit her lip and hesitated before saying, 'Last night.'

'What time?' he said, leaning forward. Had she seen the killer?

She pulled at her earlobe. 'Why don't you tell me? You film everything.'

Sanchez bristled. 'Those cameras are for our citizens' safety, so people like you can walk unmolested.'

Okoye laughed, and Sanchez stiffened further.

'The time?' Chapman asked again. Hadn't Sanchez just been lecturing him on finessing subjects?

Okoye sighed. 'About nine forty-five.'

'That's late,' Sanchez said.

'Last time I checked there wasn't a curfew.' She glared at Sanchez.

Spots of colour appeared on Sanchez's cheeks and Chapman took over before the interview got out of hand. Okoye wasn't behaving like an illegal. 'Did you see anyone else?'

Okoye glanced to her left before saying, 'Just a homeless man.'

'What was he doing?' he said, almost certain she'd lied, but why?

She studied Sanchez, her expression mocking. 'He attacked me.'

Chapman sat up straight and pointed at the lump on her forehead. 'Is that how you got the bruise?'

She nodded.

'Can we take a DNA sample?'

'Why?'

'Nothing to worry about,' he said, reconsidering his opinion about her being an illegal. 'Traces of his DNA might remain in the wound and we also need to eliminate yours. We'll destroy it once we've finished with it.'

'I've showered twice since last night.'

'We still need to eliminate you,' Sanchez said.

'I don't understand. Why?'

'Let's move on, Ms Okoye,' Chapman said; they could always return to this later.

'Why didn't you report the attack?' Sanchez said.

'Would you have caught him?'

'If you people don't report these crimes—'

'Can you give us more details?' Chapman cut across Sanchez.

Okoye took a few moments to answer. 'The man swore at me, called me a black bitch or something, and chased me. I dropped my backpack and ran.' She folded her arms and sat back.

'Can you describe him?'

She shrugged. 'A tramp. Scruffy, dirty, smelly.'

'What about age, height, colour?' Sanchez said. 'Don't you want him caught?'

Okoye glowered at the constable before saying, 'About sixty, white, under the dirt, about one eighty tall and skinny, about seventy kilos.'

'What about his clothes?'

'It was dark.'

'Did he have anything with him? A holdall, carrier bags?' Sanchez snapped.

'A bright pink sleeping bag.'

'Can you work with one of our technicians to produce a Replicant?' Chapman said, irritated at Sanchez's manner. He'd have to speak to her about how she questioned witnesses; this wasn't the way to encourage them to come forward.

'I didn't see his face.'

'Don't worry, the Replicant Generator will pick up details you didn't even realise you'd seen.'

Okoye hesitated, reluctant to comply, before agreeing. What the hell was she hiding?

◆ ◆ ◆

Antonia's thoughts churned as Chapman led her out of the building. She shouldn't have let the constable get to her. Neither of them believed her version of events, but they needed to *prove* she'd lied. Pavlo had still been alive when she left him, she was certain, but doubted they'd believe her, especially Sanchez. She shouldn't have left him in the water. A brain compression might have caused him to pass out later. The story of a mugger suing a boxer who'd resisted had been at the back of her mind, not to mention the thought of being stuck in a police station for hours, but if she'd known Pavlo would turn up dead, she *would* have reported the attack and at least they'd have her statement and couldn't accuse her of concealing their encounter.

'This way please,' Chapman said, leading her towards a small car.

He operated the remote lock and opened the rear door, gesturing for her to get in. Sanchez hovered behind her and slammed the door, which clicked locked. A sharp citrus smell of air freshener stung Antonia's nostrils. The two officers climbed in, separated from her by a glass screen. The engine engaged with a soft whirr and they moved forward. Antonia stared out of the window, worrying about the Replicant Generator. Would it create a replica of the tramp or Pavlo? She didn't know enough about how they worked. She should have paid more attention at the press launch. What did the technician who'd explained it say? If she concentrated on the tramp, it might produce his likeness.

After a short journey, the car stopped in front of a large steel barrier and with a start, she realised they'd arrived. A light flashed, then the gate slid open revealing a ramp leading downwards. The vehicle rolled forward, and as it went under the building, a tight band constricted her chest and she closed her eyes. *Don't panic, Antonia, you need to stay alert.*

'Here we are,' Chapman announced, as if they'd just arrived at a social gathering.

The doors clicked again and she heaved herself out of the seat before standing between the two officers, sweat trickling down her back. The urge to escape almost overwhelmed her, but running would make things worse. She just needed to get through this ordeal. The two officers led her through a doorway into a stark corridor with a pale tiled floor and dark-green walls. They must be under the main police station at Holborn. The thought of so much concrete above them made her dizzy. She allowed Chapman to lead her into a room accessed through two pairs of automatic doors. A fuzzy grey carpet replaced the tiled floors and soft lighting the harsh glare of the strip lights in the corridor. A machine resembling a compact photocopier in an aluminium case sat on a table. Cables linked it to a large 3D printer and a man in a pristine white lab coat waited by a seat alongside it. Chapman gestured towards the chair and when Antonia hesitated, Sanchez nudged her forward.

An hour later, the technician who'd set up the Replicant Generator removed the helmet lined with electrical contacts from Antonia's head, not hiding his disapproval of her. She ignored him and studied the figure produced by the 3D printer. Despite her attempt to focus on the tramp's image, the machine produced a remarkable likeness of the one called Arkady. *What a mess, but at least it wasn't Pavlo.* She considered how to handle this setback as the technician packed the equipment away.

'This isn't the man she described,' Chapman said.

The technician folded his arms. '*I* don't control the machine. The witness does, and that's what it produced. The witness either misremembered or . . .' He glanced at Antonia, closed the case and snapped the lock shut. 'I'll leave you to it then, Sergeant.'

'You're sure this is the man who attacked you?' Chapman said.

Now her plan of describing the tramp had failed, she had to go along with this, otherwise they'd grow more suspicious. Antonia nodded, not trusting herself to speak.

'Are you sure? Please study it again, it's very important.'

She focused on the 3D image. 'Yes, that's the man who attacked me.'

'You put him at sixty, but he's nearer thirty,' Sanchez said. 'And living on the streets would age him even more.'

Antonia glared at her. 'He might have been younger.'

'He's a *lot* younger.'

'Okay, Patience, you can go, but I may need to talk to you again,' Chapman said, ignoring Sanchez's reaction.

A grateful Antonia put her coat on. 'Do you know the identity of the victim?'

'We haven't identified her yet.'

'Her?'

'The victim's a young woman, but please keep it to yourself,' Chapman said.

Chapman headed for the office he shared with Sanchez, not looking forward to having to wade through hours of CCTV. Sanchez followed and he could sense her disapproval.

'Spit it out,' he said.

'Why did you let her go? She's hiding something and she's a suspect—'

'Did you see the injuries on the victim?'

'No. But—'

'I did, and—'

'You're saying a woman couldn't—'

'Whoever killed the victim punched her. Their hands would be a mess.'

'What if she wore gloves?'

No way could a woman have inflicted those injuries, at least not one he'd met. 'Constable, if you're unhappy at the way I'm doing my job, take it up with the inspector.'

Sanchez hesitated for a few seconds before walking on. In their office they each downloaded footage from different cameras. Chapman ignored the uncomfortable silence and studied his colleague. She had a reputation as a good copper, but she had a downer on Okoye. Maybe she had a problem with Black people, but as long as it didn't affect her job . . .

After an interminable hour of fast-forwarding footage of deserted streets, he yawned, and considered taking a break. Then a man ambled across the corner of the screen carrying two bulky holdalls. His weariness banished, Chapman sat up and concentrated on the image, studying it until the figure moved out of shot. After rewinding the footage he watched again, pausing it when the man appeared in full view. The guy looked the right age.

'Alice,' he said.

Sanchez raised her gaze from the screen. 'You found something?'

'I've found the bloke she described. The old tramp. And that pale blob could be a pink sleeping bag.'

Sanchez came behind him and studied the screen. The faint aroma of her body spray wafted towards him and her disapproval evaporated as she studied the action. 'I think you're right, Sarge. So, he could have attacked her.'

'Yeah, but why produce *him*?' He indicated the Replicant.

'If you hadn't let her go, we could ask her.'

Not rising to the bait, he pressed play. The tramp stopped at a side road and appeared to speak to someone off-screen.

A minute later a group of men came into view and surrounded the tramp. He froze the image and checked the time stamp on the film. According to the girl, this was ten minutes before the attack.

'Can you see any of the faces?' Sanchez said.

Chapman zoomed in but at this range they could just make out pale blobs. He counted six altogether. 'IT might be able to enhance it.'

'What about him?' Sanchez pointed at a figure who acted like the leader. 'He's got the right build.'

Chapman studied the Replicant, then the figure. 'It could be.'

'Why didn't she mention he was with—'

'Maybe they split up.' Although he agreed with Sanchez: why *didn't* Okoye mention the others?

The men's leader spoke to the tramp, then handed him something. He spoke to the others and four of them marched away from the camera to disappear off-screen. After a few seconds the other two and the tramp strolled down the side road until they too vanished.

'Can you check the cameras down there?' he said, but Sanchez had already returned to her desk.

The screen flickered as he fast-forwarded the images of the unpopulated streets until another figure appeared. Tall and upright, Patience Okoye strode across the screen until she reached the junction with the side road, paused, then advanced along it, halting at the edge of the picture. She seemed to be arguing with someone.

'We could do with sound on these things. Alice, you got those cameras?'

'Hmmm . . .'

'What?'

'They're not working.'

'Have you tried the next—'

'Of course, right to the end.' She returned and stood behind him.

'Sorry.' The two men came out, past Okoye.

'Why didn't Okoye mention there were two of them?' Sanchez leant towards the screen and the smell of her body spray grew stronger.

'They're leaving, I bet only one of them returned.' The two men strode away, then the leader halted. 'There, I told you.' Chapman waited for the man to attack Okoye but he blew her a kiss and walked on.

For a few seconds nothing happened, then the men returned, this time all six of them, before advancing towards Okoye and the tramp.

'What the hell happened there?' Chapman said.

'If I hadn't seen Okoye, I'd say those men paid the tramp to lure her down there to attack – shit! Did they kill the other woman?'

He slapped the desk. 'We need to find those lads and that tramp.' He brought up a map of the district and outlined the area between where Okoye went off camera and where they'd found the woman's body. 'Let's check the footage on all these cameras.' It would take the rest of the day, but the belief they'd identified the killers filled him with energy.

'What about Okoye?'

Sanchez's obsession irritated Chapman. 'This backs up her story.'

'You think? She lied to us, Sarge. No idea why, but we need to get her back in and find out.'

◆ ◆ ◆

42

Antonia didn't relax until she got on the Tube home. She'd half-expected releasing her to be a trick and them to follow her. But it must be true; Pavlo wasn't dead. Despite her relief, apprehension still gripped her and myriad thoughts swirled through her head. She shouldn't have given her DNA, but under the new Prevention of Terrorism Act she had no choice. Should she return and tell Chapman about her real attacker? But the thought of facing him, and Sanchez, made her queasy. She tried to remember what Pavlo looked like, but as she'd told Chapman, it had been too dark. Anyway, if they found Arkady using the likeness she'd created, they'd get Pavlo and the rest of the gang.

Who was the poor woman who died? Could Antonia have done anything to stop her getting killed? The thought that the body might be Monika kept intruding into her thoughts, but she refused to believe it. Although Monika often used that route, she'd gone missing weeks ago, and Antonia had to hold on to the belief she was still alive. Despite what she'd said to Eleanor, she'd carry on and would find her friend. Her disappearance *was* linked to someone she met at GRM, not a random street gang. Thoughts jittering about, she got off the Tube and walked the last stretch home, not knowing what to do. Eleanor usually acted as her sounding board, but she didn't want to explain why she'd not said anything about last night's events at breakfast this morning. By the time she reached Vincent Terrace she'd decided to tell Turner.

She walked down the stone staircase leading to the basement. The sight of the brass plaque beside the main door, with 'The Electric Investigator' in cursive script across the top, still gave her a thrill. Below, in a classic font, ran the Louis Brandeis quote that inspired Eleanor to set up the press: 'Sunlight is said to be the best of disinfectants; electric light the most efficient policeman.'

At the bottom of the steps, she unlocked the reinforced door and let herself into the reception room, taking care not to trip on the two chairs shoehorned into it. In the main office Miles greeted her with his usual cheery smile, which faded when he noticed her demeanour. A wave of exhaustion washed over her, but she knocked on Turner's door and pushed it open before she could change her mind.

'Everything okay?' Turner asked.

'No,' she said, clearing the files off his visitor's chair and slumping into it. When she finished her account of being attacked and the discovery of a woman's body in the same location, her remaining energy drained away.

Turner tapped his teeth with a pencil for several seconds. 'You think this gang is behind the murder?'

'Don't you? I'm pretty sure they'd have killed me if I hadn't escaped.'

He swallowed. 'I suppose so.'

Antonia hesitated. 'Monika used that route a lot. If they killed this woman, then . . .' Putting the thought into words took too much effort.

'You think the body's Monika?'

Although on one level she accepted her friend might be dead, the reality of finding her body wasn't something she could face. 'Possibly.'

Turner appeared to search for the right words before saying, 'Did the police say how long the body . . . Well, you know.'

Tears pricked her eyes and she shook her head. The question had coursed through her mind on her way home.

'Did you detect anything when you confronted the gang?'

'What? Like a murderous intent?'

'You're usually spot-on at reading how people will react—'

'I can't read minds.' Something about Arkady had struck her as odd, but what?

'I don't think it's Monika,' he said in a low voice. 'If they'd killed her there, would they go hunting another woman in the same area?'

'Why not? If they'd hidden her body for this long . . .' An image she'd seen, of a bloated body recovered from a disused well, flashed into her memory. The thought of Monika in the same state after lying in murky water for weeks made bile rise in her throat.

'What about the two guys from GRM you're investigating?'

'Zack and Gareth? They might be part of the same gang—'

'They were there?'

'No! They'd have recognised me.' Something Pavlo said snagged at her memory, something about money. She needed to do more research. The government hadn't introduced a bounty yet, but she'd heard rumours of white supremacist groups offering rewards for black 'scalps'.

Turner shifted in his seat and studied his screen. 'Eleanor's asked me to drop the investigation into Monika and—'

'You've discussed it behind my back?'

'She's worried about you.'

'I'm not dropping it now. If it was those men, I'm going to nail them.'

'No way. One of them almost killed you and probably killed someone else. Leave it to the police.'

'But I gave them the wrong description.'

'Don't worry, they'll have plenty of footage from the area.'

'I doubt it,' she said. 'Someone damaged most of the cameras.'

'Anti-Surveillance League?'

'Or someone who wanted the cameras there disabled, posing as the ASL.'

Turner frowned. 'I wouldn't worry about it. They've got the leader from your description, so should find the others.'

Antonia agreed, but Eleanor's accusation still stung. 'I'll find them.'

'It's too dangerous—'

'I'm doing it whether you help me or not. I'll start straight away.'

'Sorry, but I can't let you pull out of GRM yet—'

'You've got enough to run the story. We've got all those officials we can prove took money from GRM—'

'The story's got a lot bigger. I spoke to our mole. He says he can link GRM to the King's Cross bomb.'

'IS claimed they'd done it.'

'They'll take credit for *any* terrorist attacks. Our mole says GRM were about to lose a new security contract—'

'Until the King's Cross bomb,' Antonia finished for him. Were GRM instigating terrorist incidents to promote their security business? My God, this was far bigger than corporate corruption.

CHAPTER 4

Still thinking about why Okoye would lie, Chapman wandered into the conference room. The absence of chatter, despite the room being full, alerted him to the fact that the briefing had started. He searched for a seat near the back but only found space in the front row.

'Sergeant, glad you could join us.' Harding stood at the lectern, making a show of examining his watch. 'Second time today we've waited for you. Sorry we couldn't arrange the meeting to suit you.'

A few people tittered and Chapman's face grew warm as he made his way to an empty chair. 'No need to apologise, *Inspector*,' he said, and sat.

Harding scowled at him before turning his attention to his tablet. He swept his hand across the device and an image appeared on the screen beside him. 'This is the victim, an unidentified woman in her early twenties. The killer subjected her to a severe beating resulting in internal injuries and a fractured skull. Forensics tell us he used fists to inflict the damage, and from the traces of cured leather in the wounds we can surmise gloved fists.'

'So, we're searching for a man, boss?' Sanchez said.

'Let's not jump to conclusions, Constable—'

'Are you suggesting a woman would batter someone to death?' Chapman said, still smarting. 'Alice is right. Apart from the tremendous power needed to inflict such injuries, anyone who'd studied crime would know women rarely carry out these sorts of attacks.'

'Sergeant, I'm just suggesting we keep an open mind.'

'There's keeping an open mind and ignoring the obvious. Why haven't we got any DNA results yet? Are we waiting for CrimTech to pull their finger out and do the analysis?'

Harding glowered at him. 'I don't think we can accuse the professionals at CrimTech of being slow, Sergeant.'

'Really? Maybe you shouldn't let personal feelings interfere with your professional judgement, Inspector—'

'What's that supposed to mean?'

Chapman took a childish pleasure in Harding's reaction. His boss, DCI Gunnerson, glared at him, but he ignored her and Harding continued. The briefing ended and the DCI made a bee-line for Chapman. He headed for the exit, but she intercepted him.

'Russell, a word,' she said and swept off, making him feel like a naughty boy summoned to see the headmistress.

In her office, she rounded on him. 'Shut the door. So, you're unhappy about being busted from DCI to sergeant? That's not Ian's fault. If you don't like it, find another job. Don't score cheap points off him. He's a decent officer doing his best.'

'Has he come bleating to you then?'

'No, he bloody well hasn't. But I wouldn't blame him if he did.'

Chapman realised he was being an arse. 'Yeah, you're right. Sorry.'

'It's not me you should apologise to.' Her expression softened. 'I know it's tough, but kicking against the system won't make life any easier and we need everyone working together on this one.'

Chapman hurried to Harding's office, eager to get the apology out of the way, and knocked on the door.

Harding made him wait. 'Come in. Oh, it's you.' He waved at a chair across the room and Chapman sat.

The two men studied each other across the desk, empty except for a laptop and telephone, in marked contrast to Chapman's own untidy office. As he considered what to say, he scanned the room and fastened on the photo of a younger Harding receiving his top recruit's award at the end of his training course. Chapman had a similar photo but after they'd busted him down from DCI, he'd removed it from his office. Harding waited for him to say his piece.

Let's get it over with. 'Ian, I wanted to apologise. I was out of order. Sorry.' He stuck out his hand.

Harding studied it for a moment before taking it, saying, 'We all make mistakes.'

That wasn't too painful. 'Right, I'd better get back to work.' He'd got halfway through the door, thinking of Okoye, when Harding said, 'Russell . . .'

Chapman paused.

'Make sure it doesn't happen again.'

Chapman slammed the door and marched to his office, wishing he hadn't bothered.

Sanchez sat at her screen, analysing the footage of the interview. 'Anything, Alice?'

'Okoye was definitely lying about something,' she said in a tone suggesting she wasn't surprised. 'How did it go?'

Chapman entwined his index and middle fingers. 'Ian and I are like this now.'

'Glad to hear it,' she said, smiling.

'At which point did she lie?'

Sanchez rewound the footage. 'This bit, where you asked her about City Road Basin. I ran it through Polysmart and there's a ninety-three per cent probability she lied.' She leant forward and pointed at the figures across the bottom of the screen. 'I thought so at the time.'

'Women's intuition, or did you just not like her?'

'Sergeant, *I* don't let my personal feelings interfere with work—'

'And I do?'

'No, I didn't mean . . .' Her chin quivered and she blinked. 'But she *is* a suspect.'

'Witness,' he said.

'The killer wore gloves and you—'

'Don't forget someone also attacked *her*, probably the same people.'

'So she says, but she identified someone else, and anyway, why didn't she report it?'

Chapman had asked himself the same question but hadn't come up with a satisfactory answer. 'Okay, let's go back to the recording. What about when she described her attacker?'

'She lied then. It's less definite, but still about eighty per cent.'

'What have you got to hide, young lady?' he said, addressing Okoye's image in an undertone.

Sanchez ran the footage of the interview on until it finished. 'Shall we check the CCTV over a larger area?'

'It can't hurt.' And it would keep him out of Harding's way. 'Did we get any from the premises overlooking the water where we found the body?'

'Afraid not. They had a fault on the system.'

'Typical, they never bloody work when you need them.'

◆ ◆ ◆

Antonia sat across the desk from a troubled-looking Turner and placed her empty mug down. 'What exactly did your mole say about King's Cross?'

Turner leant forward, wearing what Eleanor described as his 'earnest schoolboy' expression. 'He said, "Don't you think it's convenient that every time a proposal to spend more on security encounters resistance, something occurs to make the opposition melt away?"'

'Did he mention King's Cross?'

'No, but he made it clear what he meant. GRM paid someone a lot of money, immediately before the last three bombings in the city.'

'Has he got anything we can use?'

'He claims to have evidence.' Turner checked his watch. 'He should have made contact about an hour ago.'

'You think something's happened to him?'

'He's never missed a deadline.'

'What if he's bullshitting? He might be embarrassed . . .'

'He's not the type.' His attention returned to the screen. 'I've sent a message which he should pick up tonight. In the meantime make sure you collect the papers from Reed-Mayhew's shredder tomorrow. You did disable it so it only cuts the paper into strips?'

'Of course.' The encounter with Mishkin still unsettled her.

'Great, they should help us identify the senior government people GRM is bribing, not just the small fry. Maybe even a minister.'

'What if there's nothing there?'

'We've enough evidence of dodgy financial dealings to run a story, but I want to do them as much damage as possible. And if we get evidence of a minister taking backhanders . . .'

'So, we can run a story, whether or not there's anything there.'

'We'll run the story when it's ready.' Turner's jaw had a determined set to it. 'Until then, you stay at GRM.'

She wanted to argue, but she *had* agreed to do this and she'd see it through. 'In the meantime can we investigate the men who attacked me?'

'What did Eleanor say when you told her you'd been attacked? She didn't mention it this morning.'

'I didn't tell her.'

Turner studied her, open-mouthed. 'Why not?'

'I don't want her worrying. Can we not tell her about this investigation?'

He stared at the screen. 'I wouldn't be at all happy about deceiving her—'

'We're not deceiving her, we're just not telling—'

'Come on, Antonia, it's not like you to be disingenuous.'

Her cheeks grew hot. 'You'll get Miles to start the research?'

'I'll ask him to run the names through the Zorro database. It's got a section on youth gangs. The combination of names is unusual enough to flag up; I can't imagine we'll find too many Pavlos. You up to making a start now?'

She checked the time. 'I can do half an hour. I presume you're happy with my contribution to the article.'

He looked uncomfortable. 'It could do with a bit of work.'

'Oh.' She'd spent longer polishing this piece of writing than any she'd submitted. 'What's wrong with it?'

'Nothing.' He opened a drawer and pulled out a sheaf of papers. Despite having always worked with computers, he'd adopted Eleanor's old-fashioned approach to editing, and red squiggles disfigured the text.

'That doesn't look like nothing.' She plucked the papers from his hand.

'The main issue is you're too' – he searched for a word – 'definitive.'

'I believe in what I've written. Should I be more circumspect?'

'Sorry, what I meant was, you're telling the reader who the bad guys are—'

'That's what we're here for.'

'We're here to shine a light on proceedings. Our readers make up their minds on who the villains are. Your job is to ensure they reach the correct conclusions without shouting, "Here's the bad guy, over here!"'

She glanced at the pages in her hand. 'Maybe I have been a bit forthright.'

'It just needs tweaking. It's otherwise very good, clear and authoritative, and your passion shines through.'

'Tweaking? It needs a complete rewrite. I'll do it when I get back and email it to you.'

'Oh. You going out somewhere?'

She bit her lip. 'I'm seeing Zack and Gareth tonight.'

'Are you serious? I thought we agreed you'd drop the investigation into Monika?'

'I didn't.' The prospect of meeting up with the two thugs filled her with dread, but if it helped her find out what had happened to Monika . . .

'I told you it was a bad idea last time.'

'Don't worry. I'm going with Kerry and we're meeting them in a busy bar. There'll be loads of people around.'

Chapman studied the scruffy three-storey Victorian house as the echo of the doorbell faded. Blue gloss paint had peeled off the door exposing a paler matt finish. Sanchez pressed the button again and he hoped nobody would answer. Let someone else deliver the bad news. Like all his colleagues, he'd always hated telling families they'd lost a loved one. Harding must have given him the job as a punishment for their earlier clash. Sounds from within told him he'd be disappointed.

A muscular man of about forty, wearing a hooded top and cut-off sweatpants, opened the door and scrutinised the two officers. 'I he'p you?' he said in an accent Chapman couldn't place.

'Police,' Chapman said and introduced the two of them. 'Are you Mr Rizk?'

'You want Aida?' He grinned. 'There's no Mr Rizk. Not in this country. Maybe her father.' This time he laughed.

'And you are?' Sanchez said.

'Alex. Her landlord.' He folded his arms. 'Aida's not here.'

'I'm afraid—'

'Do you know where she's gone?' Chapman cut across Sanchez.

Alex shrugged and leered at Sanchez. 'Maybe with her girlfriend.'

Chapman's dislike of the man intensified. 'Can we check her room, Alex?'

'I'm going to gym—'

'It won't take long.' Chapman stepped into the doorway.

Alex moved away and jerked his thumb upwards. 'Top floor.'

Chapman took the stairs and Alex followed. Uncarpeted, each tread had white gloss only at the edges, leaving a strip of bare timber in the centre where a runner had once lain. Peeling woodchip, painted pale blue, lined the walls. A fishy smell permeated the air, growing weaker as they ascended, until the odour of stale sweat and shower gel overpowered it. The layout resembled Chapman's old home, with the second flight of stairs narrower, reminding him of the nursery he'd decorated for Abby in the attic room. He'd quickly recognised his mistake after having to run up and down those stairs in the middle of the night. A panelled door with a crack across the right section blocked the top of the stairs.

Chapman indicated the lock. 'You got the key?'

'No need.' Alex reached past him and jerked the frame until the lock popped. The ease with which he accomplished it suggesting he'd done it often.

I bet you're a joy to have as a landlord. 'Wait here please, sir,' Chapman said and, pulling on a pair of blue nitrile gloves, pushed past him.

'What happen?' Alex demanded.

Chapman turned on the lights. This part of the house could have been in a different building. Thick cream carpet covered the floor and expensive wallpaper with stylised flamingos on it lined the walls. Chapman paused while he put on overshoes, noting Sanchez already wore hers.

Alex retreated to the landing below. 'Something wrong with Aida?'

'Please wait there, sir,' Sanchez said, and joined Chapman.

Alex watched in silence, subdued by the turn of events. Chapman realised he should consider him a suspect, but although the guy looked as if he'd be a handful, he didn't appear to present any threat.

The apartment comprised a bedsit-cum-kitchen and a small bathroom. The kitchen units and bathroom fittings were old but spotless. A large red sofa bed Chapman thought he recognised from one of Brigitte's housey magazines sat opposite a forty-inch screen mounted on one wall.

Sanchez searched the bathroom while he made a start with the kitchen units. Sanchez joined him and rummaged in a built-in wardrobe in an alcove by the bed.

'Everything's so bloody tidy,' he said. 'Reminds me of the time I shared a flat with an ex-submariner.'

'When was that?' Sanchez said, peering in the wardrobe.

'I was still a PC in uniform. The guy used to cook and eat all his meals off an enamel plate and mug—'

'Hang on, Sarge.' She brandished a tablet.

'Bag it.' Chapman opened the last drawer and found a phone under a pile of ironed tea towels. It wasn't locked and he checked the texts. Sanchez joined him as he read the latest, from someone called Benjamin. Wre fck r u bitch. Ule regret fckng me about. 'Bloody hell!' He angled the screen so she could read.

'Nice one.' She gave him a big grin.

'Bag this as well and we'll return to the station,' he said. 'I'm confident nothing's happened here, but we'll seal it just in case. Let's get Alex's details and find out what he knows and when he last saw her.'

'Shall we take him in?' Sanchez said, reaching for her handcuffs.

'I'd love to, but unless his middle name's Benjamin I don't think so.' The message gave them a great lead, but a sense of unease tempered his excitement.

◆ ◆ ◆

Chapman fought his way through the commuter traffic, each hold-up reminding him how far he now travelled to get home. He drove round for ten minutes searching for a parking space, his temper not improved when a young kid in a Fiat nipped into a gap he'd spotted. By the time he had walked to the terraced house he shared with Brigitte, he'd calmed down.

The immaculate black paint on the front door contrasted with the neglected house he and Sanchez had searched. An unwelcome thought intruded – he might have ended up somewhere like it if he hadn't got together with Brigitte – but he dismissed it. The scent from the candles she burnt every evening lingered in the hallway and Chapman removed his shoes, placing them in the bottom of the antique hallstand they'd bought on their trip to Bruges. Brigitte wasn't home yet, and he'd started his second glass of red while trying to forget about the case when the front door opened.

'Anyone home?' she called out.

'In here,' he said, cheered up by her greeting.

Brigitte appeared in the doorway, smiling. The luminous Lycra outfit clung to her slim body and perspiration dampened her long blonde hair. She saw the glass and her smile faded.

'Do you want one?' He picked up the bottle and filled a second glass.

'No, thank you.' She made a show of examining the level of wine before slipping off her backpack. 'I'm off to have a shower.'

Chapman glared at her retreating figure and slammed the bottle on to the table. He resisted the temptation to refill his glass and busied himself preparing the pasta dish he'd planned for tonight's meal.

He stood at the stove, letting his resentment simmer while stirring the sauce until she returned. What did she know of the pressures he faced? She squeezed his shoulder, the nearest he'd get to an apology, and wedged herself between him and the cooker. The smell of strawberry shampoo filled his nostrils and she kissed him. He responded, pulling her close. Under the satin bathrobe she wore nothing.

His hands slid down the fabric and came to rest below her waist, feeling the firm muscles move beneath her skin. He crushed her into him and she gripped his buttocks, grinding her groin against his. His heart stuttered, and they broke apart, gasping for breath and laughing. Her eyes shone and she slipped the robe off her shoulders. The slick material flowed off her body to gather in folds where his hands clamped it to her lower back. He let it slip to the floor and she slid a hand down the front of his shirt.

His throat thick, he stepped away and studied her, drinking in her toned body, the hint of holiday tan still visible. She smiled and licked her lips before gripping his belt and pulling. Her hand went lower, and he gasped as she squeezed him. He cupped his hands round her buttocks and lifted her on to the worktop.

They ate the overcooked pasta in an agreeable afterglow and were halfway through a second bottle of red as he finished telling her about Okoye.

'But I'm also an immigrant,' she replied.

'Yes, but you . . .'

'But what?' she said, lowering her glass.

He didn't like the direction of the conversation. 'But you're working as a lawyer, making a valuable contribution.'

'And this woman is "just a cleaner",' she said, making quotation marks in the air. 'Isn't that a valuable job?'

His face grew warm. 'Yes, I know, but you've assimilated, you speak perfect English and you embrace our customs . . .'

'So this woman didn't speak English?' Her eyes hardened.

'Yes . . .' Better than he'd expected; she spoke like a graduate and although he'd encountered many well-educated people in menial positions, something about her didn't add up. He'd get Okoye in again first thing.

Antonia hurried towards her rendezvous, a trendy bar she wouldn't normally be seen dead in, teetering in the heels she'd made herself wear. As she arrived, she checked the short queue outside the entrance. The men she'd arranged to meet weren't there and she hoped they hadn't arrived early. Although she'd briefed Kerry, she wanted a chat with her before they got here.

She handed her coat in at the cloakroom by the bottom of the stairs and pushed her way into the bar, feeling exposed in a skirt barely covering her bum. A wall of heat fortified with the odour of stale alcohol hit her as she walked into the main room. A long bar took up most of the left side. Groups of well-dressed people filled the space in front of it. Low music provided a background to the murmur of myriad conversations.

'Antonia!'

Heads turned towards the shout.

Antonia scanned the room, her insides fluttery. She'd told Kerry the men knew her as Patience. Her anxiety eased when she didn't see them. A gaggle of admirers encircled Kerry, leaving glimpses of her head visible between their shoulders, a copper cloud surrounding a pale oval. The three young men vying for her attention studied Antonia, who put on a smile and joined them. *I'm about to spoil your evening, boys.* She leant forward and embraced Kerry, experiencing a surge of comfort as the odour of Charlie enveloped her.

'Girlfriend. Let me check you out?' Kerry held her at arm's length. 'You're hot.'

'You're looking great,' Antonia said, before glancing at Kerry's admirers. 'Sorry guys, we'll love you and leave you. Women's talk.'

She squeezed Kerry's elbow and led her to a booth at the far end of the room. A waiter scurried over and Antonia ordered a bottle of Australian Shiraz.

'Not having the usual fizzy water?' Kerry said.

'I need fortifying.'

'Wow, things must be serious.'

'The first thing, you need to call me Patience and you're Kim, like we agreed.'

'Don't worry, I haven't forgotten.'

'You seemed to forget when you shouted my name. Lucky they weren't here.'

'It wasn't lucky. I've been here twenty minutes and knew they hadn't arrived yet. Chill, girl.' Kerry gave her a big grin.

Antonia returned a half-hearted smile. This wasn't a good idea. If those men were behind Monika's disappearance, they should have nothing to do with them. But it was too late to pull out now. She detailed the events of the last twenty-four hours to Kerry. Kerry's words of sympathy took Antonia back ten years, to the last time her friend had comforted her at the care home, after – Antonia blinked away tears. She mustn't think about those times.

Kerry studied the small lump on Antonia's forehead and reached across to grip her forearm, then her large blue eyes widened. 'You don't think they could have anything to do with Monika . . . ?'

'First thing I thought of.'

'What about the two we're meeting?'

We still have time to pull out, but if we stay in this busy bar, I'm sure we'll be okay. 'I still think Gareth had something to do with her disappearance. Monika said he had an unhealthy interest in serial killers and was always talking about the best way to dispose of bodies.'

'God! What was she doing with him?'

Antonia shrugged. 'You know Monika, crap taste in men. I don't think I met one of her boyfriends that didn't make my flesh creep.'

'Perhaps he's linked to this gang you ran into and they work together, preying on women—'

A discreet cough announced the return of the waiter, who opened the bottle and poured the drinks. Antonia waited for him to leave before taking a generous mouthful and explaining her plans, finishing as two figures approached: Zack, tall and wiry with small round glasses and a goatee and Gareth, shorter but with huge shoulders.

'Evening, ladies,' Zack said, his cockney accent pronounced. He bent over Kerry's hand. 'You must be Kim.'

Gareth mumbled a greeting in a thick Brummie accent. The two men joined them on the bench seat, Gareth throwing himself alongside Antonia, sitting much too close, and Zack taking a place opposite, next to Kerry. Antonia manufactured a smile and eased herself away, but Gareth slid closer. Kerry, as usual, maintained a stream of lively chatter.

Antonia struggled to hide her revulsion at Gareth's proximity while trying to read the two men, finding it harder than usual to sense their responses. Although they seemed relaxed, she detected a tension between them, Gareth glancing at Zack, as if taking cues from him. Each time she thought she'd got a handle on them, thoughts of what Monika could have gone through kept intruding and even more disturbing scenes from ancient nightmares flashed into her mind. With an effort she suppressed them and concentrated on studying the men's reactions. If they drank some more, she might find it easier.

She signalled to the waiter as he hovered solicitously, and he brought more wine. Careful to moderate her intake, Antonia topped up the men's glasses. As Kerry regaled them with a tale of being pulled over for speeding, Antonia considered how to turn the conversation round to the discovery of the young woman's body in the City Road Basin.

Before she could, Gareth said, 'I got done by a traffic camera, it flashed twice, means it's got film in it.' He shook his head. 'Going through a red light on the junction of City Road and Graham Street. There wasn't even any other cars . . .' He tailed off as Zack scowled at him. Unease emanated from Gareth, and Zack's anger hit her like a blast from a furnace.

Antonia contained her excitement. 'Wasn't that near where they found the dead woman?' It shouldn't be too difficult to find their car and track it.

'Was it?' Zack said, his demeanour warning Gareth to shut up.

'According to the police.'

Zack scowled at her. She had no trouble reading his feelings now. *Oh hell, they are involved.*

Kerry hadn't picked up on the atmosphere and stuck to the script they'd agreed. 'Patience saw the men who did it.'

Zack's expression froze and Gareth's body stiffened.

'A group of lads chased me,' Antonia explained. 'They probably had nothing to do with it.' The two men's agitation lessened but Antonia wanted to get out of there.

'Good thing they didn't catch you. Patience is really fit,' Kerry told the men.

After a few moments' silence Zack said, 'She looks it,' and attempted a leer, but it lacked conviction. He appeared more likely to hit than ravish her.

Even Kerry picked up on the atmosphere and faltered.

'This isn't a very cheerful subject.' Zack drained his glass and studied the crowded room. 'Why don't we go on somewhere quieter? I know a good place out Barnet way.'

There's no way we're going anywhere with you two. 'No thanks, I've got an early start tomorrow.'

Irritation crossed Zack's features. 'No worries. We'll give you a lift home?'

'I've got the car.' Antonia ignored Kerry's expression of incredulity and held Zack's gaze.

The sensation that he wanted to reach across the table and close his hands round her throat grew until he barked a laugh. 'Suit yourself. See you around, ladies.'

He got up so suddenly Kerry yelped in surprise. He marched toward the exit, barging through people, and Gareth scurried in his wake.

Antonia sat still until her pulse slowed.

Kerry drained her glass and refilled it before topping up Antonia's. 'Wow, I thought he was going to kill you.'

'You and me, both.' They sat in silence, sipping their drinks.

'What will you do?'

'I'm going to find their car and track it.'

'Can you do that?' Kerry sounded doubtful.

'Alan knows somebody . . .' Antonia wanted to do it at once, but they couldn't go outside for a while, not until she was sure the two men had left the area, and they stayed chatting for half an hour.

'Shall we go?' Kerry said, clearly fed up after asking yet another unanswered question.

'Sorry,' Antonia said. 'I'm not great company. I'll ask the waiter to order a cab.'

Kerry brandished her mobile and checked the screen. 'Already done it, three minutes.'

Outside, a car with the familiar illuminated roof light waited in the shadows seventy metres away. Antonia scanned the street, but didn't see any other pedestrians. 'Get him to come closer.'

Kerry pressed redial and held the phone to her ear. 'Hi, could you ask the driver to come closer to the entrance.'

She listened for a moment.

'Yes, he's here, but—' She held the phone at arm's length. 'I don't bloody believe it. He hung up. Wait until I speak to the driver.' She held the phone like a weapon and charged across the road.

'Kerry, wait.'

But she wasn't to be dissuaded. Antonia followed and they'd almost reached the taxi when the engine roared and it pulled away, tyres screeching.

'Let's go, Kerry, quick!'

The deeper note of a heavy diesel engine reverberated off the walls and a large, boxy vehicle pulled in behind them, cutting them off. The doors flew open and Antonia had no difficulty identifying Gareth's monstrous silhouette.

CHAPTER 5

Chapman yawned as he drove down the potholed lane, and the flickering blue lights evoked a feeling of déjà vu. He parked his car in the same space he'd used yesterday. The morning seemed even colder, and he recalled Brigitte's warm body, entwined with his less than forty minutes earlier. A group of vigilantes wearing orange Puffa jackets and forage caps studied the scene. He'd speak to them later, find out which one of them found the body and if they saw anyone suspicious. He picked his way past evil-smelling puddles towards the pool of bright light at the focus of operations. Shadowy figures in pale coveralls populated the scene and the sense of déjà vu intensified as Chapman moved to the water's edge. The stench of stale mud grew stronger but the knot developing in his gut since he got the call eased when he saw the figure crouched over the body-bag.

'Good morning, Sergeant.' Dobrowski straightened and smiled at him.

'We must stop . . .' they both said before laughing.

'Morning, Jo. What have you got for me?'

'Another casualty, very much like yesterday's.'

'Shit! How the hell did they get past our people?'

'They didn't, this one's been in the water longer. A day, I'd say.'

'Dumped at the same time?'

'Probably,' she said. 'I can give you a better idea later, if you wait for me to "pull my finger out".'

His cheeks grew warm. 'Right. Thanks.'

She winked and studied the body. 'Someone also beat this young man before he ended up in the water,' she said and pointed at marks on the head.

'How come the divers missed him yesterday?'

Dobrowski cleared her throat. 'I gave them the radius of search and there's no current here, so I didn't extend it so far . . .'

Chapman smiled at her. 'The senior police officer should have said something if he wasn't happy.' He bent forward to examine the victim. The nagging sensation that he recognised the waterlogged features wouldn't leave him.

◆　◆　◆

The carriage rattled as it pulled into the tunnel and Antonia hunched down in the seat next to Sabirah. Her eyes smarted as much from the lack of sleep as from the Mace Kerry had used on Gareth and Zack. Antonia had lost her heels in their headlong rush through the darkened streets, but that was just as well: she'd vowed never to wear heels again. The men's behaviour confirmed their involvement in something serious, even if it wasn't linked to Monika's disappearance. She'd have to be careful how she explained her discovery to Turner; both he and Eleanor would give her grief if they found out about her close escape. And they had a point. What would have happened if Kerry hadn't brought the can of Mace?

She'd have to make sure she didn't run into them again. That shouldn't be too difficult, but they might search for her, especially Zack. At least they knew her as Patience Okoye, so once *she* disappeared, life should become much safer. She'd discuss it with Turner after her shift. Once she recovered the financial records he wanted, he should be more amenable. Even Eleanor wouldn't insist on her staying if she was at risk, although her own recklessness had put her in this position.

A chill invaded her core at the thought of having to collect the papers. What if Mishkin had seen her coming out of the office yesterday? And if he saw her again . . . Her mind revisited the hazy nightmares that had woken her. She hadn't endured them for years, but now they'd disturbed her last two nights. Despite knowing she shouldn't, she couldn't help replaying the snatches of the latest. The memory of hiding in a pitch-black cupboard returned with vivid clarity.

'Patience, are you okay?' Sabirah asked.

'Of course. Why?' Her clothes clung to clammy skin.

Sabirah indicated Antonia's hands, twisting the straps of her spare backpack together. Antonia untangled them and smiled.

Sabirah, unconvinced, put an arm round Antonia's shoulders. 'Can I help?'

Antonia shook her head but the more she considered it, the more terrifying she found the prospect of running into Mishkin. Cleaning Reed-Mayhew's office formed part of Sabirah's work routine, so nobody would think anything of her going into it. Provided she was careful, there shouldn't be any risk to her.

'There is one thing . . .' Antonia hesitated. If anything went wrong, as a refugee Sabirah could end up in serious trouble.

'Please. I want help you.'

'You have to be really careful.'

Sabirah held Antonia's forearm. 'I have been careful all my life. Let me do this for you. You help me so much. Please.'

Antonia hesitated, but told herself Sabirah would be okay. 'I need you to collect some papers . . .'

◆ ◆ ◆

Sabirah hesitated outside the door to Reed-Mayhew's office, feeling sick. She told herself it was just normal, doing what she did every day, but memories of armed men seizing her family, and what they did to her beloved Rashid, wouldn't leave her. She took a deep breath. She must do this for her friend.

The master key slid into the lock and she checked the corridor before turning it. The latch opened with a soft click. She pushed the door open and waited, convinced her intentions would set off the alarm. As usual it beeped twice, telling the security guards the cleaner had arrived. After scanning the passage a final time, she slipped in, dragging her trolley with her.

She leant against the door, heart pounding and sweat running down her back. *Just clean the office.* She pushed away and began her work, but the thought of what she must do filled her with dread.

The only time she'd encountered Reed-Mayhew, she'd been in the adjoining kitchen when he'd wandered into the boardroom, a phone clamped to his ear. Engrossed in his call, he hadn't noticed her and sat at the conference table, facing away.

'Sorry. You've had long enough,' he'd said. He'd listened for a few moments. 'Why would I do that?'

The man on the other end raised his voice, but she couldn't make out his words.

'Tough. You signed the contract—' Reed-Mayhew stiffened at being interrupted. 'Cry all you like,' he'd said. 'It didn't stop you sticking my head down the toilet when I cried, did it?' He jabbed the handset and threw it on the table, breathing hard.

Sabirah panicked. If he saw her now, she'd be in trouble. Men like him hated people witnessing their embarrassment. She froze. If she moved, he'd hear her. He picked the phone up and pressed a button. As soon as he spoke, she shuffled further into the kitchen so he wouldn't see her unless he came in.

He ended the call. Maybe he would leave. But instead, the door opened, and another man entered.

'You wanted me, Mr Reed-Mayhew?'

Sabirah recognised the voice of the company accountant. She didn't know his name, but he seemed a kind man, one of the few working on this floor who didn't treat her like vermin.

'How much does the Honourable Gerard Lloyd owe us?' Reed-Mayhew demanded.

After a few seconds, the accountant said, 'Eight million, give or take.'

'What's our security?'

'I'll just have a look.' Another pause. 'Oh, it's his parents' ancestral home.'

'Call it in.'

'Sorry?'

'Call. Our. Loan. In.' Reed-Mayhew sounded angry.

'But they'll lose the house. Why don't we give him three months—'

'When I want your fucking advice, I'll ask for it.'

'Yes, sir. Anything else?'

Reed-Mayhew's voice had changed then. Had somehow darkened and lightened at once. 'You know, his father once shouted at me for getting mud on one of their rugs. When we've got possession, I want that rug placed outside, in the paddock. It was the one in the long hall.'

'Yes, sir.'

Remembering that tone now – the sound of a bad man enjoying an evil joke – Sabirah felt that same chill she'd felt then, cowering in the boardroom kitchen.

Just clean the office, she told herself again, but she couldn't stand the tension any more and switched off the hoover.

Reed-Mayhew's desk, a dark-wood and chrome structure, squatted on a luxurious rug at one end of the office. She approached it as she would a dangerous beast and knelt by its side, examining the panel concealing the shredder. She must have seen it every day without noticing. In the twelve months she'd cleaned the offices on this floor, she'd never emptied one shredder. She tried to remember what Patience had said, but her memory kept going blank. With trembling hands, she retrieved the key her friend had given her and put it into the lock, her ears straining for any approaching danger. The click as it released sounded like a gunshot and she flinched.

Once her pulse slowed, she reached in and pulled the metal container out. Instead of the usual confetti, thin strips of paper lay in the bottom of the bin. With great care she lifted them out and flattened them on the carpet, like Patience had told her. She folded them and slipped the bundle into her overalls, then, with trembling limbs, finished cleaning the office.

Chapman yawned and stretched, his office too warm after the early morning visit to City Road Basin. Sanchez passed him a cup of sweet instant coffee.

'Thanks, Alice. How is the search for the homeless man who attacked Okoye going?' The young cleaner occupied his thoughts again.

'Shouldn't we be trying to find this Benjamin who sent those messages to our female victim, Aida Rizk?'

'Ian's doing that while we get to do the boring stuff.' *Exactly what I used to make my sergeants do.*

'But *we* found the evidence.'

'When you're in charge, you can decide. Until then we do as we're told.'

'Yes, Sarge.' She threw up a mock salute and returned her attention to the screen. 'There's three possible candidates,' she said and reeled off the names, two of which sounded middle- European.

'Do we know where we can find them?'

'I'll use these sightings to work out which hostel they use.'

'They should be registered.'

'Yes, I know.'

He studied the image of the dead man. *How are you connected to Aida Rizk and why were you both found in the same stretch of water?* This couldn't be Benjamin, could it? A faint memory swam into the edge of his mind, leaping away when he reached for it. *Come on,* think. *Where have I seen you before?*

The notification of an incoming text distracted him and he checked his phone. 'Bloody hell, Harding, not now.' He exhaled in frustration and rose. 'I'd better see what his lordship wants.'

Sanchez entwined her middle and forefingers. 'Like that, eh?' she said, smirking.

Chapman stuck his tongue out and set off for the inspector's office. Doubtless he needed to discuss something vital like crime figures for the month, as if anyone believed them. He knocked and walked into the office without waiting for an answer, earning a look of irritation from Harding.

'Russell,' Harding said, 'grab a seat. This second body. How did they get it past our surveillance?'

'Jo reckons he'd been there a day—'

'How did the divers miss it?'

'The water's murky, so unless they ended up on top of it . . .'

'It doesn't make us appear very competent.'

'You determined the search zone.'

Harding glared at him before studying his screen. 'You interviewed a woman who works at GRM headquarters yesterday—'

'Yeah, a cleaner, Patience Okoye. Why?'

'I'm not sure it's significant, but this Benjamin Murray who threatened our female victim also works there, in the finance department.'

'Have you spoken to him?'

'He's not been in work since Friday. I'm going to his home in a few minutes, but I wanted to know what you thought of this Okoye.'

Chapman considered his interview with the cleaner. 'She's hiding something, but I'm not sure what. She might be an illegal, but I don't think she's linked to the bodies.'

'Not only did she admit to being near where we found *two* bodies, but she works with the prime suspect—'

'There must be thousands working in those offices. And anyway, she's a bloody cleaner. She wouldn't mix with people in the offices.'

'I want to question her again, and this time *I'll* interview her. I'll return with this Murray by eleven. Make sure she's here.'

Chapman seethed for a few seconds before leaving without responding.

Sanchez glanced up when he returned to their office.

'He wants us to bring—' The shrill ringtone of his phone interrupted him. 'Hello, Sergeant Chapman.'

'Russell, it's Jo. I've got an interesting match with the DNA recovered from our new vic,' she said. 'We found skin under his fingernails. It's linked to your witness from yesterday, the one who the tramp attacked, Patience Okoye.'

A surge of exhilaration at the breakthrough made him forget his irritation. 'Can you mail—'

'That's not all,' she continued. 'It's also a match for an Antonia Conti, an asylum seeker given residency rights nine years ago.'

'How come we've got her DNA?'

'Sorry, I don't know, but it's identical—'

'Are you sure?'

'Positive, I double-checked and—'

'What about the chain of evidence—'

'Watertight,' she said, her voice sharp.

'Sorry, I didn't mean . . . Can you email it please?'

'Already done.'

'Thanks for pulling your finger out.'

She laughed, making him smile, and he ended the call.

'Whose DNA have we got?' Sanchez said.

'Okoye, on this morning's vic.'

'Yess!' Sanchez punched the air. 'I *told* you she was lying.'

Irritated by his colleague's reaction, he recognised his disappointment that Okoye had lied to him. And why the hell did she have two identities? He also realised what had nagged at him. The new victim was one of the men she'd confronted on the CCTV footage.

Antonia checked the time and returned to staring at the chipped mug cooling between her hands. Sabirah was late and the conviction something had happened to her grew. She shouldn't have asked her to do it, but the fear of seeing Mishkin had loomed in her mind this morning. She put it down to the lack of sleep and the events of the last two days. Twice now she'd escaped from men intent on doing her harm. It took her back – *don't go there, Antonia.* She'd wasted too much energy trying to get justice until she'd realised she couldn't and let it go. She never wanted to relive that experience.

She dragged her mind into the dingy room. Around her the other cleaners huddled round the long table set in a room just big enough to hold it. Vapour from their lungs mingled with steam from the mugs before it condensed on the walls and ceiling.

The door opened and she spun round, smiling with relief when Sabirah walked in, though her stiff posture and fearful air suggested something had gone wrong. Antonia resisted the urge to ask her what happened as the others greeted Sabirah, who dropped into an empty chair alongside her.

'Do you want tea?' Antonia said, reaching for the large teapot still steaming in the centre of the table.

'Thank you,' Sabirah said and watched Antonia pour.

Antonia's insides knotted. She mustn't have got the papers, but at least nothing had happened to her. The others sat chatting for what seemed like an age. Antonia checked the time again. Three minutes since she last looked. She made herself join in the conversation until everyone else left.

She waited until the door closed and whispered, 'Did you get it?'

Sabirah nodded, and Antonia relaxed, but her friend's manner told how much it had cost. 'Thank you, Sabirah.' She placed her arm across her shoulder and squeezed. 'You're a good friend.' Sabirah's smile of gratitude made Antonia feel worse.

The door burst open. 'Patience Okoye?' a tall security guard demanded. 'Police here to see you.'

She stared, uncomprehending for a few seconds. 'What do they want?'

'Come on, they haven't got all day,' he said, gesturing towards the open door.

◆　◆　◆

Chapman drummed his fingers on the reception desk and next to him, Sanchez again studied her surroundings.

'I still think it's impressive,' she said.

He had the sense to keep quiet this time. The sound of footsteps broke the silence. A tall, thin man approached, dark hair parted at the side, wearing a smile that didn't include the blank eyes scrutinising them. The unmistakable smell of sandalwood preceded him like an advance guard.

'Sergeant Chapman?' he said. He had a slight accent.

'Yes.' Chapman took the offered hand. 'And this is Constable Sanchez.'

The man ignored her. 'Larry Mishkin, director of security.'

'Pleased to meet you, Mr Mishkin.' Chapman untangled his hand and flexed the fingers. 'I'm surprised they bothered you. We're here to speak to one of your cleaners.'

'Patience Okoye? You spoke to her yesterday. Nothing wrong, I hope.'

Why the hell is someone like you interested in a cleaner? 'No, I just need to clarify something.'

'Maybe I can help.'

'I doubt it.'

Mishkin's attitude hardened. 'Mr Reed-Mayhew takes a close interest in all his staff.'

Chapman imagined himself a tasty mouse facing a hungry python. 'I'm sure he does, and he can take as much interest in her as he likes once I've finished.' Beside him, Sanchez tensed. Realising he'd raised his voice, Chapman told himself to relax.

The sounds of more footsteps reduced the tension. Okoye strode out of the lift, a pace in front of the big security guard who'd gone to fetch her. She noticed Mishkin and her steps faltered.

The security guard brushed her with his shoulder. 'Come on,' he said, gripping her arm, but she shook him off and walked ahead.

'Good morning, Ms Okoye.' Chapman stepped towards her, surprised to feel so protective. 'I'd like you to come to the station with me. We need to speak to you about a body found in City Road Basin.'

The tension in her bearing eased. 'I already told you everything yesterday.'

'We found another one, a young man.'

'And we found your DNA on the body,' Sanchez added.

Before he could react, Okoye smashed her forearm into Chapman's throat. The shocking force of the blow knocked him backwards. As he fell, he saw her stiff-arm the big security guard, knocking him on to his backside. The reception desk broke Chapman's fall, and he crashed against it, fighting for air. Sanchez had stayed rooted to the spot as Okoye powered past her, but now recovered and ran after the figure charging out through the main doors.

Even with scrambled senses, Chapman realised he'd fucked up. He should have brought back-up. Like Sanchez had suggested before they'd set off. If she caught Okoye, he'd owe her a big favour. But if Sanchez caught her . . . He'd felt the power of the woman, and he outweighed Sanchez by at least four stone. He scanned the reception area. The security guard lay flat on his back and Mishkin didn't look like he was going to be any help. It wasn't worth the risk of Sanchez getting hurt.

Chapman tried to yell, 'Let her go,' but had to try it twice, the first effort a soundless whisper.

Sanchez stopped in the doorway and wheeled towards him, anger turning to concern. 'You okay, Sarge?'

He coughed and gestured to the security guard sprawled on the floor. 'Help him up,' he said.

'Glass of water, Sergeant?' Mishkin said, appearing to enjoy Chapman's discomfort.

'Yes, please,' Chapman said, noting the violence didn't faze the man, unlike the receptionist who sat stunned.

'Get a glass of water for the sergeant,' Mishkin said to her, watching Sanchez struggling to help the big security guard to his feet.

Glad he wasn't in the security guard's shoes, Chapman realised he wasn't too happy about being in his own footwear. Letting a murder suspect escape was never a good career move. *Shit! Shit! Shit!* He massaged his neck.

'You have DNA linking her to this murder victim?' Mishkin said, handing him a glass.

Chapman took a sip. 'I'm afraid I can't discuss the case.'

'Whatever you say, Sergeant. Although I doubt if losing a suspect will impress your superiors.'

Chapman blinked. *Smarmy bastard!* 'No problem, I know where to find her. Come on, Constable, we can't stay here all day. Thank you for your help, Mr Mishkin.'

He strode to the exit, determined to hide his trepidation. How the hell would he explain losing a suspect?

CHAPTER 6

Turner hurried from the Tube station and as he rounded the corner, checked behind him, making sure he wasn't being followed. He felt ridiculous, a grown man playing at spies, and he'd even left his phone behind. The fact that his mole hadn't responded to any of Turner's messages worried him and he'd begun to think Antonia was right. If the guy had been leading him on he'd . . . What would he do? Beat him up? The thought amused him. Maybe he should let Antonia sort him out.

The detective agency had given him an address in a part of London he didn't know. He'd been uneasy instructing them to follow the mole from the PO box where Turner sent his messages, but now, he was glad he'd done it. The low-rise concrete blocks of flats surrounding him sucked the colour out of the air. Built in the sixties to house the masses – with no regard for aesthetics – their occupants nowadays included well-paid young professionals and older inhabitants who'd bought when these were still affordable. He thanked his maternal grandmother again for leaving him the mews house. Although smaller than he'd have liked, it was far better than having to live somewhere like this.

He studied his map, an old *A–Z* he used on the few occasions he met informers and needed to hide his movements. His destination should be round the next corner. The short lane ended in a six-foot-high brick wall. Two rows of garages faced each other along each side. He checked the piece of paper he'd scribbled the details on. This was the right place. Not all the doorways were numbered but someone had painted a number seventeen in foot-high letters on the last one on the right.

Turner had passed a number of garages that appeared to have been converted into microscopic apartments, their metal gates replaced with windows and a small door. But this one still had the original metal gate, and he paused in front of it, searching for a bell. Feeling he'd wasted his time, and the money he'd paid the detective agency to find this place, he banged on the door. A hollow clang reverberated, echoing across the narrow lane and making Turner cringe. The sound faded and he reached out to do it again, but why bother? There was nobody here.

On a whim, he twisted the handle in the centre of the door. It turned and he pulled up the garage door. With a metallic screech it lifted. As the gap at the bottom grew, he saw first the tyres then the grille with the distinctive interlocking ringed logo above the number plate. A small red Audi sat in the front of the garage. After lifting the door all the way up and checking nobody had noticed him, he edged round the car. Although its nose almost touched the front, its rear bumper rested against the wall.

Then he spotted the opening: a door-sized panel almost flush with the back wall and with a semi-circular handle set into it on the right side. He prised the handle out with a fingernail and gripped it. Something caught in his throat and he hesitated, then knocked, holding his breath as he listened. The sound of a car horn in the distance reminded him he'd left the front of the garage open, so he stepped back and closed it, then found his way to the door by touch, wishing he'd brought his mobile, at least for the flashlight.

The door opened inward on silent hinges and Turner stepped into a darkened room. A sweet, rotting stench hit his nostrils. His fumbling fingers found a light switch and harsh light from a short fluorescent tube illuminated the space.

Ten feet by eight, a green carpet covered the floor. Two kitchen units stood along the right wall. One contained a small sink and on the other sat a microwave with a kettle on it. Dead lilies drooped in a vase of scummy water, no doubt the source of the odour. A black leather sofa took up the remaining wall space on the right, facing a flat screen attached to the opposite wall. The large cupboard next to the screen must contain the toilet.

If you lived here, why the hell give up half the space to your car?

He contemplated leaving a note but if the mole was genuine, the fact that Turner had followed him wouldn't do wonders for their relationship. He left and closed the door behind him. He was pushing the handle flat when a phone rang, making his heart jump. It sounded close. Someone must be coming. Then he realised the sound came from behind him. He returned to the micro apartment and switched on the light.

The ringing came from the big cupboard, then it stopped. He hesitated in front of it for a few seconds before pulling the door open. A man sat on the toilet lid. Blood saturated his jumper and covered the tiled floor. Turner froze, then the stench hit him and he gagged, making it to the sink in the kitchen unit before he brought up his breakfast. He ran cold water over his head and glanced at the figure on the toilet.

It must be the mole, Benjamin Murray. What the hell had happened to him? The urge to get away seized Turner but then his reporter's instincts took over. He steeled himself and approached the man. No question he was dead. A ragged wound encircled his throat and he held something in his right hand. Turner bent to examine it but the phone started again, making him start. The sound came from the man's trousers. Turner blanched; he shouldn't touch it but he'd need to phone the police.

Closing his eyes, he eased two fingers into the pocket. The man's thigh felt icy and stiff under the fabric and the phone vibrated against Turner's fingertips. Out of habit, he checked the caller ID which just showed a number, not someone in the victim's address book. He pressed Answer.

'Benjamin Murray?' a man's voice asked.

'Who's that?' Turner said.

'Police. Mr Murray, we need to talk to you.'

Antonia studied her surroundings, noticing for the first time the avenue lined with well-kept villas. She'd walked for two hours, avoiding cameras and changing direction innumerable times. She checked behind again and, confident she wasn't being followed, slowed. Her mind racing, she wasn't sure what to do. The memory of kicking Pavlo in the face kept returning. She'd left him in the water, spluttering and calling her every name under the sun, but very much alive. But they'd found his body, *and* her DNA. It wasn't surprising they thought she'd killed him. Her thoughts whirled and she doubted her memory. Had she killed him and blanked out what happened? She needed somewhere to think.

Antonia recognised the next road sign and realised she could walk to the gym in half an hour. She'd have a workout; it always helped clear her mind. Then she could hole up there for a few hours and relax amongst people she could trust. At least until the open classes started in the evening. The sensation of being watched unsettled her and she hoped the feeling wouldn't become a habitual companion again. The cheap hooded top she'd bought from the charity shop should conceal her from any cameras. She shook herself, determined not to let paranoia back into her life.

Security guards loitered by the entrance to an underground station ahead of her, the insignia of GRM Corporation on their epaulettes. If she crossed the road to avoid them they would notice her, so thrusting her hands into her pockets she carried on past them, forcing her legs not to run. Once out of their view, she picked up pace and ten minutes later arrived at the gym.

A dozen people were already training, every one of whom she recognised and would trust with her life. She collected the spare key from the empty office and let herself into the locker room. The familiar odour of mould and shampoo hit her. Was it just two days since she'd last come here? She found her spare kit in the bottom of the locker.

Someone had set up a dirty-dozen circuit, perfect for her mood. After stretching she threw herself into a set of squat thrusts and then hit the press-ups. The exertion and repetition of the exercises did the trick. Soon every muscle ached and her pulse raced. Half an hour later she moved on to the heavy bag, pounding the leather, imagining it contained her enemies. The image in her mind changed from Pavlo to Arkady before settling into the likeness of Mishkin as her punches slashed into the tough hide.

After showering she bundled up her dirty kit in the towel and left it in the office. By tomorrow it would be laundered and returned to her locker. At the far end of the gym, a door led into the health bar. Half a dozen people lounged in the moulded seats and she ordered a shake. The Dekker brothers sat at a table, dwarfing the chairs they perched on, and Antonia joined them.

'Hey Antonia, we finally met your boyfriend,' Milo said.

'Ha, ha.' Her 'secret boyfriend' was a standing joke with these two.

Milo frowned and pointed at her forehead. 'Did *he* do that?'

'The guy who did it—' *is dead,* she almost joked, but it wasn't funny. A sudden surge of panic made her want to run. 'This guy who came by. A copper?'

'Nah. The opposite, I'd say.'

'What did he look like?'

'Early twenties, one eighty-five, dirty-blond hair, pale eyes, blue or green, and a solid build but running to fat. Too much beer and curry,' Darius said. Light glinted off his scalp. 'I'm surprised, Antonia. You could do a lot better.'

The description fitted the leader of the gang who'd chased her, the one called Arkady. How the hell had he tracked her here? 'What did he say?'

'He'd found your backpack and wanted to give it to you. He asked where you lived.'

'You didn't tell him?'

'Yeah, sure,' Milo said. 'I even drew him a map.'

'Ha, ha. How did he know my name?'

'He didn't, he described you.' Milo exchanged a look with his brother. 'I told you he's a shithouse, didn't I?'

'You did, bro.'

He could be outside, waiting for her. 'See you boys later. I'd better go.'

'Don't you want to know about his wheels?' Milo said.

She sat.

'Black Nissan Navara, double cab, twin pipes,' Milo began. 'Do you want the rest?'

'Just the reg if you've got it.'

With a grin, he slid a piece of paper across the table. Antonia took it. Now they knew where she trained, how long before they tracked her home? But they didn't have her name and the gym wasn't far from where they'd attacked her. They must have guessed she probably trained and checked the gyms in the vicinity. She'd have to take care when she left, make sure she wasn't followed, and use this information to find them before they caught up with her.

◆ ◆ ◆

Sabirah completed her work in a trance. Her heart hadn't settled since the security man burst into the canteen, stuttering and lurching without rhythm. She still felt ashamed at the relief when he'd ignored her and taken Patience. The account of Patience's flight from the police had spread amongst the staff. Concern for her friend competed with anxiety over what might happen to Sabirah over what *she'd* done. Then she recalled all the times Patience had defended her. She should welcome the chance to help; it was a small thing. She opened her locker and slipped off her overalls. Her bulky overcoat took up most of the space and she bent to pull it out. The papers fell out of the folds and she stared at them, a reminder of the risk she'd taken.

Heat seemed to emanate from the bundle as she picked it up. Where could she hide it? She checked, but nobody paid her any attention. Dizzy and sick, she went into the toilet cubicle and leant against the wall before examining herself in the cracked mirror over the stained sink. She splashed herself with cold water and dabbed her face dry with the rough paper towels. She threw them into the bin and had an idea.

As she approached the staff exit moments later, she compelled herself not to hurry. The regular security guards seemed different, threatening. Were they watching her? She stared ahead, avoiding their gaze. As she drew level with the desk, one said something.

Above the pounding in her ears, she didn't hear the words. At the doors, a hand grabbed her shoulder. She spun with a cry.

The security guard, a man she normally exchanged a few words with, looked concerned. 'You okay, Sabirah?'

She couldn't speak.

'You dropped this,' he said, handing her a glove.

'Thank you,' she whispered and scurried to the exit.

She barged through the doors before anyone else could stop her. Two steps outside, she paused and took a gulp of cold air.

'Mrs Fadil.'

A tall, slim man waited by the side of the doors. Rashid would have drooled over his expensive suit. A gust of wind carried the scent of sandalwood, which she recognised from his office.

'Yes?' she said.

'Please come with us?' he said, his false smile making the hairs on her neck rise.

Then she noticed the two women behind him, big and hard-faced. Her shoulders slumped. She could see his eyes now, like those of the men who took her husband. Feeling hollow, she let them lead her back into the building.

The skin on Chapman's neck tingled as he stood in the hallway of the smart Georgian house, arguing with the old woman in the wheelchair. They'd already wasted too much time at the dead-end address GRM had given them for Patience Okoye.

'Mrs Curtis, I'm investigating a murder and I can return with a search warrant if you insist, but I'd rather have your cooperation, if you understand what I mean.'

'Sergeant, I understand you too well. Just because my legs don't work doesn't mean I've had my brain disconnected.'

His cheeks grew hot. 'I'm not suggesting anything of the sort.' He realised the old woman was enjoying this. 'So, you don't know where we could find Antonia Conti?'

'She lives upstairs and in case you haven't noticed, I can't even access her rooms, whereas you and your colleagues have just been up there. If she's not there, I've no idea where she is. I'm her land-lady, not her mother.' The old woman's eyes twinkled. 'If you've done any damage, I *will* expect compensation.'

Expect what you like, you old bat. 'I can assure you my people have been very careful. How long has she lived here?'

'A while, I would need to check my records. My accountant has them.'

He ran his hand through his hair. Acid in his throat warned him of an imminent attack of indigestion. 'Okay, I'll accept you might not know her whereabouts, but why is she masquerading as Patience Okoye?'

For an instant the old woman's mask slipped, but she recovered. 'I've no idea, I'm her landlady—'

'—not her mother. Yes, you said.' He exhaled, wondering what she was hiding, and asked Sanchez, 'Who's downstairs?'

'It's an office, Sarge. None of them are saying anything.'

'We'll see about that.'

'Sergeant Chapman, my tenants downstairs run a Licensed News Enterprise and I'm sure you're aware of the legal position and understand the sensitivity with which you need to deal with them.'

'I'll be sure to check their licence, and News Enterprise or not, nobody's above the law. Antonia Conti is wanted for questioning in connection with a violent murder. If you withhold evidence, I will make sure you're charged.'

The old lady's demeanour challenged him to do his worst and his heartburn intensified as he followed Sanchez out.

◆ ◆ ◆

Sabirah plucked at the sleeve of the paper jumpsuit as she sat behind the table in the stuffy room, staring at the blank wall. She needed to get out and go home. What would Nadimah and Hakim think if they came home to an empty house? Bile rose in her throat as she remembered the day the security police snatched their father for the last time. Then the door crashed open and one of the women who'd searched her, the fat one with spiky hair, barged into the room.

She threw a bundle of clothes on the table and said, 'You can put them back on.'

Sabirah reached for her coat; someone had ripped the lining open. 'Why do you do this?'

The woman folded her arms and glared until Sabirah looked away, her cheeks tingling. *Why do I let people walk over me?* Patience would have flattened anyone who tried to do this to her. Once they let her go, she'd attend the boxing classes. Learn how to beat up people like Spiky-hair. Buoyed by the fantasy, she leant forward and sorted out her clothes. Halfway through getting dressed, someone else came in, and she tensed, fearing it was the man, but the other one, the tall blonde, walked in. She exchanged a glance with Spiky-hair and dumped a black bin liner on the table, then both of them left.

Sabirah's handbag had spilled out of the bin liner, and a cry escaped when she saw what they'd done to it. A treasured Christmas present from her children, they'd ripped it apart. Eyes blurring with tears, she finished dressing and after trying to repair her bag, replaced her belongings.

The door opened for a third time and the smell of sandalwood told her Mr Mishkin had arrived. The blonde followed him in and closed the door behind her. Sabirah's mouth dried and she swayed.

'Mrs Fadil,' Mishkin said in a conversational tone. 'There's no need for all this.' He indicated her trashed coat and bag, still on the table. 'We know you took the papers.'

'I didn't—'

'Please don't lie.' He held up a hand. 'Where did you hide them?'

Convinced he knew, Sabirah prayed for help. 'I don't have them.'

'That much is obvious.' For the first time he raised his voice. 'You realise what will happen?' He leant forward and his stare bored into her. 'Once you're sacked, you'll lose residency rights and be sent back to the detention centre and then deported.'

'I have children.' The thought of returning to the hell they'd escaped made her dizzy.

'Ah yes, the children.' Mishkin sneered and produced a small box from his pocket, pushing it across the table. 'Do you recognise this?'

She studied the polished gold case, glittering in the light of the bare bulb. 'A case for glasses.'

'Examine it closer.'

Something told her not to touch it. Mishkin reached out and she flinched, but he just picked up the case and, as she relaxed, tossed it to her. Without thinking she caught it and before she could react, he plucked it from her fingers.

'We found it in your bag,' he said and handed it to the blonde, who put it in a big envelope. 'It belongs to Mr Reed-Mayhew. Someone took it from his office this morning.'

'I take nothing.' *Stupid woman. Why did you catch the case?*

'We'll let the police decide.' He checked his watch. 'They're on the way and once you're found guilty of stealing, they'll deport you, children or not. Back to Syria, or what's left of it. It will be bad enough for you, but what about Nadimah – she's eleven now, isn't she? She won't last long in those camps.' He shook his head in mock sympathy. 'And little Hakim, it's not a great place for a nine-year-old.'

Dreadful memories of cowering in a squalid, stinking shelter rushed into her mind and she couldn't breathe.

CHAPTER 7

Antonia hurried from the gym, not sure where to go next. Eleanor would know what to do but she must see Sabirah first, get the papers. On the Tube, she remembered with a jolt the decoy address she'd given for Patience Okoye. Could it lead the police to her? She couldn't recall what she'd told the creep who collected the rent. The guy made her skin crawl and she hadn't exchanged more than half a dozen words with him. Chances were he wouldn't even remember her. Turner had arranged the rental using a very discreet private investigator, so she didn't think there was a weak link there. Nothing connected Patience Okoye to Antonia Conti.

By the time she arrived at Sabirah's street, she'd calmed down, confident she'd get through this. She'd only visited her once before and remembered a gloomy apartment where the smell of mould hovered behind the odour of clean washing. In daylight most of the houses in the street looked in good condition. The exceptions included a row of six, seemingly untouched since the seventies. Sabirah's home occupied the lower half of the first of these. Antonia climbed the two steps to the front door and rang the bell. A figure, too small to be her friend, appeared through the pebbled glass.

'Who is it?' The high voice of Sabirah's daughter sounded afraid.

'Hello, Nadimah, it's An— Patience, from work. Is your mum home?'

A second, smaller shape joined the first. 'Sorry, my mother is not here.'

Antonia exhaled in frustration; Sabirah should have got home by now. 'Can you open the door please, Nadimah?' Would the girl remember her from the fleeting visit?

After a whispered discussion the door opened. Two pairs of big brown eyes studied her from behind a security chain.

She smiled, trying to reassure them, but this didn't work. 'Hello, Nadimah. It's good to see you again.' She offered her hand through the narrow opening, and the girl held it for an instant. 'Hi, Hakim,' Antonia said and saluted the boy, who rewarded her with a grin. 'Do you know when you're expecting your mum home?'

'Sorry, no. Can you come back?' Nadimah peered past Antonia.

'Please tell her I—' The door closed before Antonia finished speaking.

Where the hell is she? Sabirah had told her she always went straight home, so the kids wouldn't have to return to an empty house. The security checks on the Tube had increased since King's Cross, which might explain why she still wasn't back. But if something more serious had happened, Antonia couldn't just leave the kids. Sabirah had told her the neighbour upstairs sometimes helped. Antonia rang the bell, trying to recall the woman's name. She'd decided to give up and try another neighbour when footsteps clumped down stairs and the door flew open.

'What?' A large woman in a house coat stood in the opening.

'Hello, I'm—'

'I'm not buying anything and I'm in the middle of cooking so 'urry up.'

Antonia wasn't sure this was such a good idea. 'I'm a friend of Sabirah's.'

The woman's expression softened. 'Why didn't you say? She's all right, isn't she?'

'I'm not sure. She's not come home yet and I'm worried—'

'Leave it to me,' the woman said and rang the bell for Sabirah's flat. 'Nadimah, love, it's Ivy, open the door.'

The door opened again and the girl smiled at the neighbour.

'How do you and Hakim fancy burgers?'

Hakim grinned and gave the woman a thumbs-up.

Antonia hesitated before giving the woman her home number, with an injunction to ring her as soon as Sabirah arrived. Relieved at least to have found someone to take care of the kids, she set off for home. She'd speak to Eleanor and ring round the hospitals.

She reached home without noticing the journey. Several cars were parked outside the house and people were milling around them. She slowed and realised some of the figures wore uniforms. Aware it might look obvious, she nonetheless veered away and crossed the street.

The front door opened and Sanchez came out, followed by Chapman. How had they found her?

Chapman drove to the station still feeling humiliated from the run-in with the old woman. He needed to put a spin on this cock-up. Losing a murder suspect was a good way to bugger up your career, something he was becoming an expert on, starting with accusing his boss of corruption, the catalyst for the events that had ended with him getting busted from DCI. And the bastard had got away with it. He massaged his throat, sore from the blow Okoye, or Conti, had given him. The woman hit bloody hard, and despite what he'd said to Sanchez yesterday, she could easily inflict the damage he'd seen on the young man.

Sanchez interrupted his thoughts. 'What do you want me to say in the report?'

'The truth,' he said. 'I don't cover things up.'

Colour flooded her cheeks. 'I wasn't suggesting covering *anything* up, but I can either say the suspect overpowered us and escaped, *or* she got away from the security guard.'

Chapman couldn't help grinning. 'If you put it like that, Constable Sanchez, the second version is closest to what actually happened.'

She rewarded him with a smile. 'I'll get the report written. Shall I mention the suspect hit you?'

'No need, she's in enough trouble without adding assaulting an officer.'

In better spirits than at any time since he'd lost Okoye, Chapman made his way up to Harding's office. The inspector appeared to be in a good mood as well, so Chapman gave him the bad news straight away.

'The security guy from GRM lost our suspect.' He sat down without waiting for an invitation.

Harding surprised him by laughing.

'You're not annoyed?'

'We found Benjamin Murray—'

'So?'

'We also found bloodstained clothing and gloves in the boot of his car and I'm betting it came from Aida Rizk.'

'Why would he keep—'

'He'd hidden it in a garage rented under an assumed name. He probably didn't expect us to find it.'

'What's he told us?'

'Nothing. He'd killed himself.'

Typical Harding, rationing information. 'How did you find him?'

'We tracked his phone. I rang it and a guy called Alan Turner answered. He'd just found the body.'

'What's *he* said?'

'He runs a News Enterprise and Murray fed him information about GRM. He's made a statement if you want to read it.'

'I'll do it later. Now, about this Conti. I'll put out—'

'Don't bother.'

'Hang on, just because you think you've got someone for one of the killings you can't ignore the evidence—'

'I'm not. The DNA's not a match. The official report from CrimTech has arrived.'

What the hell is going on? 'Can I see?' Chapman dragged the tablet across the desk and read the report, recognising the signature at the bottom. 'That's Jo's boss, isn't it?'

'Yes.'

'Why would he sign her report?'

'What do you mean?'

'I don't believe Jo made a mistake, she was adamant Conti's DNA was on the victim and she's usually spot-on.'

'You've changed your tune.'

'Someone's covering this up?' Chapman said.

'You seriously think CrimTech would do that?'

'Don't you? Although I don't know why. Whatever the reason, there's something dodgy about this Conti girl.' *Was she Mishkin's bit on the side? It would explain his interest.* 'Shall I keep digging? See if I can find her and sort this out?'

Harding fiddled with his watch strap. 'Now she's not a suspect I don't want to waste—'

'Why the hell did she run?'

'People run for all sorts of reasons. As you suggested, she might be an illegal.'

'No, she's not, but she's got something to do with at least one of the bodies we fished out of the canal, even if she's just a witness. Don't forget she admitted she was there. I'll still be working on the case.'

Harding paused, considering the words. 'I can't allocate any extra resources.'

'Goes without saying.' Chapman pushed the tablet across the desk and rose to leave.

'You'll have to do it in your own time, and if anything goes wrong . . .'

Chapman gave a wave and left the room. *I expected nothing else.*

Eleanor wheeled herself to her kitchen table and placed the mug on the surface. Now the police had gone she could think about what they'd told her. Although Antonia had become much more even-tempered in the last few years, she'd flown into rages when younger – doubtless fuelled by whatever had happened to her as a child. Eleanor was convinced she'd been the victim of abuse, although Antonia never discussed it and had even denied it. When she recalled the tantrums Antonia had subjected her to, she knew the girl could easily have killed, especially if she came across her abuser or someone who reminded her of him. Perhaps she should have insisted Antonia sought therapy or at least talked to her. Been more of a mother to her, although thinking about her own daughter, Eleanor had no illusions as to the efficacy of her mothering skills. She sighed. She couldn't change history, and they needed to start where they were.

Turner bounded down the stairs from Antonia's flat and marched into the kitchen.

'How bad is it?' she said.

He helped himself to the other mug. 'A bit of a mess but no damage I could see.' He sat down, his appearance strained.

'Are you okay, Alan?'

'Not really.' He told Eleanor what he'd discovered in the garage.

She first thought they suspected Antonia of killing the man Turner had discovered, but they couldn't have even known about it when they turned up. 'I'm so sorry, Alan. It must have been a shock.'

'It wasn't pleasant.' He shuddered, then shook himself. 'Did they say why they want Antonia?'

'The sergeant showed me a warrant to search the flat and it mentioned murder.' She snorted. 'The Stone Age thug said Antonia was a suspect. You know, he threatened me.'

'He tried blustering with Miles, demanded to see our licence. Miles showed it him *and* gave him the card for our solicitors, told him to direct questions through them. It took the wind out of his sails.'

'It would.'

'Did he say who she's supposed to have killed?'

'No.' She didn't want to share her fears about Antonia's past without discussing it with her. The suggestion they'd been abused as kids wasn't something people wanted bandied about.

'Did she tell you about her fight on Sunday night?'

'I know she attended her boxing class, but I didn't ask the details.'

'On the way home from her class,' Turner said, and launched into an explanation.

Eleanor listened with growing concern as her nephew relayed Antonia's account of her fight with Pavlo. 'Did she say she left him alive?'

'I assumed . . . To be honest, I don't recall . . . but I would have remembered if she'd said he wasn't.' He swallowed a mouthful of tea.

'At least it had nothing to do with our investigation.'

Turner looked thoughtful. 'As far as we know.'

'What do you mean? Do you know something I don't?'

'No, no. I'm sure you're right.'

What if she was wrong? She hated the thought that they'd put Antonia in jeopardy. And if she did kill that man . . . Guilt assailed Eleanor, but the show must go on. 'I don't suppose she recovered the papers before the police . . .'

'No idea. She hasn't been in touch.'

'Run the GRM story with what we have. There's enough to embarrass Reed-Mayhew and hopefully trigger a police investigation. It will at least make sure his expansion plans are stymied. If Antonia recovered anything, we can use it in a follow-up article, really stick the boot in. But with the murder investigation hanging over her, I imagine she's got other things to worry about, poor girl.'

Antonia waited in a bus shelter down the road from Eleanor's house. As darkness fell, street lamps came on one by one. Although focused on the house, she paid attention to her surroundings, keeping alert for anyone else who might be watching. The thought that she might never be able to return here induced a wave of panic. She wanted to talk to Eleanor, tell her everything and get her advice, but couldn't risk getting her into trouble.

Turner came out of the office and set off for home at a brisk walk, never once checking for anyone following, but then, normal people didn't, did they? What had Chapman told him and what did he think of her now? She needed him to believe in her. Twenty minutes later he entered the cobbled mews where he lived and made his way towards the small cottage he'd inherited from his grandmother. As he fumbled for his keys, she called his name.

He spun round holding a hand to his chest. 'Antonia! You gave me a fright. What are you doing here?'

'Can I come in?'

He checked behind her before leading her into a narrow hallway. 'You must excuse the mess.' A door stood on the right and steep stairs led to an upper floor. 'In there,' he said and pushed the door open. 'Grab a seat while I take off my coat.'

The small room contained a black leather sofa, armchair and glass-topped coffee table. Overflowing bookshelves flanked the fireplace. If she'd accepted his offer of marriage, she would live here now. The shock when he'd asked had made her laugh and she remembered his wounded expression with shame. She left her coat on, wishing she was in front of Eleanor's fire, and dropped on to the sofa, the muscles in her neck knotted. What if he didn't believe her?

Turner came into the room. 'Can I get you a drink?'

'Something strong.'

He slipped through a narrow doorway into a galley kitchen returning with two full tumblers of an amber liquid.

'Are you trying to get me drunk?' she said, smiling.

He went bright red. 'It will get rid of the chill.'

Antonia took a sip. Although the alcohol bit her throat, the liquid didn't have the sharpness she associated with whisky. 'Very nice.' She saluted him with the glass.

'It's an excellent twelve-year-old malt.'

She took another mouthful and a silence settled on them.

Turner cleared his throat. 'What happened?'

She told him, realising the seriousness of her situation as she related the tale. 'What did the police say?' she said, wetting her mouth with the whisky.

'They wanted to speak to you about a murder. The sergeant even threatened Eleanor.'

'I can imagine her reaction.'

'Yes, she wasn't impressed.' His smile faded, and he looked uncomfortable. 'You never said if the man was still alive when you left him in the water?'

'I can't believe you're even asking me.'

'Well, was he?'

'Of course. You don't think I'd . . . Really, Alan.'

'The police will want to know why you didn't report—'

'I told you why.' *Did* she suspect she'd killed—? No, he *was* still alive.

'You need to convince the police.'

'You don't believe—'

'For God's sake, Antonia, a man's dead and you had a fight with him. No wonder the coppers have you top of their list.'

He was right. What a mess. Tears gathered to escape and she covered her eyes with her forearm.

'How did your date with the two GRM bozos go?' he said, breaking the thick silence.

'Fine,' she said, relieved to change the subject. 'They drove through a red light near the City Road Basin on Sunday night. I'm pretty sure they dumped the body.'

'What did they say?'

'It's more how they reacted when it slipped out.'

'They didn't do anything?'

'No, one of them let it slip about the traffic camera and they slunk off soon after.'

He sipped his drink. 'At least you had no problems.'

'None.' She stared into her whisky.

'You realise we can track them, see where they came from.' Turner's enthusiasm made him seem much younger.

'I remember you did it when we exposed the councillor preying on single mothers, but I'm not sure how.' At least investigating these two would take her mind off her own troubles.

'It will cost, but Eleanor won't object to paying. Have you got details of their car?'

The more she thought of it, the more she wanted to trap Gareth and Zack. 'They were driving a big SUV—'

'They wouldn't use their own car.'

Antonia's excitement faded. 'Sorry, I don't think.'

'Don't worry. They can't have caught many cars that night, we should be able to identify them. If we can find out what they were up to, we might discover if they have anything to do with the man you're suspected of . . . you know. At the canal.'

Antonia hadn't considered this and took another sip of the whisky. Could it get her off the hook for Pavlo's death?

Turner cleared his throat. 'Did you get hold of the papers?'

A spasm of concern about Sabirah filled her with guilt. 'I need to collect them.'

'Where are they?'

'A friend's got them—'

'You gave them to someone—'

'No, I got—' The words stuck in her throat. 'A friend collected them for me.'

'You got someone else involved!'

'I can trust—'

'That's not why I'm worried. If she got caught . . . Reed-Mayhew is not a man to cross.'

'It's the woman who cleans his offices. They wouldn't even notice her.' A weight settled in her stomach.

'If they caught her, she'd lose her job. And if they charge her with theft . . .'

'They wouldn't!' Sabirah would be deported, *and* her children. What had she done?

'Let's hope they don't catch her, for your sake. When do you plan to see her?'

'I've already been, but she's not come home,' she said, squirming.

'Have you checked the hospitals?'

She nodded.

'I'll ring our solicitors in the morning. If they've arrested her he can find out where they're holding her.'

Antonia stared into the fire. Was his expression contempt at her cowardice? His good opinion of her, something she'd taken for granted, had never been so important. If she'd got her friend arrested, she deserved his opprobrium.

Chapman parked his car opposite the three-storey Victorian house that had been his home for a dozen years. The resentment that he still paid for it, despite not being able to afford his own place, made him scowl, but seeing Abby in the rear-view mirror, he affected a smile.

'Thanks, Dad,' Abby said, and reached for the door handle.

'This side,' Chapman said, 'and I'll walk you to the door.'

'I'm not a child, I can cross the road—'

'I take you to the door, that's the deal.'

Abby sighed and slid across the seat to get out on to the pavement. Chapman exchanged a glance with Brigitte and joined his daughter, already halfway round the car.

'You gonna say goodnight to Brigitte?'

Abby stepped back and, crouching down, gave a small wave. 'Goodnight, Brigitte.'

'And thank you for my present – hey, where the hell is it?' Chapman said.

The jacket Brigitte had given his daughter for her thirteenth birthday lay on the rear seat. He snatched the door open and retrieved it. Brigitte hadn't mentioned she'd got her anything, but even he recognised the luxury label sewn into the lining.

He thrust it at Abby. 'Is it the wrong size or something?' His daughter stood a few inches shorter than him, but not for much longer, and the memory of the lads making comments about her outside the restaurant reminded him she wasn't a kid any more.

'No, it's fine.' She took it, holding it like she would a rag. 'Thank you, Brigitte,' she said through the open door.

'A pleasure, darling. Enjoy wearing it.'

A warning look from Brigitte stopped him from admonishing his daughter. *What the hell's wrong with the girl?* The two of them usually got on so well. Maybe this was what they could expect now she'd reached thirteen. God help them. Halfway across the road he saw the reason for her surliness: her mother, watching them from the doorway, scowling and arms folded. Chapman couldn't help grinning as he imagined a rolling pin in Rhona's right hand.

'Hi, Mum,' Abby said.

'You're supposed to bring her home before ten,' Rhona snapped.

'It's her birthday—'

'Not till Wednesday. You never bloody change, do you? Whatever suits you, regardless of what—'

'Rhona!' He gestured at Abby.

'Bye, Dad,' Abby said, fighting to contain her tears as she edged past her mother before running down the hall.

'Well done,' he said through clenched teeth, and spun on his heel.

'If you'd— Bastard!'

The door slammed as he reached the pavement.

Eleanor lay in bed, her ears straining to recapture the sound that had woken her. Max lay alongside her, his body quivering. She heard it again. Someone was in the house.

'Antonia, is that you?' she called out, her voice rising.

As she listened for a reply, she put on the bedside lamp. Max meowed and swished his tail, making a low growl she couldn't remember hearing before. The cat's reaction increased her fear. Something heavy crashed to the floor above her. She froze, listening. Max uttered another growl, jumped off the bed and waited at the door, fur standing off his body. She reached for the phone but her hand didn't want to obey her and jerked, knocking the handset off the bedside cabinet.

'Bugger,' she muttered as it landed with a hollow thud.

Pins and needles made her arm tingle and she shook it, clenching her fist to help the circulation return. The phone couldn't have fallen far. She leant out of the bed and swept the carpet with her hand, reaching ever further until she slid. Alarm made her already-racing heart jump. If she ended up on the floor, she'd be helpless. She planted her hand on the carpet and pushed, straining with the effort. She heaved herself back on to the bed and lay there panting and gathering her strength, cursing her useless legs.

The sounds from upstairs quietened. Had they gone? Then a creak. *Is someone on the stairs?* If they came down here she wouldn't let them find her defenceless in bed. Max scratched at the door.

'Don't worry, boy, we'll see them off.' She attempted to imbue her voice with a confidence she didn't feel.

She dragged the chair towards her, pulled on her dressing gown and slid into the seat, searching around for something to use as a weapon. A bronze-based lamp on her dressing table had a satisfying heft to it. She struggled to unplug it before placing it in her lap. The weight gave her a measure of confidence and she wheeled herself to the door. Max swished his tail and she eased him aside. Voices whispered, sounding close. There must be at least two of them. Fear paralysed her for a moment, but she grabbed the handle. Before she could turn it, the door rushed towards her, knocking her chair backwards. Panic made her mind go blank, but she held on to the lamp.

'I've called the police. They'll be here any minute,' she shouted.

A bulky silhouette appeared in the doorway, and then another. The figures filled the opening, huge in the darkness. A weight seemed to crush her, preventing her breathing.

'Where's the girl?' the first intruder demanded.

'Antonia?' she blurted out.

'Where is she?' The speaker loomed over her. The smell of beer wafted off him.

'She's not here.'

'I can fucking see that,' he said, and grabbed her chair.

'Get off me, you thug!' She swung the lamp. The satisfying crunch as it made contact made her feel twenty years younger.

'Shit!' her assailant cried, reeling away. 'Mad bitch.'

Eleanor gripped the lamp, ready to use it again. With a feline war cry, Max thundered past and flew at the man.

'Fucking cat, get 'im off me.'

Max's enraged yowls changed into a yelp of alarm. Something soft hit the wall behind her.

'Max!' she screamed.

A boot connected with her lifeless shins and the chair toppled. She took a wild swing with the lamp as she crashed to the floor. Winded, she lay on her side, and something solid hit her in her ribs. Bones cracked, and she grunted in pain. She needed to help Max but her body wouldn't work. Another blow and her head smashed into the floor, then blackness.

CHAPTER 8

Alan Turner sat at his desk, stifled a yawn and read his emails. Worry about Antonia had ensured he'd had little sleep. If she *did* kill that man, she could plead self-defence. It was just a shame she hadn't reported the attack. He should have tried harder to get her to go to the police. If he was honest, he hadn't pushed it because he didn't want to upset her further. Maybe he shouldn't have given her so much grief about getting her friend involved. He'd have made the same decision in her shoes. Not that he had the bottle to go undercover.

All he could do now was stand by her when she needed him. He wondered how she was getting on with the vehicle tracking. Now he'd given her the go-ahead, he needed to tell his aunt.

'Miles, have you seen Eleanor?' he called out.

'I'm afraid not,' Miles said. 'Do you want me to call her?'

'No, I'll do it.'

Getting no reply, he went up to the house. It was unlike Eleanor not to be up. The sensation of something wrong sharpened when he got no answer to the bell. She never went out without telling him. After calling through the letter box he retrieved his spare key, let himself in and called out again. Eleanor's bedroom door stood open and he paused outside it, certain something had happened. The curtains were still closed and the thought that she'd had an attack of some kind made him hesitate. The memory of his nine-year-old self finding his dead father in bed hit him like a blow.

He shook himself and fumbled for the light switch. Her wheelchair lay on its side next to her dressing gown with a lamp on it. He froze, rooted to the spot, trying to make sense of the scene until a plaintive mewing pulled him out of his paralysis. What he'd taken for her dressing gown wasn't empty.

'Eleanor! Oh God, what's happened?' He rushed to her.

She lay unmoving, and dried blood crusted her chin. Turner pushed away the panic and struggled to remember the first-aid training he'd received many years ago. Should he move her? He reached for one of her bony wrists and searched for a pulse. There wasn't one. But she couldn't be dead. Not Eleanor. His fingers probed between frail bones, scared of pressing too hard. A flicker of movement gave him hope. Eyes fluttered under papery lids and he wiped his tears away.

'Thank God,' he whispered and reached for the phone that lay on the floor under the bed.

He called for an ambulance, tears streaming down his cheeks as he answered their questions. While he waited for it to arrive he extracted Eleanor from the wheelchair and put her into the recovery position, pleased to have remembered how to do it. The low moans she made as he moved her distressed him, but at least she was still alive. Max stayed out of range, and spat whenever he got anywhere near him. Who the hell would do this? Eleanor had made plenty of enemies in a life dedicated to helping the underdog, but surely none of them would attack her. Turner punched his palm. He'd make sure whoever did this to her *paid*. The shrill ringing of the doorbell made him jump.

'Mr Turner?' the uniformed paramedic asked. 'Where's the casualty?'

'Just there, I've tried to make her comfortable.' He pointed at the blanket covering her.

'Did you find her like this?'

The tone of the question made him feel he'd done something wrong. 'I found her over there, in the chair.'

The young woman frowned and approached his aunt. A second uniformed figure arrived, an older man carrying a large valise which he placed on the floor.

'Weak, fluttery pulse and shallow breathing,' the first paramedic announced. 'Can you help me check her spine? The gentleman's moved her.' She flashed Turner an accusing look before continuing her examination.

Distressed he might have injured her further, he suppressed an angry retort before stepping aside to let the two professionals get on with their job. Eleanor's skin tone resembled chalk, turning her into a frail old woman he didn't recognise.

'This her cat?' the older paramedic asked.

Max sat against the wall, watching his mistress with a forlorn air. 'Yes, I'll take care of him.'

'He might need a vet.' The paramedic pointed out the cat's unnatural posture.

Turner hadn't noticed and another sliver of guilt cut him. 'Oh right, there's one she uses.' He studied his aunt in the scoop stretcher. 'Will she be all right?'

The woman medic answered. 'She's got severe bruising to her torso, so probably a few broken ribs, and a nasty head injury. There's compression, so it's difficult to assess without doing a scan. Have you called the police?'

'No, I suppose I'd better. It must have been burglars?'

'I'd call the Murder Squad,' she said.

His stomach did a somersault. 'Oh, right.'

He made the call to the police enveloped in a fog separating him from his actions. By the time he finished they'd loaded her into the ambulance. A plastic mask covered her mouth and a bag of straw-coloured liquid hung on a hook above her.

'Make sure you don't disturb anything else,' the paramedic said, closing the rear doors.

The vehicle pulled out into the traffic, taking away the woman who'd been in his life forever. He watched, feeling like someone had ripped a part of him out.

◆ ◆ ◆

The chink of china, clatter of cutlery and hiss of steam from the espresso machine provided a backdrop to the hum of voices in the busy cafe. Antonia cupped her hands round the large mug of cooling coffee and stared at the fat congealing on the piece of bacon sticking out of her half-eaten butty. The discovery that Sabirah hadn't come home last night left her feeling empty but unable to eat. None of the hospitals in the city had admitted a woman of her description and Antonia came to the obvious conclusion. Having watched the children set off for school, waved off by the cheery neighbour, she'd consoled herself: at least they were okay. Nadimah's serious demeanour reminded her of photos of herself at the same age, except by then *she* didn't have a mother. *I'll do everything in my power to make sure the same doesn't happen to you.*

She drained the mug and, pulling the hood over her head, set off for her meeting, visiting an ATM on the way and drawing out a thousand pounds on Turner's corporate card. Then she caught the

Jubilee line to Willesden Green, relieved there weren't any security checks at the stations. She trudged down the High Road until she found her destination, an office above a betting shop. The 'To Let' signs remained in the windows, no doubt because these guys would move on before too long. She rang the doorbell and waited.

A tinny voice said, 'Hood down, please.'

She swept it off and stared into the camera.

'Name?' the voice demanded.

Feeling silly, she recited the words Turner had told her to say. 'I'm here to see Othello. I've got a message from his cousin Olive.'

The speaker buzzed and the lock clicked. She pushed the door open and entered a narrow hallway smelling of old dust. Harsh white light illuminated stairs covered in worn blue carpet. A door opened above her and someone said, 'Up here, miss.'

A man of about sixty with thick grey hair and a dark tan waited on the landing. He studied her as she climbed the stairs then led her into an office crammed with half a dozen desks, each occupied by a worker hunched over a keyboard.

'This way.' He led her to the far corner where a rickety partition created a small office. A desk with two back-to-back screens on it split the space, a keyboard in front of the furthest screen. Once behind the desk he waved her to a chair and said, 'You got the money? Thousand.' He counted it, then locked it in a moneybox which he placed in a drawer. 'Right, what you searching for?'

She told him where the men's van had gone through the red light, and the time window. He tapped on the keyboard then the screen came to life, showing an empty road at night. The clock in the bottom corner read 21.50. The screen flickered and headlights appeared. He froze the image.

'Is that them?'

A Mini with a young couple filled the screen. She shook her head.

The next vehicle came into shot an hour later, a grey van with wide tyres and a box fixed to the roof, but the windscreen reflected the light from the camera flash, hiding the driver. The camera snapped three more cars, then the screen stayed blank.

'There's no more,' the man said. 'You sure it's this junction?'

'He said Graham Street.'

'These are the only lights on there. You sure you got the right—'

'Can you go back to the second car? The van.' She studied the image. 'I can't see the driver. Can you sharpen the—'

'No point. See the number plate?'

A pixilated blob obscured it. 'What's happened?'

'He's got a cloaking device, it hides the number plates and causes the glare on the windscreens so you can't see who's driving.'

'Aren't they illegal?' *Blast*, she hadn't considered this.

'Just about,' the man said. 'But you remember the rap singer who said he used it to protect his privacy? It's going through the courts. Now, if he'd used a scrambler . . .'

'What does *that* do?'

'Blocks all the cameras within three hundred metres. You can do serious time if you're caught using one of them.'

If they were involved in that woman's death, that wouldn't worry them. She exhaled and ran her hands over her hair.

'Do you want me to track where he goes?'

'How can you?'

The man peered round the screen, grinning. 'Easy, we follow him on the camera system. As long as he stays in sight of the cameras we can stitch the images together. It will take a few minutes . . .' The man ducked behind the screen and it turned blue.

The van came from where she'd fought Pavlo. 'Can we check where it originated?'

A few minutes later he said, 'I can go back a couple of hundred metres but then the system's down. I'll see if I can find his probable route.'

The acidic taste of disappointment filled her mouth as she remembered the damaged cameras. The sound of keystrokes accompanied his laboured breathing. An occasional cough came from the outer office and from beyond it, the sound of traffic.

'Do you just hack into the transport-system cameras,' she said, 'or can you access private security systems?'

She waited, shifting in her seat.

The screen came back on, this time a map marked with a pink line. 'This is his probable route—'

'Probable?'

'If an identical vehicle took the same route, we could have picked it up by mistake.'

'Not likely, is it?'

'It would prevent a prosecution for a motoring offence. Anyway, this is the most likely place for it to be garaged.' He zoomed in on a sign. Lincoln Road.

'Can we see the building he drove to?'

'It's on an industrial estate. They *might* have their own security cameras.'

She didn't know how to access those, but the estate wasn't big. 'Could you do me a favour? There's another car . . .' She passed him the scrap of paper Milo had given her.

'You got another grand?' he said, peering out of the side of the screen.

'Oh, I only need a trace. It's all right, we can—'

'Just joking,' he said and tapped on the keys. 'That was easy.' A printer in the corner of the room spat out paper. He spent a few more minutes clicking on the keyboard until the printer produced more paper and he fetched the sheets, placing them in front of

Antonia. 'Here's the details of who owns the Navara, and this is the van.' He produced a photo of the grey van, this time with the number plate in view.

'How come—'

'Just a hunch, but this van came out of the estate and fuelled up yesterday.' He tapped the image. 'I'd put money on it being the same one. The owner's details are on this sheet, much good they'll do you. This last is a printout of the route they took, showing where they travelled.'

'Thanks.' Antonia read the owner's name, Milton's Foods, and a PO box number. Oh well, probably a dead end, but if they'd dumped the body in the basin, she only needed to find where they'd come from. 'Could you track back so we could see—'

'The cameras were out.'

'Before they got there. They had – they'd dropped off a cargo and I need to know where they collected it.'

'Have you any idea how long it would take? Because of the break in the footage, I'd need to check every camera from where we last saw them and work outwards until we find the vehicle—'

'Can't you track the number plate? If they had the cloaking device switched off?' She smiled. 'Please.'

'Okay.' He sighed and tapped keys, but five minutes later he finished. 'Nothing, apart from their trip to the petrol station. I've checked back two weeks.'

Antonia sank into her seat. 'So, the only alternative is to check back from the dead area—'

'Or follow them from Lincoln Road.'

She brightened. 'Great, can you do that?'

'Unless you know when they left, we'd have a lot of footage to check. What's your budget?'

'You've had it.'

He held his hands out, palms upwards. 'I'd like to help . . .'

'What if you let me check it?'

'Sorry, we haven't got a spare monitor.'

Antonia suppressed her irritation. 'Can you put it on a memory stick?'

'You put that information on your laptop and go online, you could end up in serious shit.'

'I'm super paranoid. I won't download it on to my hard drive and I have a manual modem, so I'll make sure I'm offline whenever I use it.'

He didn't look convinced.

'I don't even have a mobile, *that's* how paranoid I am.'

He held up his hands. 'You've persuaded me.'

Antonia waited while he downloaded the data. Even if they proved Gareth and Zack had something to do with the woman's death, it didn't get her off the hook for Pavlo.

Chapman sat at his desk, the police radio burbling in the background. On the next desk, Sanchez tapped away at her keyboard. He'd found a few minutes to read the bio for Conti in the Bristol University yearbook, where she'd got a 2:1 in chemistry. It didn't say much, apart from the fact her mum was from South Sudan and her dad Sicilian. How had her parents met and why had they ended up in London? He didn't know much about Sudan, but either country must be a lot sunnier.

The tone of the voices over the airways changed, and he listened, then heard an address he recognised. He snatched up the radio.

'DS Chapman here, we'll take that one on Vincent Terrace.'

Sanchez looked aghast and waited until he'd finished. 'We've got enough on our plate, Sarge.'

'It's clearly related to our case—'

'Who says?'

Chapman stood and collected his jacket. 'I do.'

The door opened and DCI Gunnerson looked in. 'Russell, can I have a word about your lost suspect?'

'She's no longer a suspect, boss.'

'I'm aware of that.' Gunnerson looked uncomfortable. 'Questions have been raised about procedures, and before you ask, it wasn't from Inspector Harding.'

'Which one from upstairs?' Gunnerson wouldn't normally bother with petty point scoring, so someone high up must be leaning on his boss. Her grey streak looked to have grown wider and the bags under her eyes more prominent.

'You know I can't say.' She looked at his jacket. 'You off out?'

'Yeah, a violent assault and home invasion, linked to our murder.' He glanced at Sanchez, who focused on getting her coat.

'Okay, see me when you get back.'

'Right, boss.'

He charged out before she could change her mind.

They drove to Vincent Terrace in silence. The CrimTech team had already arrived by the time they got there. On finding out where Eleanor had been taken, he told Sanchez to contact the hospital and get an update.

Chapman watched them processing the hallway of Eleanor Curtis's home. Disappointed Jo hadn't attended, he got a strange look from the lead technician when he asked about her.

Sanchez put her phone away and returned. 'The hospital says it's too early to say, but there's a possibility she won't pull through.'

'Bastards.' He'd not liked the old bat, but didn't wish this on her.

'How are they doing?' Sanchez indicated the open doorway.

'They're being thorough, even swabbed the cat's claws. They've found blood on a lamp. Someone's tried to wipe it off so they don't think it's hers and hopefully . . .' These attacks depressed him. What sort of degenerate beats up a defenceless old woman in a wheelchair? 'Did they give a time for the attack?'

'From the state of her, between six and ten hours before the ambulance got to her.'

'Quite a wide window.'

Sanchez shrugged. 'It's the best they can do.'

'Okay, let's talk to the guy who found her.' The four people in the basement office faced Chapman as he entered. 'Who discovered the body?' he asked. One of the women yelped and the other covered her mouth. Sanchez gave him a scowl and he corrected himself. 'I mean Mrs Curtis.'

A tall, thin man of around his own age held up a hand. From his pale, pinched appearance, Chapman should have guessed. A stoop and black-rimmed glasses gave him the air of a maths professor.

'Sergeant Chapman, Murder Squad. Can we speak in private, sir?'

'Sure, my office.' The man trudged towards a door in the far corner.

Chapman and Sanchez walked past the other staff, the sullen glares of yesterday replaced with uncertain smiles. Once seated in the office, Chapman studied the cramped room. A small high window in one wall provided the only source of natural light. Why didn't a Licensed News Enterprise have smarter offices? They were usually owned by rich bastards.

'We'll record this, if you don't mind,' he said. 'Shall we start with your name?'

'Alan. Alan Turner.'

Chapman studied Turner. The man who'd discovered Benjamin Murray. Harding had said he worked for a News Enterprise. Chapman should have read his statement. There were too many links to the two dead bodies and this place, but he kept his thoughts to himself. 'Can you talk me through what you did before you found . . . Mrs Curtis?'

Turner related the events, blinking as he described finding the old woman.

'Was the front door open?' Sanchez said.

'I've got a spare key.' He studied the constable and added, 'She's my aunt.'

'How come she didn't mention this yesterday?' Chapman said.

'Because it's none of your business.'

Chapman tried another tack. 'Have you seen or heard from Ms Conti since yesterday?' Behind Turner's surprise, Chapman picked up a fleeting emotion. Guilt or fear? Or both.

'Antonia? No, why?' Turner found something on the desk fascinating.

'Antonia, is it? *She's* not related to you as well?' he said.

Turner grew red and shook his head.

'Have you seen her then?'

'No.' Turner swallowed. 'What about my aunt? That's why you're here, isn't it?'

'Yes.' Chapman opened a screen on his tablet. 'Is anything missing from the house?'

'I'm not sure. Nothing from Eleanor's apartment, and I haven't been upstairs since Ms Conti moved in, so can't say.'

'How long ago did she move in?'

'A few years, why?'

'Where did she live before?'

'Sergeant, I don't know her life story. She just works here.'

She must clean this office, but why use a different name? 'That's another thing your aunt kept from us. What does she do for you?'

'She's a reporter.' Turner examined his fingernails.

Realisation hit Chapman. 'You're doing an exposé on GRM.' This could be good news for him, especially if they'd unearthed something to derail GRM's bid for the Murder Squad. 'When will you run it?'

'Today.' Turner sounded puzzled at the change of tone.

Had someone at GRM got wind of this and decided to scare them off? Mind you, why attack the old lady? 'Did your aunt work on the story?'

'She's the majority shareholder in the business, but she doesn't get involved with individual stories. Antonia and I worked on this one.'

A sudden fit of compassion made him say, 'When you next see Antonia, let her know she's off the hook for the murder.'

'What's happened?' Hope lit up Turner's features.

He had it bad, but Chapman didn't blame him. 'Cock-up with the DNA . . . or something more sinister.' *Why the hell did I say that?*

'Sarge?' Sanchez stiffened, leaning forward.

'What do you mean?' Turner said.

'A company owned by GRM carries out the tests. You could put that in your article.'

Sanchez grew more agitated, but he ignored her and produced a business card which he slid across the table.

'Can you ask Ms Conti to call me?' This case must be linked to the two deaths, and if it somehow implicated GRM, it wouldn't harm his own prospects of hanging on to his job.

◆ ◆ ◆

Turner returned from the vet, weary and downcast, the image of Eleanor lying injured on the floor haunting him. Instead of the usual buzz that accompanied the imminent release of such a big story, a sombre mood pervaded the office. He trudged through to his room, avoiding eye contact, and collapsed into the chair.

Miles followed him to the door. The grin that normally split his bushy beard was missing and his large frame looked diminished. Even his signature colourful waistcoat looked muted. 'How is she?'

'Not great. They've done a scan. They haven't found a blood clot, but there's a lot of swelling. It will be a while before they know if she'll . . . How it will affect her.'

Miles made sympathetic noises. 'Did you see the message from the solicitors?'

'No,' Turner said, uneasy at the news. 'What do they want?'

'I imagine, to discuss last-minute legal stuff before we publish the GRM article.'

'Okay, I'll ring them. Thanks, Miles.' Turner stilled his concern as he waited for Geoff Stokes, the senior partner, to answer. His company had already checked the article, so it couldn't be much.

'Hello, Geoff, I presume you want to discuss the new introduction to our piece on GRM.'

'I'm afraid not, Alan. We received a call from the Home Office.'

His insides fluttered. 'Why would *they* get involved?'

'The bit about GRM's part in transporting terror suspects to various unsavoury regimes.'

'But that's all in the public domain and we just mention it in passing.'

'It's not in the public domain any more, I've just checked.' Stokes let this sink in. 'It's now covered by the *new* Prevention of Terrorism and National Security Act.'

'How did they find out? We haven't broadcast it yet.'

'Lucky for you.' Stokes's voice hardened. 'And I can assure you the leak isn't at our end.'

Turner's heart shrank. The leak *must* be at their end – he trusted everyone here, but no point in falling out over it. He'd been so careful, and with the new security software nobody could have hacked it. 'What happens now?'

'You can't publish the article.'

'Even if we remove the offending section?'

'Unfortunately not. The National Security Agency have sixty days to vet it and—'

'That's ridiculous.'

'I don't disagree, but I'm just telling you what has to happen. They'll remove any parts they're not happy with.'

Turner gripped the handset. 'Sixty days . . .'

'Like I said, I'm just the messenger. If they discover any hint of wrongdoing in the way you gathered the evidence, then prosecution may follow, and of course, your hard-won licence will be at stake.'

'This is fucking absurd. Sorry, Geoff, I can't believe they can just do this.'

'Believe it, Alan, and if you broadcast any material in the article before they've vetted all of it, they'll be on you like a ton of bricks.'

It felt as though a weight was pressing him into his chair. 'We've trailed it on the site, so I'd better pull—'

'No need, they've taken the site down until they have an undertaking that you'll comply.'

'Damn!' He checked his messages. All were complaints about the site being unavailable.

'Sorry . . . By the way, any news on Eleanor? Miles told me, I'm so sorry.'

'Not much. I've just got back from seeing her. She's stable but they won't know the full extent of her injuries for a few days.'

'We'll pray for her, Alan. And don't let the other business distress you. You must have scored a direct hit for them to react like this.'

Turner ended the call, not feeling the least encouraged by these last words. Eleanor had told him of Reed-Mayhew's vindictiveness and if GRM had the power to do this, maybe they had indeed bitten off too much.

CHAPTER 9

Sabirah avoided looking at the two police officers facing her and searched for something to focus on, but the small room smelling of body odour and unwashed feet had no features to hold her attention, unless you counted the scars in the dirty cream paint where someone had scratched their name. A wave of dizziness made the walls sway and she realised she hadn't eaten since they'd brought her in twenty-four hours ago. The policewoman's next words made her forget her hunger.

'If you want to see your kids, you need to cooperate.' A small woman, her manner suggested she'd found something unpleasant under her shoe.

'Are they here?' Sabirah's heart raced. If only she could see them, make sure they were safe.

'No,' the balding policeman said.

'Can I see them?' She looked from one to the other of her interrogators, searching for a hint of compassion. 'Please.'

The woman scowled. 'First tell us where you hid the remaining items you stole,' she said in a harsh voice. 'Your merciful employer has agreed to drop charges if you do.'

'I did not steal.'

'So you say, but according to your employer you told them you'd hidden them in the toilet.' The policewoman glared at her. 'You can't have it both ways.'

'Just rubbish, paper from the shredder.' The jabbing pain behind Sabirah's forehead intensified.

'Okay, let's say you took some rubbish. So, just tell us where you hid it.' Exasperation crept into the policewoman's voice.

'I tell you, I left in bin, under the liner. Someone must have moved.' Sabirah didn't know what else to say. When she'd hidden them in the bin, she'd thought it a good idea. Patience emptied the bins on that floor so would have found them. She wondered how her friend was. They said she killed a man, but he must have deserved it.

'Okay, let's move on.' The woman sighed. 'Who told you to take these papers?'

'Nobody.' She held the policewoman's gaze, determined not to betray Patience.

After receiving the same answer four times, the policewoman crossed her arms. 'So, that's all you have to say.'

'It's truth. Please can I see my children?'

The policewoman pushed her chair away without replying.

'Please,' Sabirah implored the man, who ignored her and rose to his feet.

'Okay, I tell you who asked.' She prayed Patience would forgive her, but if they already thought she'd killed someone, this couldn't harm her.

The two officers sat and noted her words as she recited them, feeling the shame of betrayal each time they made her go over her statement. When they'd finally finished she said, 'I see Nadimah and Hakim now?'

'I'll let you know,' the policewoman said, not looking at her.

'You promise.' Sabirah pushed herself out of the chair but subsided when the bald officer put his hand on her shoulder.

Tears streaked her cheeks as she watched them leave. She'd betrayed her friend for nothing.

◆ ◆ ◆

Turner stared at the screen of his desktop monitor, not taking in anything as thoughts of Eleanor crowded his mind. *Who would do such a thing?* The phone on his desk rang, dragging him out of his thoughts. A local number. He studied the readout for a few seconds before taking the call.

'The Electric Investigator—'

'Alan, I've got the information but I'll need my laptop.' The excitement in Antonia's voice would normally have energised him.

'Antonia, I've got news—'

'Sabirah? What's happened to her?'

'No, it's Eleanor.' Turner told her and waited for her to respond, picturing her distress and wishing he were with her to comfort her.

'I have to see her. Where is she?'

'Royal Free. She's in ICU.'

'I'll go now – blast!'

'What?'

'The police! Hospitals are crawling with cameras—'

'Don't worry. Chapman told me you're no longer wanted. He's investigating the attack on Eleanor.'

'Did he say why they've dropped me?'

'DNA's not a match.'

Antonia paused for a few seconds. 'I don't understand.'

'Chapman thinks someone at GRM has switched the samples to get you off the hook. The company doing the tests is part of their group.'

'Did he say why?'

'No, I think he felt he'd already said too much.'

'Could it be a trick so I let my guard down?'

'*He* seemed to believe it, and I don't see what he had to gain by saying it. I checked on the databases, and you're not on the wanted lists any more. If someone has switched your DNA, we can use it to retaliate against GRM.'

'What do you mean, "retaliate"?'

'They blocked our story. Correction, they got the Home Office to block it. The site hasn't been right since. With this—'

'What? All that work's gone down the drain?' Antonia sounded ready to cry.

The urge to hold her almost overwhelmed him. 'We can do a new story. "GRM interference thwarts murder investigation."'

Antonia snorted. 'Shall I hand myself in and insist I *am* the killer? Give them a full confession?'

'No, I didn't mean . . .' Why didn't he think before speaking?

'They'd just blame a lab technician, sack them and announce, "Lessons have been learned."' Antonia's breathing sounded loud. 'I'll visit Eleanor and come over later.'

Turner ended the call and stared at the handset. He'd let Antonia down. The notion he'd wandered out of his depth grew stronger.

Chapman sat alongside Sanchez in Harding's office waiting for the inspector to reply, mindful of the detective constable's disapproval. He'd needed all his powers of persuasion to get her to agree not to report him for what he'd said to Turner.

The inspector, who'd fidgeted with his watch while Chapman spoke, paused before replying. 'You're saying the attack on the old lady is connected to . . . what, the dead man or GRM?'

Chapman hesitated. Accusing a company as powerful as GRM of what he suspected could be dangerous. 'Both, Ian.'

Harding glanced at Sanchez.

Fuck off. I'll call you Ian in here. 'Despite what the revised DNA tests say,' Chapman said, 'I think Conti had something to do with Pavlo Helba's death. She's also been spying on GRM for The Electric Investigator. What if GRM found out and fixed the DNA tests to exonerate—'

'But why, Sarge?' Sanchez said, repeating the argument they'd already rehearsed. 'If she's arrested for murder, then she's out of their hair.'

'What if she's found something they want hushed up, a serious crime, and they want to get rid of her? If she's questioned for murder, what's to say she won't use the information as a bargaining tool to get more lenient treatment from us?'

'Don't be preposterous,' Harding said.

'Why attack the old woman?' Sanchez said.

'She owns The Investigator, so a warning, or if they came for Conti and the old lady got in the way . . .'

'You're making a serious charge, Russell,' Harding said, leaning away from him, 'accusing one of our biggest companies of kidnap and attempted murder. Do we know Conti's whereabouts?'

'No, sir,' said Sanchez, throwing Chapman an angry glare. 'The DNA result should be back from the blood on the lamp. Why don't we wait to see who it throws up?'

'Good idea, Constable. We don't—'

'That won't mean anything. First of all, GRM won't have sent anyone connected to them to do the job, and second, how can we trust any DNA results from CrimTech now? They're clearly taking orders from someone at GRM.' Chapman must take care not to sound like a conspiracy-theory nutter.

126

'What do you suggest doing then, Sergeant?' Harding said in a tone suggesting Chapman had failed.

'We get the sample retested by another lab—'

'That's not going to happen. You know how much it will cost? To say nothing of the political implications.'

Chapman expected this reaction. 'Okay, then why don't you ask Jo to check the results? We can trust her.'

Harding shook his head before Chapman had finished. 'That's not going to happen either.'

'Why the hell not?'

'Sergeant, I don't have to explain my decisions to you.'

Chapman glared at him until Sanchez said, 'I'll check if the DNA's come back then, boss.'

Harding gestured his assent and returned to his paperwork. Chapman left him to it. He'd been an idiot. If the inspector knew people high up at GRM, he was the type to go telling tales and alert them to Chapman's suspicions. It didn't bode well for either this investigation or his own future.

The sight of Eleanor lying inert in a hospital bed distressed Antonia, especially when she thought of who might have put her here. After holding the old woman's hand for an hour, she kissed her forehead and left. On the way home she kept checking she wasn't being tailed, falling into the wariness of her teenage years. The thought that nothing had changed in her life depressed her and by the time she reached home a dark mood weighed her down. Turner had told her about the state of her flat and, having no desire to tackle the clearing up, she went into the office, planning to examine the footage on the memory stick for the van. At least it would keep her mind busy.

Turner's light was on. She didn't want to speak to anyone, but he saw her before she could escape.

'How is she?' he said.

'Not great. I've never seen her so still.'

'I know what you mean, she's—'

'I'd better tidy up,' Antonia said.

'Oh, okay. I've been thinking, about who might be behind the attack. If it's GRM—'

'It's *not* GRM.'

Turner rubbed the back of his neck. 'Why are you so sure?'

'Someone came looking for me at the gym. The description fits that of Arkady, the leader of the gang that chased me. A stocky guy my age, six two with fair hair and pale eyes.'

'The description could fit any of hundreds,' he said.

'Someone searching for me?'

'But they won't know where you live.'

'It's not so difficult to trace someone. *We* do it often enough.'

'You must feel dreadful—' He turned bright red. 'I'm sorry, I meant . . .'

'I know, and I feel awful it's my fault.'

'It could still be a random burglary.'

'I'd like to think so, but . . .' She inhaled, her torso shuddering.

'Why don't you ring Sergeant Chapman?'

The mention of Chapman reminded her she'd not stayed at home because she'd seen him leaving Eleanor's. If she had been home, Eleanor would be fine now. The thought that she'd let Eleanor down led to another. 'I need to find out what's happened to Sabirah.'

'I'll find out where they're holding her. We've got a few contacts in the Ministry of Corrections.'

He made two phone calls then said, 'The police are holding her on suspicion of theft. According to the police they found a pair of Reed-Mayhew's sunglasses in her bag.'

'That's a lie.'

Turner held up his hands. 'I'm just telling you what they told me. My sources tell me they found her prints on the item and they've got three witnesses to its discovery.'

'What about the kids?' The fear she'd seen in Nadimah's eyes last night still haunted her.

'I didn't ask, but I'd imagine in care,' he said. 'And I'm afraid it gets worse. If she's found guilty, they'll deport the whole—'

'Thanks Alan, I know.' A wave of nausea washed over her as she remembered her experiences in care. 'It's my fault.'

Turner, crimson again, cleared his throat. 'I'll speak to Geoff Stokes. If anyone can get her released . . .'

Sabirah never talked of home, but Antonia could guess how awful it was from her friend's reaction whenever Syria came up in conversation. Even though the mainstream news channels no longer reported from there, you could easily find evidence of atrocities. Sick with guilt, she got up and headed for the door.

◆ ◆ ◆

Still angry, although not sure who at, Chapman sat at his desk, trying to forget his concerns about his job. He was too old to start again, and who'd want a washed-up DS with his recent record? Across the desk, Sanchez read her emails. They'd not spoken since leaving Harding's office.

'The DNA from the blood on the old lady's lamp is from an Arkady Demchuk, known to us for assault,' she said. 'We also have another match for blood found on the cat's claws. Nikolai Rudenko.'

He typed Demchuk's name into the database. 'They last arrested him for a fight outside a pub. Someone battered a young Afghan lad,' he said. 'Charges dropped when witnesses clammed up.'

Sanchez bit the inside of her cheek then said, 'I know it's not my place, but you need to sort out your relationship with the inspector—'

'You're right, Constable, it's not your place.'

She flushed before looking away, eyes shining.

'Can you please get the details of Demchuk's associates?' he said, wishing he could take the words back.

She bent over her keyboard in thickening silence as he read Demchuk's record. Grievous Bodily Harm, Actual Bodily Harm, attempted assault. Rudenko's record could have been a carbon copy, including the arrest for the assault on the Afghan youth.

'The attack on Mrs Curtis is nothing to do with GRM,' Sanchez said, sliding him her tablet.

Her tone irritated him. 'How can you be so sure?'

'Just read it, Sarge.'

The image showed Pavlo Helba and the caption underneath identified him as Arkady Demchuk's half-brother. Sanchez pulled the tablet towards her and brought up the CCTV footage. Chapman was debating whether to apologise when she pushed the screen under his nose. The frozen image showed a group of men returning to confront Conti in the alleyway. Now he knew who they were, he could identify three: Nikolai Rudenko, Arkady Demchuk and behind him Pavlo Helba. Chapman tried to work out what this meant for the two investigations.

Maybe there was no connection between the two bodies they'd found in the canal. And despite the fact they now had no evidence linking Conti to Helba, the gang who attacked her clearly believed she'd killed him. How had they tracked her down? They didn't seem the brightest. Had someone helped them? Their names sounded Russian or something, so maybe they had links to organised crime.

'Sarge,' Sanchez said, 'you might think I'm just a stupid girl but I can't work with you like this. Either sort yourself out or I'll ask for a transfer.'

◆ ◆ ◆

Antonia waited in the narrow corridor outside Kerry's bedroom, listening to sounds of movement inside. She banged on the door again. 'Come on, we need to get going.' The worry Social Services had already taken Nadimah and Hakim made her jumpy. She needed to be waiting at their home when they returned from school.

'Okay, okay.' The door opened and Kerry came out. A blonde wig hid her distinctive copper hair and she wore a sober business suit, but her immaculate make-up couldn't hide her apprehension. 'Will I do?' She gave a twirl and put on a serious expression. 'Good afternoon. Tina Smith, Social Services. I've got a Child Prevention Order—'

'Protection Order—'

'I know. Don't worry.' Although she smiled, she couldn't hide her wariness.

Too nervous to joke, Antonia said, 'This is a bad idea, Kerry, let's forget it. I'll just have to persuade the kids to come with me.'

'And if you don't? You can't let them go into care.'

Antonia hesitated but Kerry's determined air told her not to bother arguing. They took the lift down the six floors to the entrance, and concern that someone had followed her to Kerry's home made Antonia's skin tingle. Kerry's head seemed to be on a swivel as they walked to the car park and she exhaled when she got in her car. Guilt at putting her friend through this infused Antonia. On the drive to Sabirah's house Kerry tuned her sound system to a channel playing a selection of upbeat Motown hits. She parked round the corner and Antonia sat in the car staring into the distance, her hands clammy.

'You can do it, Antonia,' Kerry said.

Antonia hugged her, then headed for the house. *Come on, relax, or you'll frighten the kids.* A figure at the upper window watched her approach and waved. Antonia waved back and rang the bell, still unsure of the best tack to take. Nadimah didn't open the door until Antonia identified herself and hesitated for a few seconds before letting her in.

Hakim gave Antonia an uncertain smile and she high-fived him. 'How would you two like to go to Regent's Park?' she said.

'We should stay in case our mother returns,' Nadimah said.

Should she tell them what had happened to Sabirah, rather than just reassure them she was safe? 'We could go on to the zoo.'

Hakim's face lit up. 'Can we see the tigers and gorillas?'

'Whatever you want. How about it, Nadimah?'

'If Mother comes home and we're not here, she'll worry . . .' The girl's voice tailed away.

'We'll leave a note.'

Nadimah looked unhappy and Antonia gave the girl an encouraging smile. Hakim's eagerness swung it and they got their coats. Each would have cost their mother at least two weeks' money and Antonia couldn't help comparing them to the oft-darned charity-shop garment Sabirah wore to work. Now they were going, even Nadimah became animated.

Antonia left to tell the neighbour she was taking the children out. A car pulled up outside and something about it made Antonia hesitate. She retreated into the flat and closed the door. Her wariness transmitted to the children and they studied her. She'd almost persuaded herself she'd made a mistake when the doorbell rang. A second long ring followed, then a woman's voice.

'Hello, Nadma, Hakam, are you there?' She rapped on the door. 'I'm Julie, I'm here to take care of you.'

The *actual* Social Services. The children regarded Antonia, exuding fear, and she held her finger to her lips, trying to appear calm as her heart tripped.

'Can you open the door, love?' the woman said.

She repeated the request, then a second voice said something Antonia didn't hear. The voices faded. She held her breath, then a door opened.

'Can I help you?' The neighbour from upstairs.

The woman must know Antonia and the kids hadn't left.

'Hello, madam, Social Services. We're here to take care of Mrs Fadil's kids while she's in prison.'

Nadimah let out a sob.

CHAPTER 10

The constant background din that accompanied every moment of Sabirah's incarceration added to her sense of panic. Her mind on Nadimah and Hakim, she shuffled in line at the breakfast counter, contemplating the forthcoming meeting with the man from the Refugee Rights committee. The hope she could see her children was the only thing keeping her going. Despite all they'd been through, she'd never spent so long separated from them.

'Come on, wake up.'

Sabirah started and apologised to the server behind the counter.

'What do you want?' the woman said, and gestured at the aluminium trays of breakfast products, her doughy face arranged into a scowl.

'Porridge, please.'

The server slopped a ladle of grey goo into a bowl and threw it on to the tray. The sticky, starchy smell mingled with the underlying odour of overcooked vegetables and rancid fat. As she moved along the line, the server dropped a piece of bacon into the mess. Sabirah's stomach clenched.

'Don't you want it?' the woman behind her said.

Grateful for her intervention, Sabirah whispered, 'No.'

The woman reached over her shoulder and plucked the bacon from her bowl, then hawked and spat into her porridge. Sabirah spun round, recognising the woman, a Turk or Kurd, she couldn't remember which.

'Why you do this?'

'Your lot blew up Paddington station last night. Why don't you go back to Syria, you dirty Arab?' Other voices spoke out in support and the row of angry faces arrayed behind the woman confronted Sabirah.

Sabirah's legs trembled and she retreated, heading towards the tea urn.

'Oi, you've left this,' the server said, pointing at her bowl. Sabirah returned and picked up the tray.

Someone jabbed her in the back, making her cry out. A hand clamped to her mouth, grinding something against her lips. The bacon. Rage surged through her and she swung her arm. Her elbow sank into her attacker's midriff. The hand fell away and Sabirah spat out the bacon. A blow caught her on the ear and then another on the top of her skull knocked her to the ground.

Angry yells grew louder before fading as blows landed on her. Shrill whistles sounded and new voices shouted before a crack to her temple brought unconsciousness.

◆ ◆ ◆

The sensation of being observed made Antonia lift her head. Across the small dining table in the corner of Kerry's living room, Nadimah studied her, her serious manner making her look older than her eleven years. Antonia smiled, but the girl didn't respond; obviously still angry at Antonia's failure to tell her Sabirah was in prison and unconvinced by her assurance she'd get her out. Next to her Hakim tucked into a bowl of cereal. His reaction to Antonia suggested *he'd* forgiven her.

Kerry's flat wasn't big enough and she'd hated sharing a bed with her. Antonia had forgotten how her friend muttered in her sleep, disturbing what little rest she'd snatched between nightmares. At least she didn't have to worry about Sabirah's neighbour reporting her. Fear had changed to relief when the neighbour told the woman from Social Services that a man claiming to be an uncle had taken the children. She'd even described the man and his car. With any luck, they'd spend days searching for this mythical relative.

Antonia and Kerry spent the evening reassuring the children they'd soon get their mother released. Antonia had planned to spend the time searching for the men who'd chased her, and more than likely attacked Eleanor. Kerry said something to Nadimah and they giggled. An unreasonable irritation tempered Antonia's relief that Kerry's presence relaxed the girl. *You're* not *jealous of an eleven-year-old. Isn't it bad enough you've put her mother in danger?*

'I'll drop you off at work,' Kerry said, 'then take the kids to the academy my friend runs.'

Another pang of guilt hit Antonia. Kerry was calling in favours to help pull *her* out of a hole.

Twenty minutes later Kerry left Antonia outside the office. A dark people carrier pulled out of a side road and fell in behind Kerry's car, passing a second similar vehicle parked on the opposite side of the road. Antonia studied it, but the heavy tint made it impossible to see in.

Telling herself not to be paranoid, she went into the office. She removed her jacket and sat at her desk, unable to concentrate on work; then the phone buzzed. The call came via her line in the flat. Kerry must have forgotten something, unless the people carrier *had* followed them. She snatched the handset up and pressed it to her ear.

'Patience?'

She nearly dropped the handset. Nobody apart from the police could have connected her to the cleaner. 'Who's that?'

'Carl. Can—'

'How did you get my number?' Carl worked at GRM as a cleaner, but nobody there knew her identity, unless Sanchez, or Chapman, had said something. In which case, anyone from GRM could find her. *Oh hell.*

'Sabirah's neighbour gave it,' he said. 'Can we meet, is important?'

What the hell did he want? He struck her as a good guy, but it could be a trap. What if GRM discovered what she'd done?

'I have papers,' he said. 'From Sabirah . . .'

The documents from the shredder, thank God. Even with the story spiked she could use them. After arranging to meet him at a cafe near Sabirah's, she took a circuitous route, keeping alert for any tails. Nobody looked out of place, but someone good wouldn't. She increased her pace but didn't notice anyone hurry to keep up with her.

The aroma of toast and scalded coffee filled the cafe. Carl waited at a table against the rear wall and saluted her with his mug. His resemblance to a middle-aged Che Guevara struck Antonia anew. She ordered an Americano with an extra shot and joined him. Carl stared at her incredulously, but of course, Patience never wore tailored jeans and a leather jacket.

As she sat down, she checked out the room in the mirror above Carl. He studied the room over her shoulder, eyes darting.

'Okay, Carl, where are they?'

'Not here, somewhere safe. You think I'm stupid?'

'Where did you find them?'

'In the bin, in toilets. The man with perfume smell ask everyone if they see papers, so I know important when I find. Toilet bin is your job, so I think papers for you.'

She remembered Carl telling her he'd been a professor of philosophy in Bogotá. 'Can you take me to them?'

He hesitated. 'They arrest Sabirah, maybe they let her go if I give it back.'

'Maybe they will, but you need to negotiate with them.'

'I not negotiate, always lose at cards.' He smiled. 'I think you are not just cleaner. If I give, can you?'

'Of course.'

'You are a good friend.' He reached out, his hands trembling with emotion, and clasped hers.

Unable to meet his gaze, she blinked. 'Where have you put them?'

He pushed his cup away. 'I show you now.'

Feeling like a fraud, Antonia followed him out of the cafe. Now he'd accepted Antonia as an ally, Carl relaxed, becoming voluble and chatting to her as he strolled to where he'd concealed the papers. Antonia scanned her surroundings, feeling exposed. Carl sensed her unease and fell silent, picking up speed. Ten minutes later they arrived at a short street full of small red-brick terraced houses and he studied his surroundings.

'Over there,' he said, and led her across the road to a small newsagent/general store on one corner. 'You wait.' A bell tinkled and he disappeared into the shop.

Antonia studied the street, but nothing moved. The bell tinkled again and Carl returned, brandishing a large brown envelope.

'All in here,' he said, handing it to Antonia.

Antonia peered at the strips of paper in the packet. Much as she wanted to read them, she needed somewhere she could spread them out and after thanking Carl, returned to the office. The information on these papers should enable them to hit back at GRM and her excitement grew as she neared home.

After giving Miles a cheery greeting, she knocked on the frame of Turner's office and swept in, placing the envelope on the desk with a flourish. 'Ta da. The stuff from Reed-Mayhew's shredder.'

Turner's expression made her pause.

'What's wrong?'

'Just spoke to the hospital—'

'Has anything happened to Eleanor?'

'She's still unconscious, the swelling's not gone down . . .'

The reminder of Eleanor's condition and the thought that she might lose the old woman filled her with panic. She'd provided Antonia with stability for more than a third of her life.

'Let's see,' he said, sliding the package towards him. 'Have you read it?'

'I didn't want to tear them.'

'Come on then.' Turner's eyes glittered as he picked up the envelope and eased out the papers.

They cleared a space on his desk and laid out the strips before untangling them to create separate sheets. Antonia read the first one and her excitement ebbed. It dealt with a financial vehicle created by GRM.

She noticed Turner's posture stiffen. 'Have you got something, Alan?'

He nodded and continued reading, the tip of his tongue showing in the corner of his mouth. 'They've got a mole in the Home Office.'

'Does it give a name?'

'Margaret Gage.' He tapped on his keypad.

Antonia continued reading. The next sheet dealt with payments to someone called Hajduk Veljko for delivering a parcel. It was a hell of a lot of money. Why would they pay so much? If she didn't know better she'd suspect he'd delivered drugs, but they'd found no hint of narcotics. Antonia continued checking the remaining sheets. More financial details, not her area of expertise, or interest, but Turner might understand them. He let out a groan.

'What's wrong?' Antonia said.

'I've checked the senior staff but—'

'It might be someone junior who's got access to classified material. A PA or something?'

'It's not.' Excitement drained from his voice. 'I recognise the name. It's a pseudonym.' He turned the screen so Antonia could see it.

She read with growing disappointment the account of Margaret Gage spying on her husband during the American War of Independence. 'Sorry, Alan.'

'It's not your fault, Antonia.' He reached out and squeezed her wrist.

Memories of the ill-fated interlude when they'd dated flashed through her mind. Their easy friendship, which had developed while she grew from a young teenager into a woman, took months to recover.

Turner reddened and released her. 'Even without a name we can use this. Well done.'

Thrown by the intensity of the recollections, Antonia didn't reply.

After a few moments Turner cleared his throat. 'Let's see the rest.' He took the papers from her and read them. 'These all of them?'

'Are they no good?'

'They're very helpful. Though I'd hoped to find something linked to the King's Cross bomb.'

'It wouldn't be the first time an informer exaggerated the value of their story to get paid.'

'We weren't paying him. Anyway, these are dynamite.' He tapped the top sheet. 'Reed-Mayhew's syphoning profits through a subsidiary—'

'So what, they all do.'

'Yes, but under the new rules, all companies awarded government contracts have to pay full UK corporation tax. This refers to agreements signed since they came into force. The bastard went on TV promising his companies always play by the rules.' He grinned. 'They can't block *this*. Do you want to write the article?'

This would make up for the disappointment of having her story spiked, but what about Sabirah? 'We can't use it.'

'Why the hell not?'

'I'm hoping GRM will drop the charges against Sabirah if we give them these back.'

His excitement ebbed, making him look older. 'Do you think it will work?'

'I have to try, Alan. I can't just leave her in prison. They'll keep her there until she goes to trial, and that could be months.'

'No, you're right.' An expression of regret crossed his features. 'Your friend's freedom has to come first.'

She wasn't ready to let GRM off the hook. 'We could do both.'

Turner frowned. 'We must be careful. If we agree to return them in exchange for them withdrawing the theft charge against your friend, we can't use the information.'

Antonia couldn't understand his caution. 'We'll return the papers, but they can't expect us to un-know what's in them. We can search for other evidence. There's bound to be some. If not, we publish the story without the papers, let them sue us if they dare—'

'We'd have to agree not to use the information. From what I know of Reed-Mayhew, he'll tie us up in legal knots before they'll agree to anything. And anyway, if we make accusations without evidence, we could lose our licence, even if they don't sue.'

From the set of his jaw she could see he'd made his mind up, and Antonia exhaled in frustration. 'Okay, we'd better get in touch with GRM—'

'Don't be naïve, Antonia. We're already being investigated by the licensing authorities for the story. If it got out we'd incited an innocent woman to break the law, what do you think they'd do to us?'

Her cheeks grew hot under his scrutiny.

His expression softened. 'I'll speak to Geoff Stokes. He's already acting for Sabirah and he can contact GRM with the offer and with any luck keep our name out of it.'

The lack of sleep over the last few days and stress of being on edge all the time hit her and she sank into the chair. The need to have someone hold her, tell her everything would be all right, made her tremble. *Well done, Antonia. You've really messed up this time.*

Chapman waited in the dingy corridor wrinkling his nose at the odour of stale cooking as Sanchez bent to peer through the letter box. Scuffed lino, its original pattern obscured by ancient stains, covered the hallway floor and peeling paper lined the walls.

'There's nobody in, Sarge,' she said, straightening. 'You can see the whole flat and he doesn't like to tidy up much.'

'He must fit in here well then. I didn't realise these places still existed in London.'

He led the way to the car. It wasn't a big surprise Nikolai Rudenko had gone to ground, like the other members of Arkady's gang. Chapman hoped the team had more luck with the door-to-door near the City Road Basin, but doubted it.

A figure strolled round the corner of the building, saw them and ducked out of sight.

'With me,' Chapman said in a low voice, and set off at a run.

After twenty metres Sanchez caught up with him and forged ahead, leaving him trailing. She followed the figure round another corner and uttered a yell. *Well done, Sanchez, he's bound to stop now.* He put on a spurt and reached the corner as their quarry shot through an open gateway leading into an untidy yard.

Sanchez followed and as he reached the gateway, she vanished into a dilapidated warehouse at the far end of the yard. Too winded to shout a warning, he forced his legs across the cluttered space. At the entrance to the building he halted and peered into the gloom. Steps echoed and a figure vanished through a doorway in the far side. He crossed the floor accompanied by the sound of his gasping.

A concrete staircase led up from the doorway. 'Shit!'

Steps clattered above him and, energised, he attacked the climb. Each flight seemed longer than the last, each step higher. His thighs burned and calves knotted like steel cable. He checked how far he had to go. Almost at the top. A toe caught on the edge of a step and he stumbled, grabbing a bannister to prevent him falling. At the top he ran through an opening into a large space and paused, attempting to control his breathing so he could listen. A stitch cut into his side and the sickly smell of something rotting filled his nostrils. His vision became accustomed to the gloom, and he could make out rows of orange racking, their skeletal uprights reaching up towards the underside of the roof.

A woman's cry jolted him into action. 'Sanchez, you okay?' he shouted in between gulps of air.

Another cry pinpointed their position and he charged into a gap between the racking. Sweat ran down his forehead. He wiped it with a sleeve. The struggle sounded closer. In the centre of a pool of light, under a broken skylight, two figures struggled on the floor. The bigger one broke free and ran. Sanchez leapt to her feet and threw herself at him with a yell. Chapman ran towards them, feeling he was moving in slow motion.

The fugitive grabbed Sanchez by the throat and swung her round to smash her into the wall. But there was no wall there and for a split second they froze. Then Sanchez screamed as she fell into the lift shaft.

CHAPTER 11

Every part of Sabirah ached as she shuffled behind the warder. The worst pain came from her ribs and she hunched over to ease the discomfort. Her stomach rumbled, reminding her that not only did she miss breakfast, but she'd miss lunch.

'Come on Fadil, get a move on,' the guard following her said. Short and rotund, she seemed less harsh than the others.

The one leading heard the command and added her contribution. 'Give her a prod, Ruth, we haven't all day.'

She was the worst, a tall brunette with a furious nature and acne scars on her chin. The woman unlocked the door to the office block and stepped into the corridor before letting Sabirah pass.

'Does it hurt?' she asked, pointing at Sabirah's bruised cheek.

'Yes.' Sabirah studied her feet.

'Good.' She gave a nasty smirk and pushed Sabirah at the wall. A sharp pain shot through her side, making her gasp. The warder brushed past and led her towards the assistant governor's office at the far end of the corridor, then knocked and opened the door. 'Prisoner Fadil, sir,' she announced.

Before Sabirah realised what was happening, the woman shoved her into the room. Tears of pain came but Sabirah blinked them away and stood facing a desk taking up half the space. The man seated behind it looked about twenty-five and his pinched appearance suggested he'd rather be elsewhere. Pale hands danced over a keyboard and his gaze stayed on a screen on his desk.

Sabirah stepped forward and waited in front of a chair until he said, 'Sit.'

Not sure he was talking to her, she hesitated before lowering herself into the seat. The man cleared his throat and pushed the black plastic-framed glasses back up his nose, observing her for the first time.

'Fadil, I've got a report you've been fighting the other inmates.'

'The people attacked me.'

'It says here you elbowed prisoner Grant in the stomach. Is that a lie?'

'No, sir,' she said in a low voice.

'You also hit two of the warders.'

Sabirah didn't know who she had hit but cherished the memory of fighting back for the first time in her life.

'There's nothing funny about assaulting my staff,' he said, fixing her with a glare.

'No, sir.'

'You've got two children.'

The mention of Nadimah and Hakim frightened her. 'Can I see them?'

The assistant governor's gaze slid away. 'I'm afraid that won't be possible—'

'You promise!' The cry escaped before she could contain it and she leant forward.

Both guards grabbed her, pulling her away from the desk. The blonde twisted her arm, sending a stabbing pain through her shoulder.

'You should have thought of that before starting a fight,' the assistant governor said.

146

'I did not start fight.'

'I don't believe you, and your behaviour here just confirms your instability.'

'I have the right,' she said, determined to see her children.

'The right doesn't extend to terror suspects.'

She took a few seconds to understand the words. But they didn't apply to her. 'I'm not terrorist.'

'There is a state of emergency and the legislation covers all citizens of rogue states.'

The words didn't need to make sense; his attitude told her all she needed to know. Her insides became numb. If she couldn't see Nadimah and Hakim she didn't think she could survive being locked up for long. Sabirah's bruised body barely registered what was happening to it as the two guards bundled her from the room.

◆ ◆ ◆

Chapman waited for Sanchez to punch the numbers into the keypad outside the interview room. 'You sure you're okay?' he said. He could still feel the relief at seeing her flat on her back on top of the jammed lift car a few feet below the opening.

'No worries, Sarge, just a bit sore.' She massaged her right shoulder.

'You should think about taking a few days off.'

Sanchez pulled at her collar. 'I'd rather crack on with work than be stuck at home.' She returned her attention to the door.

Chapman wondered about her home life. He'd heard she lived with her mother.

The stuffy interview room smelt of vomit overlaid with bleach and Nikolai Rudenko didn't appear to have enjoyed the wait. His bloodshot eyes glared at Chapman from beneath thick eyebrows and his small mouth twisted as if sucking a lemon.

'I demand—'

'Shush, Nikolai.' Chapman held a finger to his lips. 'Let's go through a few things before you make demands.'

Sanchez started the recording equipment and Chapman informed Rudenko of his rights. Once Sanchez sat down, Chapman stared at Rudenko, who licked his lips.

'You're really in the shit, Nikolai. Not only did you try to kill Constable Sanchez here—'

'She attacked *me*—'

'We also know you were with Pavlo Helba the night someone killed him and you're also involved in a nasty attack on an old lady.'

'No, I wasn't.' Rudenko's eyes darted to each side.

'We've got you on CCTV, Nikolai.'

'I can't be, the cameras were—' Rudenko studied his fingernails.

'The cameras were what, Nikolai? Broken? Some were, but you're on several, large as life.'

Rudenko hesitated for a few moments, then said, 'Okay, I was with Pavlo, but I didn't touch him. The Black girl did it.'

Sanchez sat forward. 'You saw her?'

'Yeah, she did it.'

'What, you just watched while she killed your mate?' Chapman said.

Rudenko clenched his jaw. 'Yeah, they was in the water and I can't swim.'

Chapman felt an emptiness. Disappointment? 'So, what happened?'

Rudenko opened his mouth but didn't speak.

'Nikolai,' Sanchez said, 'if you want us to arrest her, you need to tell us what you saw.'

'Yeah, okay. We was walking along the canal with Pavlo in front—'

'Which way were you going?' Chapman asked.

'Errm . . . towards the bridge.'

'Where from?'

Panic crossed Rudenko's features. 'I don't remember.'

'Bloody hell, Nikolai, it was only four days ago.'

'Yes, but—'

'Someone killed your mate in front of you. I'd remember every detail.'

'You're making me nervous.' Rudenko appealed to Sanchez for help.

'Do you want a drink of water?' she said.

'Yes, please.'

Chapman glared at her, but she ignored him and got the water. 'Here,' she said. 'How come you lads hang out together?'

'You what?'

'You, Pavlo, Arkady. Where are your families from – Russia?'

He snorted. 'We hate Russians. We're from Ukraine. Well, Grandad was. He fought against Stalin.'

'So, you're part of some Ukrainian community group?'

'Nah, not really. We met at a sort of youth club. We had to go to the church every Saturday and learn folk songs.' He gave a sneer of disgust.

'A bit like the Polish—'

Chapman had heard enough. 'This is all very heart-warming, but can we get back to the question? Where were you coming from when you followed the woman you claim killed Pavlo?'

'McDonald's,' Rudenko said, pleased with himself. 'We was at McDonald's.'

'So, you walked from McDonald's, on Wharf Road, and took a detour.' Chapman knew he was lying.

'You what?'

'You went out of your way, along the canal.'

'Yeah, no, it's a shortcut.'

'No, it isn't. The quickest way to the bridge is up Wharf Road, so why did you go along the canal?'

'It's a shortcut.'

Sanchez leant forward, blocking Chapman. 'Okay, Nikolai, can you tell me what happened on the canal path?'

'We walked along and this woman just goes mad, starts screaming at us. We thought she was joking, but she knocked Pavlo in the water and then hit him.'

'What, punched him?' Chapman said.

'Yeah, well . . . It was dark, she might have had a stick or something . . .'

'If it was dark, how can you be sure who attacked him?'

'Erm . . . We saw her at McDonald's.' Rudenko smirked.

'So, you two, big scary lads, took a long shortcut along the canal, when a woman who you might have seen in McDonald's attacked you for no reason and then battered your mate to death while you watched. Is that right?' Chapman stopped himself from banging the table.

'I didn't say that. You're just trying to stitch me up. I want a brief.' Rudenko sat back, arms folded.

'Okay, Nikolai, whatever.' Chapman scraped his chair along the floor and leapt to his feet, making Rudenko flinch. 'Interview suspended fourteen forty-three.'

Sanchez paused the recording and followed him out. 'Sarge, what's up with you?'

'What's up with me? The little gob-shite is spinning us a pack of lies and—'

'He was talking, we could have teased the truth out of him. Now he's clammed up and everything will take twice as long.'

She was right. 'Yeah, it's still a pack of lies.'

'Possibly, but you can't let your personal feelings—'

'What's that supposed to mean, Constable?'

Sanchez didn't flinch. 'Conti is a suspect in a murder and you're disregarding that. She might fool you. But *I* can't ignore the evidence.'

◆ ◆ ◆

The stacks of books on the floor of her living room rebuked Antonia. She'd put them in neat piles but hadn't the energy to replace them on the shelves. The sight would have earned her a scolding from her mother. Thoughts of her dead parent led to unwelcome images. Mama running, leading the men away, then disappearing under the hooves of their horses. The bearded men dismounting and dragging her mother to her feet, blood covering her face. Antonia hiding, not daring to say anything, let alone try to help. The sense of shame felt as fresh as on that day and she could taste the dust. Desperate to dismiss the memories, she busied herself replacing the books, careless of the order.

She moved the last pile and behind it found the voice-activated recorder. She should have returned it to Alan after they'd decided not to plant it in Reed-Mayhew's office. The readout showed several messages, but she hadn't used it. She played the latest message and Turner's voice came on, telling her what had happened to Eleanor.

Antonia flicked to the first message. The sounds of objects falling then a voice, muffled. She turned up the volume.

'—we should fuck off—'

'It wasn't your brother she offed.'

She paused it. Was that the one called Arkady? The sound quality wasn't good enough for her to be sure. But who else would it be? He must be Pavlo's brother. The confirmation that the people who attacked Eleanor were linked to her fight with Pavlo made her sick with guilt. Why couldn't she have ignored the old man and walked on by? She listened some more.

Tension radiated from the recording, then the first one said, 'Well I'm here, aren't I?'

'Yeah, cos you're being paid.'

She paused it again. Their being on her route home from the gym that night hadn't been bad luck. Someone had sent them, but who? She swayed, feeling dizzy, but continued listening.

'—we fucking searching for?'

'I don't know. Papers from where she works.'

'—full of papers.'

Another voice spoke, too faint to make out.

'I'll say when we go— Sshhh. What was that?'

Silence, then twenty seconds later, the recorder switched off. Pulse racing and thoughts spinning, Antonia sat. What the hell had she recorded? She wanted to play it again, but she didn't have time. She couldn't risk missing visiting time at the prison.

Chapman sat across the interview table studying the lawyer who'd come to represent Nikolai Rudenko. On seeing the name of the company, Chapman assumed they'd send a junior who did the pro-bono work, employed to assuage the consciences of the senior partners.

But Anthony Buckley, the solicitor who'd arrived, *was* a senior partner. He wore a suit Chapman estimated cost mid four figures and his plump neck strained at the collar of his candy-striped shirt. Although Chapman guessed he didn't spend much time in police stations, his relaxed manner suggested he believed he'd make short work of the two stupid plods facing him.

Sanchez, to her credit, didn't appear fazed at having to deal with this senior member of the legal profession. Chapman read the statement Rudenko had produced with Buckley's help before studying the prisoner. *How the hell can you afford Buckley's fees?* Rudenko seemed to read his mind and studied his clasped hands.

'Nikolai,' Chapman began, 'you say in your statement you recognised the woman who attacked Pavlo Helba because she'd had words with you earlier. Tell us what happened.'

Rudenko placed his hands flat on the table then said, 'We were larking about and she turned up shouting the odds.'

'Who's we?'

'You what?'

'Who were you with?'

Rudenko looked at Buckley, who said, 'Sergeant, my client can't remember everyone there. He's still traumatised by what happened later. Anyway, none of his colleagues witnessed the attack, so their—'

'But they *did* witness the altercation.'

Buckley held his hands out. 'If my client can't recall . . .'

Chapman addressed Rudenko. 'But you can recall what she said and what Pavlo Helba said to her.'

'Yeah.'

Chapman returned to the statement. 'Okay, we'll leave that for the moment and move on to the attack. You two followed her from Wharf Road.' Chapman tried to keep the disdain from his voice. 'From about where the cameras weren't working.'

Rudenko smirked. 'Oh, yeah.'

'None of this corresponds with what you said previously—'

'Sergeant, you intimidated my client with your overbearing manner.'

'Your client is involved in one murder and—'

'Sergeant, I'm not a vulnerable young man you can intimidate. My client witnessed the death of one of his friends and is still traumatised by the experience. If you want to avoid a serious action for adding to the trauma, I suggest you stop bullying him.'

'Can you explain why you followed the young woman?' Sanchez cut in and Chapman let her take over while he calmed down.

Rudenko glanced at Buckley before clearing his throat. 'It was Pavlo's idea. She told us to stop pissing about and grow up, so he said, "Cheeky young woman. Let's have a word."'

Even Buckley smiled and Sanchez said, 'What do you think he meant?'

'Dunno.'

Chapman leant forward but Sanchez's gesture stopped him and she said, 'You must have thought something. He was your friend and if he said, "Let's have a word", what did you understand he meant by it?'

'He wanted to tell her not to be so rude.'

Chapman couldn't contain a snort but let Sanchez continue. 'Did you speak to this young woman?'

'Nah, she was too fast. I said to Pavlo we should leave it and we was walking back when she attacked him.'

'How do you know it was her?' Chapman said.

'Who else could it be?'

'So you never saw who attacked him?'

Rudenko stared at the table and his shoulders twitched.

'Can you please speak up? Did you see who attacked Pavlo Helba?' Chapman said.

After a long pause, Rudenko muttered, 'No.'

Chapman released his breath and slid the statement across the table. 'I suggest you change this then.'

Buckley scowled at him and bent over the paper making the changes.

'Why did you attack the old lady?' Chapman said. 'She's in a wheelchair—'

'I never touched—'

'My client had nothing to do with any attack on an old lady. We have several witnesses—'

'I haven't told you when it happened yet.'

Buckley reddened. 'My client is a peaceful, law-abiding citizen and isn't in the habit of attacking people.'

'He's got a history of violence.'

'Youthful indiscretions, Sergeant. He's turned over a new leaf.' Rudenko nodded and the man continued, 'He's here as a witness to the murder of his friend. Now, if there's nothing else . . .' He pushed his chair away from the table.

'You can go, but we'll keep Mr Rudenko in custody for a while yet. We can still hold him for another nineteen hours.'

'You must not question him without me present.'

'Of course, but can I ask *you* one question? How long has Mr Rudenko worked for GRM?'

The colour drained from Buckley's cheeks. 'I don't know what you're talking about.' He stood, knocking the chair flying.

Chapman couldn't resist winking at him.

The smell of damp clothes and body odour wafted towards Antonia as she waited in the queue of visitors at the prison. Surrounded by women – grandmothers, aunts and sisters, most accompanying small children – she spotted just two men amongst the crowd. The blank expressions on the women's faces suggested this wasn't their first time here. An older woman next to her struggled to control two boisterous toddlers while carrying a grizzling baby.

'Shall I hold him?' Antonia said.

The woman shook her head, then one of the toddlers screeched, so she gave a resigned smile and handed the baby to Antonia. 'Thanks love, these two are driving me round the bend.'

Antonia watched the woman's ineffectual attempts to take charge of the two tearaways, deciding she would have done a better job of it. The child in Antonia's arms stroked her hair. She smiled at him until she noticed him wiping his runny nose on his hand. *Remind me never to have kids.* She reached the front of the queue, relieved to hand him back.

'Name?' the warder demanded.

'Ant—' She remembered in time. 'Patience Okoye.'

The guard scanned the list then muttered, 'The person you're visiting. Not *your* name.'

'Ask a proper question then. I'm here to see Sabirah Fadil.'

The warder scowled at her before returning to the list, then gave a triumphant grin. 'No visitors,' he said. 'Next.'

'What do you mean, no visitors? She's on remand.' The room fell silent at her raised voice.

'Miss?' A warder tapped her on the shoulder. 'Are you here to see Mrs Fadil?' Tall, with a narrow face and pale-blue eyes, her mouth formed a smile.

'What's happened?'

'There's a slight problem.' The woman made a show of surveying the crowded room. 'Shall we go somewhere private?'

Antonia followed her through two sets of doors into a dingy corridor. The woman's evasiveness made Antonia uneasy. 'She's okay, isn't she?'

'Yeah,' she said, 'fine. If you wait here, someone will come and explain.'

She left, ignoring Antonia's questions. A short row of moulded chairs lined the left side of the corridor and she took one. Despite the woman's reassurance, she detected something deceitful about her and an uneasy feeling rolled over Antonia. Sabirah was a timid soul, an easy target for the predators inhabiting these places.

Antonia's disquiet grew and she leapt to her feet and paced the corridor.

Twenty minutes later a man in a suit came into the corridor. 'Sorry to keep you waiting, I'm the deputy governor—'

Antonia sprang at him. 'Can you tell me what's going on?'

He stepped away with an expression of panic and pushed the black-rimmed glasses up his nose. 'I'm afraid Mrs Fadil isn't allowed visitors—'

'Why not?' *At least she's not hurt*. 'She's on remand.'

'She's being held under the Prevention of Terrorism Act and will—'

'But she's accused of theft.'

'After an incident earlier today we decided—'

'What happened?'

'She attacked another inmate—'

'Sabirah hates violence. They must have attacked her first. When did this happen?'

'This morning.'

'I rang two hours ago, nobody said anything.'

He blinked and his pinched cheeks grew pink. 'Administrative error. Sorry to have wasted your time, Miss Okoye.'

She left, slamming the door behind her. Why the hell hadn't they told her straight away? *Terrorism* – there must be a mistake. She turned back, but the door had locked and rattling it had no effect. They could hold Sabirah incommunicado for months without trial. Lost in thought, she strode towards the Tube station. There must be something they could do. She moved through the barrier and made her way to her platform on autopilot.

She waited for a train on a deserted platform. A distant rumble announced the train's arrival and, suddenly uneasy, she whirled round. Four men, big and fit-looking, strode towards her. They spread out on the platform and advanced in a straight line, keeping in step. She recognised one of them, having seen him at GRM's offices, and her heart jumped. How the hell had they found her?

Pressure built up in her ears. A rush of air, the squeal of brakes and a carriage materialised. The men hesitated, ten yards away. Doors hissed and an old lady got off. Three quick strides took Antonia to the door. She jumped on and scanned the carriage. Two women, an old man reading the paper and a young mother with a pram. No help would come from there. Movement came from the far end of the carriage – one of the men, a second behind him. She stepped off, but two men still waited on the platform, now rejoined by the other two, so she leapt back on. The doors closed, followed by a buzz, then the train moved.

Two of the men had managed to get back on. Not too bad; she might handle two, if they weren't expecting a girl to fight. Then the front one moved, revealing the others behind him. All four were in the carriage. Too many. The other passengers focused on the screens in their hands. The men advanced, faces expressionless. Her insides fluttered as she retreated to the next carriage. As she passed the old man, he glanced at her pursuers and caught her gaze, but Antonia mouthed, 'I'll be fine.'

She reached the connecting door and peered into the next carriage. The grimy window reflected her pursuers, now much closer. She spun to confront them. They waited, inhibited by the witnesses. The old man gathered himself to step in, so she grabbed the handle and, pushing the door open, hurried into the next carriage.

The men rushed forward and she slammed the door behind her. As their leader fumbled with the lock, she noticed she'd entered an empty carriage. *Blast!* The door opened and the men surged through the opening. She backed up, suppressing her fear and assessing the best place to make a stand.

Now action was inevitable, her insides settled. She positioned herself opposite a set of doors. To reach her, the men needed to pass through a gap between the rows of seats. When they realised she would fight, they hesitated until one stepped forward. She crouched into her fighting stance, waiting for the first one to make a move.

The train shuddered and rocked. The stink of the brakes filled the carriage as it slowed and lights flashed past the windows before stopping. She edged towards the doors, watching the men. The button flashed green and she lunged for it. The nearest man came for her but she lashed out with her foot. He swayed away from the slashing shoe. The door slid open and she leapt out on to the platform and ran. Unfamiliar with the station, she searched for a way out.

People on the platform stared at her but then got on as the train doors beeped. The men didn't shout, but they pursued her and she ran towards an exit. She entered it without breaking stride and raced into a curved corridor. Her trainers made little sound but the men's shoes echoed. The corridor ended. Ahead, three lift doors. All closed. She jabbed at the buttons as the footsteps grew louder. Lights above the lifts moved, but too slow. She checked the corridor.

A flash of movement, then the first man appeared. She had to go. Opposite stood another door: the stairs. A yellow sign swung from the handle as she pulled it open. She raced up the stairs. After fifty steps a stitch started; she'd gone off too fast. The men's treads sounded further away. She slowed, pacing herself, and the stitch eased. The reason they'd kept her waiting in the prison now made sense. The man in the glasses must have summoned them. This knowledge filled her with panic. Was nowhere safe?

She ran round a corner and skittered to a halt. A pair of metal lattice gates blocked the stairs, a padlock and chain securing them. The yellow sign read, 'Do not use stairs.' *Blast!* The sounds of the men neared and she rattled the doors. The lock and chain didn't give as she pulled at them. Gulping air into her lungs, she considered her options. She could fight, but four would soon overpower her. She needed to get past the barrier.

The gap above the gates wasn't big enough, but if she pushed the leaves to one side, she might enlarge the opening in the lattice. She balanced on one leg, braced her other against the side wall and pushed the door towards the middle. The slapping of shoes coming closer told her she'd run out of time. The diamond she'd created in the lattice widened until it could accommodate her torso. Keeping the pressure on, she pushed her head through the opening, then her torso until most of her passed through. Then came the difficult part: once she stopped pushing against the wall, the gap would snap shut. She flexed her leg. The metal creaked as it took the strain.

With a last push she thrust herself through the opening. She fell to the floor, then gasped in agony as metal jaws seized her calf. Her leg lay jammed in the v formed at the bottom of the opening. Trapped on her back, she reached up and inserted her hands in the gap above her ankle. The men were so close she could hear their breathing. She pushed and the pain eased, then she freed herself.

She scrambled to her feet, stumbling as pain shot up her leg. Footsteps clattered on the stairs and she glanced behind her. One of the men skidded to a halt on the other side of the lattice and extended his right arm. Relief turned to terror as she saw the automatic pointing at her.

Antonia froze, her pulse thudding in her ears. She glanced back at the stairs leading up and to freedom. The gunman grinned and released the safety. More footsteps, and a second figure appeared. He stopped, breathing hard, and took in the situation.

'No!' He grabbed the gunman's shoulder and jerked his thumb upwards.

The faint sounds of a radio came from somewhere up the stairs. Workmen? Antonia pushed off her good leg and leapt up the steps.

Agony shot through her injured calf as she landed and she grabbed the handrail to stop herself falling.

'Help me move this fucking thing!' one of her pursuers shouted as the last two men arrived.

Antonia gritted her teeth and hobbled upwards. It wouldn't take them long to get past that barrier. After three more flights, the radio grew louder, accompanied by an acrid burning stench. At the next turn, two men worked on the broken handrail. She stopped, resting her throbbing leg.

'All right, love. How did you get up here?'

His companion turned a valve on the oxy-acetylene torch in his hand and straightened. Next to her, on the landing, stood a trolley with two cylinders strapped to it. Now she'd stopped, she could hear her pursuers. Not far behind. She grabbed the trolley, ignoring the protests of the two men, and pushed it down the stairs. Twin lines of hose snaked behind it, and then the torch followed, yellow flame flickering.

'Stupid bint, that will go off like a bomb!' the first workman shouted.

Antonia ignored the cramp in her calf and brushed past him. Below, cries of alarm and pain joined the sound of the clattering cylinders. Not looking behind her, Antonia ran.

CHAPTER 12

Kerry's red and yellow Mini rolled to a halt outside Antonia's office and Antonia undid her seatbelt, leaning forward to massage her calf. Although the skin where she'd ripped it free from the grip of the doors still felt tender, the swelling had gone down overnight.

'How is it?' Kerry said.

Antonia got out and tested it. 'Much better.' She waved to the sleepy-looking Nadimah and Hakim in the back seat. 'Cheer up you two, we're going to the zoo tomorrow.' This elicited a big beam from Hakim. 'Thanks for the lift, Kerry.'

'Ring me when you're ready to go, and here, take this.' Kerry pressed a metal tube into her hand.

Antonia examined the canister of Mace. 'Have you got shares in these?'

Kerry stuck her tongue out and giving a cheery toot, roared away. Antonia pocketed the can although she wasn't sure how effective it would be against those men. The one who'd almost caught her would have shot her if the other one hadn't checked him. After scanning her surroundings for anyone who might pose a threat, she made her way to the entrance. As usual on a Friday, the others came in late, but Turner sat at his desk.

'Where did you stay last night? I rang the doorbell,' he said, jerking his thumb at the ceiling.

'At Kerry's.'

He looked crestfallen. 'You can always stay at my place.'

Antonia wasn't going to tell him she'd as good as kidnapped Sabirah's kids. It was bad enough involving Kerry. 'She picked me up.' Antonia told him of her ordeal on the Tube and he paled.

'Who do you think chased you?' he said.

'The deputy governor must have something to do with them—'

'Aren't you being paranoid?'

'Why else keep me waiting?'

Turner looked even less comfortable.

'There's something else.' Antonia produced the recorder and played the intruders' conversation.

Turner played it a second time, brows knitted in concentration. 'Do you realise what this means?'

'Yeah, someone *really* wants to get me.'

'And, the attack on Eleanor wasn't your fault.'

'Yes it was, they came looking for me.'

Turner opened his mouth to protest, but shut it again.

Antonia appreciated his effort to assuage her guilt, but it wasn't working. 'GRM must be spooked.'

'They're the most logical culprits, but you've upset a few people since you started here and more than one fat cat's ended up in prison because of you.'

'Yes, but do any have the clout to get a prison governor—'

'Why not? Prison staff aren't well paid.'

'GRM owns the company which runs the prison. I'd say that moves them up the list.'

Turner picked up a pencil and tapped his teeth. 'Are you going to give the recording to the police?'

163

'I'm not sure, Alan. GRM have tentacles everywhere. Remember, they spiked the DNA results.' She still hadn't worked out why.

'Why not speak to Chapman? He told us about the DNA.'

'How much can a sergeant do? Anyway, I'm not sure I can trust him.'

Antonia retrieved the memory stick with the footage from the traffic cameras and fiddled with the cap. She hadn't even checked it.

'What's on that?' Turner said.

'The guy who accesses the traffic cameras managed to track the route taken by the van driven by the two thugs Kerry and I met for a drink. I'm hoping to find out where they travelled from.' She didn't want to mention she thought they'd dumped the woman's body in the canal. Turner would insist on giving the memory stick to the police.

'They don't usually give you anything but a printout.'

'They do if you ask nicely.' She winked at him. 'And I had to promise never to be online when I accessed it—' The shrill sound of the doorbell interrupted her.

Antonia leapt to her feet and headed for the door but Turner said, 'Someone's forgotten their keys.'

She checked the screen linked to the camera covering the front door. Two men in dark suits waited at the bottom of the steps. She stifled a cry as she recognised one of the men who'd chased her on the Tube yesterday.

The interview with Rudenko troubled Chapman and he attempted to make sense of it as he sat at his desk. What did it all mean? The toerag must have links with GRM, but how? Maybe they'd paid him and the others to scare Conti off, which made sense if they'd discovered she'd been spying on them as Okoye. The attack on the old woman also fitted, although where did Helba's death come into it? And what did Conti have to do with it? It made no sense. If she was involved, someone at GRM must be behind the cover-up of her DNA. Were there two factions at the company, one wanting her scared off and the other helping her? And why did they have her DNA on the system?

He opened the CrimeMapper database on his computer. Despite many reassurances from senior management that the new, privately run system was superior to its police-managed predecessor, he had little faith in it. Sanchez was better at this stuff, but he couldn't enlist her aid, as she wouldn't approve. His first attempt at entering Conti's details retrieved information from the current case, so he changed the date of the search. Nothing appeared until he searched back eleven years. An archived file existed, meaning he needed to re-enter his password to access it. The system refused his request, so he punched in the code again with the same result. Double-checking each character, he tried a third time. The screen went blank and he slammed his fist on the desk. Locked out.

He rang IT and gave his name. 'The system's locked me out.'

'Yes, I can see, Sergeant,' the bored-sounding technician said. 'Are you sure you entered—'

'Positive.'

'Oooh, touchy.'

Chapman didn't respond, knowing he depended on her to get him back on the system.

'Ah, I see the problem. You're trying to access a restricted file.'

Is it now? But why? He hesitated. 'I need it for a case.' He read off the case number for the investigation into Helba's murder.

'Hmmm, the investigating officer – Inspector Harding – needs to request access.'

Shit! That's all I need. 'He's in a meeting and he needs this urgently . . .' He held his breath.

She hesitated for a few seconds. 'As it's you, Russell.'

Chapman scoured his memory, trying to recall when and under what circumstances he knew her.

'There you are,' she said. 'Take care of yourself.'

He uttered a thank you and ended the call, grateful to have spoken to a technician willing to bend the rules and hoping she didn't get into trouble if it all went pear-shaped. He punched in his password and the file opened.

Conti had been in care for two years from the age of twelve, until Eleanor Curtis adopted her. With a rueful smile he remembered the old lady's insistence she was just Conti's landlady.

He'd assumed she'd grown up in Britain, but her place of birth surprised him. Malakal. Where the hell was that? The file ran to four pages and he printed them as he checked the circumstances behind her giving DNA. She'd claimed a girl called Enya, a fellow resident at the home, had been murdered by a man who'd also abused Conti. They'd dismissed the murder accusation, because, apparently, the girl in question had run away, but they'd investigated the claim of abuse. The tale of sexual exploitation of a kid in care depressed and angered him. So did the outcome, 'Discontinued due to lack of evidence'. They should have destroyed the DNA sample they'd taken from the young Conti.

'Clear evidence of sexual abuse, but unable to identify her abuser, as he wore a surgical mask. The investigating officers were able to compile a list of possible suspects and narrowed it down to three men who worked in different homes, but had access to the one where the victim lived. The victim claimed she would be able to pick out her abuser by his distinctive smell. Clothing belonging to the suspects was given to the victim, who clearly identified one item. Because of the unconventional nature of the identification, and the fact the man, Larry Videk, had a strong alibi, it was decided not to take it further.'

Larry Videk wasn't a common name, but the file didn't include his picture. Chapman spent fifteen minutes searching various databases before finding an image of him. A man stood behind a group of kids taking part in a Duke of Edinburgh Awards ceremony. He'd turned his face away, but there was no doubting who it showed. Larry Mishkin. Chapman punched the desk again. He'd known the bastard was dodgy as soon as he'd met him.

'What's this?' Sanchez said, picking up the papers from the printer.

Chapman jumped and switched to another screen, but Sanchez stayed at the printer, engrossed in the report.

'Bloody hell!'

He didn't think he'd heard her swear before. 'What?'

'Her childhood sounds horrific, but . . . bloody hell, she killed a man when she was twelve.'

Chapman took the sheets and ground his teeth as he read. He didn't disagree with Sanchez's assessment of Conti's early years. He couldn't imagine anything worse for a young girl than seeing her mother raped and murdered, then being captured by the men who'd done it. Even being abused in care must have felt like a step up. A surge of rage and helplessness overwhelmed him. On reading the passage where she claimed to have killed one of her captors before escaping, he cheered her.

'Russell!' DCI Gunnerson said from the open doorway, startling both him and Sanchez. 'What's happening with Rudenko?'

'Shit! I'd almost forgotten about the toerag.'

Sanchez said, 'We've got two hours to charge him, ma'am.'

'Are you charging him?'

Chapman said, 'Assaulting an officer and resisting—'

'Let him go, Russell.' Gunnerson held his gaze. 'His solicitor has already complained about his treatment.'

She slammed the door and left before he could respond.

'Am I being paranoid or has she been got at?' Chapman said.

'You know what it's like, his slick lawyer probably complained to an assistant commissioner on the golf course.'

He hoped that was all, but he'd always thought Yasmin Gunnerson didn't respond to such pressures.

Turner heard Antonia's cry and rushed to the front door. 'What's wrong?'

'Those men, they were the ones who chased me.'

The bell rang again and he studied the two visitors on the screen.

'Mr Turner?' one of them said through the door. 'National Security Agency, we have a warrant here to search your premises.'

The speaker held up an ID towards the camera and Turner operated its built-in code scanner. 'It's genuine,' he said, reading the data and comparing the image that came up with the man. 'I've got to open the door.'

'Don't let them in,' Antonia whispered.

He'd stall them. 'Can I check your colleague's?' he called through the mic next to the screen. He gestured to Antonia to use Eleanor's lift and get out through the house.

He took his time, then asked to see the warrant. The document mentioned stolen papers. *Damn!* It must be the ones Antonia took from Reed-Mayhew's office. Sweat ran down his spine as he continued reading, but the warrant referred to national security. It couldn't be the same papers, could it? They dealt with corruption and tax avoidance. He considered the other stories they were working on, but none fitted the bill. By the time he'd read the document, the lift motor had stopped. No way those outside could have heard it, could they?

'Sorry, gentlemen,' he said, opening the door, 'you can't be too careful.'

A scowl replaced the lead officer's professional smile. 'There's a uniformed team helping with the search. Will you want to check each of those?'

'Afraid so.'

A few minutes later, four more people crowded into the office. 'Mr Turner,' their leader said, 'you may observe the search and we will give you a receipt for anything we take, but please don't interfere with my staff.'

'Can you give me an idea of what you're searching for?'

'Start in the next office and you in the far corner of this one,' the lead officer instructed his teams.

'If you tell me, I can save you time.'

'Thank you, Mr Turner, but all I need from you is to make sure you open any locked cabinets.'

Turner flitted between the different rooms, checking on the search teams, but they seemed efficient and careful. Antonia must be mistaken about the men's identity. Further attempts to discover what they were searching for met with the same stonewalling.

One of the suited men stopped in front of a photo of the staff. 'Who's she?' He pointed at Antonia.

Turner lost the power of speech for a few seconds. 'Just one of our reporters.'

'Good-looking girl.' The man leered and carried on searching.

Turner's pulse slowed to normal and although he resisted hiding the photo, he avoided looking at it. An hour later the team assembled in the main office, their body language suggesting failure.

'Are there any parts of the office you haven't shown us?' their leader demanded.

Turner shook his head.

'What about the lift? We've only seen this floor.'

'It leads to a private house. Nothing to do with The Investigator.' Turner hoped Antonia had left.

'The lift is part of your premises.' He pressed the call button and the motor whirred.

'What do you think you're doing?' Turner stepped between the men and the lift doors. Their sour breath forced a mixture of stale tobacco and mint into his face.

'Why is the lift car upstairs?'

'I told you, it leads to Eleanor's house and she's in hospital, so nobody uses it.' The doors swished open and he turned, relieved to see an empty aluminium box.

The two NSA men exchanged a glance. 'Have you or any staff removed documents from the office in the last three days?'

'How can I know? They're reporters, so will take papers in and out every day. If you tell—'

'If you've wilfully hidden any documents from us, we will prosecute you. Do I make myself clear?'

'For it to be wilful supposes I know what you're searching for.'

'Thank you, Mr Turner.' He led his team to the entrance and once they'd filed out hissed, 'If you're fucking me about, I'll make sure you regret it.'

Before he could respond the man left and Turner watched him from the open doorway for several seconds. No longer doubting Antonia, he slammed the door and leant against it, wishing he kept a bottle of something in his drawer. He poured himself a cup of water from the cooler as the lift motor whirred, going back up before returning to the basement.

'What did they want?' Antonia said.

'Papers.'

'Reed-Mayhew's?'

'Yeah, I'm pretty sure.'

Her shoulders slumped. 'So, they've got them?'

'They never found the safe—'

'You *never* use the safe.'

'I did this time, and I've also sent a copy to Geoff Stokes.' Both Eleanor and Antonia had laughed at him when he'd insisted on installing a hidden safe behind the gas fire in his room.

'Alan, you're a star,' she said and kissed him on the cheek.

He grinned but couldn't dismiss his growing anxiety. The papers must disclose something he'd missed for them to go to this trouble, and whoever wanted them wouldn't give up.

'One hundred and forty-one,' Chapman said, and turned away from the wall.

'What you doing, Sarge?' Sanchez said, exasperated.

'Counting the parquet blocks.'

She rolled her eyes. 'Do you think we should—'

He silenced her with a gesture, certain someone was recording their words. Mishkin had kept them waiting half an hour in the room they'd used to interview Conti. Was it a deliberate choice and had they recorded the interview? He wasn't sure what GRM could have gained from listening in on the interview, and anyway, he doubted he'd ever prove it. Sanchez grew jumpier with each minute. She'd taken a lot of persuading to come with him, but if he'd left her at the office Harding would want to know where he'd gone. He still wasn't sure why he'd come here. He expected Mishkin to tell them to bugger off.

The door opened and a tall, willowy woman in her early twenties appeared. 'Mr Mishkin will see you now, if you'll follow me,' she said.

They travelled up in a lift, Mishkin's PA staring straight ahead. Chapman decided not to make small talk and Sanchez appeared too nervous to attempt it. On the twenty-seventh floor, the PA led them to a door with Mishkin's name on it. Ignoring the PA's look of surprise, Chapman stepped past her, opened the door without knocking and barged into the office.

The size of one of the incident rooms at his station, the room had décor suggestive of a gentlemen's club, with a seating area populated with comfortable-looking worn leather chairs around a fireplace at the far end. Mishkin sat behind a huge black desk on the opposite side and frowned in annoyance.

Before he could speak, Chapman said, 'Thank you for seeing us, your assistant said to come in.'

Mishkin rearranged his features and waved his apologising PA away. 'Please take a seat, Sergeant. How may I help you?'

'You've met Detective Constable Sanchez.' Chapman waited for her to sit before taking the other chair.

Mishkin kept his attention on Chapman. 'I'm very busy.'

'Let's get on then. Why didn't you mention you knew Patience Okoye?'

Mishkin couldn't hide his irritation. 'I don't know what you mean, Sergeant. She works here and I knew her name—'

'She accused you of raping her.' He'd decided not to mention the accusation that he'd killed the other girl. She'd been reported missing the day before her supposed murder.

Mishkin sat back, picking a rubber ball off the desk, the only item apart from a phone and tablet on the vast surface. Kneading the item in his right hand, he said, 'Has Ms Okoye made a complaint? I have never met the woman, so whatever she's said—'

'I'm talking about 2012, when you knew her as Antonia Conti.' Chapman thought he sensed fear in the other man. This was another reason for bringing Alice: her ability to read suspects. Now they'd started, she relaxed and focused on Mishkin.

'The name's not familiar and as I'm sure you know, neither Ms Okoye nor I worked here then.'

'Where did you work?'

'None of your business.' After a few seconds, he reconsidered. 'It's a matter of record I worked for a private company offering support for youth services in the city.'

My God, how many young girls did you have access to? 'How did you feel when she accused you of raping her?'

'I don't know what you're talking about.'

'A young refugee, accusing you of all sorts. It must have pissed you off.'

Mishkin glared at him, then laughed. 'You have been scratching around in ancient history, Sergeant. I do recall a girl made wild accusations, including that I'd killed someone.'

'Must have been a shock when she turned up here.'

'So, that was her? I didn't realise.'

'I think you did.' For a second, Chapman wondered if it was true, but ploughed on, looking round the room. 'You've done well.'

'I've worked very hard to get where I am. What's your point?'

'You've got a lot to lose. Okoye reopening those accusations would jeopardise all of this.'

'As you know, Sergeant, young girls are wont to invent things.' He glanced at Sanchez, smirking. 'If you read the report, they exonerated—'

'No, they didn't.' In that instant, Chapman recognised Mishkin's guilt. He fought the urge to batter him. 'We both know most of those cases collapsed because the system was stacked against the accuser. Nowadays we have a different approach. If we reopened the case, I'm sure more women would come forward.'

The door opened and Mishkin's expression of fury passed in an instant. 'Everything okay, Larry?' A man in his mid-thirties with hazel eyes and a side parting stood in the opening and studied Chapman. *Was he Mishkin's assistant?* But his easy confidence said otherwise. It took Chapman a few moments to recognise him from the portrait downstairs. Gustav Reed-Mayhew, Mishkin's boss.

Mishkin indicated Chapman and Sanchez with a disdainful wave. 'These officers are just asking a few questions.'

'Anything I should know about?'

'A personal— Nothing to worry about.'

Reed-Mayhew waited for a few seconds, studying Chapman, then turned to Mishkin. 'I'll leave you to it then. Come and see me once they've gone.'

The door closed, leaving a thick silence. Maybe he should speak to Reed-Mayhew next. Mishkin obviously didn't want these accusations aired in front of his boss.

Mishkin leant forward and placed the ball on the desk. 'I want you to leave.'

'I've not finished—'

'You *have*.'

'Sarge.' Sanchez gripped his sleeve. 'We'd better go.'

Chapman pulled his arm free. Reed-Mayhew's office must be nearby.

'Your constable has more sense than you,' Mishkin said. 'You mentioned I had a lot to lose, Sergeant, but so do you. Not as much as you once did, but I'm guessing enough.' The bleak glare Mishkin gave him almost made him shudder.

'No, that's where you're wrong.' He forced himself to hold Mishkin's gaze.

The door burst open and two uniformed thugs barged into the office.

'These gentlemen will see you out. If you repeat these wild allegations, I will take action.'

Chapman studied Mishkin and the skin on his neck tightened. If he thought he'd get away with it, the man wouldn't hesitate to kill them. *I bet you've got away with it on more than one occasion. My God, you did kill that girl.* Mishkin seemed to read his mind and smirked before turning his attention to his tablet.

CHAPTER 13

'That went well, Sarge.'

Chapman ignored Sanchez's barb and eased into the traffic. 'You think he did it?'

Sanchez hesitated for a few seconds. 'Probably, but—'

'But nothing. He abused Conti, and I don't know how many others. And I'm sure he killed the other girl.'

'But they reported her missing the day before Conti claimed she saw Mishkin kill her.'

'Maybe she made a mistake with the dates or someone fiddled the paperwork.'

'Someone in the police? The home reported her disappearance and the matron saw her get into a car.'

It wouldn't be the first time. He punched the steering wheel. 'I've got a daughter the same age.'

'Oh.' She stayed silent for a few moments. 'Do you think that's what she's working on, an exposé of his . . .'

'I'd assumed from what Turner said it was something to do with the company.' An exposé of GRM could halt their takeover of the squad and help his career, but an investigation into Mishkin might be the only way to make him pay for what he'd done. 'I'll ring him when we return.'

They made the rest of the journey to the office in silence, Chapman wondering if he could get Conti to restate her complaint. At the front desk he logged in and his phone beeped. 'Report to DCI Gunnerson.'

'I'd better take this,' he said.

'Okay, I'll continue the search for Arkady Demchuk.'

'Can you carry out background checks on the woman killed, Aida Rizk?'

'But we've got Benjamin Murray for her murder . . .'

'Just do it, will you?'

Sanchez flinched. He shouldn't have snapped, but she'd gone before he could apologise.

Yasmin Gunnerson didn't smile when he knocked and entered her office. 'You wanted me?'

'Shut the door and sit.'

What had he done now? He slumped into the nearest chair.

'What are you playing at? You're supposed to investigate Pavlo Helba's murder.'

'I am.' How did Harding find out?

'What has Mr Mishkin got to do with it?'

The bastard must have complained to Gunnerson. Disappointment made his limbs heavy. First telling him to release Rudenko, now this. 'What did he say to you?'

'I've not spoken to him. He's gone to the top and made an official complaint.'

He replayed what he'd said to Mishkin. Good thing Sanchez prevented him thumping the bastard. 'I did everything by the book.'

'I hope you did, Russell. Someone from Internal Affairs is on the way.'

His insides quivered as he remembered his last run-in with them. He'd started it as a DCI. 'I was following a legitimate—'

'I don't want to know. Not until they've interviewed you.'

'Who's coming?'

'Make sure you're here when they arrive.'

He marched to his office, fuming. They might have banned him from talking to Mishkin, but he didn't intend to abandon the investigation. Sanchez didn't even look up when he walked into their office. He logged into his computer and called the number for The Electric Investigator. Conti wasn't in, so he asked to speak to Turner.

'Sergeant, do you have any news?' Turner sounded shaky.

'I wanted to speak to Miss Conti—'

'She got in touch then. I got the impression she wasn't going to.'

What the hell's he on about? 'No—' This could work in his favour. 'She left a message.'

'I'm afraid you're out of luck, she's out.'

'Do you have her mobile number?' This wasn't something he wanted to discuss with a third party.

Turner laughed. 'She doesn't believe in them.'

'Do you expect her back?'

'Not today.'

Bugger. He could call in to her flat on the way from work, but Brigitte wouldn't be impressed with him coming home late again.

Turner continued, 'I'd imagine she's keen to speak to you. Do you want her friend's address? She's moved out after the break-in.'

He scribbled down the address, surprisingly uplifted at the prospect of seeing Conti.

'This might interest you, Sarge,' Sanchez said when he'd hung up. 'Someone set fire to the garage where they found Benjamin Murray.'

He clicked on the report, wondering if this had anything to do with the investigation. 'When?'

'The report's an hour old.'

'Get your coat.' He didn't expect Internal Affairs for a while, and if they turned up, they could wait.

Kerry nosed the red and yellow Mini out into the traffic and the driver of the oncoming Bentley hesitated. The smaller car shot forward and Antonia gripped the side of her seat.

'Always works when it's a flash car,' Kerry said, her eyes shining with exhilaration following her demonstration of high-speed driving through the maze of side streets. 'They're worried about denting their babies.' She gave a wave in the mirror.

Antonia checked the road they'd come out of but no vehicles followed them.

'We shake them off?' Kerry grinned.

Antonia wasn't sure if she was teasing her. 'It's not a joke.'

'Maybe they've put a bug in the car.'

'Blast! I hadn't—'

Kerry's grin turned into a full-throated laugh.

Antonia couldn't resist her friend's merriment. 'Right, girl. Drive me to Jubilee Industrial Estate and I'll batter you when we get there.'

Antonia reflected on how Turner must feel. Apart from worrying about Eleanor he must miss having her as a sounding board and support. She would love knowing they'd tweaked a big lion's tail, although this one might end up eating them.

'Antonia,' Kerry said, sounding solicitous, 'what's your problem with Nadimah?'

'I haven't got a problem with her.' Her neck grew warm.

'Hmm. I don't think *she's* noticed, but I can tell.'

Antonia didn't want to admit to resentment of the easy way Kerry and Nadimah got along. 'She's too passive and accepting, like she doesn't want to fight back.'

'You think? She's eleven and her mother's missing.' Kerry smiled at her. 'She reminds me of someone not too many miles away.'

Antonia swallowed and stared out of the side window. Had she been the same, a dozen years ago? No, she'd always fought. A memory threatened to break through but she wouldn't let it. The opening notes of 'Rolling in the Deep' burst from the speakers and a grateful Antonia lost herself in the music for forty minutes. The last track started as they reached their destination. Antonia snapped out of her reverie and focused on what she needed to do. If she'd tracked the van properly, it had come from one of the units in this industrial estate.

A board at the entrance to the estate showed a plan of the site with a list of occupiers alongside. Some had lines painted through the names and others had faded so much you couldn't read them. A circuit of the site confirmed the first impression. The place needed a serious makeover. Signs with the names of the occupiers on them hung outside some units, but none matched the board. They dismissed the ones with people in them and made a note of the others. The list ran to twenty-seven.

Antonia's stomach sank. 'Shall we start in the far end?'

A spur road led to the last few units, curving, so they weren't visible from the main section. Six of them, each with an enclosed yard at the front, and all on the list.

'Why are there no cameras on this bit?' Kerry said.

She was right. Unlike the rest of the estate, this section didn't appear to have surveillance. Did it mean anything, or had the owners just not bothered to extend the system to this part?

They drove to the far end and parked. A two-and-a-half-metre-high concrete wall surrounded the yard in front of the first unit and a pair of barred gates blocked the one opening. Antonia walked up to it, peering through the bars. Piles of scrap metal filled the yard, almost obscuring the ground. A heavy chain joined both halves of the gate. A horizontal cross-piece provided an ideal step. After checking around, she gripped two adjacent bars and raised her foot.

A brown blur flashed towards her and Antonia leapt backwards. A solid body hit the bars and teeth snapped shut where one of her hands had been. An unkempt Alsatian threw itself at the gate, making it jerk towards her. Its ambush having failed, the animal began a frenzied barking. Once sure it couldn't reach her, she relaxed, but her pulse still pounded in her ears.

Feeling sheepish, she looked at Kerry, who tried not to laugh. Antonia gave her the finger and backed away towards the next unit. The dog stopped barking. The adjacent yard didn't have a gate, but she still checked there were no dogs lurking before entering. Piles of rubbish dotted the rough concrete surface and the front of the unit had two openings, one the size of a lorry, protected by a roller shutter, and a person-sized opening with a steel door. Despite the litter, someone had made sure the ground in front of both openings remained clear. A window with thick bars across it separated the two doorways. Antonia picked her way to this and peered in, but a board covered the bottom half. She dragged an empty drum across to it and, using the bars for support, climbed up on it.

Through the grimy glass she could make out a long, narrow unit with a row of offices running the length of the left side. Near the back, facing her, she made out the shadowy outline of a van. She moved to get a better view but couldn't read the number. A pale rectangle in the rear wall indicated another window. Antonia headed to the rear of the unit, keeping away from the dog. A blue-painted steel door and a barred window above it provided the only openings in the back wall. A wheelie bin with a broken leg stood to one side and she dragged it across the doorway.

Antonia clambered on to the lid and peered into the building. The view from here was worse and she could only see the top of the van. She thumped the window frame in frustration and it moved. She pushed and, loose in its fixing, the timber moved a centimetre. If she could find something like a crowbar to work with, she could ease it out. The rubbish at the front included pieces of metal, some of which might do the job.

Antonia returned to the front and as she passed the car, Kerry called out to her, 'Have you found something?'

Antonia lowered her head to the window. 'There's a van in there but I can't see if it's the right one.'

'So, what are you doing?'

'The window's loose, so I'm going in to check. See what's in the van.'

Kerry put her hand on Antonia's forearm. 'Be careful.'

'Don't worry, I'll make sure there's no dog.' She squeezed Kerry's shoulder.

The alarm box above the front door, bashed and with peeling paint, she guessed hadn't worked for years. Antonia removed the barrel, then found a flat piece of metal about eighty centimetres long and five wide and jogged to the back door. The pointed end made short work of the crumbling mortar round the window frame. Once the mortar disintegrated, the screws holding the frame to the brickwork gave with groans as she levered it free. She stuck her shoulders in, remembering Kerry's warning, and listened.

She checked the can of Mace in her pocket then clambered in. Her feet hit something stuck to the wall. A toilet cistern. Avoiding the bowl, she lowered herself to the floor. In the gloom, she found the door and opened it. The silence echoed. She shuffled towards the van until she could read the number plate. It was the one she was looking for, and a mixture of exhilaration and anxiety made her tremble.

The van had a box on the top and a chunky rear door. Antonia tried it, but it was locked. She edged round the side and tried the driver's door. It opened and, clambering in, she rummaged around, searching for keys or a lever to open the back. She leant across to the passenger side and opened the glove compartment. There, she found a carrier bag full of paper. She emptied it on to the seat and spread the contents out. Under the cab light she identified sweet and crisp wrappers, and amongst them a receipt and two parking tickets. Elated to find something useful, she pocketed them. The dog began barking and before she could move the metal door at the front opened.

Antonia pulled the driver's door shut to kill the light then ducked. *Blast!* If they'd come for the van, she'd had it. She retrieved the Mace and waited. A roller shutter lifted and a powerful engine roared, then headlights filled the cab. The sound made the van vibrate before it cut off and the beam died. Doors slammed, then the roller shutter rattled again. Her hand gripped the canister and she held her breath.

'Home sweet fucking home,' someone said. His voice carried through the open passenger window of the van.

'At least the fucking pigs won't find us here.'

The second voice sounded familiar, although neither sounded like Gareth or Zack.

'You reckon they got Arkady?'

The name returned her to Sunday night, then she realised where she'd heard the voice.

'Nah, he's too fly for them.'

What the hell are they doing here? She raised her head to peer through the spokes of the steering wheel. Three figures gathered around a black pick-up. It must be the one they'd driven to the gym.

'Bloody freezing, I'll put the kettle on,' one of them said, and headed towards the offices.

At least if they went in there she could sneak out and escape through the window.

'I'll have a coffee, two sugars. Need a piss first.'

Antonia ducked down as he walked past, then realised he couldn't miss the big hole in the wall above the toilet.

Chapman peered into the darkened opening. The sweet stench of burnt plastic pervaded the air and the blackened skeleton of a car sat in the middle of the garage in which they'd found Benjamin Murray. A thin haze filled the space and heat radiated out of the open front.

'You sure it's safe to go in?' Chapman asked the fire officer.

'Positive. It will carry on steaming for a few hours.' He indicated the walls. 'They act like those old-fashioned storage heaters, not that you'll remember them.' He smiled at Sanchez.

Annoyed by the implication that he *would*, Chapman said, 'You've put the cause down as deliberate.'

'Follow me, you'll need a torch.' The officer walked into the opening and edged round the car.

Sanchez handed Chapman a small hand lamp and he followed, walking sideways to avoid touching the wall or car. The firefighter stepped through a doorway and shone his light round a cramped room. The haze thickened and black sludge covered the floor. Chapman studied it with distaste before spotting a clearer section and stepping on to it.

'That's where it started.' The firefighter pointed at an area of wall. 'No electric cables anywhere near.'

'I can smell petrol,' Sanchez said.

'Most of it has burnt off, but without ventilation, the residue will linger.'

Chapman shone his light round the room, trying to picture being in there with it on fire. Not something he'd fancy having to do. Someone had opened every cupboard and drawer in the place. 'Any reason your guys would open the cupboards?'

'That happened before they got here.' The firefighter directed his torch towards a mound of sludge. 'They found the contents strewn around the floor. Hadn't your guys searched it earlier? I heard you'd found a dead body in there.' He highlighted a narrow doorway in the opposite wall. 'I'll leave you with it.'

Once he'd left Sanchez said, 'No way our guys would just throw stuff around.'

Chapman agreed. 'Whoever started the fire must have done it. Maybe to help it spread.'

'Wouldn't they pile the stuff up to make a bonfire? It wouldn't burn well spread out on the floor.'

'You're probably right.' He moved towards the opening and shone the light into it. A toilet and a tiny shower filled the space and a dark stain surrounded the toilet. 'What a horrible place to end your days.'

He backed out and stepped to the far wall, where the remains of two kitchen units stood. One was missing a door. He stepped back and his foot slipped. He threw out his free arm against the side wall, catching it with his fingertips.

Sanchez grabbed his arm. 'You all right, Sarge?'

'Yeah, thanks.' Soot covered his hand and he examined what he'd trodden on. A cupboard door, covered in a thin layer of sludge. The edge of the door looked wrong and, using the toe of his shoe, he exposed it. The veneer on the front of the door didn't line up with the edge. He prised it off the floor, tapped the muck off it and stood it on edge. The small gap between the body of the

185

door and front surface admitted his fingernails, but he couldn't peel it off.

'What you found?' Sanchez said.

'I need a chisel.'

'Sure, I've got one in my handbag, what size do you want?'

She found a bread knife in the debris and he eased it into the gap. The blade strained, then shot free as the front of the cupboard door detached. An envelope fluttered to the floor. He shook it clean and studied it. Blank, but it contained a few thin sheets of paper. The murmur of voices came from outside and he straightened. A powerful beam of light swept into the room.

'Who the hell are you?' a man's voice said.

Chapman squinted. 'Police. Now turn off the fucking light.'

The lamp moved away and a chastened voice said, 'I thought you lot had finished.'

'Who are *you*?' Chapman said.

'Elliot, NSA.' The man held out an ID card.

Chapman studied it. 'Since when did you investigate fires?'

'The victim is a person of interest. We need any evidence you've—'

'You'll have to speak to my boss, Inspector Harding.' Chapman shifted his feet, grinding the door into the sludge so they couldn't tell he'd moved it. 'We're just investigating the fire.' He swept his lamp across the far side of the room. 'And you can see there's not much left.'

'We'll still have a look, if you don't mind.'

'Be my guest, but let us out first.'

The man backed out. Sanchez gave Chapman an enquiring glance, but he shook his head and, making sure he kicked the door into more muck, he followed her out. Whoever fired the place must have been searching for the envelope and he wanted to read its contents before handing it over to those bastards.

◆ ◆ ◆

The dog barked again and, in the cab of the van, Antonia pressed herself further into the floor.

'Someone's coming, Vasyl.'

The man heading for the toilet stopped and returned to the front of the unit. Antonia raised her head, watching him join the others in front of the door. With the cab in darkness, they shouldn't see her.

'Let's have a butcher's,' the one called Vasyl said.

Antonia squeezed the can of Mace. She'd make a run for the toilet while they were distracted. If she dived through the gap, she'd clear the wheelie bin and land on the grass.

'Shit, Vasyl! Where the fuck d'you get that?'

'Arkady got us one each. Fort 15, 9mm semi-automatic with 16-shot magazine. Nice, innit?'

She could outrun them, but a bullet? *Blast! Blast!* She peered through the windscreen. Three figures stood in a semi-circle facing the front door of the unit, their attention on whoever might be outside. If she went now, she might make it. Before she could make a decision, the door crashed open and one of them levelled a gun at the long-haired youth standing in the opening.

The gunman lowered the weapon. 'Nikolai, what the—'

The long-haired man stumbled inside, propelled by a shove from the massive-shouldered man stepping in behind him. 'We *told* you not to fucking go out,' Gareth growled in his broad Brummie accent.

Antonia's pulse raced even faster and her mouth dried. They *did* know each other.

The three in the unit took a pace back.

'And what's this?' Gareth said to the gunman. 'You gonna shoot me?'

Antonia gripped the door handle.

The gunman lowered the weapon, clearly deferring to the older man. 'Didn't know it was you.'

Zack appeared behind Gareth and followed him in, closing the door behind him. 'Hand it over.' He gestured to the gunman, who hesitated. 'You already in the shit. If you're found with a gun . . .'

The gunman, seeming even more cowed by Zack, passed it to him. In an effort to regain some authority, he turned on the long-haired man and demanded, 'Where you bin, Nikolai?'

'Pigs grabbed me. I smacked one of them but—'

'That's why we told you to keep out the way,' Zack said, and hefted the gun. He shot the man he'd disarmed first, a bullet in the face. The other two froze, transfixed, and he shot them. The long-haired man tried to run but Gareth grabbed him. One huge hand gripped his chin and the other arm wrapped round his chest. The echoes of the shots died away and Gareth wrenched the man's head. He fought but his neck bent backwards until with a dry crack he slumped.

'Pavlo put up a better fight,' Gareth said, and lowered the body.

Antonia dragged in a lungful of air and stopped herself retching.

'Fucking idiots,' Zack said and strode to the offices, returning with a bundle under one arm.

'Amateurs,' Gareth said. 'Should have known they weren't up to it when they fucked up killing the girl.'

The two of them put on coveralls and gloves and, working in silence, placed each body into a black bag. They carried the first one towards the van. Antonia ducked down and scrunched herself into the footwell. If they looked into the cab they couldn't fail to see her. But they continued past and moments later a door clanged open. The van shook as they shoved the body in, then shifted as someone climbed in and dragged it. Would she make it to the front door while they were at the back? Or maybe she'd go out through the window when they collected the next one. But what if Zack still had the gun? By the time they'd finished loading the bodies, Antonia still lay paralysed with indecision, bathed in sweat and her bladder demanding attention.

'Heavy cunts,' Gareth complained and they peeled off their protective clothing.

'You're just getting old and fat,' Zack said.

'What we doing with their motor?'

'Larry's scrapyard. I've got plates so we don't get pulled over.'

Antonia almost cried with relief. Once they left, she would run.

'Shame,' Gareth said. 'Nice car. I'll drive it and you bring the van.'

Her heart stopped.

'We'll come back for the van. The less time we spend driving around with them four in the back, the better.'

It started again.

'I'll put the van's cooler on. We don't want them smelling the place out. You got the keys?'

CHAPTER 14

Chapman sat at his desk and studied the envelope he'd recovered from the burnt-out garage. The contents must have been important to Benjamin Murray, assuming he'd hidden it. And someone had ransacked the place to get hold of it.

'What you going to do with it, Sarge?' Sanchez said.

An idea struck Chapman. 'Have you got Murray's home address?'

'Yeah, why?'

'Can you check on burglary reports, see if anyone's broken in there?'

She tapped on her keyboard. 'Are you going to open the envelope, or what?'

He picked it up and extracted the contents, two sheets of A4 folded in three. The first was a copy of a bank statement, and the other a memo with a cryptic message he couldn't decipher. He studied the transactions listed for the account and whistled. Three payments, each of six figures, but they barely made a dent in the balance.

Sanchez glanced up from her screen. 'What you got?'

'Not sure, but someone's shifting a lot—'

'Hang on.' A note of excitement made her voice rise. 'No burglary *reported*, but the team sent to pick him up mentioned they found the place in a mess, like someone had given it a going-over.'

'Let's see.' Chapman leant across and turned the monitor.

'Sergeant Chapman, you had instructions to stay on the station.'

He spun to face a uniformed chief inspector, and the memory of the last time he'd seen her made him squirm. 'Shauna, what the hell are you doing here?'

'Chief Inspector, to you. Interview room three and don't keep me waiting any longer.' Shauna McGee swept from the room.

He'd heard about her promotion to Internal Affairs, but she couldn't be here to investigate him, could she? *Shit!* Ignoring Sanchez's enquiring expression, he followed. 'If I'm not back in an hour, instigate a murder enquiry. Victim, Sergeant Russell Chapman.' He grinned at her, but he wanted to run away.

Shauna waited in the interview room, sitting upright. 'Close the door and sit.'

'You're looking good. Short hair—'

'I'm recording this interview, and you are under caution.' She repeated the familiar words.

'Will you interview Constable Sanchez? She accompanied while I questioned the slimy—'

'I'm here to investigate your unauthorised access of records.'

'Are you serious?'

'You lied to a computer technician to gain access to restricted files.'

'It sounds like you've already decided I'm guilty. Is that what they teach the new DCIs?'

'Talk me through what happened.'

As he related his account he had to concede it didn't sound great for him. Mishkin either made a lucky guess that Chapman didn't have permission to look at Antonia's juvenile records, or had checked and *known* he didn't. If the latter, it opened up a worrying can of worms for Chapman. Either way, Mishkin had been crafty; complaining about the interview would have meant Conti's accusation coming out and Chapman had done nothing wrong when questioning him. This way, Chapman would be done for his unauthorised access of the records. The realisation that this, combined with his past record, could leave him in deep shit made him shiver.

Half an hour later, he'd related his account twice, in painful detail. 'You can ask me again, but I'll tell you the same story. Now can I go?'

'Can you explain why you left the station, despite orders not to do so?'

'I was following a lead—'

'Under whose orders?'

'I used my initiative, it's what real policemen do.'

Shauna glared at him. 'You can go and we'll inform you of our findings in due course.'

She clearly still hadn't forgiven him for the way he'd ended their affair, although he had to admit, it hadn't been his greatest moment. 'Shauna, I'm sorry about . . . you know . . .'

'No, I don't, Sergeant.'

Chapman let himself out, realising he should have got someone from the Fed to accompany him. He always called suspects who refused a solicitor idiots. He needed to start thinking like a suspect.

◆ ◆ ◆

Antonia waited in the cab until the roar of the engine died away, then counted to a hundred before getting out. Gareth had almost reached the cab and discovered her when Zack told him to 'Bloody leave it, we'll only be an hour'. Despite the relief, she wanted to throw up. She staggered a few steps before her legs steadied. The murders she'd witnessed had left her numb and unable to think clearly, but she must escape.

Some instinct made her replace the window frame after climbing back outside on to the bin. Running to the car, at first she didn't see it and a new wave of dread hit her. Had they caught Kerry? Then with a toot it shot out from behind a row of bushes and screeched to a halt beside her. Kerry leapt out and hugged her, crying.

Antonia was only just holding herself together and pushed her away. 'We need to go.'

Kerry wiped her tears and nodded.

'Will you be all right to drive?'

'I'll have to be, you can't drive.' Kerry returned to her seat and revved the engine, racing away as soon as Antonia shut the passenger door.

'Don't catch them up,' Antonia said.

Kerry slowed. After a few moments she sniffed and said, 'What happened?'

Antonia couldn't talk about it yet. She should tell the police, but those bodies weren't going anywhere. She'd ring from a call box rather than use Kerry's mobile; she'd already involved her friend too much.

'I thought they'd caught you,' Kerry said. 'Or worse.'

The tone of accusation made Antonia want to snap back, but her friend had a right to blame her. She must have been frantic. 'Sorry, I hid in the van when the first lot arrived.'

'What was the shooting about? I was out of my head. Didn't know what to do. I wanted to call the police, but . . . well, it's awful, but I figured what was done was done. If you were all right, I didn't want to get you into trouble, so I waited.'

'Sorry. No, you did right.' Antonia couldn't tell her about the murders. 'One of the lads in the pick-up had a gun and was showing off.'

'Who were they?'

'The lads who chased me on Sunday—'

'Shit! So, they *are* friends with Zack and Gareth.'

The snap as Gareth killed the long-haired man replayed, making her nauseous. 'I think they work for the same people.'

'Bloody hell!' Kerry said. 'So, who's in the pick-up?'

'Zack or Gareth—'

'Gareth drove the car they came in. I've got the number.'

'Well done.' Antonia wondered which one of them owned the car or if it would lead to another made-up name and address.

'How did you get out?' Kerry studied her, make-up smeared on her cheek from where she'd been crying. 'If the others are still in there?'

'There's an office. They went in there . . . to watch telly.'

Kerry took deep breaths until she regained control of her emotions. 'Where do you want to go?'

'The office, please. I need to speak to' – she stopped herself saying Eleanor – 'Alan. But I need to use a call box.'

'Use my mobile . . . Oh, you can't because it interferes with your brain, or something.'

Antonia ignored her. The scene of butchery replayed and with it the long-buried memory of the bloodied bodies of her best friend's family, killed in their compound as Antonia and her mother ran. She shook her head, determined not to let them return. Getting rid of them took too much out of her the first time and she feared she'd concealed even more horrific memories behind them.

As usual, the coffee from the vending machine tasted disgusting. Reluctant to deal with Sanchez's inevitable questions, Chapman sat in the corner of the canteen lost in his thoughts. *You're an idiot, Chapman, making a mess of everything. You had a nice number as a DCI, in line for a superintendent's job, gorgeous wife, a nice house and daughter.* He realised he missed Abby the most. She wouldn't be impressed to see him wallowing in self-pity. Nor if he gave up and rolled over. Something stank about this case and the smell came from Mishkin. If he wanted to retaliate, he needed to take Mishkin on at his weakest point.

He pushed the half-empty cup away and headed for his office. Sanchez looked up when he came in, but she kept her questions to herself. He threw himself into his chair, determined to find out what had really happened with Conti's DNA test. Someone got Conti off the hook by making the results go away, but why? Someone working at GRM must want to help her but his suspicion it was Mishkin seemed to have been way off. Who else in the organisation had the clout?

After his run-in with Mishkin, Chapman decided to make sure the test mix-up wasn't a genuine mistake before he stirred up any more shit. He dialled the work number for Jo Dobrowski but a recorded message told him she wasn't available and gave an alternative contact name and number. Would they have transferred her so soon after her promotion? He rang her private number.

'Russell, what do you want? I'm on leave.'

'Sorry, I wanted to ask you about the DNA from Conti—'

'What about it?' she snapped.

'Why did you change your mind? You clearly told me DNA found on Helba's body matched that taken from Antonia Conti.'

The pause until she answered lasted so long he wondered if she'd heard. 'I made a mistake.'

'What sort of mistake?'

195

'I must have cross-contaminated the samples.'

'How did *that* happen? If I recall, you were adamant you'd checked the chain of evidence.' Chapman waited for her answer.

'It just happened.'

'Did Mishkin put any pressure on you?'

'Goodbye, Russell.'

'Hang on, Jo.' But he was speaking to an empty line. 'Well, young lady,' he murmured. '*You* are very jumpy.'

'Sorry?' Sanchez looked up from her screen.

'I'm talking to myself.' Thoughts jumbled through his mind. Several things didn't fit on this case. 'How are you doing with the background on Aida Rizk? Something her landlord said puzzled me.'

'I didn't realise it was a priority.'

'Quick as you can.' He searched for the papers he'd found in the kitchen unit. 'Where's the envelope?' He pushed away from the desk and checked under it.

Sanchez concentrated on entering data.

'Has anyone been at my desk?' he said.

'The inspector—'

'Bastard.' Chapman leapt out of his chair and charged out of the office.

'Sarge, don't do anything stupid.' Sanchez's shout followed him down the corridor.

Habit made him knock on the inspector's door, but he didn't wait for a reply. 'What the hell you playing at, Ian—'

'Sergeant, what are you doing here?' Harding's cheeks glowed red.

Chapman noticed the visitors for the first time. The two NSA guys from the fire.

One of them smirked and held up the envelope. 'Did you want this?'

'Yes.' He reached for it but the man snatched it away.

Harding jabbed a finger at Chapman. 'These gentlemen specifically told you *not* to remove evidence from the scene—'

'Who said it came from there?'

'Don't make things worse, Sergeant. Constable Sanchez doesn't share your contempt for protocol. You know NSA investigations have priority over ordinary crimes.'

No wonder Sanchez seemed sheepish. 'If I recall, *these gentlemen* asked to see any evidence we recovered and I referred them to you. They've seen you, and now they have it.' He glared at the two men.

'I suggest you return to your office, Sergeant,' Harding said in his most pompous voice. 'You're already in enough trouble.'

Chapman left, slamming the door behind him. By the time he reached his office he'd forgiven Alice; in her shoes he'd have – he should have – done the same.

'Sorry, Sarge,' she said as he entered their office.

He waved her apology away. 'Don't worry about it.'

Sanchez studied him. 'How did it go with the inspector? Still like this?' She entwined her index and middle fingers.

He made a V. 'More like this now.'

She laughed.

'How have you done with—'

The door crashed open and two dark-clad figures burst into the room. For an instant he froze, then he saw the shoulder flashes. Special Security Unit, and following them into the room, DCI Gunnerson.

'Sergeant Chapman, you're suspended,' Gunnerson said.

'Shauna's only just taken my statement.'

'This is nothing to do with DCI McGee. The NSA and Inspector Harding have made complaints—'

'Shithouse!'

'I warned you, Russell.' Gunnerson grimaced in disappointment. 'Detective Sergeant Chapman, I am here to inform you that you are hereby suspended . . .'

Chapman stood, knocking his chair into the filing cabinets, and listened to the stilted phrases.

'These officers will escort you from the building and make sure you take nothing which doesn't belong—'

'What the fuck are you talking about?'

'Don't make this more difficult than necessary.' Gunnerson's manner suggested she'd rather be anywhere else.

'Yeah. Okay, I'm on my way.' He picked up his jacket and moved towards the door.

The nearest uniformed officer stuck out a hand to bar his way and gripped the hilt of his baton with the other. Chapman clenched his fists.

'Warrant card,' the officer said, adding, 'Sergeant,' as an afterthought.

Chapman handed it to Gunnerson and went to pass him.

The officer didn't move. 'We need to search you.'

'Try it.'

Gunnerson said, 'No need, Constable. The sergeant won't take anything he shouldn't.' The officer paused before stepping to the side and Gunnerson continued, 'You'll receive notification in the mail along with instructions on when you'll be allowed to return.'

Chapman felt numb. He suspected it would be *if*, not *when*. He strode out of the room and headed for the exit. The two uniformed officers hurried to keep up with him as colleagues avoided his gaze and his face burnt.

◆ ◆ ◆

Not finding Turner at the office knocked the wind out of Antonia's sails. She realised the risk she was taking coming in, but she'd spent half an hour checking there was nobody watching the building. And after what she'd seen, she really needed someone to talk to. Miles's sympathy just made her tearful and those sights weren't something she could share with him, or Turner, she realised. She took a shuddering breath and closed her eyes. *Come on, Antonia, don't crumple now.*

She opened a news feed specialising in information from the police radio network. No mention of the discovery of four bodies in the back of a refrigerated van. Had they taken her anonymous call seriously? She'd given enough detail. The police would want to keep it quiet, but she'd be surprised if they managed to. Someone had even published a picture of Pavlo online within minutes of his discovery, still wet from his immersion. At least she knew she hadn't killed him, although if she hadn't left him – *stop. You can't take the blame.* The expression on the young man's face when he realised Gareth would kill him – a mixture of fear and resignation – replaced the sound of his neck breaking in her latest nightmare. She dismissed the thought. If the police didn't catch them, she would.

'Miles,' she shouted into the outer office. 'I put a memory stick here on my desk.'

'Alan took something, just before he left to see Eleanor.'

Antonia's heart lurched. 'Is she worse?'

'Not as far as I know, sorry.'

Insides tense, Antonia rang the ward and spoke to a nurse who reassured her Eleanor hadn't got worse. Antonia meant to visit yesterday, but following the attack on the Tube . . . She'd go on her way to Kerry's.

She got a cab to the hospital and, still jumpy, kept checking behind her until she arrived. The sight of Eleanor gave Antonia a shock, but the nurse assured her she hadn't deteriorated. Maybe

Antonia's memory had tricked her into thinking Eleanor had looked better last time. She sat at Eleanor's side, holding a fragile, unresponsive hand and trying to come up with something to say when she could think of nothing but those men's executions. She found herself talking about the first time Eleanor suggested adopting her. Tears rolled down her cheeks as she recalled the joy she'd felt, and the relief that she'd never have to return to the care home.

With a jolt, she realised she'd promised Kerry she'd not be late. Her friend hadn't seen the killings, but her ordeal had been almost as distressing. She kissed Eleanor on the forehead and hurried out of the hospital. Even though she rushed, she made sure nobody followed her, changing Tubes and doubling back on herself. Two security checkpoints added to the journey time, each delay making her more impatient.

By the time she reached Adelaide Road, a sense of dread infused her. She hurried to Kerry's flat and pressed the entry buzzer to let her know she'd arrived before letting herself in with the spare keys. Too impatient to wait for the lift, she took the stairs three at a time.

'Kerry,' she shouted through the door into the flat as she inserted the key.

The flat lay in darkness and she fumbled for the light switch. All five doors off the corridor remained closed, which meant Kerry was out. Had she got fed up of waiting and gone out with the kids? No, after what had happened this afternoon, she'd want to stay home. Unease permeated Antonia, making her skin clammy.

She tiptoed to the spare bedroom and listened. No sound penetrated the door. Would the children be asleep yet? She doubted it, and made her way to Kerry's room. Why was she being so cautious? If there was an intruder, he'd be aware she'd arrived. But who could it be? The men who chased her and searched their offices wouldn't be so quiet, unless they'd set a trap for her. But they'd have sprung it by now.

The thought that she was being ridiculous stopped her for a moment. Well, so what, nobody could see her. She listened outside Kerry's bedroom door. A faint sound came from inside, making her heart thud against her chest. She waited for what felt like an age, but didn't hear it again. With as much care as she could, she turned the handle. The lock disengaged with a click, loud as a gunshot in the silence.

After another interminable wait, she pushed the door open. A sliver of light preceded her, illuminating a figure on the bed. A flash of copper hair lay on the pillow. Relief flooded through her. Kerry and the kids must have gone to bed early. Feeling foolish, she paused, letting her vision become accustomed to the gloom. Not sensing anyone else in the room, she stepped forward.

What she saw of Kerry's face looked strange. Antonia took another step forward. What was that? She listened. Was someone else moving in the flat? An ambulance siren blared from the main road. Light filled the room, making Antonia blink. Kerry stared back from the bed, a white cloth tied round her mouth and her cheeks streaked with mascara. Antonia spun to confront the figure in the doorway. For the second time that day, she faced the barrel of an automatic.

CHAPTER 15

A steady drizzle fell as Turner walked home from the Tube station, but he barely noticed it. Thoughts of his aunt and his need to talk to her about the problems facing The Investigator made him realise how much he relied on her. She wasn't too involved in the daily running, but at times like this she was the rock they all clung to. At least the swelling of her brain had eased. He thrust his hands into his pockets and found the memory stick he'd taken from Antonia's desk. He'd examine it when he got home.

Turner speeded up but tripped on an uneven paving slab and his other foot slipped. He retained his balance, cursing his new shoes. They were useless in the wet. He'd have to take care when he reached the cobbles. He checked around to make sure nobody had noticed his stumble. A dark people carrier sat fifty metres ahead. They were taking a chance; the traffic wardens round here didn't take prisoners. He lifted his collar. Only a short distance to get home then he'd break open the bottle of twenty-year-old Springbank and have a glass or two. He'd save Antonia some, but he'd better not tell her how much it cost in case Eleanor got to hear about it.

A figure moved in the people carrier as he approached; they must be waiting for someone from the mews. As he drew level he glanced at it, but couldn't see through the dark tint. The sensation of being observed made his scalp crawl and, hunching his shoulders, he hurried by. The doors slid open and when he glanced back he saw shadowy figures emerge from the vehicle and come straight towards him. He froze for an instant, then ran. He'd reach his front door in a few steps. As he left the pavement, his foot shot away from under him and he crashed to the ground. His skull bounced on the cobbles. A metallic taste filled his mouth and voices reached him from a distance before fading.

◆ ◆ ◆

The echo of the door slamming died and Antonia recognised the intruder, even with the livid bruise across his left cheek. Arkady. And the gun in his hand pointed at her. Her already racing heart rate surged. The hatred radiating from him shocked her, but a vivid replay of his friends' massacre roused her sympathy.

He jerked the gun towards Kerry. 'Don't even think of doing anything.'

Her sympathy evaporated. 'What do you want, Arkady?'

The use of his name made him pause. 'You killed my brother.'

'No, I didn't.' A few hours ago, she hadn't been sure.

'Oh yeah, so who did?'

'A man called Gareth—'

'What you talking about?'

'Gareth boasted he'd killed—'

'Gareth's a mate.' The barrel of the gun wavered.

'Zack and Gareth dumped the woman found in the basin.' His reaction told her he also knew Zack. 'I'm guessing Pavlo saw them—'

'What you mean, guessing?' His voice rose. 'Making it up, more like. Why did the police arrest you?'

'How many times have they picked *you* up for something you didn't do?' She needed to get the Mace out of her jacket pocket, but she must distract him first.

Arkady let the barrel dip. 'Zack's helping us hide out. He wouldn't if they—'

'At the Jubilee Industrial Estate?'

Arkady thrust the pistol at her. 'How the fuck you know?'

'I was searching for Zack's van. He uses it to dump bodies—'

'You're talking shit!'

Despite his denials, Arkady was hiding something. Then it came to Antonia. 'I should have been found with the other woman. You set me up. You knew I'd be walking home that way and faked the attack on the tramp to get me away from the surveillance cameras.'

'NO!'

An expression of guilt contradicted Arkady's denial and Antonia knew she'd guessed right. 'Who gave you the information about me and paid you?'

'Nobody paid us.' His gaze wavered.

Antonia slipped her right hand into her pocket. 'Whoever it was told Gareth and Zack to get rid of you.'

'Piss off, they wouldn't.' Arkady glared at her.

She wasn't sure if she should say more. Would it distract or enrage him? Where were the kids? She glanced at Kerry. Her friend had almost freed herself.

Antonia said, 'I saw him kill them. Zack shot three of them, and Gareth killed the lad with long blond hair.'

'Nikolai?' Shock and disbelief surged from Arkady.

'Yes. I'm really sorry, Arkady.' She located the top and gripped the tube.

Arkady's hand shook and the pistol barrel drifted downward. Now or never. Her heartbeat hammered in her ears. With her thumb on the spray button, she pulled out the canister and squirted the liquid into his eyes. He cried out and reeled back against the door. Antonia leapt at him, clamping her left hand on his right wrist. The explosion as he fired the gun filled the air. Antonia froze and Kerry disappeared. With a roar of rage Antonia threw a straight right at his head. Arkady held his hand across his eyes and her fist crunched into it. She lowered her aim and hit him in the mouth and again until he dropped the gun. She hit him once more.

'I've got the gun,' Kerry screamed from under the table. 'I'll kill you, you bastard.'

'No, Kerry!' Antonia cried out.

The door opened and Arkady staggered out through it. Kerry stumbled to her feet and followed.

'Kerry, don't! You'll—'

The gun lay on the floor where Arkady had dropped it.

She followed Kerry as the front door slammed. Arkady had gone, but she couldn't see Kerry either. She wouldn't chase him unarmed. Then voices came from the spare bedroom. The children lay face down on the bed, hands tied behind their backs and make-shift gags in their mouths.

'Nadimah,' Kerry cried, untying the girl. 'I'm so sorry. Are you okay?'

Antonia shook with relief and untied Hakim, holding the boy. His thin body trembled in her arms and she made soothing noises.

Nadimah eased herself from Kerry's embrace and put a hand on her brother's shoulder. 'Hakim, the man has gone. We're safe.' She addressed Antonia. 'He's terrified of shooting. The men who took Papa . . . had guns.'

Antonia looked over the boy's head and mouthed, 'What happened?' to Kerry.

Kerry mouthed, 'Later,' then said, 'We have to go before anyone comes.'

'We should call the—'

Kerry stopped her with a gesture at the children. If they called the police, the children would be taken into care. Someone would have reported the shot. They needed to go, now, but where to?

◆ ◆ ◆

'Pull up over there,' Antonia said. 'I'll get him to lower the bollard so you can park in the courtyard.'

The car slowed and Antonia glanced into the back where Nadimah and Hakim sat huddled together. She jumped out and ran towards Turner's house. Her foot slipped on the wet cobblestones but she kept her balance. A security light came on above the front door and she pressed the bell, thinking of the last time she'd come here. The night Arkady and his gang attacked Eleanor. As she waited, she examined the spot where she'd slipped. A dark liquid glistened. Oil? She inspected it. Blood. She ran to the door and kept her finger on the bell.

'Alan!' she shouted through the letter box, and banged on the door.

The lights in the neighbouring house came on and a woman opened the door. 'Can you keep the noise down? My son's trying to sleep.'

'Have you seen Alan?'

'He's gone to hospital.'

'What happened? Did he get a call?' Eleanor must have deteriorated. *Please God, don't let her die.*

'I think he fell over. I saw blood on his forehead.'

'What did he say?'

'He couldn't really talk. Some of his friends helped him into their van.'

'What did the men look like?' Fear made Antonia's voice shrill and she described Zack and Gareth.

'No, these looked ordinary. Quite big but not unusual . . .'

Relief that those two hadn't got hold of Alan made her dizzy. 'What about their van?'

The woman described a vehicle like the one Antonia had seen outside The Investigator's offices.

'Did they say which hospital?'

'They didn't actually say they were taking him to hospital, I sort of assumed. Sorry.' The woman held out her hands.

A jumble of thoughts paralysed Antonia. Could it be a coincidence? Good Samaritans in a similar vehicle? Cold logic told her it was unlikely, but she wasn't ready to accept the alternative. She'd ring the nearest hospitals. First she must find somewhere to take the children. Then she'd worry about finding him. Antonia thanked the neighbour and jogged to the car.

Kerry lowered the window. 'Can we stay?'

'He's not here,' Antonia whispered.

'What's happened to him?'

Why hadn't they taken Turner into his house? A surge of panic accompanied the sudden conviction that whoever had taken him, it hadn't been 'Samaritans'. And wherever they'd taken him, it wasn't hospital. Pushing away the panic gripping her, she ran to the passenger side. 'We need to go.'

The car roared away. What the hell was happening to all her friends?

◆ ◆ ◆

The aroma of unwashed bodies filled the small interview room. Turner slumped in a chair, one of four at a plain wooden table bolted to the floor. When he moved his head, sharp pain fired through his skull and waves of nausea assaulted him. Dressed in a cheap tracksuit and without his watch or phone, he didn't know how long he'd been there. Concern for Antonia added to his distress. Had they got her as well? The door opened with a click and he jerked upright, setting off a blinding headache.

'Alan, how are you?' Geoff Stokes's voice lifted Turner's spirits. 'Silly question,' the solicitor said and closed the door before taking the seat opposite Turner and placing a bundle of documents on the table.

'Hello, Geoff,' Turner said, his voice sounding thick.

'Has someone seen to your injuries?'

Turner touched the dressing covering the wound. 'The doctor patched me up and declared me fit to be questioned.'

'They said you slipped and fell. Sounds like a Stasi report.'

Turner laughed. 'Yeah, it does, but actually that's what happened.'

'Talk me through it.'

'I'd been to see Eleanor—'

'How is she?'

'Fine. Well, no worse.'

'That's a relief.' Stokes opened a notebook and produced a pen. 'I need to hear exactly what happened and how you received your injuries.'

Turner related the events leading up to him falling outside his house.

'So, you were unconscious when they took you into custody. Have they cautioned you?'

'Yeah, while we waited for the doctor.'

'You understood what—'

'I passed out for a few seconds.'

'Hmm, as long as you're sure. What have you said to the boys in blue – or black, as this lot seem to favour?'

'Never talk to the police—'

'—until I get there. Well remembered. I wasn't sure if your injuries had caused you to forget . . .' Stokes indicated Turner's bandage. 'The charges against you are serious. Some relate to the Border Protection Act, which as you know carries severe penalties.' He lifted the top sheet of paper. 'It always annoys me I'm not allowed my tablet in here.' He read in silence.

Turner considered the charges they'd put to him. Assisting an illegal alien. Unauthorised possession of confidential government documents relating to national security. The documents he'd got from Antonia didn't come into that category, so it was more of the usual bullshit the NSA tried to pull to make them seem important and intimidate people.

'Who's Patience Okoye?' Stokes said.

'She doesn't exist.'

'It says here she's an illegal and you procured documents for her—'

'It's Antonia. She was working undercover using the name Okoye.'

'Oh.' Stokes raised his eyebrows. 'Where is she now?'

'I'm not sure.' Turner didn't want her involved. 'She stayed with a friend.'

'If we can produce her and show her to be the same person, you might—'

'Can we keep her out of it?'

'Alan, you don't seem to realise the seriousness of your situation. Just the assisting of an illegal alien carries a possible life sentence.'

Turner sighed and gave him Kerry's address. He didn't like the thought of officers going round to pick Antonia up, but he couldn't even phone and warn her. They discussed what Turner would say when questioned, then Stokes knocked on the door, informing his captors they were ready. They waited, now sat alongside each other.

Turner spoke into the silence. 'Have you heard anything about Sabirah, Antonia's friend?'

'Afraid not, but I'm going to a law society function tomorrow night and there's people I plan to speak to.'

'Thanks, I know Antonia's very—'

The door opened. A tall, slim man wearing metal-framed glasses, his dark hair combed back, came in and sat opposite them. The door remained ajar, then a woman entered, carrying a folder. Her lime-green outfit contrasted with her companion's dark suit. She wore her brown hair long and had piercing blue eyes. She switched on a recording device and they introduced themselves.

'My client wishes to make a statement,' Stokes said.

Turner said his piece, but neither officer reacted to his words. When he'd finished, the woman produced a sheet of paper and slid it in front of him: an enlarged photocopy of Patience Okoye's ID card.

'You're saying this is Antonia Conti?' she said.

'Yes.'

'Ms Conti has full residency rights and is a naturalised citizen,' Stokes said.

The woman scowled. Her companion produced a small tablet from a pocket and typed on it. After a few seconds he held it out to the woman, saying, 'It looks like her.'

She compared the screen with the image. 'It could be, but we'd need to speak to her. Where is she?'

Turner couldn't bring himself to tell them, but Stokes recited Kerry's address.

The man left to send someone to collect her. The woman remained, reading his tablet.

Stokes said, 'Now we've cleared it up, can you release my—'

'As I said, we need to see her to be sure.' The woman's mulish expression told them she'd need a lot of persuading.

Turner couldn't cope with being there much longer. 'But it's obviously her.'

'The two women are similar, but—'

'Similar! Same face, same age, same height. How many women over six foot and looking like her are there?'

Stokes grabbed his arm and restrained him.

'Mr Turner, even if it is the same woman, you have procured forged identity documents. Under the Border Protection Act, the penalty is up to ten years, and if she is an illegal, it's life.' She glanced down at the screen. 'And according to this report, your Ms Conti has been consorting with terrorist suspects—'

'What are you talking about?'

'She tried to visit a Sabirah Fadil, who's being held as a suspected terrorist. And, as I'm sure you're aware, under the Prevention of Terrorism Act, if Ms Conti is found to have consorted with terrorists, the government can strip her of her naturalised citizenship and send her back.'

Turner didn't need Stokes's nod of affirmation to know she was telling the truth. The Electric Investigator was at the forefront of those trying to get that law revoked. The thought of it happening to Antonia made him nauseous.

Being in a police station made Antonia uncomfortable, but she needed to report Turner's disappearance. As she waited for the auxiliary policeman to process her report, she studied the stark reception area. A woman with two silent children sat on a chair staring at the wall opposite, a livid bruise discolouring her cheek. An elderly couple sat comforting each other, whispering with heads together. She checked the time. Had Kerry found them somewhere to stay?

The auxiliary policeman punched letters on the keyboard. 'It sounds like your friend fell over and these men helped him—'

'Why didn't they help him into his house?' Antonia demanded.

The officer frowned. 'If he was injured, they could have taken him to hospital, or a private clinic—'

'Alan didn't believe in queue-jumping.'

'Okay. We'll check the local hospitals.'

'Is that it?' Antonia said.

'No.' He thrust his chin forward. 'If we don't find him there, we'll enter a full report into our database. Do you know any reason someone might want to kidnap your friend?'

He was laughing at her but she couldn't tell him about the NSA men. He'd take her for a nutter. She wasn't sure how much effort the police would put into searching for him. She'd check the hospitals herself, but there wasn't much else she could do here. After thanking him she left the station.

Kerry had returned and parked in a visitor's space.

Antonia lowered herself into the passenger seat. 'How did you get on?' she said.

'Got the keys and he said we can stay as long as we need.' Kerry put on a positive voice, but she still looked in shock.

Antonia glanced at the children in the back seat. Hakim slept, but Nadimah stared out of the window until she became aware of Antonia's attention. Antonia smiled, but Nadimah's gaze slid away.

Kerry pulled out into the traffic and Antonia scanned the road, wondering which set of headlights hid enemies. Whoever had taken Turner must have links to the men who'd chased her, and if they'd been watching his place, they might have followed her.

She didn't want to say anything in front of Nadimah but Kerry picked up on her mood and drove like a boy racer, weaving through traffic and taking so many side roads Antonia feared her friend was lost. But forty minutes later they drove into Edgware Road and the car slowed before pulling into a semi-circular driveway in front of a towering mansion block. Antonia studied the handsome building, not in the best frame of mind to appreciate it, but recognising Kerry's friend wasn't short of money.

Antonia got out and opened the boot where their luggage lay, along with one of Kerry's handbags containing the pistol they'd recovered from Arkady. Kerry had wanted to throw it away but Antonia persuaded her to keep it. She contemplated leaving it in the boot, but what if something happened to the car? She slipped the bag over her shoulder and retrieved the case containing her and Kerry's clothes. Kerry joined her and picked up the pathetically small backpack containing the children's clothes. They were still in the car, unwilling to leave the security of the metal box.

'Come on, we're staying here tonight,' Kerry said.

They got out and waited by the car, holding each other, not moving until Kerry took them by the hand. Antonia took the keys and climbed the three steps to the front door. It opened before she reached it and a man dressed in the braid-laden uniform of a Regency admiral appeared.

'Hi, Steve, could you please park the car for me?' Kerry said and he took the keys off Antonia.

'Who is he?' Antonia whispered, as he strolled to the car.

'Don't worry. He might look a prat in that uniform, but Steve's okay. Ex-forces, and my nan knows him.'

Partly reassured, Antonia followed Kerry and the children into the building. The entrance smelt of wood polish and the parquet floor gleamed. Antonia reassessed Kerry's friend's wealth upwards. A pair of ancient-looking lift doors stood facing them and the 'admiral' operated a discreet button before leaving. The doors slid open to reveal a modern interior of polished steel and dark wood.

They ascended to the third floor, the lift motor purring in the background. Relief eased the sense of dread that had haunted Antonia since she'd confronted Arkady. Nobody would search for them here.

Pale marble covered the floor and two large ornate doors led off the landing. Kerry led them to the one on the left and unlocked it before flinging it open with a flourish. Lights came on as they entered the space and Antonia paused, blinking.

'What do you think?' Kerry said.

Black marble flecked with gold lined the floors and red fabric the walls. Two huge gilt mirrors flanked the door facing them and a crystal chandelier hung down from a dark-blue ceiling inset with small mirrors glinting like stars.

'It's different,' she said. 'What the hell does he do?'

'Writes computer games or something. What do you think of it, Nadimah?'

'It's like Uncle Bahir's house,' Hakim said, recovering some of his spirit.

'Come on then, I'll show you round.' Kerry hugged Nadimah and led her into the apartment.

A huge lounge filled with pastel sofas facing a cinema-screen-sized TV led to a gym and games room where hi-tech exercise machines lined one wall. As they explored the kitchen, the doorbell rang. Antonia's heart flipped and she gripped the red handbag to her.

Both children looked terrified, but Kerry said, 'It's probably Steve, with the keys. Do you want to put the kettle on? Or there's soft drinks in the fridge.'

Antonia had just worked out how to fill the hi-tech kettle when she heard Kerry's cry. Dropping the kettle, she grabbed the handbag and rushed to her friend's aid.

CHAPTER 16

The red and yellow Mini had parked in front of a fancy apartment block and Chapman had found a spot from where he could see them. He'd turned off the engine but remained ready to go if it set off again. Chapman had to admit the redhead could drive; he'd almost lost her a few times. The women had got out of the car and gathered round the boot. Thank God. He hadn't fancied another trip through the streets trying to keep up with them.

Then the kids had got out and Dixon had taken their hands. They were too dark to belong to her, even if they had a Black father, and if she was Kerry Dixon, she wasn't old enough to be their mum. They could be Conti's relatives, but their presence made him uneasy. He'd found a parking place down a side road and sat in the car deciding how best to approach this. Mishkin's complaint could come back to bite him. Accessing the records relating to Antonia's time in care had been a mistake, unless he could use the information in them to take Mishkin down; then he could justify his actions. But he'd need Conti's help and he hoped she'd jump at the opportunity to deal with her abuser.

As he'd approached the entrance, he'd checked he had his inspector's ID, glad he'd thought to fetch it from his locker before they'd thrown him off the station. Unlike his chief inspector's card, which he'd returned when they'd busted him to sergeant, they hadn't bothered asking for the DI card back when he'd made DCI. The uniformed concierge had opened the door before Chapman reached it and waited, expressionless and arms at his sides, ready to react. Despite the fancy uniform, Chapman had got the impression this guy could handle himself.

'Sergeant Chapman,' he'd said, and produced his warrant card. 'The women who just came in, I need a word with them.'

The man had relaxed but scrutinised the ID card. 'It says here "Inspector"—'

'My promotion just came through,' Chapman said, cursing himself, 'and I keep forgetting.'

'If you wait, I'll let them know you're here.' The concierge had walked towards an open doorway beside two sets of lift doors.

'I'd rather you didn't.'

The man had hesitated before saying, 'Third-floor apartment A, the lifts are there.'

'Can I use the stairs?'

Chapman had paused on the huge landing, getting his breath back before heading for the door with a big gold A alongside it. Whoever lived here had plenty of money, probably a bean counter or banker. The bell had sounded muffled and he'd rehearsed his patter in case he'd got the wrong flat.

The door had opened and Dixon stood in the gap. Her smile had died, replaced by wariness. 'Yes?'

'Hello, I'm Sergeant—'

Her mouth had opened and she'd pushed the door. Chapman lunged forward, knocking her on to her backside, and she'd cried out. Now the door facing him was flying open and an automatic was pointing out, behind it a furious Conti.

'Ms Conti, don't do anything stupid,' he said.

She glared at him, then studied at the woman on the floor. 'Step away.'

He did so and a sob came from his left. The young girl stared from an open doorway. Dixon scrambled to her feet before going to the girl and placing her arm round her shoulders. The three females watched him, seeming unable to decide what to do next.

'Put the gun down,' he said. 'You're not in trouble. I'm here to help.'

The barrel stayed unmoving and Conti said, 'How did you find us?'

'Alan Turner gave me your address and I followed you, although it wasn't easy.'

Conti frowned. 'Why would he?'

'He thought you'd been trying to get hold of me and I didn't correct him.'

She lowered the weapon and straightened. 'Come in then, Sergeant.'

Dixon led the girl away, making soothing sounds. The noise of a football match escaped from the room behind her. Chapman followed Conti into the kitchen. Lights glinted off stainless-steel appliances and red lacquered units lining the walls.

He nodded at the automatic. 'Where did you get the gun?'

She studied it before placing it on the work surface. 'Arkady. He came to Kerry's.'

'Oh. It must have been him I saw running out of her block of flats like a scalded cat.'

She shrugged.

'Do you mind?' He retrieved the automatic. Blue metal glinted off the Fort 15. The magazine had one shot missing and the smell confirmed someone had recently fired it.

'The gun went off when I took it off him,' Conti said.

'You were brave—'

'You said you wanted to help.' She folded her arms.

'I wanted to warn you Arkady Demchuk's lot were hunting for you. They hurt your landlady and—'

'Yes, I know. It was my fault.' She looked stricken.

A surge of sympathy made him want to protect this young lady. 'It's nobody's fault, except those thugs', but how did you know?'

'I'd borrowed a voice-activated recorder and it was in my flat when they trashed it. I recognised the voices from when they ambushed me.'

'Why haven't you handed it to the police?'

'Do you need it?'

'We've got Arkady's blood on a lamp in your landlady's place, and we found traces from one of his mates in her cat's claws, but the more evidence we have the better.' Why hadn't she given it to the police? Maybe she *had* killed Pavlo Helba and they'd discussed it on the recording. 'What exactly happened at the canal on Sunday night? I don't believe the pack of lies you told us.'

Her eyes flashed and he touched his throat, still sore from her blow, but she told him what happened when the men chased her.

As she described the fight with Pavlo, he interrupted. 'Rudenko said you hit him with something?'

'Who's Rudenko?'

'Weren't there two of them?'

'Yes, but the other one left. Pavlo was alone by the time he attacked me and I didn't hit him with anything. I kicked him, but he was dragging me into the water.'

Chapman recalled the marks on Helba's face but wasn't sure what to think. She seemed to believe what she said, but she'd already lied to him. 'That's why your DNA was all over Helba. But then it *wasn't*. Do you know why?'

'No idea.' She stared into the distance.

'GRM owns the company who do the tests. Do you have any friends who work there?'

'Yes, a few cleaners and maintenance staff, I'm sure they'll have the clout.' Her glare bored into him.

Chapman resisted the temptation to snap at her. 'If it happened like you said, you could claim self-defence.'

'I left Pavlo alive. A man called Gareth killed him.'

'How do you know?'

'He and a man called Zack Wichrowski killed four of Arkady's friends earlier today. He killed one with his bare hands and said Pavlo had put up more of a fight.'

'What? How do you know this? You got an informer?' It all sounded too far-fetched.

'I saw them kill Arkady's friends in a warehouse.' She gave him the address of an industrial unit. 'I'd traced the van there and was hiding in it.'

Chapman didn't know what to think. 'When did they kill Pavlo Helba?'

'Gareth and Zack were at the canal in the van the night I got attacked. I think they were dumping the woman's body.'

How much of this was true? She looked like she believed it, but people often convinced themselves they'd seen something they'd imagined. 'Have you reported it to the police?'

She nodded, looking drained.

'What time did this happen?'

'About half three.'

Around the time Shauna had been grilling him. 'And what time did you report it?'

'Half an hour later.'

He was still in the office then. 'The discovery of four dead bodies would create a stir and the news would spread to most stations in no time.'

'Are you calling me a liar?'

'They've gone to sleep,' Dixon said from the doorway. 'Can I get you a drink?'

'How's the girl?' he said.

'Nadimah's shaken up, but she'll be all right.'

'Yes, I've got one a bit older, they're resilient.'

Conti raised her eyebrows but didn't speak.

'Could I have a small whisky please?' he said.

Dixon disappeared and he sat facing Conti across a long table. 'Whose place is this?'

'It belongs to a friend of Kerry's.'

'What about the kids?'

'They're a friend's. She's . . . away.'

Dixon returned with a silver tray, a decanter and three cut-crystal tumblers. 'I'm Kerry,' she said and shook his hand.

'Russell,' he said, then offered his hand to Conti.

She hesitated but took it, squeezing and reminding him of her strength. 'Antonia,' she said.

He didn't want to mention Mishkin with Kerry here, so asked, 'Do you mind telling me why you're investigating GRM?'

'We're investigating how they get their government contracts. They've got a contact in the Home Office feeding them information, someone senior. We're not sure who it is, but they're making sure most of their bids win. They've also been cutting corners, not fulfilling contracts but getting paid, and getting the performance bonuses.'

'It sounds like they've got more than one person on the take.'

'Yep, we've uncovered about twenty, but not the one at the top. Yet.'

'Is that why you haven't published the story yet? Your boss said—'

'No, we went ahead, but the Home Office blocked it.'

Chapman whistled. 'That *is* senior.' So much for their exposé damaging GRM's bid for the Murder Squad.

'Tell him about the other investigation,' Kerry said.

Antonia hesitated for a few seconds then said, 'Monika, one of my friends from the gym, disappeared while working at GRM. She started seeing a bloke at work just before she disappeared. Gareth, one of the men who killed Arkady's friends . . .'

Chapman tried to assimilate this with what he already knew. 'This guy you claim to have seen killing—'

'I *did* see him kill them.' Antonia raised her voice.

So you say. 'But he's also mixed up in the disappearance of your friend, and he and his mate killed and dumped the woman we found on Monday?'

'I haven't conclusive evidence of that, and I'm not sure they killed her, but what else were they doing there at that time?'

He shook his head. 'I need evidence, not half-baked theories. Anyway, we've already got someone for the girl's murder.'

She looked disappointed, then rallied. 'It's possible someone else at GRM killed them and these two just get rid of the bodies.'

'The suspect does – *did* work at GRM.'

'There you are then,' Kerry said.

'What do you mean, did?' Antonia said.

'He's dead. Suicide.'

'Why would he . . . No, he's killed others, and if he's a predator, he wouldn't kill himself. You must have the wrong man. Again.'

Her tone made him clench his jaw. 'You reporters believe we're either corrupt or incompetent.'

Antonia glared at him for several seconds, then her expression softened. 'Not all.'

'Thanks for the endorsement.' Chapman agreed Benjamin Murray wasn't the killer, despite the very convenient evidence found at his hideout. But Mishkin must be involved. 'What do Zack and Gareth do at GRM?'

'Some sort of IT maintenance.'

'It's not them. Someone got rid of the CCTV from the building overlooking the water where we found the body. Whoever did it had a lot of clout.'

'Or work in maintenance,' Kerry said. 'Zack told me, without them the company would lose millions. I thought he was bigging his job up, like most blokes, but if he takes care of the security systems . . .'

Chapman hadn't considered this, but she could be right. And if he found the killers of the two bodies in the canal, they couldn't sack him, especially as they'd already pinned one on an innocent man. It would look like vindictiveness. 'What put you on to them?'

Antonia told him about the traffic cameras. 'I hoped to find out where they'd come from, but Alan's got the memory stick holding the information and he's disappeared.' She hesitated. 'Some men in a dark people carrier snatched him from outside his house. I think it's the NSA.'

'I'll have a word with someone, get them to take your report seriously and if you've got the—' *Shit!* He couldn't use the work computers to search for the van while suspended. He'd have to ask Sanchez to do it.

'What's wrong?' Antonia said.

'Have you got the details of the van?'

'At the office.'

'Can you let me have them?'

'If you give me a lift, we can get them now.' The suggestion seemed to energise her.

'Can we collect the voice-activated recording of the break-in at your flat as well?'

Chapman followed Antonia, picking up the automatic. He couldn't leave it here, but he'd have to find a way of handing it in without getting her into trouble. He checked the time. Brigitte would be in bed, but it shouldn't take more than an hour.

◆ ◆ ◆

Antonia followed Chapman into the lift, not sure if she could trust him. He veered between wanting to help her and persecute her for something. She found him difficult to read, probably because of his years in the police. She couldn't guarantee he wouldn't arrest her for having the gun. Telling him what had happened hadn't eased her anxiety. Not only didn't he appear to believe her about what she'd seen Zack and Gareth do, but he hadn't been too enthusiastic when she'd told him her theory. What did she expect, him to say, 'Well done for making us appear stupid?'

They reached his car. 'Where's your partner?' she said.

He unlocked the doors and opened the boot.

'Don't you always work in pairs?'

He slammed the lid. 'I'm not on duty.'

'What the hell are you doing here then?'

'Do you want a lift?'

They drove to Vincent Terrace in uncomfortable silence, Chapman nervous, checking his mirrors every few seconds. Thoughts of Eleanor preoccupied her as they neared home and with them, a sense of unease.

'We'd better check nobody's watching the—'

'I've done this before, you know.'

She bit back an angry retort and peered out of the window into the shadows. They approached the house but didn't slow and he drove round the block studying the parked cars. They made two more circuits of the block before he slowed and parked outside the house. Eager to get this over and return to the flat, she reached for the door handle, but he grabbed her shoulder and pulled her back.

'Wait,' he said.

She pushed him away. 'Leave me alone.'

'Someone's trying to kill you. He's already had one go. You might have a better education than me and think you know everything, but you don't, and I don't want to get hurt because of your carelessness.'

She could smell the whisky on his breath. 'There's nobody around, so can I get out now?'

He checked their surroundings, making a show of it, before nodding and following her to the house. Infected by his unease, the skin on her neck tightened as she imagined someone watching. She unlocked the front door and hesitated before pushing it open. The beeping of the alarm reassured her.

'Hang on,' he said, and brushed past her.

'Now you're being ridiculous. The alarm's on and—'

'Easiest way to get someone to drop their guard: turn off the alarm, cover the sensor in one room, reset the system and wait for your victim.'

Heat suffused her neck as, putting the light on, she followed him into the offices, on edge until they'd checked every room. The printouts of the van details lay on her desk and, checking she had all of them, she folded them and shoved them into her jacket pocket. The recording should have been there but she couldn't find it and the thought that someone had stolen it made her panic for a moment. But who knew about it? She'd almost convinced herself Turner had taken it home when she found it in the top drawer of his desk.

'Got it?' Chapman said from the doorway.

She slipped the recorder into the other pocket, making sure she fastened the zip, and reset the alarm. Chapman was almost at the car when she locked the front door and followed, thinking she must visit Eleanor.

She sensed rather than saw the movement. A large figure dressed in black ran towards her. Instinct made her turn and she saw another, wearing a ski mask. The nearest one reached her before she could shout a warning. The impact knocked her backwards into the other man. A gloved hand grabbed her jaw. Her arm flailed and hit something solid. The man behind let out a grunt and she jerked her arm back again. The grip on her jaw loosened and she opened her mouth, biting down hard on fingers.

He snatched his hand away and she spun, thrusting herself from him. More hands grabbed at her, pulling her by the collar. Her jacket slipped off her shoulders, then she threw her arms back. The jacket slid off and her attacker swore. An arm thumped into her chest, sliding up to her throat and dragging her head back. A fist smashed into her nose and blood filled her mouth. She twisted her body and pushed backwards, making her assailant stagger. The pressure on her neck eased and she sucked air into her lungs. Through tear-blurred eyes she saw Chapman at his car, fiddling around in the boot. *What the hell is he doing?*

The grip on her neck tightened again. She resisted her powerful attacker but couldn't prise his arm away. Someone hit her in the solar plexus. The blow emptied her lungs and the pain paralysed her. Her limbs refused to respond, but a yell penetrated the edges of her fading consciousness.

'Let her go!' Chapman shouted, his voice shrill.

'Fuck off!' her captor replied, spraying spittle on to her neck.

The other man advanced on Chapman, something glinting in his hand, then a flash from the back of the car and a shot rang out. The man fell and the pressure on her throat eased. She twisted free before thrusting her hand into her attacker's face, fingers clawing for his eyes. As he staggered away, another shot rang out and he slumped, dropping the gun that had appeared in his hand. She kicked it away, then ran towards Chapman. Her jacket lay on the kerb, next to the first man.

An engine roared into life and Chapman shouted something. She wasn't leaving the papers. As she passed the fallen man, she slid on the pavement and fell. The engine grew louder and she pushed herself to her knees. Headlights swept across the pavement, illuminating one of the men, surrounded by the pool of blood she'd slipped in. Then they came straight at her but as she tried to rise, her foot slipped again.

CHAPTER 17

The cell door crashed open and Turner jolted awake, screwing his eyes up as the harsh light attacked them. It couldn't be morning already.

'Let's go,' the guard announced.

'What's the time?' he said through unresponsive lips.

The guard checked his watch. 'Midnight. Come on, get up.'

Less than an hour since Geoff Stokes had left him. They couldn't want to question him again. He yawned and pushed himself off the unyielding foam mat. The rough blanket stinking of detergent slipped off him as he sat up and swung his legs out. 'I'm not saying anything until my solicitor gets here.'

'Please put your clothes on and come with me.' *Please?* The man's manner threw Turner.

Stokes would have something to say about them waking Turner at midnight. Even with the current enhanced level of security they couldn't interrogate people at all hours. Could they? Visions of being tortured in darkened rooms by grim-faced captors swam through his mind.

'Come on,' the guard said. 'Anyone would think you liked it here.'

Turner examined his clothes. They must have finished testing them, although what they'd hoped to find he wasn't sure. He rose on wobbly legs, turned his back and exchanged the scratchy tracksuit for his own clothes. Even though they were damp and muddy from where he'd fallen, putting them on made him feel better. The guard stepped away and Turner shuffled into the corridor, where another guard waited. They led him out of the cell block but instead of going right towards the interview rooms, turned left.

'Where are we going?'

In reply he received a gentle prod in his back. They passed through a set of doors into the reception area where he'd arrived. A bulky brown envelope lay in front of the officer stationed at the desk. She pushed it towards Turner.

'Check the contents and sign this.' She indicated a tablet.

'You're letting me go?'

He emptied the envelope and picked out his shoelaces. Once he'd fastened them he felt like a grown-up and checked the desktop. They'd returned everything, including his phone, and doubtless they'd downloaded its contents. Good luck to them – apart from his music, he encrypted what little data he put on it. Although not as paranoid as Antonia, he didn't trust these devices. He wondered how she was.

'Do you want to sign here?' the woman repeated.

'Sorry.' Turner scrawled his name with the stylus and finished returning his belongings to his pockets. 'How do I get home?' he said.

'Taxis along the main road.' She pointed towards her right. 'Or there's a night bus.'

Turner thanked her and headed out on to the street, shivering as the frigid air hit him. He got his bearings and walked towards the main road. After a few minutes the recognisable thrum of a black cab cut through the night.

He dozed in the rear of the vehicle, looking forward to getting home. He paid the cab and hurried to his front door. Had it only been four and a half hours since he'd fallen outside?

He struggled with the mortise until he realised he must have forgotten to lock it. The Yale moved stiffly, but it sometimes did. He pushed the door open and stepped in, closing it behind him. He pressed the light switch but nothing happened. Had the bulb gone? Light from the streetlamp outside streamed in through the fanlight. Something seemed different. A rush of air and the door to the lounge burst open. A dark figure barrelled into him, slamming him against the wall. Turner's bladder loosened as a hand grabbed his collar and cold metal pressed into his cheek.

'Where the fuck's the black bitch?' a voice exuding beery fumes demanded.

The reverberation from the two shots echoed in Chapman's ears. The satisfaction at hitting both targets faded. What the hell had just happened? They must get out of there before someone reported the gunshots. Headlights came on, illuminating Antonia, and the roar of an engine reached him through layers of cotton wool. He shouted a warning, but she ignored him and ran to her jacket.

Stupid girl, nothing in it warranted getting herself killed. Before he could shout again, she slipped, falling into the vehicle's path. Without hesitating, he raised the automatic and fired at the driver. Three shots and the car swerved before screaming past, so close the shock wave rocked him. Antonia scrambled to her feet, seeming unhurt. He slammed the boot, ran to the driver's door and leapt in, starting the engine before his arse hit the seat.

A second later she threw herself into the passenger seat. The other car stopped and the driver's door opened. Chapman pulled away, aiming at it as he passed, but the driver dragged it shut. Relieved he hadn't shot another man, Chapman floored the accelerator.

'Are you okay?' he said.

'Yes.' Her voice shook, sounding faint above the ringing in his ears.

He gripped the steering wheel to prevent his hands trembling as what he'd done hit him. 'Fuck! Fuck!'

'Are *you* okay?' she said. A thread of blood tracked from her left nostril.

'Never better.' Chapman struggled to breathe and replayed the incident as he drove away, checking the mirror for pursuers. Not only had he shot two unidentified men while suspended, but he'd used an illegal gun recovered from an attempted kidnapping. He'd not even warned them before he did. Who was he kidding? Even if he'd done everything by the book, he was in the shit. Who the hell were they?

He switched on the police radio. They'd pick his car up on the camera system so he'd better have his story ready and it would be best if he handed himself in rather than let them find him. Ten minutes later he'd not heard any messages relating to the shooting. Puzzled, he rang Gunnerson, who should be on the twenty-four-hour rota. He couldn't believe she'd only suspended him a few hours ago.

She didn't answer for a few seconds. 'Russell?' She sounded sleepy, not someone dealing with a multiple shooting.

'Sorry to disturb you, Yasmin, I thought you were on duty.'

'What do you want?'

The question hung in the air as he thought of an answer. 'I heard someone's killed Nikolai Rudenko, the guy who attacked Alice.'

'Where did you hear this?'

'Just on the net—'

'Are you in a car?'

He didn't answer.

'Russell, can this wait until the bloody morning?'

'Yeah, sure. Sorry.' He ended the call and Antonia snatched the handset. 'Oi, what the hell—'

'Idiot, no wonder they found us. They tracked you,' she said, stripping the phone and removing the SIM card.

'Why would they track *me*? They wanted you.'

'They'll know you're here now. How will you explain that?'

He couldn't. He took a deep breath and turned up the volume. The radio traffic continued with the usual calls, but nothing about a shooting. He couldn't even remember hearing sirens. What was going on? He hadn't imagined it. The weight of the Fort 15 pulled against his jacket.

'Did you see the badge?' Antonia said, wiping at the red smudge on her upper lip.

'What bloody badge?'

'The second one you shot wore one under his jacket. I saw it when the headlights swept across him—'

'Why didn't you say?'

'It didn't sink in until I replayed it. Anyway, what would you have done, *not* shot him? He'd have shot *you*.'

She was right. 'Did you recognise the badge?'

'I'll try to remember where I saw it.' She sounded calm, but then, she hadn't just shot someone.

Who would be after Antonia? Then it came to him: the same people who'd been all over this case, the National Security Agency. No wonder it wasn't on the police channels. If they were behind this, nobody would ever know about it unless they wanted them to. *Fuck!* He'd shot two NSA men.

◆ ◆ ◆

The wet patch at Turner's crotch burned, like acid eating into his flesh. Would his jacket conceal it? At least it would in the dark.

'Where is she?' the intruder repeated, pushing the blade into Turner's cheek.

He leant away from it but the man heaved on his collar, cutting off his air and pulling him back. The steel pressed into his skin. 'I don't know.'

'Wrong answer.'

A blow to his cheek, then hot liquid ran down the side of his face before dripping from his chin. The man had stabbed him! Turner cried out. The numbness wore off and fiery agony spread from his cheek.

'Where the fuck is she?'

Blood streamed out of the wound. How much could he lose before passing out? The man's hand drew back. 'She went to stay with her friend,' Turner blurted out.

'Where?'

'Near Chalk Farm Tube station. I can't remember the address, but I've got it on my—'

'Her mate a redhead with big tits?'

He took a few moments to recognise the description of Kerry. 'Yes.'

Another blow and his head crunched into the wall. Lights flashed at the edge of his vision, but the bleeding hadn't increased so maybe he'd just punched him this time.

'I've just been there. Where's she gone?'

'I don't—' The fist drew back. 'I'm sorry but—'

'Alan!' The call came from outside the front door.

The intruder stuck the blade in the side of Turner's neck. 'Say a word . . .' he whispered and dragged him from the door.

'Alan, is that you?'

Judy from next door.

The intruder spun Turner round, releasing his collar, but before he could speak a muscular forearm pulled across his throat. 'I'll fucking cut you again if you say anything,' the man hissed into his ear.

The forearm pulled tighter, making Turner gag, and dragged him into the lounge. The intruder had drawn the curtains, keeping the streetlight from entering. With a scrape the standard lamp crashed against the coffee table.

'Shit!' The man froze.

The man's breathing sounded harsh and the blade shook against Turner's neck. His attacker's fear gave Turner a sense of satisfaction. Antonia must have either not gone to Kerry's or if she had, she'd got away. So how had he known to come here? The thought of the intruder coercing Kerry into telling him where Turner lived made him furious.

'Police are here,' Judy called through the door, sounding scared.

The man drove the blade into Turner's neck. 'You got another way out?'

'I can't breathe,' Turner croaked. The pressure on his windpipe eased. 'The kitchen,' he said, gesturing towards the door.

'Take me.' The intruder pushed him, and Turner staggered into the fallen lamp. 'Put the fucking light on.'

Turner groped for the switch and light flooded the room, making him blink. Red fingerprints smeared the wallpaper around the switch. Excited voices came from outside, Judy and deeper tones. The man pushed him towards the kitchen door and he stumbled through it. The light from the living room illuminated the small space.

'I'll be back, you bastard.' The intruder shoved him away and rushed to the door leading to the tiny yard, reaching it in two steps. He fumbled with the key, one hand still gripping the knife.

'Mr Turner, it's the police!'

The intruder stopped, fear etched into his features, then he put the knife on the worktop and returned to the lock. The image of Eleanor's broken body flashed through Turner's mind. With a yell, he leapt forward as the lock clicked and the door jerked open. Behind him a crash, and wood splintered. Turner reached for the knife but the intruder snatched it up, thrusting upwards. Light glinted off metal and the blow landed on the side of Turner's neck.

Ten minutes later they'd covered at least three miles and Antonia felt less panicky. The sight of the second man in a pool of blood kept replaying, but she told herself they'd come to kill her. The tendons in her neck ached and her right knee stiffened. She must have banged it falling in front of the car.

'Thank you,' she said.

'What for?' Chapman sounded gruff.

'The car, he'd have . . . Thank you.'

Chapman waved her thanks away, but his hand trembled and he looked like he'd aged during the drive. The car slowed and they pulled into a side road.

'Where are we going?' she said.

'I'll walk you to the flat but I don't want my car anywhere near it. I'll report it stolen in the morning.'

'There's no need, I'm—'

'Come on, let's go this way, fewer cameras.'

She jogged to catch him up. 'Here's your phone, and the SIM card.'

'Cheers.' He took it. 'I'll leave it stripped down, wouldn't want to lead anyone here, would I?'

They covered the remaining distance to the flat in silence. Nobody came to the door, so Antonia rang the bell. 'The admiral must finish early,' she said, but Chapman ignored her. 'I'm sorry I shouted at you. Someone just tried to kill me, so I was a bit stressed.'

Chapman exhaled. 'Yeah, I know, but I think those men were NSA. They've taken this case over now.'

Antonia didn't know what to think about this. Kerry buzzed them in and they ascended in the lift. After telling them not to disturb the children, Kerry led them into the kitchen and poured them a large glass of wine each.

'Do you want something to eat? I ate with the kids,' Kerry said, obviously desperate to know what had happened.

The thought of food turned Antonia's stomach but Chapman accepted, and she set up the laptop while Kerry rattled crockery. Antonia found the website. The logos displayed across the screen shared many features and she quickly found the one she'd seen on the badge, a rampant lion in a circle, representing the iris of a huge eye. Chapman came and sat next to her, bringing the odour of toast and melted cheese. Kerry hovered nearby but Antonia signalled at her to leave. She'd decide what she could tell her later.

'I'll make sure the kids are okay,' Kerry said, not hiding her reluctance.

Chapman waited until she'd closed the door behind her. 'You got it?'

'Sentinel Threat Management. Have you heard of them? It says they're a private security contractor with a category one rating.'

'Can I see?' he said, leaning over her shoulder.

She swung the screen round, conscious of his closeness as he studied the image. The smell of food made her nauseous and she leant away. She'd investigated specialist security contractors for The Investigator two years ago but couldn't remember all the details. 'Doesn't category one mean they can work for the government?'

'Yeah, they use them if they want to do something dodgy, so they can deny it if anything goes wrong.'

'Do you still think it's NSA?'

'No.' Despite the denial, Chapman sounded uncertain. 'The NSA aren't allowed to use contractors.'

She remembered the legislation, passed after the scandal when staff working for a private company used information gathered by the Security Services to blackmail businesses avoiding taxes. 'So, who?'

'You've upset a few people, but I don't see Arkady Demchuk and his mates hiring an outfit like this.'

'No, but whoever hired *Arkady* might have hired Sentinel when he messed up . . .' She remembered the rumours about Reed-Mayhew settling scores. Had he discovered Antonia's link to her Okoye identity? And he could have suppressed the DNA evidence, but why? She wouldn't be any harder to get at in custody. GRM ran most prisons, including the one where she'd visited Sabirah. An involuntary shudder travelled down her spine.

'Can we check the news channels?' Chapman said.

A trawl through the main news agencies didn't flag up any recent shootings in London, but Chapman's attitude didn't convey relief.

'That's good, isn't it?' she said. 'You're off the hook.'

'But why?' He drained his glass.

'You must be wrong. Sentinel *are* working with the NSA and if the shootings came out, they'd have to explain what they were doing there *and* why they're working with them.'

He closed his eyes and massaged his temples. 'Maybe.' After a few seconds he held out a hand. 'Let's see what almost got you killed.'

Antonia emptied her pockets and Chapman picked up the micro recorder while she unfolded the papers listing the details of the van. The recording of her apartment getting trashed started to play. 'The first one's Arkady,' she said.

'You sure?' Chapman replayed it.

'Positive. I heard him the night Pavlo attacked me and then at Kerry's.'

'Great.' He stopped the recording. 'The DNA already puts him at the house and this corroborates it . . . You got an envelope?'

She found a turquoise carrier bag with two royal crests on it. Fortnum and Mason. Of course, what else? 'Will this do?'

He wrapped the recorder in it and shoved it into his side pocket. 'So, someone paid Arkady and his gang to waylay you.'

'Sounds like it.' She still wasn't sure who.

'Whoever it is really wants you out of the way. And they've raised the stakes, first Arkady, then Sentinel—'

'Yes, I'd worked that out.'

'Sorry, just thinking aloud.'

Turner's disappearance now made sense. 'Do you think the NSA might have grabbed Alan, if they're working with Sentinel?' She wasn't sure if she preferred them to someone like Arkady holding him, but at least they wouldn't just kill him. Would they?

'I'll ring someone senior once I'm away from here,' he said. 'See if I can find out.' He didn't sound too confident.

'Thanks.' Weariness hit Antonia and her energy drained away. 'I'll let Kerry know you're going.'

'Yeah, okay.' He picked up the papers. 'And I'll need a number to contact you. I'll get a new phone myself and text you the details.'

Antonia wanted to refuse, but realised it made sense. 'You can have Kerry's, I'll get a pen.'

'No need.' He tapped his temple. 'I'll remember it.'

She found a still-sulking Kerry watching a black and white film with the sound low. Kerry came back with her and hugged Chapman goodnight, then Antonia led him to the landing. If he tried to hug her . . .

He pressed the lift button and offered his hand. 'I'll get the information on the van and come back with it in the morning.'

'Thank you and thanks again for . . . what you did.'

He smiled. 'Don't mention it.'

She stared at the lift doors long after they'd closed, feeling very lonely. Someone very powerful had her in their sights, *and* her friends. She worried about Kerry and the children, but too tired to think about it now, decided to deal with it in the morning.

CHAPTER 18

The alarm beeped as he opened the outer door to the office, and Turner keyed in the PIN. He walked with care, avoiding making sudden moves, which sent a jolt of pain across his skull. The stitches on his face felt tight and the sensation that a large piece of sharp gravel was trapped in his windpipe wouldn't go away. Although he realised he'd been lucky that only the handle of the knife had struck him, if the two coppers mentioned it once more he'd have rammed it into *their* throats. See how they liked it.

He switched the computer on and, while waiting for it to complete the security checks, wondered if he could risk a coffee. The doctor in casualty told him no solids or hot drinks for a few days. So, cold soup, great. He decided he'd have one, let it cool before drinking it. The aroma as it brewed revived him and he sniffed the mug as he logged on.

The message flashing across his screen made his insides churn. Someone had attempted to access their system. Could it be linked to their investigation into GRM? With sweating hands he ran the spyware and malware detection programmes while he checked the computer's security centre. The software claimed to have blocked the attack.

He opened the site. Still up, and with reader feedback less than ten minutes old. The programmes finished running but discovered nothing out of the ordinary. Was it a coincidence? It wasn't unusual to get these attacks. Shaken, he called ICS, their security consultants, and asked them to run a thorough check on the computers and upgrade the software. They needed a full check-up and ICS could do a sweep of the offices and the other machines at the same time.

The front door opened, making him jump. The sudden movement triggered a headache. He heard Miles's cheerful 'Morning' with relief.

'In here, Miles.' His voice rasped, sounding like he had laryngitis.

'How are— Oh, my God.' Miles halted in the doorway, hand across his mouth. After a few moments he rushed forward and sat on Turner's visitor's chair. 'What happened?'

Turner told him, omitting to mention he'd wet himself. Lucky he'd already ruined those trousers when he fell. Miles presented a rewarding audience, reacting animatedly as Turner related his ordeals.

'I could *never* stay there again,' Miles said, 'knowing that animal had violated my— Oh, sorry Alan.'

Turner agreed. He'd stayed in his house long enough to get changed and have a shower, but he'd hated every second. He'd book into a hotel until he sorted something long term. 'We've got another problem. I've got ICS coming in later to check our system. Someone tried to hack my computer.'

'It will cost. You sure we need them? We get attacks all the time and our security software is good.'

'After what happened recently I don't want to take any chances. They're doing a full security scan, including the offices.'

'Oh well.' Miles sighed. 'I won't get much done today then. So much for coming in on a Saturday . . .' He rose to go, but hesitated at the door. 'Why don't you get security guards?'

'Not my scene.'

'At least until they catch the animal. ICS have a sister company which carries out personal protection.'

Miles closed the door behind him and Turner tapped his teeth with a pencil as he contemplated the idea. A guard would make him feel a lot safer. He rang ICS, who told him they no longer owned the subsidiary, but they'd ring him back with a recommendation.

He decided not to risk going through his emails until they'd completed the security scan, and trawled the news channels for details of stories worth investigating. The crime reports brought up an address that snagged his attention – the report of a shooting and a man seen running from a block of flats off Chalk Farm Road. He checked the time. Antonia should have arrived by now. Something his attacker said came back to him. He'd claimed he'd been to Kerry's and he'd said Antonia wasn't there, or was it that she'd got away from him? Had he been the gunman? But he didn't have a gun, otherwise why use one of Alan's knives? Maybe he'd shot Kerry. But the report didn't mention casualties.

The phone rang and a voice he didn't recognise said, 'Mr Turner?'

'Yes. How can I help you?'

'Nigel Harrison here. I understand you need personal protection,' the man said in an Essex accent.

'Oh yes.' They discussed Turner's needs and the terms, and agreed Nigel would arrange a safe house for Turner before coming to the office in two hours.

'Fantastic,' Turner said, feeling a weight lift off him, 'and what's your company called?'

'Sentinel Threat Management. I'll see you later, Mr Turner.'

The powerful jets of water from the hi-tech shower revived Antonia. Despite the luxury of the huge bed and silky sheets, she'd hardly slept. Apart from images of the man Chapman shot, nightmares featuring Mishkin disturbed her sleep. She could tell he presented a threat, but each time she almost saw why, she woke, covered in sweat. She dismissed the dreams, didn't believe in premonitions. Dreams only reflected your preoccupations and imagination.

Convinced Chapman wouldn't come up with the footage of the van, she wondered if Turner— Oh God, she still didn't know what had happened to him. She jumped out of the shower and fired up her laptop, drying herself as it searched the internet. After ten minutes she still hadn't found any news that could relate to Turner, but if whoever took him didn't want him found . . . She mustn't think of that and she got dressed, her insides trembling.

Kerry had set the table for breakfast and the aroma of fresh coffee filled the kitchen. On seeing Antonia, she frowned. 'Smile,' she mouthed, indicating Nadimah and Hakim tucking into bowls of cereal.

Never having to be sociable at breakfast – Eleanor shared her disposition and they'd often sat in silence – she found this a strain. Motherhood obviously wasn't for her, unlike Kerry, who embraced the role. She produced a smile, receiving a tentative response from Hakim. Although quiet, Nadimah seemed happier today, but the sadness wasn't far beneath the surface, especially when she looked at her brother. Antonia had to find out how Geoff Stokes was getting on with Sabirah's case.

'Russell rang while you were in the shower,' Kerry said.

'Why didn't you tell me?' Antonia demanded.

Kerry glanced at the children. 'He said he'd meet you for brunch later, about eleven, and bring your laptop.' She gave her the name of a restaurant in Covent Garden.

'Did he say anything about Alan?'

'No, sorry.'

Trepidation made Antonia light-headed.

'Who's Russell?' Hakim said.

'A friend of Antonia.' Kerry winked at him.

'Like her boyfriend?'

'We-elll . . .'

'No!' Antonia snapped. 'Just someone who's helping me.' She drained her coffee. 'I'd better go.'

'Are we going to the zoo?' Anticipation lit up Hakim's face.

Kerry looked at Antonia, who shook her head once. 'Antonia can't come, but we're going.'

Hakim's head dropped in disappointment and he continued eating his cereal. Antonia ruffled his hair and said goodbye. As she rode down in the lift, a sense of loss settled on her. She'd visit Eleanor and check up on her.

At the hospital entrance, she checked behind her, convinced someone was watching. She shook herself, determined not to let paranoia return to her life, and went through the doors. Then she saw him and stopped dead: one of the men who'd chased her on the Tube, sitting on a bench opposite the main entrance. He spoke to someone out of her sight. A second man wearing similar clothes appeared, but she didn't recognise him.

She retreated out of the building, but decided those bastards weren't going to prevent her seeing Eleanor. Checking they hadn't followed her out, she headed for the accident and emergency entrance. An ambulance crew wheeled a stretcher towards the doors and Antonia strode ahead of them, holding the doors open. The

243

paramedics thanked her and, keeping alert, she followed the signs for Eleanor's ward.

Antonia recognised the nurse on duty. 'Hello, Sister, has there been any improvement?'

'She's suffered a minor setback but we've arrested—'

'She's worse?'

'You mustn't worry too much, she's bound to have bad days.'

Filled with apprehension, she rushed to Eleanor's room. Her face seemed thinner even than last time, a tiny skull surrounded by a halo of wispy grey hair. With an empty sensation in her guts, Antonia reached for a hand that felt brittle and light, like the bones were hollow. Her own troubles forgotten, she sat with the woman who'd been part of her life for the last nine years. The fact Eleanor might not survive hadn't sunk in until now. She'd worried her injuries might diminish the old lady, but if she deteriorated any further, she feared they might have to consider switching off the life-support system.

As she passed the lifts, one opened. The two men from the main entrance stood in the doorway. They looked as surprised as she was. She reacted first and punched the nearest one. He reeled away with a grunt and the back of his head smacked into his companion's face with a sickening *thunk*. The doors swished closed as Antonia ran for the stairs.

The scruffy shop smelt of dust and stale tobacco and Chapman waited for the owner to descend the wooden stepladder with a box from a top shelf, crammed, like those below, with electronic gadgets. The owner blew on the box, dislodging a small cloud of dust, and passed it to Chapman before retrieving a cellophane envelope from under the counter.

'SIM cards in here with credit,' he said. 'The phones don't have internet or GPS, like you asked.' He produced a bulky envelope. 'Spare batteries, fully charged.'

'Thanks.' Chapman counted out the pile of notes and left.

In the car, he assembled a phone and punched in Sanchez's number.

'Hello, who's this?'

'Alice, it's Russell, sorry to disturb you on a Saturday.'

'No problem, Sarge. I'm in the office, a bit of a flap—'

'What's happened?' Had they kept the shooting out of the news?

'Arkady Demchuk attacked Turner, the guy from The Electric Investigator.'

'How is he?'

'A few stitches and a headache, but he's home.'

Chapman exhaled in relief. At least the NSA weren't holding him. 'I need a favour. Can I get information emailed to you—'

'At work?'

'Can you put it on a memory stick?'

Sanchez hesitated. 'I don't think I've got—'

'There's a couple in my desk. Top right drawer, use either.'

The sounds of her searching carried over the airways. 'What's on the email?'

He'd contemplated telling her but decided she was better off not knowing. 'A zipped file, but it's nothing dodgy.'

'Why can't they send it to you?'

'It's from Traffic. I thought I saw someone we've been after for a while. I want to make sure it's him before I cry wolf.'

Sanchez hesitated for a few seconds before saying, 'Okay, I'll do it. How do I get the stick to you?'

He told her where to meet him, then rang the company that monitored the traffic cameras. After introducing himself he gave the crime number for the attack on the old woman and the registration of the van.

'So, Sergeant, what dates do you want the footage for?'

'Last four weeks please?'

'You can have a period no greater than seven days.'

'Okay, a week starting on Tuesday fifteenth.' It would cover the days he wanted. 'And can you email it to my assistant? My mailbox is full.'

He ended the call and the images of him shooting the two men flashed through his mind. His hands still trembled at the thought of what he'd done. Whoever had instigated the attack had covered their tracks. The fact that nobody he'd spoken to this morning knew of a shooting confirmed they'd done a good job. A cover-up that big needed a lot of clout and they hadn't done it to spare him and Antonia. He doubted they'd give up, and worried about her. But now he'd shot two of them, they'd also come after him.

Antonia peered out of the rear window of the cab. She'd already changed cabs twice since escaping from the hospital. Having got the others to take her to a shopping centre then Euston station, she hoped she'd have lost any tails. She tapped on the partition and redirected the driver to the office. Once she'd paid him she had only twenty pounds left, but she'd borrow from petty cash.

Two men in white overalls and carrying aluminium cases came out of the office as she crossed the pavement. Her muscles tensed, but she recognised the logo on their pockets. Something must have happened to the computers. She let herself in and Miles greeted her.

'What did ICS want?' she said.

'Alan called them—'

'He's in?' She headed for Turner's office, eager to find out what had happened last night.

'Alan's . . . I'll let him tell you, but prepare yourself.'

Antonia knocked on Turner's door and rushed in. A large plaster covered his left cheek, the flesh round it discoloured. The dark shadows under his eyes told of his exhaustion and she walked round the desk to give him a hug.

He coughed and they broke apart. 'Well, that was a pleasant surprise.'

'What happened to your voice?'

She listened with growing concern as he brought her up to date. If she'd reported Arkady, he might not have attacked Turner. But she couldn't allow herself to think like that. 'What did the police say?'

'They already wanted him for the attack on Eleanor, so they've upped the priority.'

'I've just been to see her.'

'How is she this morning?'

'She looked empty, like she'd given up.'

'I'm sure she's still fighting.'

'I hope so, Alan.'

After a short silence Turner said, 'I've got news about your friend. Geoff Stokes told me her kids have disappeared. An uncle's taken them.'

'At least they're safe,' she said, unable to look at him. 'Any news on her?'

'Nothing concrete, but Stokes said there were hopeful noises, whatever that means.'

Disappointment vied with irritation at the vagaries of the legal system. 'What were ICS doing here?'

'I got them to sweep the offices and check the computers. We had a cyberattack.'

'Is the memory stick affected?' She remembered the warning not to use it online.

'It was in my pocket when I fell. It must have dropped out. Unless . . .'

'Unless what?'

His eyes flicked sideways. 'The NSA emptied my pockets when they arrested me.'

'You must have signed for anything they took off you.'

'I wasn't exactly compos mentis, sorry!'

A moment of panic passed. Compared to what had happened since, having illegal access to the security camera system wasn't worth worrying about. 'Don't worry, Chapman's getting me a copy. What did ICS say?'

'The computers were okay. Although someone had carried out a determined assault on mine, the firewall blocked them. Twenty grand a year well spent. Oh, and they found a camera by the front door.'

'That explains—' He didn't know about the shootings. But it explained how they knew someone was in the offices. She'd have to apologise to Chapman.

'Explains what?'

'I just had a bad feeling about those men.'

'The funny thing is, the guys who found it said NSA didn't use that make of camera.'

'You're sure the blokes were NSA?' she said, thinking about the one who'd chased her.

'Positive. I scanned their ID and it all checked out.'

But were they doing GRM's bidding?

Turner winced and touched the plaster.

'Will you be okay staying at your place tonight?' she said, wondering if they could fit him in at the flat.

'I've got bodyguards. They're arranging a "safe house".' He made quotation marks. 'A company called—'

'Sorry to disturb you, Alan.' Miles appeared in the doorway. 'Someone from Victims of Crime . . .'

Antonia checked the time. She needed to go, and borrowing four hundred pounds from Turner, she gave him another hug and left. At least he'd be safe. But the feeling of loss returned as she made her way to meet Chapman.

CHAPTER 19

Covent Garden Tube station thronged with tourists in London for the weekend. The security guard took an age examining Antonia's ID and searching her backpack, but she resisted the urge to say something. He'd only find a pretext to delay her further. She scanned the passengers behind her. If anyone was following her they'd stand out. When he'd finished, she zipped up the bag and hurried out of the station. In front of her stood the Nags Head and she turned right. The restaurant Chapman had suggested had good reviews and she was looking forward to a good meal.

He waited outside, examining his watch. 'Where the hell have you—'

'Why didn't you get a table?'

'We're not eating here.' He set off, leading her to his car, parked in a loading bay. A sign in the windscreen stated, 'Police on duty'. He slipped it into the glove compartment as he started the engine.

'I thought you were reporting it stolen?'

'I was going to, but I've other plans.'

'Where are we going?' Antonia said as she fastened her seatbelt.

'To see a friend.'

When he didn't elaborate she said, 'Are you going to tell me why?'

'It's best if you don't know.'

Curiosity overcame her irritation. 'It'd better be worth it.'

Half an hour later they'd made innumerable changes of direction and Chapman slowed before turning into a narrow side street.

'Is this it?' she said, studying the scruffy buildings lining the lane.

'Just a bit further.'

Her irritation needed little rekindling, but she kept it in check. A few more twists and turns down ever more potholed roads brought them to an industrial unit in a railway arch. The sign above the graffiti-covered roller shutter read 'Garage'. Chapman got out, and the gate at the side of the shutter opened. A small bald man in grease-stained overalls came out, giving Chapman a welcoming smile.

Chapman told her to wait and followed the man. She thumped the dashboard and the glove compartment fell open. A phone sat amongst the clutter and her pent-up anger exploded. She snatched it up, clambered out of the car and headed for the gate. It opened before she reached it and Chapman came out.

'What the hell are you playing at, you idiot,' she said, shoving the phone at him. 'Don't you learn—'

'Hold your horses.' Chapman's cheeks reddened. 'It's a pay-as-you-go with no GPS. They can only track you if you make a call.'

They stared at each other and the anger drained from Antonia. *You're not being fair, girl.* Behind Chapman, the roller shutter rose and the overall-clad man watched them, an amused grin playing across his features.

'Come on, let's eat. And bring the laptop,' Chapman said, holding out his hand for the phone. 'Right, Sammy, I'll see you in an hour.'

She handed it over and collected the backpack as Sammy slid the driver's seat forward. Chapman set off for the far end of the row of arches where a cafe sign hung. This wasn't what she'd pictured when he'd offered brunch, but too embarrassed to argue, she followed.

The aroma of frying bacon made her mouth water as she scanned the room. Formica-topped tables surrounded by rickety chairs with tubular chromed legs filled the front of the space. A stainless-steel counter with a large coffee maker on one end divided the front from the cooking area, where a skinny man wearing a spotless white apron tended a huge industrial cooker and grill. An opaque layer of condensation rendered the red-checked curtains covering the lower part of the windows redundant.

'You set the laptop up while I order,' he said. 'What do you want?'

'Where's the menu?'

He pointed at a blackboard with a dozen dishes chalked on it hanging off the opposite wall. Every meal included chips. 'I'm having the full English,' he said, 'with chips and extra bubble.'

She nodded. She could return to a sensible diet once this was over. He held two fingers up to the chef and headed for the counter. She started the computer, surprised the caff had high-speed Wi-Fi. Chapman joined her and placed two mugs of tea on the table before sliding into the chair opposite.

'There's obviously something dodgy going on with your mechanic friend,' she said. 'But why did you want me to come?'

He placed a memory stick in front of her. 'The footage of the van you requested.'

'Thanks.' After going offline, she plugged it in and checked the contents, identical to the data Turner had lost. 'It will take a few hours to go through it—'

'Take your time.'

'Why couldn't you drop it off?'

'Let's say I've been thinking about your theory and I want to see your research notes,' he said, making it sound a challenge.

She opened a spreadsheet she'd created to collate the information on the disappearance of Monika and the other two women, and angled the screen so he could see.

He craned his neck and read. 'Very impressive, but what is it?'

'These are the three women who've disappeared. Two worked at GRM—'

The chef cleared his throat and the smell of cooked bacon filled the air. She pushed the laptop aside so he could deposit two huge oval plates piled high with steaming food in front of them. Chapman turned the screen so he could read whilst he ate and she squeezed a dollop of brown sauce on the corner of her plate before attacking the mountain of food.

Chapman swallowed the last of his egg and pointed at two columns on the spreadsheet. 'What are these dates?'

'The first column is for the dates they disappeared.'

'And this one?'

'The dates they found the bodies.'

'But you've only filled in one date. Next to Sofie Stoltz.'

'Apart from the one you're investigating, Aida Rizk, hers is the only body they've found so far.'

'So, the other two are just missing? Do you know how many young women go—'

'Yes, I do. Do you want to listen, or . . .'

He held up his hands before returning his attention to the screen. 'Who's Latif?'

'He's a private investigator looking into GRM.'

'I meant, why is he on here?'

'He's in prison for killing Sofie Stoltz.'

'Let's rewind here. You have two women missing and, if you include Aida Rizk, two dead. Their killers are in prison or dead—'

'What if they didn't kill her?'

'I don't know about Latif, but we've found conclusive evidence against Murray, Rizk's killer.'

'I think the killer framed them.'

'And your evidence?'

Antonia hesitated. Her theory wobbled here. 'That's your job.'

Chapman grinned. 'I thought you'd say that.' He sipped the dregs of his tea. 'Did Turner say what made him go to the garage?'

'What garage?'

'He found Murray's body in a tiny apartment at the back of a garage.'

'Alan?' This didn't make sense. 'He never said. Anyway, he doesn't know Murray.'

'Murray worked for GRM and was feeding Turner information. Didn't you know?'

'Oh my God. Alan said he had a source.' Her mind raced, putting pieces into place.

'Shit!' He slapped the table, making the crockery jump. 'I bet Murray had those papers to give to—'

The chef came over and scowled at Chapman before removing the empty dishes.

Once he'd left, Chapman continued, 'I found papers hidden, well hidden, where we found Murray's body. They didn't make much sense to me, but if he'd given Turner other information, I bet he could work them out.'

'Have you got them? I recovered documents from GRM which I couldn't decipher. Maybe if we put them together . . .'

'The NSA took them.'

Blast. They always seemed one step ahead. 'They put a camera in the office. That's how they knew we were there.'

Chapman slammed his fist on the table.

Antonia checked the rear of the cafe, but the chef ignored them. 'Thought you'd be relieved it wasn't your fault—'

'I *knew* it wasn't.' He ran his fingers through his hair.

Antonia wanted to lift his spirits. 'Shall we go? If we can find the van's destination . . .'

'Yeah.' Chapman sounded resigned and pushed his chair away. 'Let's get those documents. I can remember some of what was on the ones I found, so we might make sense of them.'

Antonia waited by the door as Chapman paid, exchanging a joke with the chef, who studied her. Did he think she was *with* Chapman? She left, not bothering to hold the door open. Chapman trotted to catch up with her.

'I meant to ask you—'

'What?'

'I found out about Mishkin—'

A phone rang and she took a moment to realise it was coming from her pocket. 'It's a pay-as-you-go with no GPS,' she said in response to Chapman's raised eyebrows. Only one person knew the number. 'Kerry?'

'Antonia, you have to come,' Kerry whispered. 'Some men were waiting by the car—'

'Is it Arkady?'

'I'm not sure.'

Antonia didn't think Arkady had the resources to track Kerry's car, and anyway, his mates were dead, so he'd be on his own. 'Where are you?'

Kerry gave Antonia the address. 'We'd gone for a burger so I've taken the kids back into the restaurant, but it's closing soon.'

'Wait there, we'll come and get you.' She ended the call. 'Someone has followed Kerry,' she said to Chapman. 'She's trapped in a restaurant.'

'Who—'

'Does it matter?' Fear made Antonia dizzy as she ran towards the garage. Should she call the police? What could she tell them? Could she trust them?

◆ ◆ ◆

Chapman pushed the car but kept to a speed that wouldn't get them stopped. He wasn't worried about cameras, not with what Sammy had fitted. He'd be in the shit if they caught him, but so what, he still had the Fort in the boot. Stupid, but he might need a gun and until he got another, he'd have to keep it. Losing his job would be the least of his worries, but he couldn't allow himself to dwell on it. *Let's get to the end and then deal with the fallout.* They passed a bank of traffic cameras.

Antonia said, 'They must have tracked Kerry's car and they might have yours—'

'Sammy fitted new plates and a cloaking device.'

'That's illegal.'

'So is shooting people,' he snapped.

Antonia blinked. 'Yes. Sorry.' *Well done, why don't you think before you speak?*

They covered the last mile in silence. Chapman didn't know this part of town and said, 'Could you get the *A–Z*? It should be in the door.'

'You've got satnav.' She reached forward to switch it on.

'Sammy disconnected it. They work by GPS.'

She snatched her hand away as if scalded and he could have sworn she blushed.

With her directing, they drove down a street parallel to the one they wanted and pulled up. 'Ask Kerry if she knows where they're parked. Also ask her if she can find out if there's a rear entrance, and if so, where it comes out.'

Antonia exchanged terse words with Kerry. 'She says it's a big van-like thing opposite the restaurant, about eighty metres away. She's asking the owner about the exit, he wants to throw them out and close— Yeah, okay, so it goes into the courtyard?' Antonia listened then covered the mouthpiece. 'What do you want her to do?'

'Wait, but be ready to leave by the back.'

Antonia ended the call and chewed her bottom lip. 'What now?'

Chapman outlined his plan – simple but, he hoped, effective. He approached the restaurant and let Antonia out a hundred metres from it. Antonia covered half the distance to the entrance and he spotted the people carrier just as two men got out and crossed the road.

Antonia reached the door of the restaurant and pulled it before rapping on the glass. 'Come on, let her in,' Chapman muttered. The door opened with the men still fifty metres away, and she disappeared. *Time to go.* He gunned the engine and accelerated, passing the restaurant with the two men banging on the door. Just before he reached their vehicle, it swung out into his path.

'Shit!' The driver must have spotted him. But if he swerved to avoid him he'd hit the parked cars across the road. He held his line and braced himself for the impact. Chapman's head snapped forward when it came, but the seatbelt stopped him before he hit the steering wheel. Fortunately he didn't have airbags. Sharp pain spread from his chest where the belt hit him and suffused his neck. The slower-moving people carrier whipped away towards the pavement and crunched into the car in front of it, setting off an alarm. His car crossed the white line before he regained control of it. The engine juddered, but to his relief, didn't die.

Chapman continued to the next junction. Behind him the men ran from the restaurant towards their car. He screeched round the corner, ignoring the engine lights flashing on the dash. He eased the car into a cobbled courtyard and scanned the doors opening on to it. The restaurant's should be near the far end. Movement at a door, then Antonia charged out, followed by three smaller figures. He drew alongside them. Antonia bundled Kerry and the two children into the back, then leapt into the passenger seat.

He threw the car into reverse. More warning lights came on and the car shuddered. *Don't die on me now.* The engine coughed, then caught – but then a car screeched into the mouth of the court-yard and stopped, blocking the exit. The people carrier.

Two men got out and advanced towards them. One of the children in the back sobbed.

CHAPTER 20

The text on his screen became blurred and Turner closed his eyes as the headache that had accompanied him all day intensified. He should go home and get a good night's sleep. After warning his guards he was coming out, he packed up his laptop.

Nigel Harrison waited outside a people carrier with the rear door open and helped Turner into it. The driver spoke to a tall dark-haired man through the open window. The man's voice rasped, like he smoked tar. Turner recognised it but before he could identify the speaker Nigel slammed the door. Turner realised with a start where he'd heard the voice. It belonged to one of the men who'd grabbed him outside the house.

What had he got himself mixed up in? The engine fired and the car pulled out. Panic paralysed him and he sat rigid, oblivious to his surroundings. The car had stopped for several moments before he realised they'd parked near his house. *What are we doing here?*

'Do you want to collect clothes for a few days?' Nigel said.

'Oh, right.' Turner fumbled for the door handle but Nigel jumped out and opened it.

He collected his things in a trance and contemplated making a run for it, but a solicitous Nigel followed him everywhere. They returned to the car, Nigel carrying the weekend bag. Unfamiliar streets rushed past and Turner stared out of the window. Where were they taking him? An hour later, the car slowed and pulled into a quiet road lined with detached bungalows set back from the road. They pulled up alongside one before reversing up the drive.

'A bungalow?' Turner said, feeling foolish. 'Shouldn't we be above the ground floor?'

'Don't worry sir, we *have* done this before,' Nigel said, smiling. 'If anyone comes near, we'll know about it.'

Nigel checked the house then led Turner into it. Solid bars protected the front windows. Turner hesitated, seeing a prison, not a refuge. In the hallway Nigel keyed a code into a sophisticated alarm panel with a large screen above it. The place smelt musty and the décor whispered show-home, bland and characterless.

They showed him to a bedroom with an en-suite shower and, above the double bed, a big red alarm button. He left his bag just inside the door and, begging tiredness, closed it and lay on top of the bed. Jumbled thoughts battled in his mind. Concern for Eleanor competed with worries as to whether he could trust his bodyguards. Was he mistaken about the man who'd been talking to the driver? He'd heard 'The Smoker' say a few words. The last time he thought he'd heard that voice, he'd been lying in the back of the people carrier, groggy, while the man sat in the front. He couldn't even remember his hair colour.

Someone passed the door to the room and he tensed, but they carried on. He had to get out of here and he examined the barred window. There must be a way to get away from these two. Although he'd left his phone in the office at Nigel's suggestion, he'd brought a cheap disposable, which he'd slipped into his bag without his guards knowing. But who to call? The police. And say what? 'I've hired security guards but they're linked to the NSA.' So what? He didn't even know his location. The headache returned and he retrieved a packet of painkillers from his bag.

He couldn't find a glass and stepped out into the corridor, unsure of where to find the kitchen. A voice came from behind a half-open door on his right, and he listened.

'They've found the kids,' the other guard was saying. 'Denton must be pleased. Let me know if we can knock this on the head.' He ended the call.

Turner froze. What did the exchange mean? What kids? Did they mean Sabirah's kids? But why would they be looking for them? Someone moved behind the door, coming towards it. Turner rushed to his room and made a show of stepping out of it, coughing as he did so. The guard stepped into the corridor and glared at Turner.

'Where's the kitchen?' Turner said, trying to sound natural.

'I'll show you.' He brushed past Turner and led him into a stark kitchen with oak-effect units and grey worktops.

'Where's Nigel?'

'Out,' the guard said, scowling, then seemed to remember his role. 'He's checking the outer perimeter, shouldn't be long. Can I make you a drink?'

'I need a glass of water, to take these . . .' Turner brandished the painkillers.

The man produced a glass from a cupboard and filled it from the tap. An idea of how he could both see Eleanor and shake off his guards came to him.

Turner took the tablets, then said, 'I need to go to the hospital.'

'We'll get a doctor to come here, it's safer.'

'It's not for me. I want to visit somebody, my aunt.' Why would it be safer to bring another person to the hide-out?

'Not a good idea.'

'Why not? I am free to go, aren't I?'

The guard's phone beeped and the doorbell rang three times before the front door opened and Nigel appeared. 'Feeling better?' he said.

'I want to visit my aunt in hospital.'

Nigel exchanged a look with his colleague. 'Okay. Which one?'

Turner told him and collected his jacket, confused by the differing attitudes of the two men. On his return, he found them engaged in a whispered argument in the far corner of the room, ending it when they noticed him.

'Ready to go then,' Nigel said, smiling.

They travelled to the hospital in silence, the unresolved tension between the two security men like a fog in the vehicle. Turner concentrated on his surroundings. What did the half of the telephone conversation he'd heard mean? He worried they weren't taking him to the hospital until he saw the buildings. Outside the main entrance he got out and Nigel joined him.

'I'll be a while,' Turner said.

'That's all right, sir. We have to wait for you.'

'I'll be quite safe in there.'

'I'm here to make sure.'

Turner set off for the ICU, frustration making him hot. The back of his neck itched as Nigel's footsteps echoed behind him. How the hell could he get rid of him without arousing his suspicion? He almost walked past the unit and stopped so suddenly Nigel stepped on his heels, apologising.

'Nigel, I know you're just doing your job, but I'd rather have some privacy.'

'Sure, I'll wait out here.'

Had he made a mistake and was Nigel just a conscientious security guard? The nurse on duty did a double-take, studying his bandaged cheek.

'I'm here to see Eleanor Curtis,' he said.

The nurse smiled. 'I've got good news for you then. She's regained consciousness.'

Turner forgot his own troubles and rushed to Eleanor's room. He first thought nothing had changed, but he spoke and her eyelids fluttered open. A tired smile transformed her strained features and her lips moved. He put his ear next to her and she whispered a greeting, her breath fluttering against his cheek. Too weak to speak for long, she closed her eyes and lay back as he held her hand.

Within a few minutes, the need to escape from Nigel and his sidekick made him restless. Eleanor's steady breathing and slow heartbeat confirmed she'd fallen asleep and, apologising to her, he left. He peered through the door on to the corridor but saw nobody. It didn't mean Nigel wasn't out there.

Turner returned to the nurse's station and asked, 'Is there another way out?'

She looked at him quizzically.

'Please, there's someone I don't want to see.'

She led him to an emergency exit at the back of the unit and, thanking her, he set off down the stairs, listening for sounds of pursuit. At the bottom he stepped into a corridor. On his left, he saw the main entrance through two sets of doors, then the taxi rank. People filled the entrance lobby, most moving with purpose, and he couldn't see either of his minders. Insides churning, he darted forward, keeping his head down until he reached the exit where the taxis waited.

He cursed when he saw the empty taxi rank, and scanned the road. A pair of headlights came into view. He held his breath until he saw the light on the roof and stuck out a hand.

'There you are, Mr Turner.' Nigel's voice made his heart lurch.

◆ ◆ ◆

'It's a dead end,' Chapman said, peering at the corner of the courtyard Antonia wanted him to drive into.

'Just do it!' Antonia shouted, checking behind them.

The men were now thirty metres away, the automatics in their hands visible. Shots would attract attention but they wouldn't hesitate to fire if he drove at them. He floored the accelerator and steered away. The courtyard turned through ninety degrees and the end wall loomed. His foot hovered over the brake as he passed a row of wheelie bins on his right and then an archway.

'There!' Antonia shouted.

The car juddered as he turned and braked, the rear wheels sliding on slippery cobbles. He steered through the opening, turning left on to the road. The men ran after them, waving their arms but growing smaller in the mirror. 'Up yours!' he shouted, exhilaration making him light-headed. Antonia grinned and punched the air. He glanced at the rear seat where Kerry held the two sobbing children, her hunted manner making him embarrassed at his reaction.

'Thanks,' he said to Antonia.

'I had the map.'

At the apartment, Kerry disappeared with the children and he sat in the kitchen with Antonia. The sense of panic that had infused him since he'd shot the men made thinking impossible. He stared into the glass of whisky. How could he get out of this jam? If Mishkin was behind this he needed to take him down, although even if he did, he couldn't imagine Sentinel would forget about him shooting two of their men.

'Do you want to collect the papers from the safe?' Antonia said.

He'd forgotten about them. 'Yeah, sure, I'll finish this and we'll go.'

He studied Antonia. Despite her tiredness, she wore a determined expression. He needed her help, but unsure how to broach the question of Mishkin, he sipped the whisky and smiled. Her expression didn't change; not unfriendly, but calculating.

Well, here goes. 'I spoke to Mishkin.'

Antonia looked uncomfortable. 'And?'

He pressed on. 'You might remember him as Videk.'

'Larry Videk!' Kerry cried out from the door.

Bugger! When did you return? 'Do you know him?'

'I never met him. Is Mishkin really Videk?' Kerry stepped into the room.

'Mishkin's his mother's maiden name. He changed his name eight years ago.'

'I'm not surprised, after what happened.' Kerry stared at Antonia.

'What happened between you?' he asked Antonia.

Antonia eyes clouded, but she didn't reply for a few seconds. 'Nothing. Mishkin caught me on the twenty-seventh floor—'

'I meant at the Towers children's home.'

She leapt out of her chair, grabbed his collar and thrust her face into his, moving so fast he didn't have time to react. 'Nothing happened.'

Chapman pushed Antonia's hands away. 'I'm sorry to drag up old memories, but you *did* make a complaint about him.'

Releasing his jacket, she shook herself and left the room. Kerry started after her, but shooting him a venomous glance went instead to the sink, returning with a cloth. With trembling hands, she wiped away the splashes of whisky he'd spilt on the table.

'Videk, or Mishkin if he's calling himself that, is at GRM?' she asked.

'Head of security. You knew about . . . what happened between him and Antonia?'

Kerry's gaze stayed on the table. 'Everyone knew.' She took a shuddering breath. 'I told the people running the care home about it but they accused me of lying, making up malicious lies.' She returned the cloth to the sink and spoke over her shoulder. 'Antonia put up with it, said she'd been through worse. *I* persuaded her to complain to the police, told her they'd put him away, but she told them he'd killed my sister—'

'Enya?'

'I think he must have tried it with her, but she ran off. I don't know why Antonia said he'd killed her, but they decided she must be lying and dropped the case. It devastated her. She hasn't spoken about it since.'

'Things have changed. I'll help her.'

'She won't go through it again.'

'So, Mishkin gets away with it.' Chapman recognised that some of his anger reflected his disappointment.

'Men like him always do.' She returned to the table. 'I appreciate you want to help, but . . .'

'What about Enya, did you ever hear from her?'

'She must have got far away and made a new life for herself. I wouldn't have wanted to remember anything about those days if I'd escaped.' Tears welled, but Kerry kept them under control.

'Sure.' Experience told him Enya was probably in a hole in the ground somewhere, but no point in destroying Kerry's fantasy. He leant on the table and rose, limbs heavy. 'If Antonia changes her mind.' He handed Kerry a card.

'She won't, but thanks.'

Antonia appeared in the doorway, eyes red but exuding an air of controlled anger. 'Shall we get those documents?'

'Are you sure you're—'

She spun on her heel and strode to the exit, her rage almost palpable. What had he unleashed?

◆ ◆ ◆

The people carrier slowed and pulled into a road Turner now recognized. With its detached thirties bungalows, it looked like a typical suburban street. Now he knew where he was going, he made a note of the name. Nigel made his usual checks before returning to the car and opening the side door. Turner followed him, his disappointment at not shaking them off at the hospital fading as he planned his escape. Nigel had appeared to believe his story of suffering a dizzy spell and forgetting he'd got a lift. His bruised and bandaged face doubtless helped convince him.

'Do you want something to eat?' Nigel said. 'I'm not much of a chef but the freezer's well stocked.'

Turner panicked. He needed to get them out of the kitchen. 'Shall we get a takeaway?'

'Whatever, there's quite a few that deliver.'

If one of them left the house, his plan had a better chance of success. 'I fancy a curry. Is there a dosa house?'

Nigel looked at him blankly.

'It's gluten-free. There's a place in Tottenham.'

'Right . . . We'll see about it.'

Great, the driver would be gone for ages. 'Thanks, you won't regret it. I need to take another tablet.' He fingered the bandage on his cheek.

'I'll get you water—'

Nigel's phone rang and Turner rushed into the kitchen. After pouring water into a glass he rummaged through the drawers nearest the cooker.

'You all right?'

The driver! He had to think. 'I wanted a corkscrew. Nigel suggested a takeaway and I fancied wine.'

'You find one?' The driver's manner suggested he didn't believe him.

'No, I'll check the other drawer . . .' Great, he'd found what he wanted; now to get it out unnoticed. He dropped the glass and as it shattered, he pocketed the matches.

The driver swore, then fetched a dustpan.

'Sorry,' Turner said and rushed to his room, slamming the door before collapsing on the bed, bathed in sweat.

Exhilarated by his success, he retrieved the matchbox and examined it. At least a dozen matches – plenty to start a small fire. Once the alarm started, he'd run. He'd have to start it in the bathroom and let it develop. It wouldn't work if Nigel extinguished it in seconds. What would he do once he got out? Get a taxi, go to a hotel. What if no taxis came? He'd ask Miles to give him a lift. He didn't want him involved, but if Miles picked him up in a nearby street, it should be safe. Miles's mobile transferred straight to voicemail; Turner rang again with the same result.

Then Nigel knocked on the door. 'I've downloaded a menu, do you want to choose?'

Turner shoved the phone under the pillow. 'Sure, come in.' He chose something, not caring what, but remembered the wine. 'Who's going?'

'Me,' Nigel said. 'I won't be long.'

Turner made sure the door was shut and sat on the bed, disappointed, but it should work regardless of who stayed. Miles still didn't answer, so he rang the office.

'Yes, what is it?'

'Antonia?'

'Alan, I thought you were Chapman. What do you want?' She sounded stressed.

Containing his curiosity about why she was at the office, he told her, explaining his plan.

'Who did you say provided the security guys?'

'Sentinel.' Did she gasp? No, he must have imagined it. 'ICS recommended them.'

268

Antonia hesitated for a few moments then said, 'Don't start the fire. We'll create a diversion when we arrive and get him out of the house.'

He lay back and placed the phone on his chest. The thought that Antonia and Chapman were on the way improved his mood. He'd soon get out of there. The front door shut; it must be Nigel going out, but someone spoke. Turner pressed his ear against the door.

'I hope he's getting enough for us.' The Smoker. What was he doing here?

And he wasn't alone. If they were still here when Antonia arrived . . . He called her back but the phone rang out until the office voicemail kicked in. Too late; she'd left. How could he stop her?

CHAPTER 21

In Turner's office, Antonia banged the phone down and jumped to her feet. She'd expected the call to be from Chapman, telling her to get out. Her relief had evaporated as she listened to Turner explain his situation. Why hadn't she warned him about Sentinel? She picked up the papers she'd retrieved from the safe and charged out of the office, remembering to set the alarm before she slammed the door. The telephone rang again. She hesitated, but it would take a good couple of minutes to open up and answer it. Probably a sales call from the other side of the world, and Turner didn't have long before the second guard returned.

Chapman, slumped in his seat with his eyes shut, sat up as she approached. 'Did you get the papers?' he said as she opened the passenger door.

'We need to go, Alan's in trouble.' She threw herself into the seat and shoved the documents into the glove compartment.

Chapman started the car. 'What's happened?'

She told him of Turner's predicament and where the men from Sentinel had taken him as she searched for their destination in the atlas.

Chapman did a U-turn. 'What the hell's he doing hiring them?'

'How was he supposed to know?'

She resisted the urge to tell Chapman to hurry. Images triggered by Chapman's mention of the name Videk flashed through her mind, getting more vivid and persistent each time they returned. Concern for Turner and concentrating on what might happen when they found him helped keep them at bay. They reached the road where they'd find the safe house.

'Thirty-two, on my right,' Chapman said. 'There they are.' He pointed at a black people carrier parked at the kerb fifty metres ahead.

Blast! The one who'd gone for the takeaway must have returned. It still could work. 'Have you got a knife?' she said. 'If we slash the tyres, they can't follow us.'

'How will we get him out?'

'If you smash the windows, the alarm will go off and they should come out—'

'Not both of them.'

'The other one's supposed to be out. I'll have to overpower him.'

'You're a strong girl but these are trained bodyguards. I'll do it.'

'I can't drive.' Chapman was probably more powerful than her, but he didn't have the fitness to take on a trained bodyguard and she also hoped being a woman would give her an edge.

Chapman studied her for a few seconds before sighing and reaching under his seat. 'Take this. Press this button and it extends. Hit him hard before he can react. Don't mess about.'

'Thanks.' She took the retractable baton and got out, fear and apprehension making her hands tremble.

Chapman followed and waited by the people carrier. After checking around, he jabbed at the tyres and gave her the thumbs-up. With the baton held beside her leg, she made her way towards the bungalow. A bare expanse of block paving separated the house from the pavement. If they kept watch, they couldn't miss her. The front door was near the left corner and next to it, alongside the end wall, a carport. Why hadn't they taken the car on to the drive? Maybe they wanted a clear field of view. Feeling exposed, she made herself stroll, suppressing the urge to run. Her pulse hammered in her ears. She reached the door without triggering an alarm and stepped into the carport.

She could just see the back of the people carrier and, preparing herself, she extended the baton. The vehicle emitted an ear-splitting shriek and the hazard lights flashed. She scrunched against the wall. Once the first one came out, she'd charge in.

◆ ◆ ◆

Turner sat on the edge of the bed staring at the phone, unable to decide if he should phone the police. The wail of a car alarm cut into his thoughts and confused him for a few moments, then he realised what it meant. Antonia had told him *not* to create a diversion, but she didn't know about the extra men in the house. If he could distract even one, it would even the odds.

He rushed into the bathroom and, picking up the matchbox, struck the match he'd left on top. The head exploded in a shower of sparks before flying off, leaving him holding a broken stump. He cursed, and with trembling fingers retrieved another match. This one flared into life. He applied it to the mound of screwed-up toilet paper in the bin. Blue flames edged in yellow climbed up the sides of the crumpled sheets.

From outside the room came the sound of voices raised in anger. He pulled the door shut to stop the smoke alarm going off too early. A flickering mass filled the bin but it would soon consume the paper, so he lowered the edge of the hand towel into it. Flames leapt, blackening the fibres before getting a grip on the fabric. He let it fall into the container. The smoke thickened, making him cough, and he left, closing the door behind him.

The car alarm still shrieked, but the voices had fallen silent. He pressed his ear against the door.

◆ ◆ ◆

Raised voices came from behind the front door and Antonia gripped the baton, her palms damp. The voices quietened and after a long pause, the door opened. A man with reddish-blond hair ran down the drive, yelling. Antonia waited until he'd reached the pavement and rushed into the house.

She found the hallway empty and lowered the baton. Where was the second man? Voices came from behind a door. She crept up to it and listened.

A voice she didn't recognise said, '—bloody kids, they'll break into anything nowadays.' The speaker sounded like he smoked forty a day.

She didn't hear the reply but it must be Turner. She lowered her shoulder and charged. The door crashed open and she burst into the room. A man faced her, a pistol in his hand. She slashed down with the baton and the man cried out. A flash came from the pistol and an explosion made her ears ring.

Before she could work out if she'd been hit, a fist smashed into the side of her head. Stars sparked before her and she crashed to the floor. Instinct took over, but before she could scramble up an arm wrapped round her neck and cold metal pressed into her temple.

'Miss Conti, I presume,' The Smoker growled into her ear.

◆ ◆ ◆

Chapman had returned to his car and crouched down in the driver's seat. Curtains twitched in the bungalow opposite, then a man appeared from the drive where Antonia had disappeared. The man slowed and studied the people carrier, examining the broken front windows before silencing the alarm. Something about the way he behaved made Chapman suspicious, but he couldn't work out why.

The curtains opposite closed, then it came to Chapman: the man was acting, and not very well. He obviously recognised this as a distraction and whoever remained inside would be waiting for Antonia. Chapman needed to warn her. The man finished his act and returned to the house. Chapman leapt out of the car and recovered the automatic.

The man reached the door and Chapman ran up the drive. A crack like a pistol shot came from the house and the man disappeared through the front door, slamming it behind him.

The stench of stale tobacco made Antonia gag as her captor dragged her upright. Her right palm stung but she no longer held the baton. She must have dropped it, but couldn't see it. The man she'd hit bent down to pick an automatic off the floor with his left hand, cradling his right wrist. He winced, glowering at Antonia. She hoped it really hurt.

'The fucking bitch has broken it,' he said in a pronounced estuary accent.

'The *fucking bitch* will break the other one if you come near me,' she said.

Estuary-Man made a threatening gesture, but The Smoker stopped him and said, 'You can discuss it with her later.'

Antonia guessed she'd not enjoy the discussion. The front door slammed and for a fleeting second she thought Chapman had arrived.

'You get her?' a new voice said, dashing her hopes.

'Who's out there?' The Smoker demanded.

'Guy about forty, five ten, brown hair, needs a shave and a haircut—'

'Chapman.' The Smoker spat the name out. 'We want him.'

He dragged Antonia round, pushing her into the hallway but keeping the gun against her skull. A red-haired man stood by the door. So much for luring one of them out. He studied a screen by the front door showing four views of the outside, including the carport. They must have been laughing at her attempt to hide against the wall. Nauseous, Antonia realised she'd walked into a trap. A figure appeared in the centre of one screen, growing bigger, then the front door shook as someone kicked it.

'Come on, mate, put your back into it,' Red-Hair said, his accent pure East London.

'Let him kick it again, but the third time open the door and get ready to take him,' The Smoker said, screwing the pistol barrel into her scalp. 'Just in case you were thinking of warning him.'

The door shook again but didn't give. Chapman receded on the screen, then he gathered himself, wearing a determined expression. The man by the door stepped to the side and flicked the lock. Would The Smoker shoot her? If she did nothing, they'd hurt Chapman. Sweat trickled down her spine. Estuary-Man came into the hallway, the pistol in his left hand and his right arm held against his body. How well could he shoot with the wrong hand?

Chapman began his run-up. A shrill beeping noise came from behind a door on their left. The three men froze and stared at the door.

◆ ◆ ◆

Turner had waited behind the door in an agony of indecision. The sound of the shot had paralysed him until Antonia's angry voice confirmed she wasn't hurt. He wanted to charge out and rescue her but they had guns. He'd searched for a weapon. A chair sat under the window and he'd picked it up. It felt reassuringly solid, but what chance did he have against a gun? If he escaped, he could get help.

He'd pulled the curtain open but the thick bars across the window mocked him. Maybe a neighbour had heard the shot. How long would the police take to get here? He carried the chair to the door and, holding his breath, pressed his ear against the wood. A crash, then the driver had said something. Someone was trying to break in.

One of the newcomers had growled an order. The words chilled him. He needed to do something. Gripping the chair, he'd hesitated. Visions of him charging out and rescuing Antonia wouldn't coalesce, but one of him getting shot did, and he could almost feel the agony of the bullet ripping through his guts.

The smell of burning grew and the alarm beeped, dragging Turner from his trance. If he did nothing and they hurt Antonia, he couldn't live with himself. He opened the door to the en-suite and a black cloud billowed out. The beeping became a shriek. He must do it now before his courage deserted him.

A door at the side of the hallway flew open. Smoke poured out and Turner charged through the doorway shoving a chair in front of him and screaming a war cry.

Estuary-Man lifted the pistol but the chair hit him, knocking him backwards. The front door crashed open and Chapman flew in, knocking Red-Hair off his feet. The Smoker dragged Antonia's head back with his forearm and pointed his pistol at Chapman. She bit down on his sleeve, forcing teeth through the fabric into flesh. He yelled and released her. Balancing on one leg, she swung her foot back to where his knee should be. Her heel hit him with a satisfying crunch and The Smoker collapsed with a cry, hitting his head on the doorframe as he fell.

The Londoner lay face down with Chapman on top of him, smashing his skull into the floor. Turner stood over Estuary-Man with the chair held above him. Time stopped and the sounds of battle faded as Antonia watched Estuary-Man lift the pistol and point it at Turner. She strained every sinew to throw herself at the gun, knock it out of the way, but she moved as if in slow motion. The pistol flashed and her senses returned. The roar of an explosion filled her ears, then a second. Turner wore a surprised expression, then the chair fell from his hand as he crumpled.

Estuary-Man dropped the gun and raised his hands to protect himself from the falling chair. Antonia kicked him in his face, snapping his head back. She rushed to Turner, who lay on the floor face down, and turned him over. A red hole in his right cheek leaked blood and for a second he looked at her, then his eyes lost focus.

'Antonia, we have to go.' Chapman gripped her arm.

She shook him away. 'We have to get help.'

A second alarm joined the first as the smoke thickened.

'He's dead. Come on, we have to get out.'

Turner stared up at her, a smile on his lips, but lifeless.

'Come on.' Chapman pulled her to her feet.

A body on the floor moved – The Smoker, reaching for his automatic. Chapman kicked it away and stamped on the man's knee, then pushed her towards the door. Antonia allowed him to do so and stood on the drive, her legs like lead pipes joined with elastic bands. He put his arm across her shoulders and led her to his car. He helped her into the passenger seat and she slumped in it, shivering.

'Put the belt on,' he said, and started the engine.

As if in a trance she fumbled for the seatbelt. A large dark car raced past them and pulled on to the drive. The driver leapt out and ran to the house as Chapman gunned the engine and raced away. The sight of Turner falling replayed in Antonia's mind.

CHAPTER 22

Chapman finished dressing in the tiny wetroom, attempting to keep the cuffs of his trousers out of the water. He eased the door open and stepped out. Faint light leaked in round the edge of the blinds covering the two skylights illumining the bedsit. Antonia slept on in the large sofa bed. Even in sleep she appeared agitated. When he'd brought her here last night she'd veered between wanting to sleep and fight until she'd collapsed on the bed, exhausted.

The cushions he'd slept on lay scattered on the floor. He stacked them, remembering her sobbing in the night. He'd resisted the urge to comfort her, fearing a broken arm or worse if he touched her. She moaned and stirred. Time to make coffee. By the time he returned from the compact galley kitchen with two steaming mugs, Antonia was sitting.

'Didn't know how you took it,' he said, passing her a cup.

'Whichever way it comes. Thank you.' Her voice sounded thick, like she had something in her throat. She sipped the scalding liquid, grimaced and said, 'What's the time?'

'Ten.'

Antonia surveyed the large room. 'Whose place is this?'

'A friend's. Nobody else knows I use it. Do you want to get dressed and we'll go for breakfast? There's a good shower in there' – he indicated the wetroom – 'and clean towels under the sink.'

'Where are my clothes?'

'Kerry put them in that.' Her case sat in the corner of the room. 'And your laptop.'

'What did you tell her?'

'It's safer for us to stay away from her and the kids—'

'But those men tried to snatch them.'

'True, but they'd tracked her car and that's still outside the burger restaurant. They don't know about the flat, but every time we go there, there's a chance they'll spot us. Even though Sammy fitted my car with a cloaking device, it won't help if they've got eyeballs on the ground.' He'd taken an hour to get there, using the tricks he'd picked up in twenty years on the force. The car seemed to be running well, despite the damage, but he should think about getting another. 'I've told her not to go out. Reduces the chances of being spotted.'

'They won't stop, will they? They'll hunt us down.' For the first time she sounded despondent.

The same thought had crossed his mind. 'We'll find a way.'

Antonia's expression told him she believed him as much as he believed it himself. She threw the bedclothes off and trudged to the case, wearing only a long-sleeved vest and knickers.

'Can I use your laptop?' he said, looking away.

'You'll need the password.' She gave it to him and headed into the wetroom.

Chapman made the bed up, and powered up the computer, rereading the papers they'd recovered from Turner's safe, trying to make sense of the financial records while he waited. He'd not suspected the young man had it in him to take armed men on with a chair. You could never tell what people were capable of until you painted them into a corner.

The laptop beeped and he entered the password, then logged on to the building's secure Wi-Fi. Turner's shooting provided the lead story on most news channels. 'Controversial News Editor Found Shot Dead' one headline said. The report stated the NSA had questioned him in connection to 'girlfriend-killer' Benjamin Murray. It must have been them who grabbed him outside his flat. The tone of the report suggested Turner deserved what he got because of his involvement in something dodgy. It continued, saying he'd employed bodyguards but gave them the slip. The report mentioned no one else at the scene. Chapman wondered who would investigate the case. If it was someone he knew, he'd make sure they investigated Sentinel, but he'd have to give them the information without incriminating both him and Antonia. The last line of the report depressed him. Because of earlier links to national security, the NSA were in charge. Great, they'd bury the case in layers of secrecy and obfuscation.

'What do the reports say about him?' Antonia said.

He'd not heard her return. 'Not a lot. They don't mention the others at the house.'

'Let's see.' She came and stood behind him.

'Someone's pulled strings to blacken his name,' he said. 'You know what these news channels are like . . .'

She reached across and scrolled down the page. The smell of shampoo wafted off her. The story continued, mentioning that the NSA had investigated The Electric Investigator for jeopardising national security. Tears ran down her cheeks, but she said nothing.

'What Alan did took tremendous courage,' he said. 'If he hadn't done it, one or both of us would be dead.'

'Uh, huh.' Tears dripped on to the keyboard.

'We'll sue the bloody—'

She sniffed and disappeared into the bathroom. The tap ran for a long time, then she returned, her expression unreadable. 'What they've published is true. Anyway, dead men can't sue.'

'There must be something—'

'What? Everything we've done so far has made things worse.'

Chapman couldn't disagree.

◆ ◆ ◆

Antonia finished cleaning the wetroom and returned to the bedsit. Chapman had already made up the sofa bed and she tidied the room. With few items of furniture and no ornaments, apart from a vase and four generic pictures on the wall, it didn't take long. The galley kitchen took even less time. She searched for something to do, needing to keep busy. Her mind drifted. The door to the flat opened, making Antonia start. Chapman walked in and brandished a grease-stained paper bag.

'Croissants and more coffee,' he announced and disappeared into the minute kitchen.

Antonia drifted back into her daydream, thinking of Turner. She remembered their first meeting. She'd been a gangly fourteen-year-old, wary of everyone. Turner had burst into Eleanor's kitchen, full of enthusiasm and warmth. It had alarmed her at the time but once she'd worked out he wasn't a threat, she'd welcomed his visits. He'd insisted on taking her round London, introducing her to the city he loved.

She came to regard him as a big brother, but once she became a woman his feelings for her changed. But even then, he never once pushed it, knowing she didn't reciprocate his feelings. The sight of him dying in front of her wouldn't leave and her eyes stung. She chased the vision away and recalled the last time she'd spoken to him, hugging him in his office. It was a good memory.

'Coffee's brewing,' Chapman said, placing a plate on the table.

A stab of resentment at his interruption passed when Antonia's stomach reminded her she'd not eaten. The stale, woolly croissant wasn't great, but she'd started on the second by the time Chapman returned with the coffees.

'You were ready for those, weren't you?' Chapman said, helping himself to one and releasing a shower of crumbs as he chewed it. He ate it in silence then took a swallow of coffee. 'I had a good look at these documents. Makes me furious, a company making huge profits and avoiding paying tax.'

Antonia didn't have the energy to raise any indignation. 'So what, they all do it.'

'They may do, but it's still wrong.'

She shrugged. What did it matter, compared to people losing their lives?

'What about this woman, a senior civil servant taking back-handers? I'd throw away the key. Such a distinctive name should be easy enough to—'

'It's a pseudonym. Margaret Gage was the wife of a British general who spied on her husband during the American War of Independence.'

'Oh, right.'

She experienced a perverse satisfaction at his disappointment.

Chapman laid the documents down and exhaled. 'Shall we concentrate on the disappearance of your friend? You can't believe it's okay for people to get away with murder.'

'I don't—' She took a deep breath. 'Okay, I'll show you.' At least it would take her mind off Turner. She opened the 'Monika' folder on her computer, fighting the feeling that this was a waste of time. She angled the screen so Chapman could see it. As she read through her notes the enthusiasm for the investigation rekindled.

'You said another woman went missing, apart from your friend Monika,' Chapman said, wiping his fingers on a piece of kitchen towel.

'Agnes Sanders. Her sister Julie reported her missing. I put a request on a women's forum for anyone who'd had a bad experience at GRM and Julie got in touch.'

'Was she the only one?'

Chapman's tone made her defensive. 'Yes, but others might not have seen the shout-out.'

'What did she do at GRM?'

'She attended an interview but didn't take the job.'

'Who interviewed her?'

'I didn't ask.'

'You serious? What sort—'

'I worked on the theory the killer saw her there, *not* he interviewed her.' Her cheeks grew hot. 'Anyway, I've been working on another investigation and believe it or not, I've been rather busy.'

'You got her sister's address?'

'Yes, why?'

'We need to see her, find out who carried out the interview.'

Antonia wanted nothing more than to stay here and return to bed. 'Why don't you go on your own?'

'She doesn't know me from Adam. And I'm not leaving you here to mope around.'

'You're unbelievable, my friend's been—' She couldn't say the words. 'Anyway, I'm not moping.'

'Not now you're not. Come on, I'll buy you a proper lunch when we finish.'

He set off for the exit and, realising he was right, she followed.

◆ ◆ ◆

Chapman followed Antonia up the path to the small 1950s semi and waited behind her as she rang the bell. A faint tinkling sounded in the distance. What the hell was he doing, playing at coppers while suspended? Mind you, if what he'd already done came out . . . The lights came on in the hall and chains clanked before the door opened.

'Hello?' A pale narrow face topped with greasy black hair appeared in the gap.

'Julie, it's Antonia from The Electric Investigator.'

'Oh, hello.' The worried frown changed into a smile and the door closed before opening wide to show a tall girl wearing a loose-fitting jumper and jeans.

'Thank you, Julie,' Antonia said. 'I've brought Russell Chapman, from the police.'

The frown was back as she turned on him. 'Oh, you're interested now, are you? What's happened? Someone famous gone missing?'

'I'm sorry if you think my colleagues haven't given you the attention you deserve. I'm here to remedy that.' He held out a hand, which she gripped before stepping aside to let him enter.

Antonia brought up the rear and closed the door, which Julie checked before saying, 'Go through to the kitchen, I'm just preparing lunch.'

The odour of garlic and onions grew as they walked into a long room lined with pale kitchen units. At the far end a small round pine table stood in front of patio doors overlooking a tidy lawn surrounded by a panelled fence. Julie guided them to this and they sat while she prepared drinks, stirring a pot bubbling on the range until the kettle boiled. Chapman had told Antonia to let him take the lead. She'd better. Julie placed two mugs on the table.

'Julie, do you have a picture of Agnes?' he asked.

She returned a few seconds later with a photo in a pewter frame, showing her and a woman of about twenty-five. 'Dad took it in Corsica last summer.'

Both wore bikinis, Julie tanned and looking far more attractive than she did now. Although the same height, Agnes appeared shorter due to her build. Her sculpted body exuded power.

'Looks like she took care of herself,' he said, placing the photo on the table.

Julie picked up the frame and stroked it. 'Oh yes. Aggie's super fit, she's always training. Bodybuilding, rugby, Taekwondo, you name it.'

'Can you tell me about the interview she had at GRM?'

Julie sat in one of the remaining chairs and replaced the photo frame before starting. 'She'd applied for a job as a security consultant, it wasn't just a guard. Aggie's bright, she's got a degree in sports science.'

'How did the interview go?'

'It *started* well. A woman from personnel interviewed her and then they gave her tests, including a physical. She did a beep test and reached level fourteen five.'

'Very impressive,' Chapman said, not sure what it meant but reacting to Julie's tone. 'What went wrong?'

'The chief of security interviewed her. The guy freaked her out and she came home saying she'd never work for someone like him.'

'Mishkin?' Antonia blurted out.

Chapman glared at her.

Julie said, 'Is he someone you suspect? Has he done—'

'No,' Chapman said, 'Mr Mishkin has no police record.' *Not that he didn't deserve one.* Antonia avoided his gaze and he continued, 'So, they never offered her a job—'

'But they did.'

'What happened?' Chapman said.

'They phoned and she refused. Told them why. Then he came here. Mum let him in but Aggie blew her top and threw him out.'

'What did he do?' Chapman couldn't contain his excitement.

Julie shuddered. 'He didn't get angry, just smiled at her and said, "You'll regret this, girlie."'

Antonia stiffened, seeming about to speak but subsided and withdrew into herself.

'What happened then?' he said.

'Aggie thought she saw him on a night out, and then out of the blue someone offered her a job as a personal trainer, great money.'

'Who?'

'She never said. They made her sign a confidentiality clause. Mum and I used to tease her it was one of the Cabinet – she hated politicians – but she never even hinted who it was . . .'

'Did she say how they found out about her? Was she applying for those jobs?'

'No, she'd applied for your lot' – Julie tilted her head at him – 'the army and GRM. She complained there weren't any jobs out there.'

'But she took it?' he said.

'We thought so, but then we got the letter—'

'What letter?' both Antonia and Chapman said.

While Julie disappeared to fetch it, Chapman said, 'Mishkin *is* behind this.'

Antonia didn't react.

'He came here and threatened her,' he said.

'To say you'll regret something isn't a threat.' Antonia sounded despondent.

'What's wrong with you? How can you defend him after what the guy did to you—'

'Here it is.' Julie returned and placed a sheet of paper on the table.

Chapman read the letter. From a firm of solicitors, it informed Agnes Sanders that because she hadn't attended at the agreed time, their client would withdraw the job offer. The name on the letter seemed familiar but he couldn't remember where from.

'Have you shown it to the police?' Chapman said, passing it to Antonia, who took it without enthusiasm.

'They said it was a dead end,' Julie said.

'Can we borrow this?'

'Keep it, it's a copy.'

Antonia's lack of interest dampened Chapman's excitement. Mishkin must be behind this, and Turner's death. If someone killed one of his friends, Chapman would make sure they paid. What the hell was wrong with her?

A familiar ballad sung by someone Antonia didn't recognise issued from the speaker attached to the faux beam above their table. The heavy, chunky furniture carried on the medieval theme of the dining room, as did the Gothic script used on the menu. The waitress hovered beside the table and Antonia studied the menu, unable to muster interest in the dishes on offer. Julie Sanders's words had released a torrent of memories that demolished her appetite.

'Don't you know what you want?' Chapman said, sounding impatient.

'Just a coffee.'

He frowned at her. 'They do a great roast—'

'Order what you want.'

He ordered two roast-beef dinners and waited until the waitress moved out of earshot. 'I understand you're annoyed you missed an important lead by not asking who'd interviewed—'

'You don't have a fucking clue.'

Chapman looked ready to snap at her but instead said, 'Why don't you enlighten me?'

The urge to tell this smug bastard exactly what they'd done to her seized Antonia. See how he enjoyed the 'great roast' afterwards. A dark cloud settled on her and tears threatened to break out. She leapt to her feet, rushing to the toilets before they escaped.

She charged into the ladies' cubicle and leant against the door, locking it behind her. Tears poured down her cheeks, dragging out sobs that seemed to bring up pieces of her soul. She closed her eyes and found herself in the linen cupboard, terrified and helpless as she hid from monsters in human form. She tried to conjure up her safe place, but she hadn't needed it for so long she couldn't recall how.

Antonia made herself study the image in the mirror. A frightened girl stared at her, face streaked with tears. Behind her a dark figure. Mishkin, his cruel eyes shining above the blue surgical mask. A black weight paralysed her.

'*How do you know it was him?*' *the policewoman with the perm said.*

'*His eyes . . .*'

'*Right, his eyes. Anything else?*'

'*The smell. He wore—*' *How to describe it.* '*He smelled like aftershave.*'

The policewoman waited for Antonia to continue. '*Quite a lot of men wear aftershave.*' *She looked at the social worker on Antonia's right.*

At that moment, Antonia knew nothing would happen to her abuser.

The vividness of the recollection took her breath away and the urge to roll into a ball and rock herself overwhelmed her. Then the vision of a frail woman in a wheelchair appeared. Surrounded by looming figures, the woman fought them until they disappeared.

Antonia uttered a roar of rage and smashed her fist into the mirror. Mishkin disappeared as the glass shattered, the pieces remaining glued in place.

She studied her crazed reflection until a bright-red drop splashed into the sink. Dragged out of her reverie, she examined her knuckle. It didn't look too bad, just a graze. She sucked the wound, then held it under running water until it ran clear. After washing and drying her face, she studied it in an undamaged corner.

A haunted girl stared back. She might have banished him for now, but Mishkin was back in her head. Getting rid of him last time had been the hardest battle she'd ever fought and she wasn't sure she had the strength to do it again.

CHAPTER 23

Antonia crouched in the corner of the linen cupboard and held her breath. Heat radiated from the huge hot-water tank above her, bathing her trembling body in dry metallic air. Footsteps sounded outside, then an angry voice.

Through the door she couldn't identify the speaker but knew it was him. Her heart seemed intent on battering its way out of her ribcage and her pulse whooshed in her ears. She pushed back into the corner, trying to burrow into the walls and become invisible.

Then a cry, a young girl. Forcing herself to move, Antonia shuffled to the front of the cupboard. Light shone through a crack in the door and she pressed her eye against it. Her vision adjusted until she could make out the scene.

The small figure of a young girl lay on the bed, and on top, thrusting at her, was the man who'd done the same to Antonia. Again, he wore a surgical mask, but she'd know those eyes anywhere. Bile filled Antonia's throat. He grabbed the girl by the neck and repositioned her, using her like a toy. Now Antonia could see her face. Enya. She seemed to be staring straight at her, pleading.

Tears poured down Antonia's cheeks. She should help, but her body wouldn't obey her. Enya cried out again and the man clamped his hand over her mouth. Antonia closed her eyes. The disgusting sounds he made stopped, then he swore. She looked again. Enya lay still, her eyes open, but she couldn't see. Antonia held back a cry of terror.

The man pulled his trousers up and ran from the room, panic wafting off him. Antonia stared at Enya. She should help her, but wasn't Enya already dead? What if he came back and caught her? She stayed hidden, unable to decide, then excited voices came closer. The man barged into the room, behind him the matron and someone else Antonia didn't recognise.

The matron checked Enya's neck, then shook her head. Antonia shuffled back into the corner of the cupboard, placing her hands over her ears so she couldn't hear them.

Antonia sat up and stared about her, breathing as if she'd gone twelve rounds. Light leaked in through a skylight and after a few seconds she recognised the bedsit. Did she cry out in her sleep? Fortunately Chapman wasn't in the room. She untangled her clammy limbs from the bedding. Sweat soaked her knickers. But it *wasn't* sweat. She leapt off the bed, heat suffusing her skin. A small damp patch on the sheet condemned her.

The murmur of Chapman's voice came from behind the door to the kitchenette. She picked up a discarded top and wiped at the patch. When she'd done all she could, she stripped the bed. The stain on the mattress seemed huge, but covered an area smaller than her hand. She closed the bed and folded the bedding, making sure the incriminating mark on the sheet stayed hidden. After replacing the cushions, she rushed into the wetroom and, leaving her knickers and top on, stood under the shower.

When she finally came out, she couldn't hear Chapman. A note on the side of the tiny fridge said he wouldn't be long. She made coffee and toast as her laptop fired up. She resisted the temptation to log on to the news channels and stayed offline before plugging Chapman's memory stick into a port. The memory of her dream kept intruding, but she pushed it away.

She took a few moments to get the hang of which camera covered which section of road but once she did, she examined the footage from the camera on Lincoln Road positioned at the entrance to the Jubilee Industrial Estate. She started at dawn eight days earlier. Had it already been a week since Arkady and his men had chased her? Even at high speed it took an age and she had to keep pausing when a likely vehicle appeared. A vivid memory of Turner telling her that most investigative work consisted of painstaking research flashed into her mind.

Thoughts of Turner and the fact that she'd never see him again made her breath catch. Then the notion she might also lose Eleanor hit her. She forced herself to concentrate on the screen. Her eyes stung and she yawned. Despite going to bed early, she'd hardly slept. Mishkin appeared in an early dream and the fear he'd return whenever she let consciousness slip away kept her awake, until near dawn she'd lost consciousness and then – she shook her head and focused on the screen.

At 14.43 a van left the estate and she slowed the footage until she could make out the distinctive box on the roof. She froze the image and zoomed in but couldn't see the number plate or passengers. She compared it to the printout of the image of the van and let out a small whoop. It was the same vehicle and the success drove away her fatigue.

She followed the vehicle from one camera to the next, engrossed in tracking it as it headed for the outskirts of north-east London. A sound from outside distracted her. The lock clicked and the outer door opened.

Chapman appeared. 'Morning, Miss Sleepy. While you've been in your lazy bed, I've got us a new car' – he brandished keys – 'spoken to the officer who put Latif away, and Jo Dobrowski, the crime-scene tech who identified your DNA, has agreed to see me at lunchtime—' He cocked his head. 'You got something.'

'I've found it.'

'Well done.' Chapman sat next to her. 'Where were they?'

She brought the map up and found the camera on a long straight stretch of road. She retrieved the footage from the next camera and found the van, tracking it until she ran out of cameras.

'Did you get material from all the cameras?' she said, disappointment and irritation making her voice sharp.

'All the ones you wanted.'

'You can't have done.' She indicated the area where the van had disappeared. 'You didn't get these.'

'Are you sure?'

'I'm positive.' She opened the list of cameras. 'There' – she tapped the screen – 'there's no more from that road.'

'Let's see?'

She called up the map and Chapman studied it.

'There aren't any more,' he said after a few moments.

'I thought the government put safety cameras on all roads?'

'They're supposed to, but country lanes like this one aren't a high priority.'

Antonia wanted to throw the laptop out of the window. All that work for nothing.

Chapman studied the map and pointed at a building in the section not covered by cameras. 'That's where they went.'

'Sears Farm? How do you know?'

He tapped the side of his nose. 'I'd have to kill you if I—'

'Not funny.' Antonia remembered saying the same to Turner.

'The papers I found at Murray's place mentioned Sears. I can't recall the context but remember wondering if it had anything to do with the department store.'

They had nothing to lose. 'Let's check it out.'

'We'll go after I've met up with Jo. I'll pick you up, and in the meantime you see if you can find the—'

'I'm coming with you.'

'She's expecting me alone.'

'It will be a nice surprise for her then.'

Chapman glared at her.

'It's my research which found the link. And anyway, I'm not sitting here waiting for you.' With nothing to occupy her mind, she feared Mishkin would visit her, even when awake. 'We'll see your friend, then go to this Sears Farm.'

Chapman led the way into the restaurant and scanned the tables. Covered in white linen with black crockery arranged on them, they filled the centre of the room. A series of booths lined the walls. The aroma of fresh baking and herbs infused the air. Dobrowski waved from a booth but faltered when she saw Antonia.

Despite the way their last conversation had ended, Dobrowski had been happy to meet him and hadn't objected when he'd asked her not to mention the meeting to Harding. Maybe she and the inspector were no longer together. He'd been looking forward to this but not with Antonia in tow, especially in her current mood. She'd been in an evil temper since she'd come out of the toilet yesterday lunchtime, her expression blank, like a shutter had descended, and had eaten as if forcing broken glass down her throat. He hoped not to have to endure a repeat performance.

'Jo, how are you?' He went to shake her hand, but she offered her cheek and a clumsy dance ensued. 'Thanks for seeing me at short notice.'

'What you said intrigued me,' she said, her gaze fixed on Antonia.

'Hi. I'm Antonia. Russell and I are working together.'

Dobrowski's brow furrowed. 'Antonia *Conti*?'

Antonia nodded.

'I didn't agree to this.' Dobrowski gathered her bag.

'Jo, please stay.' He knew this had been a mistake. 'Antonia's done nothing wrong. She's a victim here.'

Dobrowski stared at Antonia. 'Why is he protecting you?'

'I don't know why anyone would make you change my DNA—'

'I refused to do it. My boss changed it and told me I'd "made a mistake" after he got a call. And only one person could have been behind that. Reed-Mayhew,' Dobrowski said. 'Nobody in any of his companies does anything without his say-so.'

'I've never even met him,' Antonia said.

Dobrowski glared. 'I don't believe you.'

Chapman said, 'I think it's Mishkin.'

Antonia stiffened and stared at nothing.

Dobrowski hesitated then said, 'That creep's the only other one it could be. But why would he protect—' She nodded at Antonia.

'That's one of the things we need to find out,' Chapman said, hoping Jo would agree to help them.

Dobrowski studied Antonia's stricken expression before seeming to accept this. They arranged themselves around the table and a waiter took their orders, leaving behind an uncomfortable silence. Dobrowski retrieved a pink folder from her briefcase and placed it in front of her, holding the flap as if reluctant to release it.

'These are the autopsy reports on Sofie Stoltz and Aida Rizk.'

'Great, did you have any trouble getting them?' Chapman said.

'Now I've undertaken suitable retraining after my *mistake*' – she glanced at Antonia and made a face showing what she thought of it – 'I have full access to the records.'

Chapman sympathised, having undergone a few bouts of 'retraining' himself when he'd deviated from standard procedures. 'I appreciate it. Thank you.' He took the folder.

She hung on to it. 'If it gets out I've given you these . . .'

'They won't go any further, Jo. And you can trust Antonia.' He hoped he was right.

Dobrowski hesitated for a moment then released the folder, and he opened it while Antonia produced a notepad. Their order arrived and he read the documents before passing them to Antonia. She scribbled a few lines of incomprehensible marks on the pad. He finished the last document, with a growing sense of excitement. Antonia's theory that Latif and Murray had been framed made sense.

'Are you going to tell me what's going on?' Dobrowski said. Despite accepting Antonia's presence, she still appeared uneasy.

'We think there's a link between the victims,' he said.

'What sort of link?'

He hadn't discussed what to say with Antonia, but she sat back, letting him know it was his decision. 'We don't think the two men in here' – he tapped the folder – 'killed the young women—'

'The evidence is incontrovertible. Each man had blood and tissue from his victim on his body. In addition, you found other evidence—'

'Conveniently left next to Murray's body,' Antonia said.

Realisation struck Dobrowski. 'You're saying someone also killed *him*?'

Chapman nodded.

Dobrowski shook her head. 'There was no doubt he killed himself. We found no sign of him being forced—'

'The killer drugged him,' Antonia said, taking the reports out of the folder. 'I quote, ". . . had ingested a cocktail of drink and drugs . . ."'

'What about Latif? He's serving—'

'I spoke to the investigating officer this morning,' Chapman said. 'She told me they found Latif unconscious, having apparently tried to hang himself. He seemed well out of it, like *he'd* been drugged, and he's maintained his innocence—'

'Well *that's* a surprise.'

'—claiming GRM framed him to stop him investigating them.'

'Why not just buy him off or kill him and bury the body under a motorway? They're involved in building the new one up north.'

'As a warning,' Antonia said. 'Everyone's scared of upsetting GRM. They're notorious for litigating, but I've also heard rumours since I went undercover.'

'Antonia's right. If he'd just disappeared, nobody would have noticed. But this way . . .'

'But he survived, so why hasn't he spoken about what he uncovered?'

'He endured a vicious beating while on remand and "vigilantes" firebombed his family home, supposedly in retaliation for killing Sofie Stoltz. He's said nothing since.'

Dobrowski leant forward and lowered her voice. 'You're saying GRM, the company I work for, arranged for the murder of two women so they could get at their partners.'

'Rizk and Murray weren't a couple.' Chapman remembered something Rizk's landlord had said. 'She was gay.' Was that what linked the victims? He was sure the Sanders girl batted for the other side.

'That doesn't preclude her having a relationship with—'

'The women were killed for another reason,' Antonia said. 'Framing the two men was a bonus. Other women have gone missing – let's go.' She swept the folder and papers off the table and rose in a smooth motion.

Chapman said, 'What's up – shit!'

Two men in dark clothes approached from the entrance. Another two appeared from opposite sides of the rear of the restaurant. Dobrowski turned red and mouthed 'Sorry' before backing away.

Other diners stared as Antonia slid out of the booth and charged towards the rear of the restaurant. Adrenaline banished the lethargy that lay on her like a heavy blanket. Without consciously making a decision, she ran towards the left where a door led to the kitchen. Something about the body language of the man approaching her told her he wasn't up for this. When she'd halved the distance between them, he faltered, torn between standing his ground and coming forward. She lowered her shoulder and accelerated towards him.

His indecision left him off balance and he went down with a grunt, crashing on to an empty table and scattering glasses. Antonia rode the impact, keeping her feet, and checked on Chapman, who followed three paces behind her. The door to the kitchen opened and a waiter holding three plates emerged, took two steps and halted, rooted to the spot. Antonia swerved, missing him by centimetres, and he recovered in time to dodge Chapman, but not the figure pursuing him.

With the sound of angry yells and smashing crockery following her, Antonia ducked into the kitchen. The odour of roasting meat and cooking fat assaulted her nostrils and hot, steam-laden air engulfed her. She wove her way through the crowded kitchen, passing the huge ranges, and into a prep room. Two doors stood at the far end and she hesitated. A young man in checked trousers stood between them and pulled one open, revealing a courtyard. Antonia ran past him mouthing her thanks.

Realising it appeared Chapman was chasing her, she shouted 'He's with me,' over her shoulder.

Bins lined the yard and at the end it opened into an alleyway. Antonia hesitated and checked both directions. Chapman caught her up and with a breathless 'This way', ran left. She followed and they reached the road. Chapman swore. Only thirty metres away, two more men dressed like their pursuers waited on the pavement, studying the entrance to the restaurant. One held something up to his ear.

'Come on,' Chapman said, heading for an alleyway between two shops. He ducked into a doorway and pulled Antonia to him. She let him and stood listening to his breathing. The stink of stale urine seeped out of the brickwork. Yells came from the mouth of the alley followed by feet slapping on the pavement. She froze, exhaling when they continued past the entrance. Chapman let out a loud breath and put a hand on her shoulder.

'The way you blasted through that guy.' He laughed. 'You don't play rugby, do you? Maggie Alphonsi would have been proud.'

'He was off balance.' Exhilaration made her grin.

'Still, you did well.' He released her and stepped away. 'Let's get the car. We should be able to get out at the far end.'

They returned to the car without incident and within half an hour had left the North Circular, driving away from the city. What would they find at the Sears Industrial Estate? Would it enable them to make sense of what they'd discovered? With a mixture of hope and trepidation, Antonia directed him using the map, but roads had changed since its publication.

After criss-crossing the area for several frustrating minutes, Chapman spotted a sign and took the turn. The road narrowed and the buildings lining it became less frequent. Traffic thinned until they no longer encountered vehicles.

'Are you sure we're going the right way?' Antonia said.

Chapman didn't answer but pointed to a rustic wooden sign reading 'SEARS FARM' in faded letters. The road grew more pot-holed until she worried they'd get stuck. They rounded a bend to find a dilapidated collection of buildings ahead of them. A 'For Sale' sign hung askew above the front door. Broken windows gave the double-fronted grey building a derelict air and the gutters sprouted greenery. Beyond the house she saw a range of barns and outbuildings in a similar condition. They got out and, picking their way round puddles and dried cowpats, inspected the site.

'Nobody's been here for years,' Chapman said, sounding as disappointed as she felt.

'It might just be camouflage.' She peered into an old milking parlour. Battered milk churns and rusty bits of machinery covered the floor and the place stank of manure.

Chapman kicked a stone that bounced against a metal drum, making rats scatter. 'Ugghh, let's go.'

A Land Rover pulled up behind their car, blocking them in. Antonia tensed as two men got out. Mishkin's heavies? Probably not. They didn't look the part, dressed in stained overalls and wellies.

'Can we help you?' The words didn't match their demeanour.

'We heard the place is for sale,' Chapman said.

The older of the two men answered, 'There's no land, just this.' He jerked his thumb at the yard and buildings.

'That's a shame.' Chapman glanced at Antonia. 'We were saying how much potential it had.'

The men stared.

'We'd better get going then.'

Without another word the men returned to their Land Rover, reversed and parked on the verge, waiting until Chapman and Antonia passed them.

Once they were out of sight, Antonia burst out laughing.

'I kept hearing the theme tune from *Deliverance*,' Chapman said, joining her.

Antonia sank into the seat, her limbs heavy. 'What a waste of time.'

'Maybe not.' Chapman grinned and pointed to a sign directing them to Sears Industrial Estate.

Unwilling to raise her hopes again, she stayed silent as Chapman followed the sign. A concrete roadway lined with hedgerows led to an orange roof visible over the trees. On each side of the roadway a narrow strip of green separated it from the hedge. Four hundred metres from the road, the strip of concrete opened out. Several small industrial units surrounded a larger building.

'This is more promising,' she said.

He slowed, crawling up to the main building before stopping in a parking bay. Red roller shutters protected each opening and large 'To Let' signs adorned each corner. 'Which one do you reckon we should check first?'

'Shall we try the biggest?' She undid her seatbelt and reached for the door handle.

'Hang on, there's someone coming.'

'We'll say we're thinking of renting it? They can't be any worse than those two—' The car shot forward, pushing her back into her seat. 'What the hell—'

'Wait!' Chapman gunned the engine and threw the car into a tight turn.

Antonia wedged herself against the door and fumbled for the seatbelt. A dark van approached from her left and they shot past it, heading to the main road. Chapman's anxiety transmitted to her and her mouth grew dry. The engine raced and they hit the concrete track leading back the way they'd come. She glanced over her shoulder. A second van emerged from behind one of the other buildings. Chapman swore.

A third van waited in their way. Chapman didn't slow and she realised he intended going for the narrow gap between it and the hedge. She saw the ditch too late to cry out a warning. The front wheel left the roadway and the car shot off to the left, aiming at the hedge. He snatched at the wheel, cursing as he dragged it to the right. The van loomed in the windscreen and Antonia braced herself. She still hadn't refastened her seatbelt. Chapman wrestled the wheel, to no avail. With the screech of tearing metal, his car ploughed into the side of the van, bouncing off towards the hedge. Branches grabbed at the car, then an irresistible force shoved her forward. Antonia threw her arms in front of her and waited for the impact.

CHAPTER 24

Antonia heard a loud crack then the hedge disappeared and her forehead smacked into the airbag. The car rocked back before settling, and powder filled her mouth. The bag collapsed, revealing Chapman, slumped in his seat with blood flowing from his nose.

She leant across and shook him. 'Russell, are you—'

He coughed, then shouted, 'Get out. Run!'

Angry voices sounded close and she snatched the door open. A man stood at the side of the van they'd smashed into, trying to open its door. More vehicles raced towards her and she ran towards a gate in the hedge. At the gap she checked on Chapman, but he hadn't got out. She stopped, but he waved her away, and she vaulted the gate, landing on a divot and rolling her ankle. A spike of pain shot up her leg.

A large field sloped upwards towards a wooded copse. The road ran alongside the bottom edge and a muddy patch at the far corner led to another gate. Raised voices came from behind her. Three men ran at her, less than ten metres away. Ignoring the pain from her leg, she set off towards the far corner. The men shouted something. An engine started, but she ploughed on over the rough, rutted ground. She'd covered less than fifty metres when a blur passed the hedge.

A car, cutting her off. She changed direction, going uphill towards the copse.

'No shooting!' a man shouted.

Her heart jumped and she pushed herself harder. The terrain tested her ankle and she picked her way over the ruts, not daring to check on her pursuers. What was happening to Chapman?

Movement came from her right, and she risked a fleeting glance. In the distance a man picked his way through the mud at the far gate. The trees were less than a hundred metres away, twelve seconds on a track, but she'd take nearer a minute on this terrain and her damaged ankle would slow her further. At least her heavier pursuers would struggle more. At fifty metres she noticed the fence, five strands of barbed wire on wooden posts, half-hidden by undergrowth.

Her gasping drowned other sounds. She held her breath, but the echo continued. They were right behind her. A surge of adrenaline pushed her faster. The fence loomed and knowing she couldn't slow to negotiate it, she ran at the nearest post. She reached for the top, pushed off with her sound leg and pulled. Something stung her palm, but she left the ground and sailed over the barrier.

She landed on her hands and knees, then struggled to her feet. On the other side of the fence, an athletic man of about thirty studied her. Further down the field, two more came, moving towards them in slow motion. Antonia backed away, testing her ankle. The man ran at the fence with a determined expression. He mistimed his leap and landed on the wire. His coat snagged on the barbs and he struggled to pull free, a giant fly in a metal spider's web.

A heavy branch lay by her foot and she it snatched up, holding it in both hands. The man saw her and stopped struggling. She stared at him and he swallowed, exuding fear and regret. The men in the field came closer; she needed to run, but she daren't leave him. Once he slipped his jacket off, he'd be free. She took a step toward him and he reached under his jacket. She charged, ignoring the pain from her ankle, but the pistol appeared before she reached him.

One of the men in the field shouted. 'No, Eddy! We need her alive.'

The man gestured at the branch. 'Go on then,' he said, grinning. 'Take a free shot with your twig, darlin'.'

She threw the stick away and ran, his mocking laugh following her. The path descended, taking her down. Towards a road? Branches snatched at her as she brushed past, masking other sounds. The undergrowth thinned and then the path petered out. In front of her, another fence, two metres high and made of concrete planks. She reached for the top and pulled herself up. Behind it stood an industrial building, a concrete-covered yard between it and the fence. Then the bonnet of a tractor appeared, trundling across the concrete. A farm, thank God – she could get help.

Her relief didn't last long. The vehicle rumbled onwards, towing something: Chapman's car and, following it, one of the dark vans. She must have doubled back and ended up at the rear of the Sears Industrial Estate. She lowered herself to the ground, fighting to contain tears, and leant against the fence, chest heaving, listening for her pursuers.

◆ ◆ ◆

Chapman had listened to Antonia clambering out of the car, and then she was gone. At least she hadn't argued when he'd told her to run.

Blood filled his mouth and it felt like someone had kicked a giant football into his face. The smell of hot metal mingled with a more agricultural odour. He'd pushed against the driver's door, which opened a few inches before stopping. Then the passenger door opened and for a moment he thought Antonia had returned. He opened his mouth to remonstrate but realised his mistake as a handgun barrel pointed at the centre of his torso.

'Get your hands where I can see them.' The speaker, a man in his mid-thirties, wore a dark jacket, like the men he'd shot, and didn't look as if he had much patience.

Chapman released the door handle and lifted his arms.

'Hands behind your head, lace your fingers together.'

Chapman had done so, studying the gunman. The guy handled the weapon with the easy proficiency common to military types. How had they got here so quickly? They couldn't know which car he was driving unless . . . No, he wouldn't believe Sammy would betray him. How would he explain he'd totalled his car? Shouts from outside told him Antonia was getting away; he hoped she'd have the sense to keep going. The gunman stared at him unblinking until a rough diesel engine came closer.

A minute later the gunman had stepped away and the car jerked backwards. Chapman wedged his elbows against the roof to prevent himself falling. Once the car had escaped from the grip of the hedge, his door swung open. Two more men appeared, dressed the same. One carried a handgun. The unarmed man reached in and dragged him out, making sure he didn't block his mate's line of fire. Chapman fought to keep his balance, but a boot kicked the back of his knee and he landed on his backside, jarring his spine. By the time he'd regained his senses, a cable tie secured his wrists behind his back.

The one with the gun came closer, limping on his right leg, and Chapman had recognised him. 'Sergeant Chapman,' he said, sounding as if he marinated his vocal cords in nicotine. 'We meet again.'

Chapman's limbs shook. The Smoker grimaced each time he put weight on his knee and came to a stop a metre away, staring down at Chapman. He couldn't detect an expression in his eyes, just an iciness that filled Chapman with dread. The man drew his arm back and, moving with surprising speed, struck him on the cheek. Chapman reeled, but a knee hit him in the back, keeping him upright. Tears blurred his vision and he couldn't feel the right side of his face, then the heat spread, like he'd been branded with a hot iron.

'That's for Terry,' the limping man had said. 'And for Ivan.' He'd raised the gun and Chapman cringed, bracing himself for another blow, but the man laughed. 'Nobody liked Ivan much.'

The man stepped away and Chapman relaxed, but the man's shoulders tensed, then came a blur as the gun descended. Chapman swayed to the side, but it caught him on the side of the head. Lights flashed at the edge of his vision. The band holding his wrists together bit into the flesh as he fought to free his hands.

'Put him in the van,' the voice had said.

Still groggy from the blow, he hadn't resisted when they hauled him to his feet and dragged him to one of the vehicles. Someone had pulled a canvas sack over his head and thrown him into the back. The front doors opened and the vehicle rocked as two heavy bodies got in. The side of his face felt numb and on fire at the same time. He'd tried to gather his thoughts. These men didn't care if he recognised them. His insides fluttered as the implications of this hit him.

Lukewarm water spluttered out of the showerhead and Sabirah bowed her head under it. The sounds of the other inmates faded as she thought of her beloved children. When she'd heard an 'uncle' took them, she'd been certain it was the creepy man who'd arranged their passage to London, telling Nadimah she was beautiful and asking her to call him uncle. She'd vacillated between telling the authorities all she knew about him and keeping quiet, hoping he wouldn't hurt her children. If she told how she'd entered the country they'd cancel her Permit to Reside, regardless of what happened with this trumped-up charge. She also knew closing down his operation would remove a lifeline for people like her, but her children came first.

She'd almost convinced herself he offered no threat and his affection for Nadimah was innocent, but the memory of an aunt who'd allowed her husband to abuse her daughter wouldn't leave her. Once it had all came out, the pathetic woman had told everyone she hadn't suspected him, and even after her sister warned her about him, she'd believed his protestations of innocence. Sabirah still thought of the woman with contempt.

Now she'd told the governor what she knew about the man, there was no point in dwelling on it. When they found the children they'd take them into care, but, however bad that was, it couldn't be worse than . . . Sabirah couldn't allow herself to think of what might happen to her daughter.

The water cooled, telling her she should get out. Soap clung to her hair and she rinsed it off, hurrying before the guards shouted at her. With her eyes screwed up, she reached for her towel but couldn't find it. Blinking the soapy water away, she peered at the hooks where she'd left the rough cloth. The soap stung but even through the blurred vision she didn't have trouble recognising the woman who stood in front of her. The Kurd who'd attacked her. Fear and the vulnerability of being naked made her insides shrink.

'Is this what you're after, snitch?' The woman brandished a cloth.

'Please.' Sabirah reached for it but the woman snatched it away.

Other figures crowded behind her and Sabirah realised with dismay they were friends of the woman. The guards who hung around the showers scrutinising the inmates had disappeared. A tight band constricted her chest.

'We don't like snitches, do we, girls?' the Kurd said. The others agreed.

'I don't snitch.' Sabirah had learnt early this was the worst crime you could be accused of in here.

'Oh yeah, so why did you ask to see The Lech?' she asked, using the name the inmates gave the assistant governor.

'About my children. I need to find them.'

'So, you dropped someone in it—'

'He is pervert, child molester.' How did this woman know what she'd said? Of course, the guard who'd taken her into the office. She'd seen her talking to the Kurd.

Some of the other women lost their enthusiasm. A child molester had even lower status than a snitch.

'Yeah, so you say. And anyway, what you doing letting a nonce take care of your kids?'

'I don't let. He took them—'

'You're still a snitch,' the woman said, and lunged at Sabirah.

Sabirah, sick of cowering and remembering the exhilaration of fighting back, dropped her shoulder. The woman crashed into her, sending her into the wall. Winded by the impact, Sabirah dragged air into her lungs. The woman attempted to grab her but couldn't grip her still-soapy flesh. Sabirah thrust her hand in the woman's face and pushed but her foot slipped on the wet tiles. With nothing to support her she crashed to the ground. Before she could scramble to her feet, a blow hit her in the side, then another. She curled up into a ball, praying for the guards to come.

◆ ◆ ◆

Antonia hesitated for a few moments, not sure what to do. But she couldn't stay here and, rousing herself, she tracked along the wall. The undergrowth thickened, forcing her away from it until she found another path. Then she came to a fence, this time low with three strands of wire, and beyond it a road. She waited and listened, hearing a car coming fast. Something told her to stay still and a dark-blue van with a dent in the side raced towards her.

She ducked into the undergrowth, waiting for it to pass, sick with disappointment. Her body ached and her palm hurt like hell. The pain of the 'sting' came from a cut oozing blood and, dismissing fears of infection, she considered her options. If she wanted to help Chapman, she needed to get out of this wood.

She jogged into the trees, determined to find a way out. She should have paid more attention to orienteering classes in the Girl Guides, not that she'd lasted long before they'd thrown her out. After ten minutes of fighting through branches and listening for sounds of pursuit, she found herself back where she'd jumped the fence. The field now lay empty, but then she noticed the sentry, waiting by the road. He'd see her long before she reached safety.

She'd have to wait for dark, still many hours away. Her ankle sent jolts of pain up her leg with every step. Now she'd stopped moving, cold seeped into her and she shivered. She stepped into the trees to wait, then she saw movement. A van parked by the gate. The sentry approached it, greeting the two men in the front. After talking for a few moments the driver opened the back doors and a large dog leapt out, excited to be free.

Bile rose in her throat. The dog would find her in no time. The three men locked the van and advanced up the field. She set off for the concrete fence, hoping the men on the other side had gone by now. The dog couldn't follow her over it. She ran until she reached the barrier, fear overcoming her aches and giving her strength. The dog barked; it must have picked up her scent.

She peered over the top of the fence. A removal lorry was parked next to the tractor and men milled around it. Two heavy planks formed a ramp into the rear. Chapman's car sat in the lorry, near the back. The men loaded the planks into the lorry and stood congratulating themselves, like men do when they've done something unfamiliar. The lorry driver pulled the shutter down, securing it with a hook on a chain, while the other men climbed into the van.

Loud barking came from the trees, sounding closer. Antonia tried to work out how near it was but saw only undergrowth. The van drove off with a blast of the horn and disappeared round the corner. After checking the lorry driver wasn't looking in her direction, she swarmed over the fence, lowering her body to the ground. Even this short drop made her gasp in pain.

The lorry's engine turned over and caught, expelling a cloud of black smoke. She hobbled to the back of it before it moved off. Frozen fingers made clumsy with panic struggled to unsnap the shutter's hook as the vehicle rolled forward. The barking grew louder, but she ignored it and concentrated on the task. Then the hook came free and she pushed the shutter open. The lorry picked up speed and she threw herself forward, landing behind Chapman's car. As she congratulated herself on getting away, the barking stopped. She saw why. The dog was charging at her, less than ten paces away, and she froze as it gathered itself for a leap, jaws agape.

CHAPTER 25

Chapman lay on a hard floor under heavy boots. The thickening air trapped in the sack made him light-headed. The vehicle stopped and the engine died, then the door opened. In the background a chain rattled.

'Get him out,' The Smoker said.

Hands grabbed him and hauled him upright. Made dizzy by the sudden movement, he swayed.

'Take it off,' the voice said.

Someone pulled the hood off, not bothering to untie the draw-string. The wound on his cheek opened, dripping blood down his chin. Chapman blinked and gulped fresh air as a roller shutter finished clanking shut. Light seeped in through muck-covered skylights, illuminating a large space. A warehouse with the musty odour of age. Three men stood in front of him and he sensed more behind him.

'This way,' one of them said in an Australian accent, gripping his upper arm and dragging him towards the back corner.

His legs still unsteady, he followed, but too slowly and received a smack round the ear. A second man grabbed his elbow and the cable tie securing his wrists cut into the flesh.

'Hey, there's no need—'

'Shut it,' the Australian said, prodding him in the kidneys.

They pushed him towards a doorway twenty metres away at the rear of the space. One of the other men hit a switch on the wall. A row of strip lights flickered and he opened the door.

Stairs led down and Chapman resisted. 'Where are you taking me?'

'Wherever we want,' the Australian said, and the others laughed.

They dragged him down the stairs and the odour of mould and damp increased. At the bottom, they waited for The Smoker, who struggled down, favouring his injured knee. Chapman's vision adjusted to the dim light. A bare bulb in the centre of the ceiling illuminated a basement room six metres square with whitewashed brick walls, the paint flaking and patchy. The vaulted brick ceiling was over two metres above the stained concrete floor and dirty puddles occupied two corners.

'What do you want?' Chapman said.

'The girl, and any copies of the documents,' The Smoker said.

'What do I get?'

'You're not in a position to bargain.'

'What's my incentive?'

'I don't do carrots.' The Smoker grinned. 'Just sticks.'

Chapman swallowed and the Australian said, 'Don't bother making a noise. There's nobody to hear you down here.'

Chapman knees quivered. '*You* know where the girl is, and she's got the papers.'

'So you say.' The Smoker signalled and the men flanking Chapman dragged him to the far corner of the room.

A chunky chair sat four feet from the wall. Ugly but functional, a sheet of plywood formed the seat, and the legs, resembling fence posts, supported solid arms. It had no back and bolts secured it to the concrete floor. The two men positioned him in front of it and the Australian released his arm before shoving a pistol into the side of his neck. He passed a clasp knife to the other man, who hacked at the cable tie until it parted, releasing the pressure on Chapman's wrists. He flexed his hands.

'Easy.' The Australian ground the barrel into his neck.

They spun him round and pushed him into the chair. He gripped the crude arms to break his fall. With practised ease the two men secured his wrists to the chair. Brown splashes of dried blood marked the floor. He sensed movement behind him and before he could react the two men hit him in the kidneys with what felt like hammers. The agony emptied his lungs and his cry came out a gasp. He slumped forward, breathing hard but trying not to move until the pain receded.

'Now I have your attention, Sergeant Chapman, I'll ask you a few questions,' The Smoker said.

Once he could speak, he said, 'My colleagues will wonder where—'

'You think so, *Mr* Chapman, now you're suspended?'

Fear made Chapman's bladder loosen. He didn't want to die, especially not like this. The opening notes of 'The Teddy Bears' Picnic' rang out and Chapman thought he was hallucinating, but The Smoker produced a phone and it stopped.

'Yes,' he said. 'Hang on, signal's crap.' He hobbled over to the bottom of the stairs. 'Go on.' He listened for a few seconds. 'What about the dog?' He listened again. 'She can't have. We've got a car on each road out of there.' He held the phone against his body and stared up at the ceiling, muttering before continuing, 'Right, we'll get more guys out there and a proper tracker dog. I'll return and take charge.'

He spoke to the men behind Chapman. 'You two, stay with him, and Eddy,' he addressed the Australian, 'let's have your gun.'

The two men glared at each other but after a few seconds Eddy grinned. 'Sure.' He passed over an automatic. 'I won't need it to deal with this drongo.'

'We might still need him, so don't overdo it.'

The Australian saluted and smirked at Chapman. 'Don't worry, I won't.'

Dread drowned the relief that Antonia had evaded their men. The Australian studied him like a hungry predator while sounds of the others leaving carried down the stairs.

'I'll lock the shutter,' Eddy said. 'Don't go away, Sergeant.'

Chapman waited as the roller shutter rattled to a close, then Eddy reappeared. He held something in his hand and Chapman tried to see it, his body tense. Eddy walked up to him and threw a liquid at Chapman's face.

He jerked away, but fire flowed into the wound on his cheek. Someone yelled in pain, and recognising his own voice, he clamped his jaws shut.

'Sorry, did I use too much?' Eddy said with mock concern. He held up a bottle half-full of brown liquid. 'Don't want to get an infection, do we.'

Chapman recognised the distinctive green label as the disinfectant ate into his flesh. Eddy placed the bottle on the floor and produced an extendable baton from his pocket. With a flick of his wrist the baton extended more than half a metre. He swung it in a lazy arc and it whipped into Chapman's jaw, snapping his head sideways. His vision blurred as he hung on to consciousness, then the right side of his face became numb.

'Eddy!' the other man said in a high voice. 'You heard what Lia— Just leave 'im.'

With another flick of his wrist Eddy housed the baton and slipped it into a pocket. The other man relaxed and stepped away.

The loud banging on the gate made them jump. His guards froze, then Eddy said, 'You get it.'

The other guard hesitated, giving a backward glance to Chapman before leaving the room. Eddy grinned and reached into his jacket.

◆ ◆ ◆

Antonia recoiled from the dog, backing against the rear of Chapman's car. As the animal launched itself, another cloud of black smoke shot out of the exhaust and billowed around it. Both front paws landed on the load bed as the lorry jerked forward. The dog's massive chest hit the floor, its jaws half a metre from her nose. The animal's fetid breath enveloped her as claws scrabbled for purchase. Unable to get a grip, it slid backwards.

The dog fell off the lorry on to the concrete and performed a somersault before trotting a few steps and coming to a halt. The excited shouts of his handlers grew louder. A short loop of webbing hung down from the shutter and she reached up, dragging it down as two figures appeared behind the dog. The lorry picked up speed and she huddled on the floor, hoping the men hadn't seen her.

She hooked the webbing over a peg and hunted for something to hold. The roof let in enough light, so she could see the lorry contained nothing except the car, and edging towards the front she clambered in. She eased herself into the passenger seat, taking the weight off her ankle before massaging it through her jeans. The flesh felt swollen and doughy but she mustn't think about the damage.

She wanted to rest but needed to get out of there before the lorry arrived at its destination. It stopped and she panicked for a moment, but they were in the wilds and she'd seen nowhere it could have reached so soon. When it moved off she relaxed, but she would have to get out sooner rather than later. She'd wait until it stopped in traffic and climb out. But she didn't know where to find Chapman. She had to assume they'd captured him, and staying to the end of the journey, hoping they took the car to the same destination, gave her the best chance of finding him.

There'd been at least four other men loading the lorry, and she'd need help to tackle them. Chapman's phone wasn't in the glove compartment and a frantic search of the car ended in failure. A sense of helplessness hovered at the edge of her mind but she pushed it away. She'd survived worse. With a surge of hope she remembered the handgun and heaved herself out of the car. It lay in the boot, hidden under an old anorak smelling of Chapman. She was freezing, so she put it on and slid the gun into the side pocket.

In the car, she examined the weapon. She'd handled a few firearms during a story on illegal gunsmiths and although not an expert, knew how they worked. She weighed the magazine in her hand – her only ammunition, so she must make every one count.

Lulled by the motion of the vehicle, she let the tension leave her body. With a start she realised the lorry had stopped. She scrambled out of the car, her legs unsteady, and made her way to the back, listening to the sounds outside. She heard voices but no traffic. They must be at their destination. Her fingers trembled as she retrieved the pistol and held it to her side, then with a jerk, the lorry moved forward before stopping again. The brakes hissed and the engine died.

Nothing happened for a while, so she pressed her ear against the side wall and heard a rattling noise. It ended and the voices started again but she couldn't make out the words. They came closer and stepping away from the shutter, she tightened her grip on the pistol. The shutter lifted a few centimetres before snapping shut. Antonia stared at it, then the webbing, still fastened over the peg. Before she could free it, a man swore and pushed the shutter up again, this time inserting his fingers underneath. The loop jammed against the peg.

A man with a high voice said, 'Let me have a go.'

The shutter slammed shut and Antonia unhooked the webbing before stepping back with the gun raised. The man grunted and the shutter flew upwards. Bright light blinded her. A body lurched forward into the lorry, and supporting her weight on her good ankle, she smashed her heel into the side of his head. He grunted and collapsed on to the cargo bed, lying face down with his feet on the floor.

Another man watched open-mouthed and by the time he'd regained his senses, she'd trained the pistol on him. He raised his hands. Around fifty with thinning grey hair and a paunch, he wasn't like the men who'd chased her. The other man groaned and stirred. She kicked him again, taking out her anger at what these men had done. Her ankle complained, but the man stopped moving.

His companion stared, terrified. 'Don't shoot—'

Her sharp gesture silenced him. 'How many others?' she whispered. 'Answer without speaking.'

His eyes widened in panic, then he mimed driving and mouthed, 'I'm only driver.' The other one might know, but he wasn't likely to talk anytime soon. She gestured to the driver to step away and lowered herself before sliding on to the rough concrete floor. The lorry sat in a warehouse that smelt of mould and diesel fumes. Roller shutters protected the three large openings in the front wall.

Two doors led from the rear and she pointed at the nearest. 'What's behind there? Whisper it.'

'Toilet,' he said.

She pointed at the second and he hesitated so she jabbed him in the side with the pistol.

'Cellars.'

She hit him on the temple with the butt of the pistol and he crumpled to the floor. A thin red ribbon leaked from the wound. The other man still hadn't moved. She checked the toilets before heading for the second door, which stood ajar. The light showed stairs leading down and after checking behind her, she descended, limping on her injured ankle. The earthy stink hit her and from halfway down she could see it opened into a room. As her vision adjusted to the light, she saw a figure in the far corner, a man in a chair. Chapman, and he looked in a bad way. With the pistol held in front of her, she stepped off the stairs.

Chapman spoke but there was something wrong with his voice. She sensed someone behind her and spun, seeing a man holding a stick. The weapon became a blur as he aimed a blow at her. She moved to block it and it smashed into the automatic, knocking it from her grasp and making her stagger. As she attempted to keep her balance, her ankle gave way and she fell. Her attacker raised his right arm.

Sparks flashed against the ceiling above him as metal scraped across brick. The man swore, but the expected blow never made contact; instead a metallic object landed on the concrete floor a metre away. She rolled towards it, kicking out at the man's legs. Her heel hit him and the man grunted.

She focused on what he'd dropped and seeing the retractable baton, grabbed it. Her hands still stung from the blow but her fingers closed on one end. Chapman shouted a warning then a heavy body landed on her. The impact almost dislodged the baton, but maintaining her grip, she swung it backwards. It landed with a hollow *thunk* but apart from making him snort, didn't have any effect.

An arm wrapped round her neck cutting off her airway. She swung the baton again but couldn't get power behind the blow. Dizzy from lack of oxygen, she gathered herself for a last effort, but this time stabbed backwards with the bar.

With a cry of pain, her attacker released her. She rolled over, gasping, and rose to her knees. The man came at her, his foot raised, and she ducked under it, swinging the baton upwards between his legs. He grunted as it made contact and before he recovered, she swung it again. He fell to his knees, clutching at his groin and made a grab for her with his other hand.

A punch from her free fist pushed him away, giving her space for a swing. Her first blow hit him below the ear and blood sprayed from the wound. The second, with all her weight behind it, crunched into his skull and he fell sideways. The force of the strike ripped the weapon from her hand but she wouldn't need it again. With her vision now adjusted to the gloom, she recognised her opponent.

'Will that do as my free shot?' she said, between gritted teeth.

Chapman mumbled something and she studied him. He looked more than in a bad way. Battered features bore evidence of the beating he'd endured, the swelling on the left side of his face balanced by an angry wound disfiguring the right side. She staggered to her feet and went to him.

'You okay?' she said, out of breath, and searched for something to cut him free.

'Gweat,' he said, adding, 'His pocket. Wife.'

She took a second to realise what he meant and returned to her attacker. A pool of blood surrounded him, flowing from the centre of his ear. She found the knife in the second pocket she searched. After hacking off the fastenings, she helped Chapman to his feet, her ankle complaining at the extra weight.

'Can you walk?'

Chapman mumbled something before taking a step and stumbling. Between them they made it to the stairs. Near the bottom lay the automatic and, ignoring Chapman's gesture to give it to him, she pocketed it. Using the rickety bannister for support, they struggled up to the ground floor, Chapman's progress even slower than hers.

Fearful the others would soon return, she wanted to rush, but her ankle couldn't support his weight. The driver was sitting up, groaning and holding his head. When he saw her, he shrank away. The other man still lay in the lorry.

'Keys,' Chapman said, pointing at the vehicle.

Antonia stepped towards the driver, who retrieved a bunch from his pocket and threw them to her. She stared at them. She didn't know how to drive a car, let alone a lorry. Chapman seemed to read her mind and gestured for them. He wasn't in any state to drive but what options did they have? Chapman swayed when he took the keys but ignoring her ankle's complaints, she stopped him falling. The cab of the lorry seemed impossibly far, then an idea.

'You' – she pointed the pistol at the driver – 'help him.'

The man scrambled to his feet and swayed before steadying himself. He supported Chapman and they made their way to the cab, taking an eternity to cover the fifteen metres. Once he'd helped Chapman into the driver's seat, she waved him away.

'Move over there,' she said, gesturing to the front of the vehicle and ushering him round to the other side. 'In the corner,' she said before backing up to the passenger door and, keeping her gaze on him, she clambered aboard. The engine burst into life, filling the bay with black smoke.

'Get him to open the front,' Chapman said.

She opened the window to shout the instruction but a loud banging came from the shutter in the next bay. 'Open up!'

The driver hesitated, torn between waiting for her order and responding to the shout. Another bang made the slats quiver. The lorry leapt forward, throwing her into her seat. It ploughed into the shutter, which gave way with a scream of tearing metal. A curtain of steel obscured her vision, then it was snatched away to reveal the brick wall of the building opposite racing towards them. Chapman stamped on the brakes and the engine stalled.

Outside the adjacent bay, the occupants of a blue people carrier hesitated and then exploded into action, reaching for weapons as their engine turned over with a dull click.

CHAPTER 26

Chapman turned the key again, but nothing happened. *What the hell's wrong?* Antonia fell into the footwell. *Is she hit?* But she sat up, frightened but unhurt. Then he remembered he needed to apply the brakes before he could start it. They hissed, then the engine coughed before catching with a roar. He released the brakes and the vehicle lurched forward, heading for the wall again until he pulled on the steering wheel, aiming towards the people carrier.

Figures scattered out of his path and the lorry clipped the corner of the smaller vehicle, swatting it aside with a crunch. A lamp post loomed in the windscreen but he spun the wheel and missed it by a miracle. In his mirror, the men swarmed into their car and he hoped he'd done enough damage to disable it. He slowed as he approached the main road, saw a gap and pulled out into the stream of traffic, leaving his torture chamber behind.

'You can get up,' he said and Antonia scrambled on to her seat, wincing as she put weight on her foot. 'What's wrong?'

'Damaged my ankle.'

'Looks painful.'

She grinned at him. 'Less than your face, I'd imagine.'

He attempted a smile, but his jaw hurt too much. He hoped he'd not broken it. A road sign told him where they were, so finding the warehouse again wouldn't be a problem. Up ahead lights changed and he braked, checking the mirrors, but nobody had followed them.

'We've lost them,' he said.

'Where's the nearest police station?'

'Forget it. After what you did to the man in the basement—'

'But he was trying to kill me.'

'I'm not blaming you, the opposite, but you've laid yourself open to excessive use of force. And you had a gun.' These men must work with the two he'd shot and he didn't want that can of worms examined.

'But they'll find my DNA on both of them.' Antonia sounded despondent.

'Don't worry about it, whoever is paying that lot will make everything disappear,' he said with more confidence than he felt.

'We need to change vehicles. How far can you walk?'

'I should be all right,' he said, but he'd struggle to cover any distance.

Antonia massaged her calf. 'I won't get far on this.'

'Thank you for getting me out. How did you find—'

The car behind flashed him and Chapman panicked until the Porsche raced past him, the driver tooting his horn and gesticulating towards the rear of the lorry.

'Blast!' Antonia said. 'Stop.'

'Why, what's—'

'Just do it.'

Another car flashed its headlights, and suppressing an angry retort, Chapman pulled into a layby. 'What's the—' But she'd gone, leaving the door swinging.

She disappeared behind the vehicle, hobbling back a few seconds later and pulling herself into the cab before slamming the door.

'I'd left the shutter open,' she said as she fastened her seatbelt. 'Why the panic?'

'I left one of them in the back but he must have fallen out.'

'Left him—' He replayed what she'd done to Eddy and decided not to ask any more. Thank God she was on his side. 'How did you find me?' he said, noticing she was wearing his jacket.

'Your car's in the back so I guessed, *hoped*, they'd bring it to the same place.'

'Good guess.' A wave of pain and exhaustion made him tremble. He just wanted to lie down in a darkened room. 'I can't drive far.'

'We'll get a cab, there's plenty on this road.'

Five minutes later they abandoned the lorry in a side street. He struggled out and leant against the side, his head pounding and jaw throbbing. Antonia clambered into the back, returning with her backpack before flagging down a cab. The first one refused to take them when he saw Chapman's face but the next one examined them, shrugged, and let them aboard. Exhausted and in pain, Chapman collapsed on to the seat.

After what seemed like no time at all, Antonia shook him awake and helped him out. The walk to the front door of the block drained him, then the stairs waited. Climbing them took an eternity, with Antonia supporting him, emitting low whimpers with every step she took. An overwhelming feeling of gratitude made him want to hold her. The climb ended and Antonia left him propped up against the wall as she prepared the sofa bed, then, as he was about to fall, she helped him to the bed and lowered him on to the mattress before collapsing next to him. Despite knowing they were far from safe, sleep overcame him.

◆ ◆ ◆

Antonia woke with light streaming through the skylights she'd forgotten to cover. Not wanting it to disturb Chapman, she slid off the bed, wincing as she put weight on her injured ankle. After limping to the skylights and closing the blinds, she made her way to the bathroom. In the shower, she avoided looking at her ankle. It wouldn't be pretty. Washed and refreshed, she hopped to the kitchen and found a tray of ice cubes which she wrapped in a tea towel and pressed to her ankle as she lay on the bed.

Twenty minutes later, she removed the ice pack and examined her ankle. The blackened and swollen flesh resembled an aubergine. Helping Chapman up the stairs had drained her more than she cared to acknowledge and the intense pain lingered. Mind you, he looked even worse than she felt. He mumbled but slept on and she wondered what he dreamt of, hoping it was something good. At least her exhaustion had stopped her dreaming.

She got up and hobbled to the kitchen to get rid of the half-melted ice. Every part of her body ached, but the shower had woken her. She made her painful way to the chair, taking with her the papers on the case and her laptop. Chapman stirred again when the computer beeped, but he didn't wake.

The fear that whoever had arranged the ambush at the Sears Industrial Estate could track them to this flat made her panicky, but she needed to focus on finding out who had murdered the missing women. The fact that Monika had worked at GRM and Agnes Sanders had been offered a job there had to be significant. But Agnes hadn't taken up the job offer, and she'd failed to take the other one she'd been offered. Why?

Antonia read the letter the solicitors sent to Agnes, withdrawing the job offer. She'd not paid it much attention, but as she studied it, the logo stirred a memory. She found it on the papers she'd recovered from the shredder and checked the details. A frisson of excitement made her want to wake Chapman and tell him, but he needed sleep. Another thought deflated her. How was Sabirah coping in prison? The best way to help her friend would be to take GRM down, and if she could link them to the deaths of these young women, she'd be halfway there.

A phone chirruped, signalling an incoming text. Chapman stirred but carried on sleeping. It came from the chest of drawers across the room. She found the mobile under Chapman's clothes, a basic pay-as-you-go. How many did he have? The text message said WHERE THE HELL R U. She'd forgotten he lived with someone. The poor woman must be frantic with worry. Should she ring and tell her he was okay? But she didn't want to get into a long explanation and contented herself with a short text: I'm ok explain later.

'Who's that?' Chapman croaked, making her jump.

'Sorry, I didn't know you were awake.' She held the phone toward him. 'Brigitte, asking . . . wanting to know how you were. I said you're okay . . . I put it from you . . . Sorry.'

'Thanks.' He waved the phone away and tried to sit, grimacing with the effort.

'Don't get up—'

'I need a piss.'

'Right.' She helped him get to the door of the wetroom. The thought that he'd need help in there made her face hot. 'Will you be okay?' She gestured at the door.

'You offering to hold it for me?' He saw her expression. 'Sorry, inappropriate. I'll be fine, thank you.'

While she waited for him to return, she read through the files Dobrowski had given them. Considering the woman's treachery, could they trust the documents? They appeared genuine. Were Latif, the private investigator framed for murdering Sofie Stoltz, and Murray, Alan's mole, the real targets and the women just camouflage to deflect the investigations? But why had Monika and Agnes Sanders disappeared? Their bodies hadn't been found.

Perhaps there was no link. She checked the descriptions of the two dead women. Neither resembled Monika nor Agnes, and they didn't have much else in common with each other. There must be another reason they'd been targeted. The realisation that Monika was probably dead made her breath stutter. But why? She exhaled in frustration and returned to researching the two men.

Latif had been investigating GRM for a client, maybe a news outlet like theirs, and Murray had been working *for* GRM, and leaking information to Turner. What could Latif have discovered that justified trying to kill him? Once Chapman returned, she'd ask him to see if they could arrange to visit Latif in prison. He said Latif had refused to talk after the attacks on him and his family, but it must be worth trying again. What about Murray? She studied the papers again. The disclosure that GRM had dodged taxes would embarrass Reed-Mayhew, but would it justify killing someone? There must be something she wasn't seeing. But what? She wanted to scream.

She studied the document listing the payment to Hajduk Veljko. What had he done for GRM to justify such large fees? A search brought up thousands of references to an eighteenth-century figure, but nothing more recent. She read the first entry: 'Hero of the first Serbian Uprising against the Ottomans.' So, another pseudonym, like Margaret Gage. A snatch of conversation came back to her, Mishkin and Reed-Mayhew mentioning a Serb carrying out a task for them while she hid in the cleaner's cupboard. It must be linked to Alan's assertion that they had connections to the recent bombings. That was the day of the Paddington bombing. The implications made her thoughts race. Murray died before he could speak to Turner, but Chapman had found papers at Murray's place. They might shine a light on what made it worth killing him, but as the NSA had taken them off Chapman, there was no chance of examining them.

The door opened and Chapman appeared. 'God, that was difficult. You got any painkillers?'

She helped him to a seat and gave him two extra-strength ibuprofens, taking one herself, and made coffee while he caught up with her notes. 'What do you think?' she asked, placing a mug of coffee next to him.

'Your theory that these payments were for the Paddington and King's Cross bombings are pretty explosive.' He grinned. 'But I wouldn't publish it if you want to avoid a big defamation lawsuit.'

'Believe it or not, we don't put anything out if we don't have the evidence.'

'The account where these payments came from' – he tapped the sheets – 'I found the statement in the envelope I discovered at Murray's place.'

'Shame you couldn't hang on to them. Did you find anything that might make it worth killing Murray and framing him for killing Aida Rizk?'

'Sorry, I can't remember seeing anything else.'

She tried to hide her disappointment. 'Let's find out who owns Sears Industrial Estate.' She carried out a search as Chapman sipped his coffee, her frustration increasing as she read. 'A shell company based in Bermuda, but no link to GRM . . .'

'That's not a surprise,' Chapman said.

'I'd love to see inside those units.'

'Too dangerous to go back.'

'Couldn't we get your lot to search them?'

'On what pretext?'

'What about if we check if the van went there in the days before they discovered the woman "killed" by Latif? The footage you gave me didn't go back far enough.'

'I'm not sure if we can get it that far back, but even if we did, what would it prove?' He placed the mug down and crossed his arms.

'There's something dodgy going on. For them to drive from there to where you found one body might not mean anything, but if it happened twice . . .'

'But why kill those women? They could have got rid of Murray and Latif without killing two more people.'

'I don't know.' Chapman's negativity pissed her off. She wished she could talk this over with Turner, but that would *never* happen again. A wave of grief made her want to howl, but she fought through it. Who'd organise his funeral? Whatever happened to her, she'd go. But what about Eleanor? Someone would have to tell her about her nephew. And it had to be Antonia. She hadn't even seen Eleanor for a few days. Was she awake yet? Or maybe she'd got worse. The certainty something had happened to her struck Antonia.

'Can I borrow your phone?'

'Hmm.' Chapman slid it to her. 'Sure, yeah.'

She rang the hospital demanding they put her through to ICU.

'Can you tell me how Eleanor Curtis is?' she said as soon as someone answered.

'Curtis? Hang on,' a woman with a Northern Ireland accent said. After a few seconds of clicks she returned. 'When was she admitted?'

'A few days ago. Why? What's wrong?'

'She's not on the ward—'

'What do you mean?' A surge of panic made Antonia leap to her feet.

'Sorry, I'm from an agency. If you want, I'll make enquiries and get back to you.'

Antonia gave her Chapman's number and ended the call.

'Something up?' Chapman said, his voice sounding slurred as if he was struggling to stay awake.

'I'm not sure.'

He closed his eyes again and after a few minutes began snoring. Unable to stand waiting any longer, Antonia rang a cab. After strapping her ankle, she hobbled downstairs and waited in the car park. *Please don't let me be too late.*

◆ ◆ ◆

The clamour of the prison faded as the inmates concentrated on eating their breakfast. The smell of the food made Sabirah nauseous, but thinking of Nadimah and Hakim in the hands of the people trafficker would have removed any appetite in any case.

'Sabirah Fadil!' the guard shouted.

Sabirah cringed as the other inmates turned their attention on her.

'Assistant governor wants to see you.'

Jeers and catcalls broke out and her face grew hot. Had they found her children? She pushed the bowl away and struggled to her feet.

The guard spotted her and gestured at her to hurry. 'Come on, don't keep him waiting.'

Sabirah shuffled along the row, bent over to ease the pain of her ribs. Comments of 'Dirty Arab' and 'Snitch' followed her as she passed. Although she ate with the others, the regulations forbade her talking to them, and that suited her. She kept her head down and fell into step behind the guard. If they'd found Nadimah and Hakim, they might let her see them. Could they be here now? She told herself not to let the hope grow. The disappointment if they weren't would make everything that much harder. The more likely explanation was they'd reviewed her refugee status and were going to deport her – a fate made far worse if she didn't have her children with her.

Once in the corridor, the warder smiled at her and didn't shout when she struggled to keep up. She realised there wasn't a second one behind her. This must be good news. She hurried, but her knee still hurt from when the Kurdish woman had attacked her in the showers. The guard halted outside the assistant governor's door and knocked, receiving the instruction 'Come in' straight away.

Sabirah stepped in, surprised to see another woman in front of the desk. The assistant governor said, 'Mrs Fadil, please sit—'

'Have you found my children?'

He frowned at the interruption. 'Meet Mrs Ellis,' he said, gesturing at the woman.

The woman gave her a smile, but it lacked sincerity. They couldn't have found the children or – please God, no. They'd found them, but something had happened.

'Good news, Mrs Fadil,' Mrs Ellis said. 'We're releasing you.'

It must be a trick. 'What about my children?'

The woman studied her blankly. 'I know nothing about . . .' She looked at the assistant governor.

'The police are searching for the man who posed as their uncle.' His gaze didn't meet hers. 'Don't worry, they'll find him.'

'Thank you.' Although desperate to believe him, Sabirah suspected she couldn't.

'As Mrs Ellis said, the police have withdrawn all charges so you're free to go.'

'I can go home?'

Still grinning, he nodded.

Tears cascaded down Sabirah's cheeks and she sobbed. Her prayers had been answered too late. Nadimah and Hakim had gone. At least if she got out, she could find them. Patience would help her. But she didn't have money for the Tube and didn't know where the nearest station was.

'—will make sure you get home.' The assistant governor held out an envelope, which she took.

In it she found a thin sheaf of notes, then Sabirah noticed the bag in front of his desk. Her clothes. 'Thank you, sir.'

He waved her thanks away. 'Once you're changed and have collected your belongings, you can go with Mrs Ellis.'

Still in a daze, she followed the guard and twenty minutes later arrived at the gates of the prison in her own clothes. She'd dreamt of this moment since she arrived. A large dark car, a van with seats, arrived and Mrs Ellis slid open the rear door.

'Do you want to jump in, Mrs Fadil?'

Two men wearing dark clothes sat in the front seats. Sabirah hesitated, not wanting to get in, but she must find her children. Mrs Ellis got in and patted the seat next to her. Sabirah followed and the woman slammed the door. The car pulled away and Sabirah fastened the seatbelt. Her insides tensed; she wanted to run away.

Mrs Ellis offered her something. The windows were dark, so it took Sabirah a few seconds to see it. A phone. 'Sabirah – can I call you that?'

Sabirah nodded.

'Your friend's number is on there,' Mrs Ellis said. 'Patience, you call her, but she's called Antonia.'

How did this woman know Patience and what did she mean? Sabirah dismissed her words. 'I have a phone.' She found it in her handbag and switched it on, but nothing happened.

'The battery's dead. Take this.'

Sabirah took it and stared out of the windows. The notion that the children hadn't been taken but were hiding grew, and by the time she arrived at her home half an hour later, she'd almost convinced herself they'd be waiting for her. She raced up to the house and with shaking hands, opened the front door.

'Nadimah, Hakim!'

No answer. The place smelt musty, as if nobody had been in it for a while.

She searched the rest of the flat, knowing she'd find nothing, and returned to the living room. Sick with disappointment and exhausted by her ordeal, she sagged against the wall. The van left and she retrieved the phone. She hadn't liked the Ellis woman and didn't trust her, but she needed to find her children. Patience's number was the only one in the memory and she hit dial.

CHAPTER 27

Still high after the relief of finding Eleanor awake but weak in a general ward, Antonia paid the taxi. The bandage the nurse had applied at the hospital supported her ankle, making negotiating the stairs to the flat easier, and the analgesics were taking the edge off the pain. She found Chapman slumped on the sofa, snoring, and resisted the urge to wake him. Did the people at The Investigator know about Turner's murder? She retrieved Chapman's phone, taking it into the kitchenette.

His girlfriend's reply to his last message just said: Leb wohl. Wondering what the hell it meant, she rang the office.

'Hello, Electric Investigator—'

'Miles, it's Antonia.'

'Antonia, oh my God, have you heard about Alan?' Miles's professional tone evaporated.

'Yes.' She swallowed a sob. 'How is everybody?'

'Devastated.' Miles's voice broke. 'We're keeping going, but just. How about you?'

'The same,' she said, her breath faltering.

'Before I forget, your friend rang—'

'Kerry?' Had something happened to the children?

'No. She confused me, asking for Patience. Her name was Sabirah or something like—'

'What did she say?' Questions raced round Antonia's mind.

'She said to tell you she's home, and asked about her children. She had a strong accent and I missed some of what she said. Sorry.'

Thank God. 'Did she leave a number?' Antonia memorised it and rang straight away. The phone purred in her ear. What had changed to make them release her friend?

'Patience?' Sabirah shouted.

'Sabirah, how are—'

'Patience, bad man take my children,' Sabirah wailed.

'No, he didn't—'

'Police say man who—'

'Nobody's taken them, they're with—' Antonia wanted to reassure her, but clung to her habit of not giving too many details by telephone. 'They're safe. I'll take you to them. Did they say why they released you?'

Sabirah sobbed for a few moments, then took a stuttering breath. 'The woman say all charge dropped.'

'The woman at the prison?'

'She bring me home—'

'Where did you get this phone?' Antonia hadn't recognised the number and her scalp crawled.

'Woman gave. My battery dead—'

'Sabirah, don't use this phone again. Charge your own phone. I'll contact you. And don't worry about Nadimah and Hakim.'

Antonia ended the call and stared at the phone for a few moments before switching it off. Whoever gave Sabirah the phone must have traced her. She'd been an idiot, ringing an unknown number from here. Now she and Chapman must get out, and quickly.

◆ ◆ ◆

Chapman heard the murmur of voices and experienced a moment's panic before recalling where he was. He remembered an interminable climb before passing out, but why wasn't he lying down? He was sure he'd spoken to Antonia, but where was she?

'Antonia,' he called, and she burst out of the kitchen brandishing his phone.

'We have to leave.'

'What's happened?'

'I'll tell you on the way.'

'Where are we going—'

'It doesn't matter. We have to go, now!' She threw his clothes on to the bed beside him.

Chapman wasn't in the mood for this. Every part of him hurt like hell, especially the side of his head. 'What's the time?' Daylight seeped in through the edge of the blind on the skylight, so he guessed morning.

'What the hell.' Antonia threw up her hands. 'Eleven. Now get dressed.'

His brain seemed loose and his tongue was stuck to the roof of his mouth. 'I need a shower.'

Antonia grabbed his shoulders and pulled him forward.

'What the fuck!' Pain shot through his ribs then seared through his skull, making the room sway. Antonia released him and he closed his eyes until the dizziness passed.

She crouched down in front of him. 'We have to go because the people who did this to you might be on the way here. Do you understand?'

Fear replaced the surge of anger and he said, 'Help me up. Slowly.'

Her body vibrated with suppressed energy as she helped him upright. Despite her gentleness the pain made him gasp.

She disappeared into the kitchen, returning with a glass of water. She thrust two white pills into his hand. 'I got them for my ankle, they're stronger than the ones you took earlier.'

Chapman swallowed both and drank half the water in one gulp. With Antonia's help he struggled into his clothes. She let him spread toothpaste on his teeth and rinse his foul-tasting mouth out while she packed. He'd avoided his reflection earlier but this time caught a glimpse in the mirror. He'd make a great child-scarer.

He waited at the entrance to the flats, guarding their bags while Antonia went to find a cab. If those men found them he didn't give much for their chances of survival. The tension in his guts increased as he waited and he fondled the automatic in his coat pocket. He'd always been confident he could deal with any problems he encountered, even without the force behind him, but look at him now, relying on a girl to keep him safe. This must be what getting old did to you.

The thrumming of the taxi engine soothed Antonia into a trance-like state. She needed to find somewhere safe to take Chapman. How could she have made such a basic mistake? *Stupid, stupid.* Her options were dwindling. She couldn't stay with Kerry and the kids. What about Turner's place? No, although empty, the men responsible knew about it. Images of a very alive Turner tumbled through Antonia's thoughts. She'd brought these men into their lives. They'd killed Turner and put Eleanor in hospital where, despite her improvement, she remained in a bad way. The thought of *her* dying filled Antonia with terror. She couldn't lose any more people who mattered to her. Last time she'd lost her family, the people responsible carried on with their lives, unmolested, as if their victims had no worth. She wouldn't let it happen again.

'Antonia?'

She jumped. Chapman studied her through his right eye, the left closed by bruised and swollen flesh.

'Yeah?' she said.

'Where are we going?'

She glanced towards the driver. 'Aylesham Shopping Centre.'

Chapman leant toward her and whispered, 'But where then?'

She didn't have a clue. Did Chapman know somewhere else they could stay? But if he did, he'd have suggested it. Could they sneak into Kerry's flat, just for one night?

The taxi pulled up and the driver said, 'Sixteen seventy.'

'Here, keep the change.' Chapman shoved a twenty at him.

'We need to be careful with money,' Antonia said as the taxi left. 'We can't risk using our cards.'

Chapman gave her a sour look. They paused at the entrance to the shopping centre and she studied the unprepossessing choice of shops. Her ankle hurt as the painkillers wore off. 'Shall we grab a coffee and a bite?'

They found seats at the back of a cafe that smelt of old oil and overcooked vegetables and she took two painkillers, offering Chapman the same. A huge Black man with a shaved skull passed in front of the window and for an instant she mistook him for Milo Dekker, but this man wore an earring. The thought of having the Dekker brothers at her side gave her a boost; then she remembered something Darius had said.

'Drink up,' she told Chapman. 'We've got a home to find.'

The taxi dropped them outside a mini-mart two hundred metres from the gym. She left Chapman with their bags and went to see the Dekkers. The familiar odour of liniment and leather made her want to get changed and complete an intense workout.

Blow the cobwebs away and forget her troubles. The clank of heavy plates from the far end told her where to find her friends.

Milo, spotting a bench-press bar for his brother, shouted, 'Hey Antonia, what's up with your leg?'

The bar stopped and Milo eased it on to the stand. The high-tensile steel flexed as the eighty-kilo plates on each end settled. Darius sat up, a sheen of sweat on his forehead. 'You okay, kid?' he said, wiping it with his wristband.

The temptation to say 'No, I need taking care of' passed in an instant. 'Sure, I just need somewhere to lie low, just for a few days.'

'Just you?'

'I've got a . . . friend.'

The brothers exchanged a glance. 'You're in luck. We've a new place above a hair salon, just renovated, ready to move into. Two beds and very private. I'll get the keys.' Milo headed towards the changing rooms and as always his gracefulness surprised her.

Darius stared at her, concern in his demeanour. 'What happened?' He indicated her ankle. 'Trouble with the asshole who came searching for you?'

'No.' She laughed. *If only.*

'You know you only have to ask—'

'How's everyone here?'

'Here you are.' Milo handed her the keys and gave her the address.

After thanking them, she hugged each brother and left. Tempting as it was to have their help, she couldn't get any more friends involved.

◆ ◆ ◆

'Who owns this?' Chapman said, studying the tiled entrance to the flat above a small parade of shops. A steel staircase enclosed in corrugated-iron sheeting led directly from the car park behind the shops to the flat. The odour of paint and wallpaper paste filled the air.

'A friend,' Antonia said, putting the luggage in the hall and locking the door behind her. Chapman followed while she inspected the apartment – two bedrooms, a large living room with kitchen and a new bathroom. Basic, but clean and much bigger than their previous hideaway. She carried his bag to the first bedroom and dumped it on the bed. *He* should be doing that for her, but just the walk up to the flat had exhausted him.

'Separate rooms already?' he said.

A scowl told him what she thought of his attempted joke. 'I need to get Sabirah together with her kids.'

'Your friend in prison?'

'They've released her.' She explained what had happened.

Irritation at what she'd done made him explode. 'That's why we had to scarper. After those bloody lectures you—'

'Yes, okay.' She slashed the air with her hand, then the tension drained from her. 'I'm very much aware it's my fault.' Tears gathered in her eyes.

The thought of her crying knocked him sideways. 'You were worried about her. I'd have done the same. And anyway' – he gestured around them – 'you've found us a better place *and* you can get away from my snoring.'

She returned his smile, but it didn't hide her remorse. 'I'll get milk and a few bits. Do you need anything?'

His headache persisted, but the tablets she'd given him played havoc with his guts. 'Soluble painkillers and a Mars bar.'

'Sure. I won't be long. And while I'm gone, can you try to remember anything from the papers you found at Murray's place?'

'I'll try.' At the moment, he couldn't remember anything he'd read yesterday.

'Thanks. And lock the door behind me.'

He resisted the temptation to lie down, knowing he'd fall asleep despite the pain that infused the bones in his face. He suspected they'd released her friend to use her to trap Antonia, but she wouldn't listen if he tried to stop her going. The best way to guarantee her, and *his*, safety would be to make the investigation official. If he ended up being prosecuted for shooting those men, so be it.

He went to his case and dug out a phone, glad he'd bought three. Gunnerson answered straight away.

'Yasmin, it's Russell.'

'Good afternoon, Russell,' she said, her tone wary.

'Have you discovered where they killed Aida Rizk?'

'It's not your case, Russell. In fact, you're suspended—'

'Have you?'

She hesitated before replying. 'No, why?'

'I've got reliable information she died at Sears Industrial Estate—'

'How reliable?'

If he was wrong, he'd lose all credibility with Gunnerson. 'Very.'

'Okay, I'll send someone to investigate and get back to you, thanks—'

'Wait.' Although he questioned the reliability of Antonia's research, he ploughed on. 'Do you remember a PI called Latif? He's doing life for killing his girlfriend.'

Gunnerson didn't reply for long seconds and he pictured her entering the name on her PC. 'Why are you interested in that one?'

'I think the two cases are linked.'

'In what way?'

Chapman hesitated. Up to now what he'd told Gunnerson could be classed as credible speculation. 'Someone framed him and they're trying to do the same with Murray.'

'But Murray's dead—'

'They also tried to kill Latif.'

Gunnerson took so long to answer he wondered if he'd lost the signal. 'That's quite a serious accusation—'

'I haven't made an accusation.'

'No, but you're suggesting we wrapped up three deaths and put away an innocent man, but the killer or killers are still on the loose.'

'Yes.' Chapman held his breath, waiting for her reply.

'Why are you doing this, Russell?' She sounded exasperated.

'I believe someone has got away with several killings.'

'Are you going to tell me who this someone— Shit! You think it's Mishkin, don't you? I told you to stay away from him—'

'The man's a child molester and killer—'

'Alleged, and dismissed as unfounded.'

Chapman paused. He needed Gunnerson's support. 'We've got details of the vehicle used to dispose of Rizk's body.'

'Go on, I'm listening.'

He told her about the van and listened as she tapped the details into a keyboard. 'The van's linked with another incident,' she said. 'A woman made an anonymous call. Hang on, is that the "we" you mentioned?'

'What happened?'

'We investigated but found nothing—'

'Did the forensic examination—'

'No, Russell, you know how these things work. We found nothing to justify a forensic examination. Have you and your . . . what do I call her? Co-accuser? Have you compelling evidence to justify me authorising a forensic examination of the vehicle? Bearing in mind the owners have already made a complaint—'

'Who *are* the owners?'

'Their solicitors made the complaint.'

'Who are they?'

She mentioned the firm who'd sent the letter to Agnes Sanders.

'They're the same—' He realised if he mentioned Mishkin or GRM again, Gunnerson would put the phone down.

Gunnerson broke the silence. 'I take it you have *no* evidence—'

'I've got the van on camera near City Road Basin around the time Rizk was dumped. A witness heard the driver boast he'd killed Pavlo Helba—'

'The *witness* isn't the suspect we questioned about Helba's killing, is she?'

'Yasmin, if I can have access to the traffic camera system I'll find the van near where we found the woman Latif is accused of killing.'

Gunnerson took a long time to reply. 'If you can show it near *both* bodies, I'd stick my neck out.'

Relief made his hand tremble. 'Thank you, Yasmin. And can you let me know how you get on at Sears Industrial Estate?'

'Hmmm. And Russell, be very careful. Your suspension is being monitored from the top. You're already in bad odour with a lot of the high-ups, so don't give them any more ammunition.'

Had she made the right decision? But after what she'd put Sabirah through, getting her together with her kids was the least Antonia could do. Chapman took his time negotiating the stairs from their new flat but her ankle didn't complain too much. The two extra-strength painkillers doubtless helped, detaching her from reality. Now she needed something to kill the emotional pain. She waited as he made his way down the last flight like an old man. He must have damaged his back in the accident. The large plaster covering the gouged wound in his cheek gave him the air of a cartoon villain and she couldn't suppress a grin.

'Something funny?' he said, trying to scowl, but a twinkle in his eye betrayed him.

'Any bad guys who see us coming will run for it.'

'Once they've stopped laughing.'

She became serious. 'There's no need for you to come with me. I'll be okay.'

'I'd only worry about you.'

The thought that he'd worry about her hadn't occurred to Antonia and she didn't know how to react. 'We're meeting Sabirah in a shopping centre.'

'Good idea, more people around and more ways to escape.'

His approval made her feel better. 'I've ordered a cab. We should change at least once. I don't want anyone tracking us here.'

'Do you want these?' he said, handing her the keys to the flat.

'You hang on to them.'

Kerry and the kids were waiting outside a fried-chicken take-away. Antonia's cab pulled up alongside them and, telling the driver to wait, Antonia scrambled out. Kerry's expression when she saw her made Antonia realise how tough her friend had found the last couple of days. The enthusiastic greeting from the children, especially Hakim, lifted her spirits. After promising them a big treat, Antonia said goodbye to Kerry and took the children to meet Sabirah.

Nadimah and Hakim, at first wary of Chapman's battered appearance, warmed to him during the journey, helped in part by his promise to buy them a pizza. At Chapman's insistence, they changed cabs once more, telling the children it was part of an elaborate game. The second taxi drew up outside the entrance to the shopping centre and Antonia set off, leaving Chapman and the disappointed kids in the cab. She checked each entrance for suspicious-looking cars, then traversed every walkway, taking more care as she neared the cafe where she'd arranged to meet Sabirah. The thought that Sabirah's neighbour had been unable to pass on the message, or worse, had betrayed Antonia, lasted an instant. She had to trust somebody.

She had to ignore the urge to greet her friend when she spotted her in a booth, huddled over a table. Careful not to be seen by Sabirah, she circled the block containing the restaurant three times. She scanned the shoppers as she passed, but none stirred her suspicions. Sabirah had kept her promise to be careful. Antonia rushed back to the cab and paid the driver. Chapman set off with the children, attempting to walk without limping like an old crock. Antonia followed them, her senses on edge despite her earlier recce.

Hakim spotted Sabirah before his sister did and cried out. After staring in disbelief, the two children rushed at their mother to form an excited but tearful scrum. Antonia hesitated, her joy at seeing the reunion tempered by the guilt at what she'd put them through. Sabirah waved and beckoned her. Antonia joined them, embracing her friend. Sabirah's tear-stained face showed marks of its own.

'Sabirah, I'm so sorry,' Antonia said.

'Thank you for taking care of my treasures.' She hugged Antonia again, crushing her.

Antonia introduced Chapman and led them to a pizza restaurant in the food hall where he made good his promise. Although Sabirah said little about her incarceration, Antonia could see it had been an ordeal. Regret and guilt robbed her of her appetite but she couldn't change what she'd done and would have to make it up to Sabirah. When they'd eaten, Antonia insisted on giving her the residue of Turner's money before waving them off in the last taxi at the stand. The offices populating this district had closed, leaving the streets almost empty and after five minutes, they were still waiting.

'I'll go up to the junction with the High Street,' she said. 'There's more chance of getting a cab on the main road.'

As she stood on the corner scanning the traffic, Chapman shouted to her. She jumped in alarm, but he waved and pointed at a black cab waiting across the road. A pair of city types emerged from a doorway near the cab and headed for it. Chapman yelled and limped towards them. The three men squared off.

A people carrier with a taxi sign pulled up next to Antonia.

'Come on, Russell, leave them, we'll take this one.'

The side door slid open and two men wearing black jumped out. She spun round. Two more came from behind her. Before she could escape, huge arms wrapped round her, lifting her off the ground. Unable to free herself she snapped her head back but hit a bony forehead. The impact stunned her and more hands grabbed her. Chapman shouted, then a needle pierced her buttock. The shouts and grunts faded to nothing.

CHAPTER 28

The excitement outside the shopping centre died down and the spectators drifted away. Chapman waited for the three senior officers standing in a huddle. At least they'd taken him seriously and sent a decent attendance. Despite his impatience to find out what they were doing to locate Antonia, he recognised his input wouldn't be welcomed. One of them glanced at him, then they separated and Gunnerson came towards him.

'What's happening?' he said.

'We're winding it down—'

'Why haven't you got CrimTech down here?'

'What was the row about?' Gunnerson said.

'What row?'

'Those two guys' – she indicated the men who'd tried to take his taxi – 'said you—'

'They were trying to grab my cab. But what's that got to do with Antonia's kidnapping?'

'According to them, you and the girl argued.'

'No, we didn't. Hey, you two!' He started towards them, but Gunnerson grabbed his arm.

'Don't make things worse, Russell. Some people already want to do you for wasting police time.'

'What?'

'Just listen, Russell. I'm on your side. But they think you had a row with Ms Conti and she took a cab—'

'Those men snatched her. Ask those two, or the cabbie.'

'He saw nothing. He was watching you shouting at the two men and *they* dispute your version.'

Heat filled Chapman and he recognised the frustration and anger he'd often seen in others. Not so great being on the receiving end. 'The men in the people carrier grabbed her.'

'One thing the cabbie noticed, the other car was an iTaxi. The black cabs hate them, so he noticed. You were the only person who saw a kidnapping.'

'What about CCTV?'

'Scrambled.'

'That proves it.'

'Afraid not. Traffic caught a German diplomat using a scrambler about half an hour ago. She drove through this area when . . . at the same time, so . . .'

Chapman wanted to kick something, preferably those two bastards. They must be involved with the other two who'd snatched Antonia. 'What happened with the raid on Sears?'

'Russell, I've not had time to organise a raid.'

'So, you've done nothing.'

'I sent two cars to check every unit, and all they achieved was to piss lots of people off.'

'Great, you've warned them now.' Had Gunnerson done it deliberately? No, he needed to trust somebody, and he'd known her for years.

Pink spots appeared on her cheeks. 'There was nobody to *warn*, Russell. It was just an industrial estate full of people trying to make a living. And I don't appreciate the innuendo. I stuck my neck out to get two cars to go.'

'Sorry. I'm just disappointed. What about the van? Did you check its location the night they dumped the first woman?'

'Not yet.' Gunnerson's gaze avoided his. 'You said they'd used a cloaking device, so it's a big job.'

The implication wasn't lost on him. He could expect no more help from her. *Great, what to do now?*

Bright light shone into Antonia's eyes and she closed them again. Cotton wool filled her skull. She raised her head and grimaced – the cotton wool possessed sharp edges.

'Sorry about that, Ms Okoye, or do you prefer Conti?' Mishkin. This must be a nightmare.

She opened her eyes, but this wasn't a dream and her insides shrivelled. Next to him stood another man she recognised from the portraits scattered throughout the GRM building: Gustav Reed-Mayhew, the big boss. Mishkin examined her like he would a specimen in a jar. The strength drained from her. She avoided looking at him. More figures stood around, but she ignored them. Despite Sabirah's reassurances, they must have followed her friend. The fact that Antonia hadn't spotted them made her feel worse.

'Do you want water?' Reed-Mayhew's voice revealed his expensive education.

Through a mouth full of sand, she said, 'Yes, please.'

He gestured to a figure behind her and the drink appeared. She took it and sniffed the liquid before swallowing a mouthful. Shards of glass jabbed her brain when she tilted her head.

'The effects soon wear off, so I'm told,' Reed-Mayhew said, his tone reasonable, as if explaining something to a child, 'but we needed to subdue you before you did any damage to my staff. Or yourself.'

She followed his gaze and recognised the big security guard she'd knocked over during her escape from Chapman seven days earlier. An even bigger specimen stood next to him, leering at her.

'What do you want?' Had they grabbed Chapman, and if so did anyone else witness the attack?

'I have a proposition for you.'

Reed-Mayhew gestured to Mishkin, who operated a remote control. A screen emerged from the ceiling and as a scene unfolded upon it, she abandoned her speculation and concentrated on it. She took a few seconds to recognise the tableau, shot from across a canal basin. Mishkin slowed the action, and it clearly showed her kicking Pavlo in the face as he dragged her to the water.

'Very impressive, Ms Okoye,' Reed-Mayhew said. 'He was quite a powerful specimen.'

'Why did you pay him to attack me?'

Reed-Mayhew seemed puzzled. 'Why would we have anything to do with a thug like him?' He gestured at the men arrayed behind her. 'We don't use amateurs.'

The tips of Mishkin's ears turned pink and he stared at the floor.

'Where's the rest of the footage?' she asked, her mind racing.

'The rest?'

'Yes, the part where he attacked me, and where I leave him in the water. Still alive.'

'I'm sorry, there's no more.'

'Why does that not surprise me? What do you want from me to encourage you to find the rest?'

Reed-Mayhew's laughter rang out. 'You *are* bright. I want the papers you stole from my office, plus any copies. I imagine you're the only one alive who's seen them.'

They can't know Chapman's seen them, so he must be still free. 'Those papers for the footage?' She couldn't believe it could be so simple.

'Not quite.' He signalled to Mishkin.

A new scene appeared on the screen. In the foreground, two athletic women wearing short leather tunics fought in a ring surrounded by a cage. The camera focused on the spectators across the ring. Antonia ignored them and concentrated on the women fighting, realising with a shock the tall blonde woman could be Monika. The other woman, a muscular woman with red hair, laid into her, urged on by a baying crowd. The blonde woman couldn't defend herself and Antonia tensed as she waited for the referee to intervene.

'Not enjoying it? Maybe too raw for you,' Reed-Mayhew said. 'I want you to participate in one of my contests.' He gestured to Mishkin and the screen switched off.

'You made my DNA disappear.' And the men's reluctance to shoot her at the Sears Industrial Estate suddenly made sense.

Reed-Mayhew grinned. 'Women with your fighting ability are rare creatures.'

Get rid of these guards and I'll show you what sort of creature I am. 'What if I refuse?'

'Not a good idea. We still have the footage of you attacking the young man, and the touching reunion between your friend and her children. The Home Office hasn't renewed her residency permit, and with her recent record . . .'

Ice spread down her spine. 'When?'

Chapman sat in the flat and took a sip of beer. His attempt to question any witnesses to Antonia's kidnapping had come to nought and almost got him arrested. He considered what Gunnerson had said. From the sound of things, they weren't taking him seriously. And they wouldn't unless they uncovered evidence to support his claims.

He swallowed the last of his drink and stared at the bottle. A wave of hopelessness overwhelmed him. However tough things had been in the past, he'd never felt powerless. An image of his incarceration in the basement flashed before him and he imagined the same happening to Antonia. She wouldn't sit here staring at a bottle. A surge of self-disgust propelled him out of the chair.

Mishkin was the key. Chapman would find out where he lived and pay him a visit. What he planned would take him so far over the line he doubted if he'd ever return, but he couldn't just leave Antonia. First, he rang Sammy, arranging to meet him with a replacement car. He realised how much Sammy must think he owed him when he didn't even ask what had happened to the last car he'd lent him. Mind you, if someone rescued *his* daughter from child traffickers, he didn't think he'd ever consider the debt settled. Then he called people who owed him favours until a contact from the DVLA promised to ring him with the address.

Sammy delivered the car at eight. Chapman found Mishkin's address on the *A–Z* the mechanic had left in the glove compartment, took another two painkillers and, after checking the automatic, began the drive to Enfield. He arrived forty minutes later and drove past the house, taking his time to study it. A detached sixties architect-designed residence with a steep pitched roof and dormer windows, it stood out amongst the thirties villas flanking it. Situated well back from the road, high hedges concealed it from its neighbours. Although there wasn't a car on the drive, several cars could fit in the integral garage.

He wanted to check the back and parked fifty metres away where a narrow lane ran past Mishkin's neighbour's house, leading to the rear of the properties. He pulled on his gloves, psyching himself up. Despite the hour, several vehicles passed, their headlights raking the interior of the car. As he opened the car door, a vehicle arrived at Mishkin's. Chapman closed the door. He'd have to wait until it went away. The driver carried a package to Mishkin's house, then returned to his car a couple of minutes later. The car drove slowly past him, then pulled into the lane. Chapman swore, then realised it was turning round. The name of an Italian restaurant decorated the sides of the Fiat 500. As it reversed back out of the lane, the man stared at Chapman, as if memorising his features.

Again, Chapman swore. Feeling the man would more than likely call the police, he lowered the window and gestured for him to stop. Mind whirring as he searched for a convincing story, he got out of the car and approached the Fiat.

Chapman produced his warrant card and held it up, gesturing for the driver to lower his window.

'A'right, chief,' the man said. 'How can I help you?'

After swearing him to secrecy and telling him Mishkin was a suspect in a major people-trafficking ring, Chapman questioned the driver, who confirmed he would be back there with a delivery the same time the next night. Once satisfied that the man wouldn't mention this encounter, Chapman waved him off. He waited a few minutes until his heart rate returned to normal and his eyesight became accustomed to the darkness. Then he set off down the lane, relying on faint moonlight and fighting the urge to hurry. It opened out and he paused, peering into the blackness at Mishkin's place.

Chapman walked to the back fence. The house stood in darkness and he searched for signs of intruder protection, but saw none.

He'd expected someone in Mishkin's position to have the latest technology but he wouldn't be the first head of security to neglect his own home.

He lifted the latch and pushed the gate, but it didn't move. That would have been too easy. The fence on each side reached over six feet in height and in his current state he had no chance of scaling it. Who was he kidding? Even before the crash he'd have struggled. He found a loose panel and slid his fingers underneath. He lifted it eighteen inches before it jammed and, wedging it, he crawled through the gap. A flagged path set in a wide lawn led to the house. A light came on upstairs and a man appeared at the window. Mishkin? He didn't even know how many people lived here. He checked the automatic in his jacket and edged closer.

A sound from behind made him freeze. An amber light flashed in the alley and an engine growled. The car stopped behind Mishkin's house, doors slammed, then a dog barked.

The young girl stood in the centre of the circle of men, trying in vain to avoid their grasping hands. Someone pulled at her top and she spun to face him, an enormously fat man with bad breath and greasy hair. The memory of his stink, stale sweat and tobacco, made her gag. He laughed as she took a swipe at him, catching her thin wrist in a large paw. Another hand pulled at her from behind, dragging the scratchy cotton pyjama top, faded from too many washes, away from her back. She tried to protect herself but the fat man seized her, pulling her arm. With a sound of tearing fabric, the material parted, ending up in the hands of her tormentor. Tall and slim, she hated him the most. Like the others, he wore a surgical mask, but she couldn't mistake the smell of his aftershave. He laughed, pointing at the scars on her back, and the others joined in, jeering like hyenas.

'Come on. WAKEY, WAKEY!'

Antonia jerked awake, bathed in sweat and blinking until the light became bearable. The large security guard bent over her.

'Get out,' she said.

He ran his gaze along her body, tangled in the blankets and partially exposed, then said, 'Ten minutes,' and stepped away.

'And close the bloody door, you pervert.'

He chuckled, then slammed the door and drew the bolt.

Antonia shivered. How long had he been there? She should have wedged the chair against the handle. The fact that she hadn't woken until he shouted made her uneasy. She'd always woken when someone entered her room. The memory of a dream rushed at her but she concentrated on her anger.

She got out of bed and stood. The swelling round her ankle had reduced overnight, but the flesh still felt tender. The room reminded her of her study bedroom at uni, except that had had windows and the books had been on chemistry, not mass-market paperbacks. A set of new underwear and a grey fleece tracksuit in her size lay on the chair next to the bed.

She took these into the bathroom next door and locked the door. As she let the shower wake her, she revisited her meeting with Reed-Mayhew. He obviously didn't have a clue about Mishkin's attempts to kill her. Could she use that knowledge to help her get out of here? She finished and dressed, still trying to work out how she could get to see Reed-Mayhew.

Two guards arrived and led her to a small dining room. The whole place smelt metallic, as if they filtered the air. They were underground, she guessed. She didn't know how long she'd be here and none of the guards would tell her. The food was good and she tucked in, washing it down with weak coffee. The police raids on the Sears Industrial Estate must have happened. What had they uncovered? Once they got the evidence they needed, they'd come for her. Chapman wouldn't let Gunnerson and the others rest until they found her. Unless they had snatched him, too – no, she couldn't think that.

She finished eating and the door burst open. The large guard who'd watched her in bed barged in, followed by a smaller companion. 'Time to go,' the larger guard announced.

'Where are we going?'

Instead of replying he grabbed her upper arm. She pushed him away and leapt to her feet, fists clenched.

'To get your ankle checked out,' his companion said.

They led her down a corridor ending in a set of double doors. The stink of exhaust fumes increased as the doors opened and she found herself in a small car park. A grey van with wide tyres waited in the nearest space. Antonia's stomach dropped, but then she saw the roof; to her relief, this van didn't have a box.

The large guard slid the side door open and pointed at a bench bolted to the bulkhead between the cab and back. She clambered on board and the door slammed, plunging her into darkness. A moment of panic, then she took a deep breath. She needed to stay calm. She shuffled to the seat and fell on it as locks clicked. Not knowing where they were starting from, she didn't bother memorising the turns and relaxed, wondering what Chapman was doing, imagining he'd initiated a city-wide manhunt for her.

After a short drive, the van stopped and the door opened into another underground car park. The two men led her to a lift and they rode up three floors. The pale corridor stank of disinfectant and they showed her to a small examination room, leaving her alone. A stocky bald man in a white coat came in and inspected her damaged ankle.

He questioned her about the injury while manipulating the joint with cool hands. He then massaged her foot and ankle before applying a beige bandage. She flexed her foot; it felt much better. At this rate she'd be fit to fight in three or four days. The memory of watching a fight with the Dekker brothers seemed a long time ago. Now, she'd not only missed ten days' training, but she'd abused her body. Despite this, she experienced little trepidation. Chapman would find her before she got anywhere near a ring.

'It doesn't seem too bad,' he said, 'but I'll still give you this.' He produced a plastic box and removed the lid to display a syringe full of clear liquid.

'What's that?' she said, recoiling.

'Synthetic cortisone.' He lifted the syringe.

'No, thanks.'

'I recommend you use it. Otherwise you'll be in no fit state to fight tonight.'

Fear filled Antonia's throat with acid and her insides with fluttering moths. She would be fighting in just a few hours. She lay on the narrow bed in her cell attempting to occupy her mind with one of the paperbacks, but couldn't remember one thing about the page she'd just read for the fourth time. The screen on the wall opposite showed just combat sports or snooker.

She switched it off and lay on her back, wishing she could listen to her music. She'd trained hard for her forthcoming bout until a week ago, and even though the last few days had taken a toll on her body, she was still in good nick. Who was she kidding? The thought of fighting a nineteen-year-old had made her nervous, and that was with the Dekker brothers in her corner. Whoever she fought tonight would be a far tougher opponent, *and* she'd be on her own.

Come on, Antonia, don't defeat yourself before you start.

She focused inwards and inhaled, trying to reach her safe place. Her frequent recent attempts made rediscovering the sanctuary easier. After a few minutes her worries drifted into the distance as her body grew heavy.

Someone entered the room. Mishkin stood at the foot of her bed. Terror sliced through her, then a surge of anger. The man faded into the distance, getting smaller until he disappeared. A bang on the door woke her and she sat up, gasping, a sheen of sweat coating her skin.

'Time to go.' The guard who'd come this morning seemed to have learnt some manners since then.

Her ankle felt numb when she put weight on it, but it worked. The two men led her to the van in silence, a sombre respect replacing the cocky attitudes of the morning. Once in the van, she performed the relaxation routine Milo had instilled in her. His voice filled her mind. *Fear will rob you of energy. You must eliminate it, drive it out of your body.* She hummed the music he'd used to get her in the right frame of mind. Each time they stopped, Antonia hoped they'd hit traffic, but eventually the engine died and the side door slid open, flooding her with light. She squinted before stepping out on wobbly legs. As her vision adjusted, she studied her surroundings. Another subterranean car park, but this time full of vehicles.

'Go with them,' the driver said, pointing to two uniformed guards who stood by a doorway studying her.

They led her through a pair of swing doors and along a well-lit corridor. After passing through two more sets of doors they encountered a gnarled man of around sixty with his nose zigzagging across a scarred face.

'You one of the new girls?' he said, his voice a hoarse whisper.

'Women,' she corrected him. 'Where do I change?'

'Darlin', at my age, you're all girls.' His blue eyes twinkled and despite her nerves she returned his smile. 'Through there,' he said, pointing at a door with a silhouette of a man on it. 'And don't worry, it's just girls tonight. You're on at ten.'

The odour of liniment and eucalyptus oil enveloped her. Finding a bank of light switches alongside the door, she hit them. Wooden benches with clothes hooks above them lined two walls of the changing room. An opening in the opposite wall led to a tiled room with a trough urinal, two wash basins, a toilet cubicle and a large shower.

She sat on one bench. Her lungs didn't fill, however much she inhaled. Two bags sat on the bench opposite, but the effort of checking them seemed too much. The thought of what Milo would say if he saw her like this drove her to her feet. One bag contained a choice of black knickers and sports bras and the other bandages and liniment. They must be bringing the costumes later; she wasn't fighting in just her underwear.

She filled her lungs and stretched. As her muscles warmed up, her anxiety decreased. She felt good, despite the ankle. The door opened and a blonde woman stood in the doorway.

'Wrong room,' Antonia said, confronting the newcomer.

'Hi, I'm Sian.'

Keep them on the back foot, Milo's voice said. 'Wrong room.'

The blonde stared back, pale eyes unflinching. Although not as tall, she outweighed Antonia and it looked all muscle.

'This is *our* changing room. The others are in the ladies,' the woman said, stepping through the doorway.

'Our?'

The blonde thrust out a hand. 'Yeah, Sian. Pleased to meet you.'

Antonia took this in as she introduced herself, shaking the warm damp hand. The woman had a strong grip. 'Do you know what's happening?'

'Tag,' Sian said. 'You and me against Macha, and her partner—'

'I don't do teams.'

'I didn't choose you either, but that's the way it—'

'We'll see.' Antonia brushed past and stepped out into the corridor.

The broken-nosed man stood outside the door, speaking to two women – a stocky redhead of around her height and a shorter, muscular Asian woman. They eyeballed her, the women sizing her up. Antonia thought she recognised the redhead.

The man said, 'I'll get your kit brought—'

'What's this about a tag team?'

'You'd better get ready. You're on in an hour,' he said, and the two women gave her a last look before heading for their changing room.

'I said—'

'I heard you. Now get ready or you can take the consequences.' A cold glare had replaced the amused twinkle.

In the changing room Sian had stripped down to her knickers and bra and stood like a marble statue with pale muscles and veins showing blue through her skin. An ugly knife wound disfigured her flat stomach. Antonia realised she'd have to change in front of this woman. Nobody had seen her scars, not since Mishkin and his cronies . . . *This isn't the time, Antonia.*

'Did he say anything about our costumes?' Sian asked.

'No. Have you done this before?'

A knock on the door and a woman came in carrying a holdall and two suit carriers, each containing a skimpy fantasy of a Roman soldier's uniform. The outfits matched those in the footage she'd seen in Reed-Mayhew's office. The scenes replayed in her mind and she remembered where she'd seen the redhead from the corridor. She swallowed, but her mouth was dry.

Sian answered her question. 'Nah, I'd heard rumours, but never been lucky enough to get picked.'

Antonia noticed the scars on Sian's forehead, and her nose had stopped a few punches. 'So you don't know what happens tonight?'

'Someone comes at me and I fight. That's all I need to know.'

Antonia examined the knife scar again. Was her new partner an untrained street fighter? 'Have you ever fought in a ring?'

'Plenty. Kick-boxing, a few cage fights. Twice nude. The blokes who watch it disgust me but the money's good. What about you? Done much?'

'Similar to you,' said Antonia, not wanting to admit her inexperience. 'Except for the naked stuff. Boxing and Taekwondo.'

'You got the legs for it,' Sian said, seeming to believe her. 'What you going to do with the money?'

'Money?'

'Yeah, fifty thou for taking part. Quarter mill if we win.'

'Not thought about it.' That was a lot of money, but she didn't think she'd see any, win or lose.

'If I win, I'm buying a house, big enough so the kids can have a room each.'

Antonia studied Sian again and realised she'd underestimated her age. She used Sian's visit to the toilet to slip into the costume and checked herself in the mirror, feeling ridiculous in the short black tunic. The knee-length sandals with it incorporated shin guards and instep protectors but the soles were unforgiving. She made a note not to get caught with a kick.

They helped each other bind their hands and then stretched, each performing their own routines. Antonia began shadow-boxing and her body relaxed as her muscles executed choreographed moves. The door flew open and Antonia, executing a series of kicks, changed direction, stopping her right foot ten centimetres from the intruder's chin. Broken-nose flinched before scowling at her.

She lowered her foot. 'Knock next time.'

'Your gloves,' he said, and threw them at her.

Made of heavy-duty leather, they had cut-off fingers and firm pads on the knuckles. She examined them with growing dread. These weren't to protect their hands but to inflict serious damage, and their opponents would have the same.

CHAPTER 29

After spending a frustrating day at the Sears Industrial Estate searching for Antonia and trying to persuade the police to do the same, Chapman decided on a full-frontal assault. A second night's rest had done his battered body good and the intense headaches he'd suffered yesterday had receded. Now he knew Mishkin lived alone, he intended to get the information out of him. By any means necessary. He hobbled to his car, his knee still sore from the fall into a neighbour's pond when he'd escaped from the security guards and their dog. Despite his ignominious getaway, his recce had been fruitful.

On the drive over, he rehearsed his plan. The conversation with the delivery driver had given Chapman the idea. He planned to intercept the driver and drop off the food himself. It meant another person could identify him if it went pear-shaped, but he'd already gone beyond such concerns. He didn't want to arrive too early and attract attention, so checked his speed, pulling into Mishkin's road fifteen minutes before the meal was due to arrive.

The sight of a car with lights on near Mishkin's house made him panic. Had he mistimed it? Then he noticed the taxi sign. Shit! Was Mishkin going out? But the car pulled away and came past him, its 'For Hire' light on and the back empty. Had it dropped someone off? That would complicate things. But Mishkin's hall light wasn't on. Wouldn't he be greeting guests if anyone had arrived? It must have been at a neighbour's house.

Even if he had guests, Chapman didn't dare delay finding Antonia, and telling himself to stop worrying he pulled over to wait. Almost exactly on time, headlights appeared in his mirror and the liveried Fiat drove past towards Mishkin's house. Chapman pulled on the baseball cap he'd brought, got out and, ignoring stiff legs, intercepted the driver before he got out.

'A'right, chief,' he greeted Chapman, 'you still keeping an eye on matey?'

'I'm going to need you to let me deliver that.' Chapman pointed at the insulated food container on the front seat.

'You raiding him today? Where the others?' The driver grew animated and peered into the darkness.

'Don't make it obvious.'

'Sorry, mate. Here.' He opened the passenger door for Chapman to collect the food. 'Do you mind letting me have the insulated pack back?'

'Take it.' Chapman removed a carrier bag of food. He didn't give a damn if Mishkin's dinner got cold. The aroma of rosemary and garlic made him salivate. 'What's in it?'

'Rigatoni with a spicy sauce and veal chops with rosemary potatoes and zucchini.'

More saliva flooded his mouth, and he swallowed. 'Now, beat it before anything kicks off, but leave quietly.'

The driver looked disappointed, but didn't argue and pulled away, leaving Chapman on the pavement.

Chapman hefted the bag in his left hand and hurried to the front door. The bell echoed through the frosted glass and he waited for Mishkin to answer, the weight of the Fort 15 pulling at his jacket. A small camera in the corner of the porch followed his movements, and he tilted his head to hide beneath the cap. Lights came on and a shadow approached. Chapman gripped the stock of the automatic. The doubt he could go through with this assailed him again.

'Yes?' a voice demanded through a speaker.

'A'right, chief, got your rigatoni and veal.' A chain rattled, locks clicked, and the door opened. Mishkin stood in front of him, his jacket off but tie still fastened and a fiver clutched in his fist. His expression turned to puzzlement as he recognised Chapman. 'Sergeant, what do you want?'

'A word?'

'Make an appointment.'

Chapman thrust the bag at Mishkin, who instinctively reached for it, then pushed the door open.

'Go away.' Mishkin pushed back.

Chapman shoved with both hands, stepping into the hallway and forcing Mishkin to retreat.

'What the hell are you playing at?' Mishkin raised his voice.

'I won't take long,' Chapman said, taking a deep breath.

Mishkin looked ready to attack him, then his gaze darted to a blue door on the opposite side of the hallway. 'Make it quick.'

The hallway was wider than Chapman's house and his feet sank into a cream carpet. A wrought-iron hall stand full of sticks and umbrellas stood beside the door, a row of shoes under it. He wasn't removing *his* shoes. The blue door opened and a young woman, no, a girl dressed in school uniform, stood in the doorway. Shit! He didn't think the man had kids. This was a bad idea. Then he saw the drink in the girl's hand and the heavy make-up. He wouldn't let *his* daughter dress like that.

'I want you to leave. Now!' Two spots of colour showed on Mishkin's pale cheeks.

Realisation hit Chapman. 'How old are you?' he said to the girl.

'None of your business,' Mishkin said. 'Leave now or deal with the consequences.'

Chapman ignored him. 'You're not in trouble. Just tell—'

'Go now, Sergeant, or you'll—'

The girl cried out and dropped her glass, spilling red wine on the carpet before disappearing back into the room. She rushed out a few seconds later, clutching a fake fur coat and holding a Barbie-pink phone to her ear. She couldn't have been more than fourteen. Not much older than—A surge of rage seized Chapman and it took all his willpower to wait until the girl left. The door slammed and he punched Mishkin on the bridge of his nose. The man grunted and fell, clutching at the wound.

Chapman kicked him in the side. 'Get up.'

Mishkin took his hand from his face and stared at the blood. Fear appeared for the first time. 'Please don't—'

'Get up.' Chapman drew the automatic and aimed it at Mishkin. *What the hell do you think you're doing, Russell?*

Mishkin scrambled to his feet. 'Please—'

Chapman remembered what he'd come for and regained control of himself. 'Where's Antonia?'

'I don't know who you're—'

'Where is Antonia Conti?' Chapman jerked the barrel of the automatic.

Mishkin's expression changed again, his calculation almost visible. 'Sergeant, there's no need for this. Can't we behave in a civilised way?'

'Cut the bullshit. Now where is she?' Chapman shoved the barrel at the man and Mishkin stepped away, hands raised.

'You're deranged. I don't know what—'

'I don't care about myself. Where – is – she?' Chapman said, jabbing him in the chest with the end of the barrel to emphasise his words.

'I know you've been under strain, Sergeant, but you're making things worse for yourself. If you leave now, we'll forget about it.'

'You think you can talk your way out of this?'

Mishkin's supercilious smirk betrayed his thoughts.

Chapman hit him on the temple and Mishkin fell, knocking over the hall stand. Cold fury gripped Chapman as he waited for him to rise off the floor, then he hit him again. A small voice said, *He's got to talk. Don't kill him.* Chapman stopped himself, but the fury stayed and he knew he'd do whatever it took to make Mishkin crack.

'Get up,' he said, his voice calm. 'Tell me or I'll hurt you in ways even you couldn't imagine.'

Mishkin wiped blood from his lip, his look telling Chapman he'd do the same to him if he ever got the chance. He must have recognised the determination in Chapman's manner, and he subsided. 'She's agreed to take part in a – a contest.'

'What you talking about?' Chapman raised the pistol.

Mishkin cringed and in a flat voice he told Chapman the details.

Confused thoughts raced through Chapman's mind. 'Where's the fight?'

Mishkin hesitated. 'Sears Industrial Estate. We've got a unit there—'

'It can't be. I went there this afternoon and we searched it yesterday.'

Mishkin couldn't resist a smirk. 'We expected you. By the time your lot arrived . . .'

That explained why the two crews Gunnerson sent had found nothing. Someone in the police must have warned them. 'Who's your mole?'

Mishkin's grin faded. 'I genuinely don't know.'

Chapman didn't know whether to believe him and even if he named someone, he wouldn't put it past the slimeball to give him the wrong name. 'So, the fight's in the big unit with the orange roof?'

'No, it's the smaller units. They've got inspection pits, but they lead to an underground complex. Goes under the car park.'

'You're lying. They wouldn't dare use it after yesterday's raid.'

'But, Sergeant, that makes it the safest place to use.' Mishkin's smug grin had reappeared. Chapman resisted the urge to remove it. It made sense.

Chapman could picture those units and the jolly man who'd showed him round. He retrieved his mobile. If he told Gunnerson, she'd have to act. The sound of the doorbell made him jump. Two silhouettes appeared through the opaque glass of the front door and then he saw movement to his left. A stick flew at his head.

Antonia followed Broken-nose down the stark corridor, her body numb. She'd accepted Chapman's theory that Mishkin killed the women. The memory of the sadistic games he'd made her play returned with full clarity, reinforcing the belief. But now she knew the killings happened in the ring. That explained the women's injuries. And neither she nor her tag partner was supposed to survive. Sian's loud panting told her she'd realised it too.

A low murmur came from in front, growing louder with each step. Antonia's insides fluttered. Broken-nose studied her, a leer touching the corner of his lips. The corridor widened and twin doors flanked by uniformed sentries blocked their path. When they got near, the guards flung them open. The noise exploded, making the hairs on Antonia's arms rise. A tunnel of clear plastic cut a path to a large circular cage with a boxing ring in the centre. Despite their enthusiasm, the crowd surrounding it seemed too small to produce the sound assaulting her. They must use amplifiers. Antonia examined the space, the right size to be the orange-roofed unit she and Chapman had discovered, but the ceiling seemed too low. But hadn't the police raided it? They would have found evidence. Maybe they were keeping it under observation and waiting until the contest was in full swing.

The size of the ring eased her apprehension. Despite her damaged ankle she could still use her reach. Broken-nose led them through the tunnel and the cacophony increased. Eager faces pressed against the walls of the tunnel and fists hammered against the sides. She caught sight of a few faces, familiar from magazines and news reports. Broken-nose stopped at the edge of the ring and gestured to the two women to enter it.

Antonia fought the urge to flee and climbed into the ring, followed by Sian. They waited in the centre and Antonia kept moving to prevent her muscles tightening. Two figures appeared at the far end of the tunnel and when the crowd noticed them, the noise changed and a chant started: 'Macha! Macha! Macha!' Antonia tried to shut it out and concentrated on controlling her breathing.

The newcomers advanced towards the ring. The redhead, dressed in a white tunic, her hair coiled on top of her head, led. Behind her followed the Asian woman, muscles defined like a bodybuilder's. At the edge of the ring, the redhead acknowledged the crowd before executing a backward flip over the top rope to raucous applause. Her companion followed and finished with three flick-flacks, passing less than a metre in front of Antonia. The sprung floor of the ring shook when she landed and she bowed to the cheering crowd who chanted, 'Ning! Ning!'

As she waited for the fight to start, Antonia glanced over at the crowd, hoping to see signs of alarm as the police arrived to break up the contest. She checked out the two women in the white tunics. Both looked fit, but built for power. She hoped they lacked stamina. In which case, she *just* had to avoid being hit until they tired. Provided her ankle held up.

All too soon the build-up ended and she followed Sian to the red corner in a trance. She tried to picture Milo and Darius in the corner, giving her advice and keeping her calm. The fight would start with one of them outside the ring. If she let Sian fight first, could she make a run for it? It meant leaving Sian to her fate but if Antonia escaped, maybe they'd abandon the contests.

A cheer from the crowd ended her speculation. Two people remained in the ring, her and Ning.

For a second Antonia stood rooted to the spot. Ning charged and Antonia reacted without thought, moving to one side and firing a jab at the woman's jaw as she rushed past. The sense of satisfaction as the punch made contact gave Antonia a boost. She followed up with two more stiff jabs, catching Ning in the back of the head before she could turn. Antonia paused for a second, expecting the referee to caution her, but Broken-nose remained outside the ring. Her hesitation let her opponent escape from the corner and she rushed at Antonia, who fired off another jab. The two women circled each other, Antonia's confidence growing as she picked off the shorter woman and Ning lunged to get her punches in past Antonia's jabs.

The stocky woman soon started blowing, sucking air through her open mouth. She lunged again and Antonia evaded her before swinging a right fist into her jaw. The woman, reacting faster than Antonia expected, shot out her left foot, which smacked into Antonia's thigh. Her leg went numb and Antonia staggered before countering with a left hook, catching her opponent high on her forehead. Without the padding of normal boxing gloves, each punch told on her fists. Another hook and Ning fell against the ropes, panting.

Antonia rushed in for the kill, dropping her guard, and didn't see the uppercut that caught her on the chin. Her skull snapped back and she staggered. Her arms fell to her sides. A fist hit her in the centre of her torso, driving into her organs and emptying her lungs. Agony spread from the impact. Unable to breathe but remembering her training, she somehow got her guard up. Another pile-driving blow hit her forearm and knocked her backwards. Arms flailing, she fought to stay upright. If she fell, she'd be finished. A rope stopped her descent and she clutched at it. Her fleeting relief lasted until Ning swarmed over her, aiming punches to her head and upper torso. Every impact carried the full power of the woman's muscular body and propelled Antonia backwards.

Trapped on the ropes, she covered up. Each blow, even the ones she blocked, sent shock waves through her. Beyond thought, she knew she needed to do something, but what? She swayed away, avoiding the worst of the blows, her body moving without direction. Ning paused, arms lowered and gulping air. Antonia recognised her chance and threw out a jab, then another, using her reach against the shorter woman. Her punches drove her tiring opponent backwards, giving her more room.

She sprang away from the edge of the ring, panting but boosted by her escape. Freed of the ropes, she stayed out of range and rained blows on to the retreating Ning. The woman blinked and stepped back, unsteady as she took another rest. *Got you.* Antonia stamped her heel into the woman's torso. Ning rode the blow, grinning, and Antonia realised her mistake too late. Hands seized her ankle, pulling her off balance. Antonia stayed upright but a sharp pain surged up her leg as Ning tightened her grip. Fuelled by fear, Antonia swung a desperate punch. Her attacker swayed out of reach and twisted Antonia's leg. Tendons strained against joints and panic swamped Antonia. The woman wouldn't let go until she'd dislocated Antonia's knee. *Where the hell is Chapman?* A voice reached her above the screams of the crowd.

'Antonia, here!' Sian yelled from their corner and reached out to her.

Antonia stretched out an arm. A gap of less than a metre separated them. Ning grimaced and pulled, but Antonia lunged for her partner and their fingertips touched. Sian leapt into the ring and, confronted by a second fighter, Ning released Antonia's leg. She fell in a heap before dragging herself into the corner and slipping under the bottom rope.

Pulse hammering in her ears, lungs straining, Antonia examined her ankle and knee. Both hurt like hell but she grabbed a sponge from the bucket in their corner and squeezed icy water on her joints. The yelling of the crowd reminded her that the battle continued.

Blood streamed down Ning's forehead, but Sian wasn't unmarked, either – a cut on her cheek oozed red. Ning landed a blow in her midriff but Sian countered with a knee in her ribs. With a gasp, audible above the sound of the crowd, Ning went down, sprawling face-first on the canvas. With a yell, Sian landed a kick in her fallen foe's side.

Antonia grimaced and cheered her partner. Sian leapt on the prone woman and slammed her skull into the canvas. She raised her fist to the back of Ning's head and the chant of 'Macha!' started. A figure entered the ring and flew at Sian. The crowd drowned Antonia's shout of warning. Sian's fist crunched into Ning's neck at the same moment Macha hit her with her shoulder.

Sian fell, landing on the canvas in a heap. Macha followed up with a kick to her head. Antonia pulled herself on to the skirt of the ring, but a hand grabbed her foot, pulling her away. Fire surged from her injured ankle. Holding on to the top rope to keep her balance, she jerked her leg and the grip loosened.

Broken-nose clutched her ankle. She reached down, thrusting her extended fingers into his eyes. With a yell of rage he released her foot and after kicking him in the mouth, Antonia fell into the ring. The crowd were by now baying at full volume, the cacophony hurting her ears. Sian lay on the canvas, a red pool spreading from the back of her skull.

Antonia advanced towards Macha, who faced her wearing a grim expression. The woman matched her for height and reach but her muscular frame outweighed that of Antonia by at least fifteen kilos. They circled each other, avoiding the section of the ring where the two fallen women lay. The reduced ring favoured the heavier woman, although the way her legs felt, Antonia doubted if she could have made use of the extra space.

Macha came at her and Antonia used jabs to keep the woman at bay. Three landed in quick succession and pink indentations appeared on her opponent's forehead. Macha grimaced, adjusted her footing and threw a punch. Antonia blocked it. The force numbed her forearm and then came another, driving her back with frightening power. Antonia's right foot hit something soft and she lost her balance. Sian. By the time she recovered, Macha had leapt on her.

Antonia twisted away and smashed her elbow into Macha's neck. Macha grunted but still advanced, and Antonia saw her opponent would corner her. She stepped to her left and landed a hook on the side of Macha's jaw. Then she lunged past, using the momentum of the punch to spin right and take her away from danger.

Macha followed and Antonia directed a kick at her body. The woman blocked it, but the blow still knocked her backwards into the corner of the ring. Before she could recover, Antonia attacked. Desperation and rage gave her blows extra venom. The powerful punches jolted her arm and forced Macha against the ropes.

The redhead stood dazed and Antonia, hoping her knee and ankle wouldn't give way, spun on one leg and released a roundhouse kick. It snapped Macha's head back and she fell against the ropes, still conscious but ready to fall. Determined not to make the same mistake again, Antonia kept her guard up as she went in for the kill. The crowd fell silent.

Antonia teed up her next punch, a straight right to Macha's heart. The pinprick in the top of her leg didn't register at first. She drew her fist back to finish her opponent, but her limbs seemed encased in thick treacle. Her body became impossibly heavy but her head floated. Unable to continue, she halted her attack. Macha's expression changed as fear transformed to hope then triumph and she came off the ropes. Although she knew she must stop her, Antonia's arms, too heavy to lift, flopped by her sides.

She saw the punch but couldn't avoid it and a fist smashed into her face. The taste of blood flooded her mouth and tears blurred her vision. Another blow smashed into her and her legs gave way. She fell, crashing towards the floor. Frantic messages to her arms to break her fall went unheeded, and a roar filled her ears as she hit the canvas.

CHAPTER 30

Chapman ducked but the heavy stick hit him on the temple before clattering off the wall. Mishkin followed the projectile and his head struck Chapman in the ribs, emptying his lungs. While Chapman gasped for air, Mishkin gripped him round the waist and drove him backwards. They both crashed into the wall but Chapman held on to the automatic. He swung it down, hitting his assailant in the middle of his back. A second blow and Mishkin let go, falling to his knees.

'Mr Mishkin, are you okay?' A concerned voice came through a speaker by the door, cutting through the sound of their ragged breathing.

Chapman shoved the barrel into Mishkin's neck and whispered, 'Tell them to go.'

Mishkin hesitated for a few moments, panting. 'I'm fine, it's just a misunderstanding.'

'Right?' The speaker paused, sounding uncertain. 'What's the safe code—'

'He's supposed to tell us without us asking,' a second voice said.

Chapman couldn't help smiling and gestured to Mishkin to answer. 'Tottenham Hotspur,' Mishkin said, unable to hide his fury.

Chapman listened to the men leaving, keeping his gaze on Mishkin. His temple felt numb and his hand came away wet when he touched it. He had to admire the man's guts. He wasn't sure he'd tackle an armed intruder with a walking stick.

'We'll take my car,' Chapman said. 'Now get up.'

To his relief the security men's vehicle had gone and he prodded Mishkin in the back, keen to go before they returned. He made Mishkin drive and sank into the passenger seat. Exhaustion drained him as adrenaline leaked away and the aches suffusing his body returned.

He rang Gunnerson. 'Yasmin, Antonia's in Sears Industrial Estate.'

'Russell, please don't embarrass yourself. I heard you went there today. Have you been drinking?'

'No, I bloody—' He stopped himself. 'Please, Yasmin, there's an underground complex—'

'Run by a man with a white cat.'

'Did you check the inspection pits in the smaller units?'

Gunnerson's silence gave him the answer.

'Antonia's down there now. They're making her fight. That's what those dead women are, the losers.'

'What's your source?' She sounded less scornful.

'Someone senior in GRM.' Mishkin stiffened and Chapman threatened him with the automatic. 'You must trust me on this.'

After a long pause, she said, 'I'll send someone to investigate.'

'We'll need more than one car. It's a big complex—'

'I'll send someone, Russell.'

He ended the call with a sense of relief, but the fear they'd arrive too late to save Antonia gnawed at him.

◆ ◆ ◆

Intense cold seeped into Antonia and a metallic tang filled her mouth. She swallowed but her stomach heaved and, clenching her teeth, she held it in. She lay panting, acid burning her throat. Consciousness diffused through her and pain started at her head, spreading to her body. An uncontrollable tremor shook her. She opened her eyes but couldn't penetrate the dense blackness.

A distinctive taste and a surge of nausea evoked the recent memory of standing in Reed-Mayhew's office, groggy and confused. The bastards had drugged her. She shivered again, but her limbs continued to quiver outside her control. A sound penetrated her consciousness: wheels thrumming and the growl of an engine. She was in a car.

The darkness remained complete and she attempted to investigate her surroundings, but couldn't move her arms. She pushed until a wall of fabric gave way. Uneasy, she explored with her right hand. The wall enclosed her. What was it? Then she knew. A bodybag. Terror made her chest constrict and she tore at the fabric until she collapsed, exhausted.

Antonia made herself relax and gather her strength. *Go to your safe place.* Her mind took her to a hidden valley until the panic passed. There must be a zip. Fingers probed until they found it, tracing it to an opening. The hole admitted three fingers and she eased the zip forward until she could thrust her head out. She lay on her back gulping air. Even out of the bag, the blackness persisted and the freezing air made her throat hurt. She must be in the grey van.

Gripped by a new terror, she lay paralysed, but something had changed. The floor no longer vibrated. A door slammed and a man spoke. For a second she hesitated – hide or fight? – but she didn't have the strength for the latter. She gripped the zip and it took all her willpower to pull it shut. She dragged her fingers back in as the doors opened.

'Come on ladies, let's put you to bed,' a cockney voice said. Zack!

A bulky object bumped against her foot before sliding past her. Another body; Sian must be in here. Antonia lay there, unthinking, until they grabbed her ankle. She stifled a cry. Hands hoisted her off the floor and someone shoved a bony shoulder into her torso. She bounced with each step and clamped her jaws together to prevent herself from crying out. At last they stopped and she fell, landing hard, the air expelled from her lungs.

'Fuck! This one's heavy.' It sounded like Gareth.

A kick smashed into her side, but she held back the cry of pain. The zip opened and she closed her eyes, resisting the urge to gulp. The odour of decay made her gag, then they tipped her on to the floor. Steps receded, followed by silence. Had they gone? She stared into the blackness. A light flickered, growing brighter, and the voices returned, the conversation incongruous as they discussed Chelsea's chances in tomorrow's game. A sound she couldn't identify, and then liquid splashed. A pungent odour filled the air, drowning the stench of corruption and burning her eyes. Bleach.

Zack complained and she attempted to work out what they were doing. The fumes attacked her mucus membranes and a cold spray hit her, almost making her cry out. A boot pushed her, turning her on to her back, and then they sprayed her hands. The skin tingled and the spray moved up her arms. The stringent chemical attacked her throat and she couldn't contain her cough.

'Shit! This one's still alive.'

◆ ◆ ◆

A river of headlights flowed towards Chapman and Mishkin. The deserted road he'd traversed over the last two days teemed. A siren sounded behind him and he checked in the mirror. Blue lights.

'Pull over,' he told Mishkin, and they stopped in the entrance to a farm.

A police car raced past and then another. He rang Gunnerson. 'Yasmin, what's happening?'

'A patrol car went. The place was swarming and people were already leaving. They must have received a warning—'

'Did you find Antonia?'

'Nothing yet, they struggled to gain entry.' A man's voice said something in the background. 'I'll ring you back—'

'Yasmin!' But she'd gone.

He rang again, listening to the ringtone as he imagined what might have happened to Antonia. The call went to voicemail and he redialled. More emergency vehicles passed, on their way to the scene. What would he do if they arrived too late? He suppressed the urge to batter Mishkin.

Gunnerson answered the third call, sounding out of breath. 'Russell, I *am* busy here—'

'Why aren't you searching the cars leaving? Check she's not—'

'You're joking. On what grounds? Do you know how many—'

'She'll be in a refrigerated van.'

Gunnerson's voice faded and she shouted something before returning. 'We're checking now, Russell. I have to go.'

Mishkin smirked as Chapman listened to the empty air. *Shit! If she's in the van, it means she's already dead.*

◆ ◆ ◆

Bright light shone into Antonia's streaming eyes as fumes from the bleach filled the air.

'You!' the two men said in unison.

Antonia stared back, unable to speak.

'What we going to do?' Zack said.

Gareth shrugged his huge shoulders. 'Dunno.'

The men studied her and, satisfied she wasn't a threat, Zack gestured with his thumb and they withdrew to the far corner of the room. Their bodies threw grotesque shadows against the walls and they spoke in hushed tones. Antonia searched for an escape. The room had just one opening, a door behind the men. Even if she were uninjured they'd cut her off before she reached it.

She needed a weapon. Beside her she saw three mounds, two body-sized but the third far larger. The odour of earth overcame the bleach for a moment and she noticed the spade in the top of the big mound. The men's voices stopped and they studied her, wearing expressions needing no interpretation. Fear gave her a jolt of adrenaline and she struggled to her knees.

She'd scrambled a short way to the spade before they reached her. A blow to her side sent her sprawling. Hands grabbed her shoulders and pinned them to the floor. Other hands seized her wrists and she fought to free herself. Lamplight gleamed off glasses as Zack forced a knee between her legs, pushing them apart. The short tunic rode up, exposing her knickers. Neither man spoke, grunts and the sound of their breathing the only accompaniment to their struggle. Zack's fingers bit into her wrists. Helplessness assailed her as she fought to escape his grip. But she wouldn't let them do this to her. A desperate heave and she freed an arm. She swung her fist and his glasses crunched.

She tore her left hand free and clawed at Gareth's face. The hand gripping one shoulder let go before clamping to her wrist and forcing it away. Zack hit her in the side but she was beyond pain. She rammed the fingers of her right hand into his eyes. With a cry, he reeled away, landing on his backside. Once free of his weight, she bucked her hips, jerking her body. Gareth swore, then her other shoulder came free. She twisted and swung a fist at him. It smacked into his skull with a solid clunk and she kept punching until he released her wrist.

Zack seized her ankle, pulling her on to her back and dragging her across the floor. He loosened his grip, searching for a better hold, and she thrust her free leg at him. Her heel crunched into bone. The force of the strike jarred her joints and she didn't need to see him to know she'd damaged the cockney.

'Zack, you okay?' Gareth shouted, alarm in his voice.

Zack didn't answer but with both legs free Antonia swung them up in a scissor kick, catching Gareth a glancing blow and knocking him backwards. Ignoring the pain, she scrambled to her feet and scuttled towards the door. After a few wobbly steps she steadied. The door led straight to a stone staircase and she clambered up to the next floor. At the top she paused. The only light came from below, a faint glow through the gaps in the floorboards. She searched for an exit, arms outstretched. Her left hand hit a wall, then a doorframe. She groped for a handle, but couldn't find one. *There must be. Come on Antonia, find the hinges.* She ran her fingers round the frame, desperate to get out before her captors recovered.

Voices came from below and a beam of light cut through the darkness, swaying as it approached. It illuminated the nails stitching the edge of the door. *Blast!* Wooden stairs led up and with a cry of frustration, she took them, pausing at the next landing. Faint light shone from above: another floor. The staircase shook as the men ascended. She charged up the stairs and through a doorway into a large room. Moonlight shone through holes in the roof and a high window, but it was too small to let her escape. Antonia pictured herself stuck halfway through, helpless while the men dragged her back.

She'd have to make a stand, and searched in the gloom for a weapon. The door stood fully open against the wall on her left and she pushed it shut. A piece of furniture threw a dark shadow on the wall. Muscles complaining, she dragged the chest of drawers across the rough floor and jammed it against the door. She leant against it, panting. A phone trilled and voices grunted before receding. Were they leaving? She strained to hear, then a new sound reached her: a car starting. Not daring to hope, she pressed her ear to the door. No voices, but another sound and a distinctive odour. Smoke.

◆ ◆ ◆

Consumed by a mixture of frustration and helplessness Chapman replayed what he'd done, seeing how he could have done better.

Mishkin glanced at him. 'If you let me go now, you might at least save your—'

Chapman slammed the barrel of the automatic into Mishkin's head. The man grunted and bounced off the side window. A thin red stream flowed from the cut above his eye.

'That's to make sure you're paying attention,' Chapman said, adding, 'Where have they taken her?'

Mishkin clutched at the wound. 'I don't—'

Chapman struck again and Mishkin half-blocked the second blow with his forearm, but the impact knocked him into the door and the tip of the barrel opened the cut. Chapman studied him, not conscious of any emotion. 'I'll ask again, where is she?'

'Don't hit me again,' Mishkin panted, wiping blood from his cheek. 'I genuinely don't know. They don't tell me. It's safer.'

This made sense, but Chapman wasn't sure he believed him. 'Can you get hold of them?'

Mishkin dabbed at his wound before saying, 'Yes.'

'Find out where they've taken her.'

Mishkin reached into his jacket.

'Slowly,' Chapman said, pressing the barrel into his neck.

With trembling hands, Mishkin retrieved a phone.

'Put it on speaker,' Chapman said.

A man with a strong Birmingham accent answered.

'Where have you taken the parcels?' Mishkin said.

'You said you didn't—'

'Don't make me ask again.'

The man dictated an address, breathing hard between words. 'While you're on, boss, we'll need extra for sorting out the one that's still alive—'

'Antonia?' Chapman blurted out.

'Who the fuck's that?' the man said, and ended the call.

Chapman swore, telling Mishkin to take him there before ringing Gunnerson, hoping they weren't too late.

Antonia pushed the chest of drawers aside and opened the door. An orange glow appeared in the opening. Tendrils of smoke cast silhouettes against the light. Paralysed by memories, she stared at the fire, her mind conjuring figures running from huts in the flames and echoes of screams. A crash from below broke the spell. The glow filled the doorway and heat hit her, forcing her to the floor. She must get out. And the stairs provided the only escape. She'd have to advance towards the flames. If she hesitated, she'd never do it. She crabbed forward, keeping low. At the top of the stairs she stopped. Flames attacked the staircase, twisting, hungry serpents leaping towards her. *Oh hell!* She stayed low and retreated into the room, dragging the door shut behind her.

She sat, back against the woodwork, fear gripping her as she realised she was trapped. Thick haze filled the room and her eyes watered. Half-remembered instructions returned to her and she lay on the floor, gulping down the clearer air. Smoke collected under the tiles until it obscured the holes in the roof. At the far end, the window faded to a faint rectangle, almost indistinguishable from the surrounding wall. It offered her only hope and, staying on all fours, she set off towards it. Her head smacked into the wall, stopping her with a painful jolt. No longer able to see the window, she guessed its position and rose. Heat hit her like a physical barrier. She fell to the floor, gasping and inhaling acrid smoke. She lay for a while, retching and coughing. The fit passed, leaving her even weaker.

A wave of despair washed over her. *Come on Antonia, you can't give up.* She extended her arm upward, this time prepared for the searing temperature. The skin on her hand tingled as she searched by touch. Unable to find the opening before the temperature became unbearable, she snatched it back. She must have gone off line, but left or right? She was right-handed, so must have veered to the right. Aiming left, she shuffled along the floor and tried again, each attempt scorching her skin. Then she reached a corner.

Blast! She must have missed it. The fear she'd never escape paralysed her, but she had to fight it. She went back, her ears crinkling and sweat pouring off her, until she reached another corner. She can't have missed it *again*.

A thud came from below and she listened. Had someone seen the flames and called the fire service? After a few seconds she realised it was just the fire. Not letting disappointment strike her down, she attempted to work out where she'd seen the opening. It must be to her right. The air grew thicker, smoke attacking her throat. Her hand touched a wooden panel. *Oh no, the door!* She slumped against the wall, weeping. After what could have been seconds or minutes, she roused herself and returned, this time keeping a hand on the wall.

Even at floor level, her body seemed to cook, and she imagined she could smell her hair burning. Her hand hit a corner. This must be where she'd gone wrong. Another crash from below shook the floor. She didn't have long. But she mustn't rush. Making herself take one small step at a time, she continued her search.

After what felt like an age, she thought she must have passed it again. Then her fingertips touched the windowsill. Unable to believe it, she pushed her hand further, shaking with relief when she touched the frame. She crouched under the opening, gathering her strength. The memory of the heat made her hesitate and her courage ebbed until visions of Eleanor lying in a hospital bed flashed through her mind. *Come on Antonia, people need you.* She filled her lungs then propelled herself through the layers of scalding gasses.

Her hands found the window frame, its glass long gone, and she gripped it, ignoring the nails digging into her palms. She pushed with exhausted legs, heaving with her arms. The frame bent, but held, and her feet scrabbled against the wall until they found purchase.

She dragged herself into the opening, but halfway through she jerked to a stop. She writhed, struggling to release herself. A stream of superheated smoke flowed round her, scorching her bare legs. Lungs starved of oxygen threatened to burst. Her body, abused and weakened, begged for rest as the heat drained her remaining energy. Then she shot forward, accompanied by a tearing sound. She emerged into the night air and refilled her tortured lungs. Relief changed to alarm as she slid on smooth tiles. She pushed down, trying to slow her descent. The roof ended, and she grabbed the gutter. It crumbled into rust and she sailed into space.

CHAPTER 31

Chapman peered into the darkness, searching for the street sign, and then he saw it. Mishkin slowed and they turned into the narrow unlit road. They'd almost reached the far end when headlights exploded from an alleyway and the van shot out before racing past them. Although unable to identify who was in the front, he could see the box on the roof.

'Go down there,' Chapman said, pointing down the alleyway the van had burst out of. At least they were in the right place.

The alleyway ended in a low brick wall and Mishkin killed the engine, leaving them in darkness. Chapman found a small map-reading torch in the glove compartment and opened his door. The stench of burning hit him straight away. He got out and edged round the front of the car, keeping the pistol trained on Mishkin, who sat illuminated by the courtesy light.

'Get out.'

Mishkin didn't hurry to comply and Chapman pulled his door open before prodding him on the neck with the pistol. Mishkin clambered out and stood by the car, hands by his side. The smell came from their right and a confusion of footprints covered the muddy pathway leading towards the fire. Chapman dismissed the instinctive thought that they mustn't contaminate the scene.

'Over there.' He used the feeble light to direct his prisoner.

Mishkin hesitated, but a shove in the back with the automatic made him stumble down the path. The smoke grew thicker and then a glow appeared through the haze. Distracted by the fear of what they'd find, Chapman blundered into Mishkin.

'Get a fucking move on.' He pushed him.

The path ended, opening out into an untidy lawn in front of a dilapidated house on a large plot. Chapman stopped. Flames leaped out of the lower windows, filling the garden with a flickering orange glow. He'd arrived too late. The bozo Mishkin had spoken to must have fired the place. Chapman couldn't even get near the building. If Antonia was in there, she had no chance. He used Mishkin's phone to summon the emergency services and stood watching, feeling sick.

A clatter came from the side of the house. *What the hell was that?* He prodded Mishkin, pushing him towards the corner. As they rounded it, the illumination from the flames faded. A street-light glinted off metal security shutters blocking the lower windows and containing the fire. More illumination came from a small opening in the roof, above a bay window. A column of thick smoke poured out of the opening. Fire chased it, lighting up a pile of bin bags stacked against the side of the house. The flames flared up, growing brighter, and a shadow moved across the bags. Below the opening, on the flat roof of the bay, something stuck out. An arm? As he watched, a hand moved.

'Antonia!' he cried out, and took a step forward.

Then he remembered Mishkin. Chapman spun and saw a blur of motion, then a wooden post smashed into the side of his head and he fell into the pile of bags.

◆ ◆ ◆

Antonia opened her eyes. Hazy stars filled the sky and as her memory returned she lay still, unable to believe she was still alive. She tried to get up but didn't have the strength. Every part of her hurt and she rolled over on to her side, the effort bathing her in perspiration. She lay on a flat roof. Smoke and flame pumped out of a window a few feet above her. Another sound carried above the noise of the fire.

She pulled herself to the edge of the roof and looked down. The glow from behind her illuminated a pile of black bin bags. A body lay on top, face down. Then a shadow moved, a second man, searching for something. The body groaned and the second man lashed out with his foot before continuing with his search. As her vision adapted to the light, she recognised Mishkin.

She didn't think she'd made a noise, but he stopped and studied her. Bloodied and bruised, he raised his hand and she saw the automatic.

'Come down, Miss Conti,' Mishkin said, and edged away.

The voice, familiar from nightmares, made her heart freeze. A whoosh from the window, followed by a shower of sparks, stirred her out of her paralysis.

'I'll shoot you up there, it makes no difference.'

She rose to her knees and backed to the edge. More flames and a blast of heat streamed out of the opening. She lowered her legs before crashing into the pile of rubbish, releasing a cloud of evil-smelling gas.

'Get up,' Mishkin said.

Beneath her, polythene slid as she struggled to her feet, using the wall for support. The skin of her lower arms tingled and the back of her legs prickled.

'Go to him,' Mishkin said, gesturing to the unmoving figure.

Antonia gritted her teeth and staggered towards the body. As she came closer, she recognised it and cried out. Chapman *had* come for her, but now Mishkin would kill both of them.

'Don't worry, this will soon be over,' Mishkin assured her.

'What do you want?' Her voice sounded slurred, and even those few words exhausted her.

'Pick up his hand.'

She hesitated. What sick game was he playing?

'Just do it.'

She reached for Chapman's hand, almost passing out as she bent forward.

'Get your blood on it.'

The icy hand felt too heavy to lift, but she raised it to her battered lips and kissed it.

'Very touching. Now the other.'

She did the same then moved away from Chapman, falling against the rough brickwork. Despite the fire behind it, the masonry chilled her. All she wore was the gladiator's tunic, ripped where she'd snagged it and exposing her front. Unable to even imagine the intense heat she'd so recently endured, she shivered.

Mishkin scrutinised her for a few moments, making her skin tighten. He walked across to something on the ground and prodded it with his toe. After wrapping a handkerchief round his hand he picked it up. A metal bar, a metre long. As he advanced, Antonia pushed off the wall.

'I'll shoot you if I have to, Miss Conti. This is *his* gun, so it doesn't make much difference how *he* killed you.'

Light-headed with exhaustion, she considered these options. She had no illusion she'd reach him before he shot her, but a bullet through the brain would be painless. She suspected Mishkin wouldn't make it quick if he had the choice. At least after the first blow with the bar, she wouldn't know anything about it. She stepped towards Chapman's body and fell to her knees, welcoming the thought of resting at last. She gazed at Chapman and smiled. Mishkin would have traces of her body fluids on him and she hoped a conscientious officer would investigate.

In the corner of her vision she saw him advance, moving cautiously over the pile of rubbish. In the distance sirens sounded but too far away to help her now. The helplessness she'd felt as a girl and, worst of all, the betrayal when they told her they were dropping her complaint against Mishkin overwhelmed her. She bent forward to offer an easy target, taking the weight on her arms. Mishkin stood over her and lifted the rod.

'Goodbye, Miss Conti. I can't say it's been a pleasure.'

She moved her hands and a sharp pain made her wince. A broken bottle cut into her hand. Had Chapman injured himself falling on to it? What did it matter? He'd be dead soon. And his daughter? Another young girl left without a father, prey to Mishkin and his ilk. Rage galvanised Antonia and she snatched up the bottle.

Mishkin, arms raised over his head, saw her lunge at him and with a cry of surprise, jerked away. Antonia thrust the bottle at him and it caught him in the neck. She shoved it into the soft flesh. Mishkin fell to his knees with a gurgle. She kept pushing, twisting the bottle, driving it further in and watching his eyes dim while his blood jetted out over her hand.

CHAPTER 32

Sunlight streamed through the tall windows lining the side wall of the day room. The door opened and the excited young voices made Eleanor Curtis smile. She operated the control on her motorised wheelchair and spun to meet her visitors. Although the rate at which her body responded drove her crackers, she took pride in her proficiency at controlling her new mode of transport. The ability to get it to spin on a sixpence gave her great satisfaction.

'Mrs Curtis,' Sabirah greeted her. 'You are looking well.'

'Compared to what?' She'd given up telling her to call her Eleanor; apparently it wouldn't do to address her employer by her first name.

Sabirah seemed puzzled.

'Thank you, dear,' Eleanor corrected herself before greeting Nadimah and Hakim, who gave her bright smiles. Both children appeared much more at ease, although Nadimah still possessed a haunted air reminding her of the young Antonia. 'How did you get on with the refugee agency?'

'Good.' Sabirah beamed. 'We have Permit to Reside for twelve months and woman says we can apply for citizenship when you transfer apartment to me.'

'Geoff's on the case, so it won't take too long.'

'Is too generous—'

'Nonsense, I can't use it and after what your family's endured . . .'

'When will they let you come home?' Hakim said.

'Not soon enough. Maybe a week.'

'Max will be happy,' Nadimah said.

'She let him sleep on her bed,' Hakim said.

Eleanor winked at the girl, who blushed. The worst thing about being here was not seeing Max. He'd have to get used to sleeping downstairs when she got home, not upstairs in Sabirah's flat. It would be strange sharing her house with these people. Strange but good. She couldn't dwell on what she'd lost, and having young people around would help her heal.

The too-hot and stuffy interview room stank of stale sweat. Antonia scanned it with distaste. A carafe of water and three glasses stood on the table in front of her, next to the recording machine. Across from her Gunnerson and Harding took their seats, seemingly unaffected by the environment.

Gunnerson started. 'Ms Conti, thank you for coming. I understand you only left hospital this morning. If you need to rest, let me know. As you know, you're here as a witness and are not under caution. However, if I believe you've committed a crime, that may change. We will record the interview.'

Harding started a recording machine and the two officers stated their names and ranks.

'Can you talk us through what happened three weeks ago, on the thirtieth of March?' Gunnerson said.

Antonia had replayed the events innumerable times and, after clearing her throat, began. Still weak from her injuries, she paused often but declined the offer of a break. She didn't want to do this again. She'd rehearsed the story so many times that it seemed to have happened to someone else until she reached the end. Then she returned there, smelling the garbage and smoke and seeing Mishkin. She paused and swallowed a mouthful of water, draining the glass.

'Ms Conti?'

She focused on Gunnerson, almost surprised to see her.

'What happened then?' Gunnerson said, leaning forward with her hands interlaced on the table.

'When I bent forward, I cut my hand on a bottle under Russell . . . Sergeant Chapman.' She described how she'd killed Mishkin, but didn't tell them the tremendous feeling of freedom the act had given her. Like a huge shadow dominating her last ten years disappearing as his life ebbed.

Harding cleared his throat. 'You're sure Mishkin had the metal bar in his hand when you attacked him?'

She looked at him for the first time. 'Yes, I'm positive.'

'We found none of his fingerprints on the—'

'He wanted to make it appear Russell had . . . done it. He'd wrapped a handkerchief round the end.'

'Did he *tell* you that's what he intended, or are you surmising?'

'No, he told me.' She then recounted Mishkin's words.

Gunnerson spoke. 'Thank you, Ms Conti, we've got enough for now. We'll let you know if we need to speak to you again.'

Antonia didn't think she had the energy to stand, let alone go home. She gathered her strength, ignoring a developing headache.

'One more thing,' Harding said. 'Do you know how Sergeant Chapman found you?'

Antonia knew they'd questioned him at length and although he'd told her, she didn't intend to share the information. 'You must ask him.'

Out in the corridor, a woman waited for her. 'Ready to go?'

Antonia didn't recognise her for a few moments. 'Yes, thank you, Constable Sanchez.'

'Alice, please,' she said, smiling, the animosity from their earlier encounters forgotten. 'If you wait in reception, I'll get the car.'

'Is Russell here?'

'He's up at the big house seeing the chief super.'

Antonia wondered if this was good or bad news.

◆ ◆ ◆

Chapman sat in the anteroom staring at the wall opposite, contemplating his future. His determination to have a bigger role in Abby's life had started well. Even Rhona had grown more tolerant, especially when he'd been in hospital. How much of her changed attitude was down to his newfound notoriety? He'd find out once things quietened down, but in the meantime he'd make the most of it. Footsteps clacked on the tiled floor and echoed off the walls.

'Sergeant Chapman?' the woman said.

He followed her to the borough commander's office. The chief superintendent greeted Chapman with a smile, which he took as a good sign. 'How are you feeling, Sergeant?'

'Fine, sir, keen to return to work.' Chapman didn't need to fake his enthusiastic response. He was going stir-crazy.

'Good, good. Just a few formalities before we can allow you to start. Now, DCI Gunnerson tells me you won't explain how you came to be at the fire where we found the dead women and this Mishkin attacked you.'

Chapman swallowed. *I attacked him in his home, sir, and forced him there at gunpoint. Now, could I possibly get a cup of tea?* That probably wouldn't do. 'Can I be frank with you, sir?'

The chief superintendent adopted a grave expression. 'If you tell me of a crime, I will have no choice but to act.'

Unless I was in your lodge, you pompous hypocrite. 'It's a bit embarrassing.' Chapman cleared his throat. If the old git didn't take this bait, he could face dismissal, but hopefully not have to do time. 'I didn't believe my suspicions about Mishkin and my report of Ms Conti being kidnapped were taken seriously—'

'You're making a very grave accusation, Sergeant.'

'I haven't made it lightly.'

The commander nodded for him to continue.

'I took precautions and intercepted Mishkin's calls—'

'That *is* a crime, Sergeant.'

'I understand, sir. But I judged it better than letting a very brave young woman die. When I heard him discuss dumping the bodies with his accomplices, I warned DCI Gunnerson and made my way there.' After the way his last meeting with Dobrowski had ended, he'd not felt able to consult her, but hoped nobody had carried out a forensic check of his car. Sweat slicked his palms and Chapman held his breath, waiting for the officer to respond.

'Without making a judgement on why decisions were made, you *did* find her alive. On that basis I have to say you did the right thing and we will therefore not take this any further.'

'Thank you, sir—'

'However, you're forbidden from speaking about this case to anyone. Is that clear?'

'Yes, sir.' A huge grin split Chapman's face.

Antonia sat at Turner's desk and flexed her knee. She would have to get used to calling the desk hers, but not for a while. Although exhausted by the interrogation and unaccustomed exercise, she intended to do some work before going home. God knows when she'd have recovered enough to start training again.

The doorbell rang and Miles greeted the visitor before showing him in.

'You've not wasted much time,' Chapman said, brandishing a bottle of champagne.

Her cheeks grew hot. 'I just thought it made sense—'

'No. Sorry, I meant returning to work. Not moving into Alan's old office.' He waved round the office. 'Shall I start again? Welcome home, Antonia. Good to see you out of hospital.'

'Thank you, Russell.' She pecked him on the cheek.

'Could you run to glasses?' he said.

She didn't want any alcohol, but she didn't want to disappoint him. Once they each had a full glass, he raised his. 'To Inspector Chapman.'

'Well done.' She took a sip. 'I wondered if it would be *Mr* Chapman.'

'Or prisoner Chapman.' He gave an uncertain smile. 'Yasmin told me it's not confirmed yet, but they couldn't have a mere sergeant solving such a high-profile crime.'

'Or a mere reporter.' She winked at him.

'Touché.' He took another sip. 'What's happening here, then?'

'I'll be running things. Alan left me his shares and his house. I've moved in there and Sabirah's moved in upstairs with the kids. Eleanor will be more hands-on until we can afford to hire another reporter. Once she's better.'

'How is the old lady? I quite liked her, despite her being a pain in the arse.'

Antonia laughed. 'The hospital is keen to see the back of her but she'll need a power chair, at least for a few months.' Eleanor was still weak and the doctors had warned her she might never improve, but she was alive and her brain worked. 'What about you?'

'Back on the Murder Squad, with no stain on my character.'

'I meant, are you home? Your girlfriend didn't seem happy . . .'

He gave a rueful laugh. 'You can say that again. If a German tells you to "live well" they don't expect to see you again.'

'So, you're on your—'

'They've caught the man who killed Turner, I mean, Alan.'

Typical Chapman, still cagey. 'What about the men who interrogated you in the cellar?' She indicated the scar on his cheek. Those events still hung over her future. She'd killed at least one man there.

'Vanished. So have Arkady's gang. They've excavated the whole of the basement where they were going to bury—' Chapman blushed.

The events of that night still gave her nightmares, but she could handle them. 'You know they found Monika's remains there and Enya, Kerry's sister.'

Chapman nodded. 'Mishkin told me he didn't know about the place, but he must have been using it for years.'

'If they'd followed up my claim, they could have stopped Mishkin years ago.'

He looked embarrassed. 'There's an investigation into how the police acted.'

Antonia guessed she'd have to be satisfied with that. She wasn't sure she wanted to focus on the past. 'What about the men you killed – I mean the people from Sentinel?'

Chapman gave a rueful snort. 'They've disappeared as well. They must have another hiding place, but nobody's talking.'

'You're not in trouble?'

He shook his head. 'Anyway, Sentinel is no more. Their CEO disbanded it, claiming rogue elements had infiltrated the company, and he's now doing Mishkin's job.'

The mention of Mishkin no longer disturbed her, but she hated the fact that Reed-Mayhew had escaped unscathed. 'I don't understand why you haven't prosecuted Reed-Mayhew.'

'All the evidence pointed towards it being Mishkin's operation.'

'So, Reed-Mayhew didn't know what was going on? They took me to his office—'

'Your word against his. Five people, including a junior minister, were with him at the time you claim—'

'They're bloody lying.' She wanted to kick something, but resisted. It wasn't Chapman's fault.

'I'm sorry, Antonia. The decision is taken way above my pay grade.'

'It stinks.'

Chapman held up his hands. 'I'm on your side.'

'What about the National Security Agency?'

'Not involved at all. It was just a coincidence their, quote, "investigations intersected this case", unquote.'

'They were bloody well working with Sentinel.'

'I'm not disagreeing, but at least the powers-that-be are reconsidering whether they should outsource security services, including our lot.'

'That's just hot air until the fuss dies down but I'm not letting them get away with it. I've still got the papers from the shredder proving Reed-Mayhew has been dodging taxes and possibly paying terrorists — have you had any joy finding the papers from Murray's flat?'

'Vanished.' Chapman looked embarrassed.

Disappointment weighed on her, although she wasn't surprised. 'We can still make so much noise—'

'Your DNA is all over two of the women found in the basement and you admit to killing Mishkin. They're treating it as self-defence, but that can change. Add the evidence from Pavlo and things could become serious for you. Some people would be happy to see you in the dock.'

'What are you saying?'

'Let it go.'

She swallowed half the glass. Much as she hated to admit it, he was right. She had more than herself to consider.

'Anyway, someone like Reed-Mayhew is bound to overreach himself. And then . . .' Chapman raised his glass in a toast and Antonia clinked hers against it.

She'd have to be satisfied with that. At least Mishkin was off the planet.

Acknowledgements

Although my name is on the cover, the process of writing and then publishing a novel involves many people.

The support of my family and friends has always been important and I want them to know I never take it for granted. Members of my writing group, South Manchester Writers' Workshop, continually give me constructive advice on my writing, and contribute greatly to my development as an author.

My beta-readers. Thank you, B E Andre – Boz, Mark Thomson and John Keane, talented authors all, who read the early drafts and gave me such valuable feedback, especially Boz, who bravely read two versions.

My editors, who knocked my manuscript into shape in its earlier stages. The team at Fiction Feedback, especially Dea Parkin, and Richard Bradburn of Editorial.ie. Both not only improved the manuscript immeasurably, but gave me plenty of pointers to make me a better writer.

My agent, Clare Coombes from The Liverpool Literary Agency, who not only believed in me enough to offer to represent me, but improved my manuscript before selling it to a fabulous publisher. Her continued support is much appreciated.

Finally, the people I've dealt with at Thomas & Mercer. Starting with Victoria Haslam, who persuaded her colleagues to give me a three-book contract and has been so positive and supportive. This wouldn't have been published now without your support.

David Downing of Maxwellian Editorial Services, Inc., who gave me such positive feedback and, apart from improving my manuscript, made the editing process a pleasure. And he put up with my English slang without too many complaints.

Gill Harvey, who copyedited the manuscript whilst also suggesting changes that have made it even better. Her thoroughness has given me confidence that very few, if any, of my many mistakes have slipped through.

Sadie Mayne, who did the proofread and not only corrected my questionable grammar but identified some timeline and technical errors I'd made.

Dominic Forbes, whose excellent cover designs made choosing the final one so difficult.

I've taken some liberties when describing our world, as I'm sure many of you will have noticed. I wrote the first draft in 2013 and while some of my 'predictions' haven't materialised, I've treated them as if they have.

About the Author

Photo © 2021 Steve Pattyson Photography

David Beckler writes fast-paced action thrillers populated with well-rounded characters. Born in Addis Ababa in 1960, David spent his first eight years living on an agricultural college in rural Ethiopia where his love of reading developed. After dropping out of university he became a firefighter and served nineteen years before leaving to start his own business.

David began writing in 2010 and uses his work experiences to add realism to his fiction. David lives in Manchester, his adopted home since 1984. In his spare time, he tries to keep fit – an increasingly difficult undertaking – listens to music, socialises and feeds his voracious book habit.